Lightwood

Brainard Cheney

MM John Welda BookHouse

2014

ISBN: 978-0-9892491-71 (Trade Paperback Edition)
Library of Congress Control Number: 2014942832

First Paperback Edition
The Lightwood History Collection: Book 2
Cover Illustration: from Forrest W. Orr

For more information:
www.lightwood.com

TO

THE MEMORY OF

MATTIE MOOD

Contents

Brainard Cheney on the Ocmulgee River in Georgia
circa 1941

Foreword to *Lightwood*

Brainard Cheney

The persistent trickle of inquiry for this book over the forty-five years since its first appearance, bringing about its republication, is undoubtedly due to its historical content. It is substantially a pseudonymous history of the South Georgia *Squatters War*. The enveloping action is largely factual. The dramatic action, I believe, symbolically true of the fate of these last victims of the *Lost Cause*.

I won't pretend to be unbiased in this war, but I will reveal that I changed sides during my digging into the background, in preparation for the writing. It was a personal relationship that originally inspired me. My father in his early years as a lawyer was a member of the lumber Company's legal staff. Moreover, he and my mother—his Charleston bride whom he was introducing into this wild back country, for a time lived with the Company superintendent—the *fated* Company superintendent! And, the Company story I cut my teeth on was quite different from what appears here.

But I had the accidental (I believe *fated*) good fortune to fall heir to the complete legal record of the Company's operations in Georgia. That is, all of the legal documents of that long war were left behind by the Company's last agent, for me to find and examine. And the account I give of how the Company came by its enormous holdings of Georgia land and its legal battle with the *squatters* is based on these records.

With your indulgence for my sympathies, I will add another small incident. I also learned from these papers that my father (of brief acquaintance, since he died when I was eight) in the beginning a Company lawyer—twenty years later was representing a group (twenty-five in number) of "squatters," trying to hold onto their land.

I found the *relicts*—the children and grandchildren—of the "squatters" (those who lost land to the Company) very reluctant to talk about it. The cause of the *Squatters* had lost respectability utterly with them. And this last battle of the Civil War was, indeed, a *lost cause.*

Editors Note: This Foreword appeared in the 1984 reprint of *Lightwood*. The italics used in the Foreword were Cheney's own.

The Lightwood History Collection

The *Lightwood* area as of 1860

Characters and Places

Micajah Corn, Farmer and Fighter

Calhoun Calebb, Attorney for the Squatters

Captain Ian McIntosh, Coventry Company Superintendent

Kathleen McIntosh, The Captain's Daughter

Christopher C. Coventry, Northerner, Company Owner

Proudfitt Coventry, Christopher's son, Company Head

Mathias Hurd, Sheriff of Telfair County

John Casement, Company Attorney

Zenas Fears, Land Agent for the Coventry Company

Trigger Fowler, Scuffletonian Assassin

Jere Corn, father of Micajah

Littleton Corn, son of Micajah

Ardel Cone, killed by Land Company agents

Judge Cassius Crow, Federal Court in Macon

Lancaster, county seat of Coventry County

Pineville, headquarters of Coventry Company

LIGHTWOOD

1

Micajah Corn sat in a duck-legged chair before the fire in the big double-pen house on Cedar Creek. Behind him the great square room was dim with wavering shadows, but the circle of firelight was bright. On the wall above the mantel was stretched a catamount skin. The chair Micajah sat on had a deer-hide bottom. The hide had been worn slick and black by years of sliding backsides, but the chair was still Micajah's favorite. He tilted it forward now and, carefully picking up a blazing splinter from the hearth, lighted his pipe.

The flaring splinter revealed a long man whose body had the lean, twisted look of an ironwood tree. His graying hair almost brushed his shoulders. His face was complacent yet melancholy. The gray-streaked, yellowish mustache, curving down over his lips, then gently upward to loosely twisted ends, gave the illusion of a fixed, mild smile.

Across the wide hearth from him Jere Corn, his father, rocked and slowly chewed his cud of tobacco. Micajah had often thought that his father's head resembled a shuck broom—an old broom with its shucks twisted and bleached white by lye and water. Like shucks the hair grew in clumps, baring cheeks and mouth and the top of his head which an Indian scalping-knife had once despoiled.

But Micajah was not thinking of his father nor of the clatter of dishes from the back room nor of the squeak of the well-sweep in the yard that at this moment were the only sounds in his ears. He was thinking of the word a neighbor had brought him that afternoon in the Sugar Field. While he was laying off rows, Ben Cameron had come by looking for his pied heifer. He was full of some news Zenas Fears had told him. Micajah thought that the thing sounded like a scared-nigger story. Ben thought that, too, though he pointed out that Fears was no scared nigger. Fears had told Ben that he was working for the Yankees, had a job on the surveying crew. He said he had seen the Yankee surveyor's map and the Corn land lots were marked in green on it. Green—the same color as the Yankee holdings!

Micajah exhaled a cloud of smoke and gazed through its haze into the fire. Suddenly, and it seemed of its own volition, a picture had come into his mind: an army of blue-coated fig-ures, busy as ants, sweating, bustling, moving big pine logs and heaving them into wagons. Among the sweating workers other bluecoats with gold-braided sleeves moved, gesticulating with drawn sabers. The mules that drew the wagons were close-clipped and bore the brand *U.S.* on their hips. They drew the wagons up to where the logs could be loaded onto railroad cars—an endless train of cars that disappeared in the distance.

This, he knew, was not an accurate picture of the Yankee sawmillers he had been hearing about. But the report of their mammoth operations on the railroad stumped him. Shipping trainloads of logs all the way to Brunswick—more than a hundred miles! He could only envision them as an army—a uniformed antpile.

So the Yankee army threatened him again! It was nine years since the war. Nine years since the April day in '65 that ended his long walk home from Macon.

And he had grown cotton in the Sugar Field every year since then, undisturbed by anything else except high water and low prices. The Sugar Field flooded often, though the flood years weren't plumb-gone destruction; the flooding of it now and again kept the field sweet, put power to the cotton roots. But the years since the war had been close years. There had not been one in which a man could afford to lose a crop. He hoped the creek wouldn't take a notion to rise this year and fertilize the field.

He leaned toward the fire and tapped his pipe against a brick to make it drop its ash, still thinking of his talk with Ben. They had stood there near the gate while they talked. After Ben had had his say, Micajah had turned to gaze at the field. He saw it now as he had seen it then: wide, even rows of grayish-black earth stretching as straight as a martin pole off to the distant wall of the swamp with the sun ball, red as a lightwood fire, dipping at the edge of the moss-tailed trees.

Yankee sawmillers claim the Sugar Field! Coonshine! Ben said Fears admitted he wasn't sure. He didn't know Pa's lot numbers. He got at it by saying the whole district was marked green. What did a little green paint on a linen map make up? The railroad was sixteen miles away at its nearest point. The Yankees would never send log-cutters out to Cedar Creek. Still he didn't want surveyors running lines through his place.

Taking his pipe from his mouth after a brief puff, Micajah raised his drooping eyelids to look at his father. He spoke in a slow drawl that had in it a note of tenderness.

'They're a-goin to have big doin's up in the new county, Saturday, Pa.'

Jere's voice was pitched in a higher key, but it had the same slow drawl, like the idling of a weathervane in slack wind.

'Whatch-a-way, Son? Whose a-doin-'s?'

Micajah prolonged his meditative pause before he replied. 'It's the people a-cuttin' the timber over on the railroad. The man behind it all—that un they named the county after—is a goin' to be there. His name's the same as the county: Coventry. The meetin' 'll be at the new county site, Lancaster. Ben Cameron, he was tellin' me about it this afternoon.'

His father asked what the meeting was for. Micajah was silent for several minutes. Finally he spoke.

'Ben said he's been a-buildin' a courthouse for 'em and Saturday he's a-goin' to give it to 'em.'

Jere made no comment. Micajah got up, opened the shutter to the right of the fireplace, and drew in a lightwood log from the rack beneath the window and threw it into the fireplace. He waited until a bright blaze broke from the log before he resumed the conversation:

'They tell me his hands are a-sendin' off logs by the hundred every day. They load the whole train down with 'em some days, there on the Macon and Brunswick Railroad. And a-raftin' and a-driftin' 'em too, down below here on the Ocmulgee River. That there mill of his'n on the coast must be the master big.'

4

'What in the name o' lead-' n-powder can he do with all that there timber?'

Micajah watched his father rub the old scar on top of his head in his habitual gesture of doubt, and wondered with him. Ben Cameron had said that the timber was all shipped North, to the Yankees. Well, there wasn't anybody down South who could buy it anyhow. And who in the name of common sense would want to buy it when he could haul his logs to mill and get them sawed into shares, like Ben sawed for him, Micajah?

'He's a-borin' with a mighty big auger,' he commented finally. 'Think of haulin' them logs all the way to Brunswick on railroad carts! Ben says it's a-goin' to be a big thing for this piney-woods country, but his wits is always wool-gatherin'. Ye recollect the old Lumber City mill away back yonder? It didn't last more'n seven aer eight year. And there ain't a Yankee of 'em left now, they a-tell me—'less it's pore little Cal Calebb and he's a half-breed.'

He looked up. Civil, his wife, and his son, Jethro, had come into the room and were taking seats about the fire. Jethro sat down in a rocker that was a companion to the one Jere sat in, but Civil went silently past the men to take a seat a little back of the semicircle.

There was no sound in the room except the clatter of Jet's rawhide boot soles. He was called Jet by everyone except his mother who usually used his full name. But for his close-cropped, reddish beard and his green eyes he might have been his father at twenty-five. His face had the Corn mildness and the Corn calm.

Jere spoke. 'I reckon there'll be a-plenty of pine trees left on the barrens when they're all dead and gone.'

5

Micajah's next words came in his usual deliberate drawl. 'I been a-thinkin' I might go up there to Lancaster and see that there man, Coventry.'

'To Lancaster!' Exclamations of unbelief came from Jere and Jet. Civil gave a wordless gasp.

Jere recovered himself first. 'Why, Micajie, it's forty mile up there, if it's a foot. It 'ud take three days at the leastest, a-goin' and a-comin.'

Micajah looked into the fire in front of him as if he had not heard his father. 'I won't plant no cotton afore next week,' he said meditatively, 'and I reckon I can see most of the corn and tobacco in before I go.' After a pause he turned his face a little in Jere's direction. 'Zenas Fears was a-talkin' over at Cameron Shops, Ben told me today. Fears has got a job with that Coventry crew surveying land lines and claims to've seen the plat of the Coventry holdings. Coventry's got his mark on our lots, he says.'

Silence filled the room as water wells up in a spring. Jere's rocking-chair slowed quietly to a stop. Jet and Civil sat motionless in their seats.

But there was no change in Micajah's voice when finally he went on. 'More'n apt Fears was wrong. He didn't know our lot numbers—just said the whole district was marked. But I ain't goin' to take a chance on havin' them a-chainin' and a-blazin' lines through our land.' He paused as if he might say more, but he did not.

Jere broke the silence. 'Reckon I'll go along with ye, Micajie.'

And after a briefer pause Jet joined in. 'Pa, can't I go, too? I ain't never got over to McRae yet and seen that there railroad business. I wouldn't mind a-goin' along.'

During Tuesday and Wednesday and Thursday of that week the Corns all set out tobacco plants and planted seed-corn with a sense of time. Even Civil and Jet's Mary Ann worked in the fields most of the day. And ten-year-old Little-ton, Micajah's youngest son, labored savagely, hoping against hope.

There was business to be done and Micajah did not want to be bothered on so long a trip with a 'youngun.' But he capitu-lated finally in the face of Civil's persistent will. She said only, 'It'll do the boy a lot of good and we can make it without 'im.' But Micajah saw that her heart was set on it, that she really wanted this favorite child of hers to go. He had said simply, 'All right, wife, let 'im earn it.'

The guineas in the chinaberry tree had just begun their first soft potracking when the Corn household stirred on Fri-day morning. Before they had well subsided, Jet was out, with the lantern swinging its circular bands of white light across the hard swept yard, as he walked toward the barn to feed the horses. The kitchen fireplace crackled with flames as Civil and Mary Ann got breakfast ready and finished with the basket of food they had begun fixing the night before to feed the Corn men on their first day's journey. Micajah, aided by Jere, put supplies in their wagon: feed for the horses, blankets for sleep-ing out, spider and coffee-pot, meal and side meat and the guns. Then he helped Jet hitch Old Gray and Dan, the gelding, to the wagon. Littleton, dressed in jeans breeches that came almost halfway between his knees and ankles, shivered in the early morning dark as he piled into the wagon after his grandpa and was followed up by Micajah and Jet. The hounds, locked in their pen, whimpered as the wagon creaked into motion.

Micajah gave the horses a pretty free rein to find their way over the trail to Cameron Shops in the dark, but they moved slowly, fearing that in the dark they would wrap the wagon around a tree. Going was better on the old Blackshear Trail that led on to McRae. The way had been cut out here, a three-path road. About a half-hour after they passed the shops, the gray sand of the wagon ruts grew dimly visible. Micajah figured that it was seven o'clock when the sun got up enough to come through the pines, sending slivers of gold through the great trunks that stretched up like the strings of a harp. Straight the sun streaks came through the trees, leaving one in shadow and washing the brown bark of another as bright as a knife blade. And as the road came slowly on, slipping under the horses' feet and disappearing behind, it turned into sight countless other stems that reared upward toward the sky. The sky over Blackshear Trail was green pine boughs, a hundred feet high, or near it. In the sun-up stillness they uttered a faint drowsy swish.

Three deer moved at an easy lope ahead of the team for a quarter of a mile, but Micajah stopped Jet when he reached for his gun. They hadn't time to bother with deer meat. The sun was already two hours high when they passed the first clearing in the pines—a cow-penned pitch with a pine-pole shack on it.

More than a mile beyond the clearing the road skirted the head of a bay. Here the pine trees thinned out and a scrubby growth of palmettos and gallberry bushes covered the flats bordering the morass. They followed a twisting curve for a half a mile before rounding the bay, and Micajah enjoyed the spring sight of it. Tyty blooms sprinkled the thick growth with a bright frost and the bay trees turned silver-bottomed leaves to the sun. Here and yonder, high up in the tree-growth, white bay blossoms were opening. And nearer the edge were the black gum saplings, sending out green leaves tender as twilight.

A bay is a pretty thing of an April morning, Micajah mused. It was a relief to break the monotony of the pine woods even if the road were pushed a half-mile out of the way to get around the bay. He had a vision of himself and his party, twisting through the pine trees like a redbug climbing along the scruff of a dog's neck. This was wild country sure enough when old General Blackshear and General John Coffee blazed this trail— all the way from Dublin to Jacksonville, slap across the pine barrens. There had been Indians crawling around amongst the pine trees then. His old grandfather, Jonathan Corn, had been there with the trail-blazers. And there was nothing along this trail except the blazes on the trees even when his father moved out to Cedar Creek. Now it was settling along. Soon it would be like the River Road.

Micajah and Jere were the only members of the family who had ever been over the trail to McRae since the county seat was moved there from old Jacksonville three years before. It was five miles nearer from Cedar Creek to Jacksonville and the Corns had always gone there to trade. It was still a better trad-

9

ing town, even if the courthouse had been moved. Besides they had never had any lawing to do.

Everything was moving out to the railroad now, Ben Cameron said, but Micajah did not believe that. Railroads were all right, but the river had always been there and always would be there. He would sure like to see one of those trainloads of logs, though. This Coventry crowd was boring with a might big auger. Fears told him they owned pine woods all over Telfair and the new county and even over in Montgomery and Laurens. And they were going to survey every blamed lot of it. That was the unreasonablest thing ever he'd heard of—it would cost more than a lot of that wild land was worth. Well, they'd better not come over on any of his and Pa's land with their compass and tree-blazing!

They came to McRae. The Corns ate there and rested their horses. It was here that Jet and Littleton got their first look at the railroad. Littleton had never seen a clearing so long and straight as the one in which the railroad ran. He marveled at it. Micajah watched his excitement with gentle tolerance. The carriages that ran on the railroad had wheels made out of iron, same as the rails, he told the boy. An engine pulled them and it ran with steam same as a steamboat. It ran very fast, some said forty miles an hour, but Micajah doubted that.

The road from McRae to Lancaster extended along the edge of the railroad clearing. To their left the pines made a wall. They had passed the stump-stubble of great clearings and the new-boarded houses of a place called Pineville, and the sun was swinging low toward the tree line, when they heard it. It wasn't much of a noise at first, just a faraway rumble above the wash of the pines. Then it was a racket, like a big wind coming up from behind along the railroad clearing. The Corns could not see down the clearing because of the trees, but the roaring was coming on terrifically fast. It was like nothing Littleton had ever heard before. It grew louder, louder, louder. His eardrums seemed about to break, his head buzzed. The horses began to run. Micajah grabbed the lines and tried to saw them down, for the road now ran close to the tracks.

A black locomotive, spewing steam and smoke, rounded the bend with its wind-rifled coaches and hurtled along the clearing toward them. It came on, right at them—like a steamboat boiler shot out of a gun.

Micajah yelled something and dived out onto the wagon tongue between the horses. But Littleton did not wait to hear, or see. He hit the ground and bounced up at a run. Jet's eyes caught the flash of Littleton's moving legs and he followed him over the side of the wagon. They knew vaguely that the horses were rearing and running, but they took no heed. Hissing, beating, clangor, was exploding at their backs, shaking the ground about them. They strained their legs to make the woods.

From the depths of the pines they heard the roaring recede. Jet stopped first. He looked behind and then about him. He rubbed his hand over his face and yelled at Littleton. He started back toward the road kicking up pine straw as he walked. When they emerged from the woods, all was quiet along the railroad. Micajah stood at the horses' heads, still soothing them, and Jere was in the wagon holding the lines. The railroad tracks were still there. Nothing had been hit or blown up. The train was nowhere in sight.

Micajah stooped to glance underneath the horses. 'Dan's busted his belly-band,' he said. 'We might as well a-make camp some'ers nigh here.'

2

WHEN the Corns reached Lancaster the next day, the sun was straight overhead and already a crowd had gathered in the village. They drove through its street of stores, assembled like a ragged row of drygoods boxes, crossed the railroad track, and turned into a thinned-out grove of pines. In the center of it reared the brand new Coventry County courthouse. It was box-shaped, clapboarded and painted white with green window-blinds and a green shingle roof. The building was two-storied, but the façade was a single-floored narrow porch, ornamented with rococo wooden trimmings around the eaves and spindling pillars. Wide steps gave entrance to the porch and front door.

'Look, Pa, it's painted!' Littleton exclaimed.

Micajah conceded that it sure was a fancy got-up edifice.

He was astonished at the crowd. It was such a big gathering and there was so much show and dress to it. He had expected something of the sort, but he hadn't seen anything like this since the war. There had been vehicles and animals tied behind the stores all the way, but here they were thicker than potato bugs. And all sorts. Horses and ponies and oxen, yearlings and old steers, and a sprinkling of mules. Rough, block-wheeled carts, like the one Micajah used around the place, wagons, buggies and even surreys. Some of the more elegant-looking ones had fringe around their tops. Some even had negro coachmen dressed in linen dusters standing about them.

The crowd, in the grove and going in and out of the court-house, was as mixed in kind as the teams. (The sky overhead was clean-washed as a china plate and there was an April sun, but the wind blowing had the tooth of March in it. The ladies in the courthouse, however, did not seem to mind the weather's briskness.) The ladies looked as bright as calico horses, in blue and pink and yellow and white and silver-colored dresses, of rustly silks and thin spider-webby stuffs. These ladies had tiny waists and skirts sticking out behind and trailing after them. Many of them walked along, with gay-colored parasols in their hands, on the arm of some prancing young fellow with a broadcloth suit buttoned up to the knot of his wide scarf and a derby on his head. There were men strutting around there, too, in jimswinger coats and striped breeches. Micajah knew that these were people from along the River Road, and from Hawkinsville and Lumber City, and from as far away as Mount Vernon and Dublin, probably.

Hay-and-straw with them were ladies whose dresses were of the same style, but were of cotton, and were not so small at the waist, not stuck out so far behind. These ladies wore home-made hats of wattled shucks, or palmetto with ribbons on them. There were others whose loose dresses were made of

14

homespun and dyed with wild indigo, who wore long sunbonnets stiffened with tupelo strips.

Their men wore brown jeans britches and rawhide shoes and homespun shirts and jackets. They did not prance along with their women, but squatted on their heels and squirted tobacco juice into the pine straw, or sauntered about the grounds.

But it was neither the size nor the diversity of the crowd that caused Micajah to stare about him for a long moment before starting to get out of his wagon. Thinking things over on the way here, he remembered having heard that Calhoun Calebb was teaching school in the new county seat. He didn't take much stock in a half-Yankee, but Calhoun was a little bit kin on his mother's side. Micajah had thought that he might at least get directions from him, anyhow. But now that he was here he realized that it would be as difficult to find Calhoun as to get hold of the man Coventry.

He decided that he would not do anything about it now and mingled with the crowd. As he went he marked the gray of Confederate uniform salted through it, sometimes on a booted-and-spurred planter, sometimes on a backwoodsman with wild-grown beard and hair. Micajah himself wore over his homespun shirt the jacket of an old uniform. It heartened him to see the gray on the other men.

The Corns had eaten, but the presence of dinners spread on the ground stirred appetites in Jet and Littleton and they found a man with a gingercake wagon and a keg of persimmon beer near the courthouse. Micajah had no money to be spending on that trash, he said, but Littleton had a half-dime Civil had given him and Jet had his own money. While they ate,

15

Micajah learned from the vendor that Calebb not only taught the school, but was mayor of the town and would preside at the exercises in the courthouse. Micajah was relieved, but told his sons to make haste. He said that not more than half of the people in the grove could squeeze into the courtroom and they had better go ahead and get seats while the getting was good.

Micajah heard that old man Coventry and his three sons had come all the way from New York City to take part in the doings. He had supposed they lived somewhere near-by to look after their business, but it seemed that Yankee-like they stayed up North and only came down here to tell people how to run things.

It was almost two hours before the speaking, but Micajah determined to await his men in the courtroom. The courtroom filled early, the same crowd with the wild hair and whiskers and sunbonnets mixed in with the fine store-bought hats and barbered heads all over the house. The rostrum, too, became tightly filled with dignitaries of the town and county and of Coventry and Company. The closeness of the place filled Micajah with vague unease and he felt sweat about his eyebrows. The place began to stink in his nostrils. The aroma of pine sawdust that covered the floor had the sharp scent of tobacco spit in it. With this were mingled stale body smells, the odor of bear grease and of sweet extracts. He mopped his face and looked about him. There was no way to get out. Nobody else seemed disturbed.

The people behind the railing sat facing each other from either side of the judge's bench. Some looked straight ahead, as if they were in a market pen to show, but pretended they didn't know it, Micajah thought. Others limbered their necks

16

about to pick out folks they knew in the benches. A stiff-backed man with a little girl at his side held Micajah's eyes. The little chap had red in her cheeks even sitting there quiet. She was sure a rosy-cheeked youngun, as fair-colored as wheat straw. His dwelt on her for a moment, then went on. There were only three people behind the railing he remembered ever having seen before.

A man whom he had been watching in profile now stood up behind the judge's bench and faced the audience. The man had been getting up and down and whispering to different ones on the stage. Micajah picked him out as Cal Calebb when he glimpsed a scar on his face, though there was little about him that looked like the boy he had seen twenty years ago. From his unscarred side, Micajah thought Calebb a fine looking man. He was almost a giant in size with a dark glossy coat of hair and a jaw like a millrock. Among the others he stood out like a hilltop pine.

The man turned about full-face. Micajah felt a breath of pain at the bridge of his nose. The scar on Calebb's face stretched from the black shield he wore over his left eye to the corner of his mouth in a purplish, twisting course. It looked like a gnarled, burnt 'catface' on a pine tree, Micajah thought. He hadn't remembered it was so rough-looking.

Calebb was speaking. He said that a great history was dawning for this piney-woods section. Micajah's mind wandered after a moment; he himself had had enough to do with history when he fought the Confederate War. But Calebb didn't talk long. He put up a man he called Major Alan Rhea, who read a deed from Christopher C. Coventry to the Ordinary

17

and his successor in office, in trust, for the people of Coventry County. It was for the courthouse they were sitting in.

Micajah eyed curiously the next man who came forward. It was Coventry and Company himself!

Some people in the audience applauded, but Old Jere leaned and whispered shrilly to Micajah, 'He looks like an Abolitioner!' Micajah did not reply. The pupils of his eyes were pin-points. He watched in solemn immobility.

The man before them was old, as old as his father, Micajah guessed, though not as bent. His wide mouth smiled in kindness. He had gray mutton-chop side whiskers, and the smile made his face look wide, when it was really long.

So this was the old man who was giving the backwoods people around Jones' courtyard a courthouse, because Carpetbagger Bulloch and his crowd had named the county after him! This was the man who would have land lines run out over other men's land!

The old man's mouth was kind, but Micajah thought his eyes, glinting under shaggy eyebrows, had a shrewd, trader look. And that plow-point nose wasn't one to leave other people's business alone. He did look like an Abolitioner! But maybe he wasn't.

This section between the two rivers had as fine a climate and as fine a people as were to be found anywhere, Coventry was saying. He wanted to see them, 'through industry and integrity, grow a greater and fuller prosperity.' If he could be 'an instrument in God's hands for the realization of this dream for the people of Coventry County,' he would feel an humble gratitude.

18

Those were high-sounding words—preacher's words, Micajah thought. As soon as this meeting was over and he could get hold of the old man, he would get an idea of just what Mr. Coventry and Company meant by them.

The next man both Micajah and Jere had seen in court at Jacksonville: Colonel Tom Coffee. His name for oratory was well known from the Oconee to the Ocmulgee. He wore a black jimswinger coat and a boiled shirt and shoestring tie. His silvery beard was close-trimmed to a point and his nose was as keen as his beard. He cocked them both up like a rooster about to crow as he slipped a hand into the front of his buttoned coat.

'I have been requested by the Ordinary, on behalf of the officers and that of the whole people, to make acknowledgements and to return their kindest thanks.' The speaker's voice began to move from naturalness into histrionic tones...'And express their gratitude to you, sir, for the rich and noble gift you have made them in giving the courthouse to the county that bears your honored name.'

Micajah looked away. These highfalutin speeches were pretty, but somehow he never could get much sense out of them. It put him in mind of shouting in the church.

Finally the speaker was closing. 'You will carry with you to your own beautiful home far away, the warm regards and affection of this people who, with their hearts on high, will give you a deep libation of love and wishes for your future health and happiness.'

He sucked in his breath, bowed sweepingly, and walked to his seat. The speaking ended and people rose and began jamming their way toward the doors. The Corns remained seated and waited for the crowd to thin.

'I never expected to live to see such carryin' on over a dang Yankee in Georgie!' Jere shrilled into Micajah's ear, then added as an afterthought, 'But I reckon it might of been looked for here—nothin' but deserters used around this swamp during the war!'

3

THE stuffed courtroom disgorged its crowd and was almost clear of people and foul air when Calhoun Calebb came down from the dais and along the middle aisle bearing two law books under his arm. Twenty-nine years of life had left no trace of boyishness about him. His features were cavernous. A solitary gray eye glowed from the depths of its crater and the scar broke and twisted one side of his face like lava. Bare beneath a cross-bar mustache, his wide mouth was drawn out of line by the scar. As he walked toward them, his head was bent, his lips were pursed, meditatively.

Thus engrossed he did not hear Micajah's first call to him and when he did look around he gazed at the Corn men with blank absent-mindedness. Micajah had not expected recognition so he repeated his own name: Micajah Corn. Calhoun was collecting himself; Micajah presented Jere and told him they were the Corns who lived on Cedar Creek in Telfair, and added, for good measure, 'You most like a-don't recollect Pa and me a-seein' you that time in Jacksonville—you'uz just a shirt-tail boy.'

Calhoun jerked up his big head. He recalled that his mother had once told him she was distantly kin to Jere's wife. He told Micajah he remembered the Jacksonville meeting clearly. He said it with hasty loudness and called them Cousin Micajah and Cousin Jere, Cousin Jet, and even Cousin Littleton, shaking hands all around. He questioned them about the Corn family and fortunes, about their trip to Lancaster and the day spent there.

No one was left in the courtroom except his group, though feet still clomped down the stairway to the ground floor of the building. After shaking hands with the Corns, Calhoun had turned about in the direction whence he came, bringing the unmarked side of his face toward his listeners. It was a habitual action. He now eased into a loose posture and looked off toward the empty benches in front of the Corns. He spoke in an authoritative way.

'I tell you, Cousin Micajah, the railroad and the Coventry enterprises are going to be the salvation of this section and they are going to bring undreamed-of development to these piney woods—not only to this county, but to Telfair and Montgomery.'

His voice was easy and mellow, a big wind that paused fitfully to play with a paper bag. His words coming with effortless emphasis had behind them the weight of his big head and towering frame. He spoke with measured deliberation.

None of the Corns had offered to reply. He went on. 'The war and what come after it has left us flat on our backs—and no shirt on the back, either. Of course this section in here has never been opened up. Just a few farms scattered over a wilderness of piney woods. Coventry's sawmills will bring more cash money into these backwoods than any of us ever dreamed of.

'We don't want to accept the conqueror on his terms—I resent it as much as any man—but what can we do about it? Old Joe Brown was right, as he's always been right. The people hated him for it and they still hate him, some of them, but what he said was the plain truth—the unvarnished facts. We've got to admit we're licked and take the hand that is being extended us, or we'll never get on our feet.'

Seeing silent disaffection in the faces around him, he paused. Micajah lifted his drooped eyelids and brought pinpoint pupils to focus on Calhoun's face deliberately. 'Brown a-got a job from the carpetbaggers, did't 'e?' His tone was casual, but his drawl was emphatically deliberate.

'Governor Brown merely acted on his own advice,' Calebb said. 'But I don't aim to argue politics...What did you think of our meeting here?' He spoke good-humoredly, shifting his deep-set eye to Micajah's face and smiling.

'It was right smart a gatherin'. Howsomever, I didn't a-know 'em—hardly aery one of 'em.' Micajah said, and paused. The pause was so long that Calhoun was about to take up the conversation again, but Micajah resumed. 'There was a man a-sittin' over there close by ye, Calhoun, who had his little girl a-side him. She was about the red-cheek-dist youngun I ever seen. Look like she might a-put something on 'em.'

Calhoun had been conscious of those cheeks, too. He felt a trivial sense of guilty discovery at Micajah's remark. He smiled a little self-consciously. The man, he said, was Ian McIntosh, Coventry general superintendent, and his daughter. They came from Canada—that was why the girl's cheeks were so red. He added that she was one of his scholars at the academy, and then changed the subject.

'How did you like Mr. Coventry?'

'He made a pretty good speech—pretty good,' Micajah replied without warmth. 'He's a mighty smooth exhorter.'

Calhoun now raised his voice a trifle and spoke in the manner of a public man making known his views.

'He's a really big man, Cousin Micajah. I know he's a New York Yankee, but if all Yankees had been like him we wouldn't have had any Civil War or any Reconstruction, either.' He went on several minutes talking of Coventry's position, accomplishments, and good deeds. He, Calhoun said, had had a talk with Coventry only that morning about his plans. Coventry was going to build another sawmill at Pineville, just a few miles below, bigger than the one on the coast and would extend his railroad all over Coventry and Telfair Counties to get our logs. The operations would furnish work for hundreds of men, he said.

Micajah's interest sharpened. 'Is the man Coventry a-goin' to stay here aer down at Pineville?'

Calhoun had turned and taken a step toward the doorway, but he shifted about again and spoke with tolerant willingness.

'He won't stay down here in the piney woods. He's got too many other interests—mercantile, banking, railroads.' He went on talking of the railroad built through Lancaster. That had been Coventry's influence. Governor Bulloch's railroad bonds had financed it.

Micajah halted as the group began to move slowly toward the courtroom door and spoke. His drawl had lengthened and there was a slight formality in his manner. 'I a-come to see this Coventry, Calhoun. I come to see him on account of some information I got from Zenas Fears. Fears said he saw a plat of the Coventry holding and he a-had his mark on our land lots.'

Calhoun jerked his big head in Micajah's direction. There was surprise in his solitary eye. 'There must be some mistake about that, Cousin Micajah,' he said, after a pause. 'You-all have lived there—well, let's see how long? I've heard Mother say that Cousin Jere and Cousin Araminta moved out there on Cedar Creek before the Indians were moved West. Anyhow, you have titles to that land, don't you?'

Micajah gave a slow, dry smile and there was a flicker of a twinkle in the thin blue of his eyes, but his voice was unchanged.

'It's a mistake all right enough. I wanted to see him and a-tell him about it a-fore his surveying crew got into our woods. I thought you might tell me where I could get a-holt of him? I don't want to have no trouble and I a-come to see him.'

Calebb looked through the doorway ahead of him. A faint air of tolerance had come into his face as he lifted his head, but he did not look directly at Micajah.

'Cousin Micajah, the man you want to see is Major Rhea. He is looking after all of the surveying and land claims for Coventry and Company. You saw him here awhile ago in the

25

ceremonies. That's the man. You may know him: he comes from over about Mount Vernon.'

The group had reached the bottom of the stairway and paused for parting words. Micajah nodded his thank-you and the Corns all shook hands with Calhoun again.

He stood by the door of the Ordinary's office looking after them reflectively as they disappeared. Old Jere was a queer-looking codger with that brush heap of beard in front and gnarled bald top poking through. Micajah was unusual, too—was there something going on behind that placid mustache? He had not seen or thought of them since that meeting in Jacksonville twenty years ago. But there was one thing about it still in his mind. Old Jere had said, 'What happened to this boy, Marthie? His face looks like it might've been busted with a gopher plow!' He had shuddered and got behind his mother.

By God, that was always the thing he remembered!

4

THE Corns had made a round of Lancaster's streets and stores and dinner-house when Micajah finally espied the men he sought crossing the railroad track in a top buggy. He hallooed them and the conveyance pulled up to a stop by the sawdust pile across the track. There were two men in the buggy. One was a young man with a bald, brusque look about him. His lead-colored eyes with the large copper-ringed pupils looked boldly and impatiently out upon the scene around him.

'Hello, Corn,' he called from the buggy as Micajah approached, followed by his father and sons.

'Howdy, Mr. Fears.' The common title Micajah gave Fears assumed a cold formality under his tone and emphasis. He had reached the front buggy wheel when he added, after laying a hand on the wheel and looking up into the faces of the two men in the seat, 'I'd a-like to be made acquainted with the gentleman with ye, if ye don't mind. I got some business I'd a-like to talk to 'im about.' His voice was courteous, but casual.

Fears introduced Major Alan Rhea, who was seated on the side of the buggy near Micajah. Major Rhea shook hands with him and immediately got down out of the buggy.

The Coventry and Company woodsman-agent was a man of Micajah's age. His height was less, but as he alighted on the ground his body straightened into an erect, almost stiff, bearing. He wore a well-tailored, double-breasted suit of Confederate gray and a black slouch hat. His Vandyke beard and mustache, almost white, were neatly trimmed.

He now looked intently at Micajah with his large-pupiled blue-gray eyes. His eyes had a way of absorbing the gaze of the person speaking to him that brought them into close relationship. His voice contributed to this effect. It got lower as the conversation progressed and increased in intensity. There was a steel-like timbre within its softness.

'Well, now, I don't have that plat with me, Mr. Corn,' he said, in a manner that gave polite form a tone of sincerity. He went on, 'If you can give me the lot numbers and all of you'— here he lifted his head and voice to include Fears as well as the other Corns—'all of you supply such facts as you can, I think we should be able to come to an understanding—amicable of course.'

Micajah's manner, if a little stiffer, was no less polite than Rhea's. He felt that Rhea was a *real gentleman*. He was pleased that he would have to deal with no dang Yankee.

'Pa here owns the home-place, Major—that's lots 180, 181, 145 and 146, in the first and a-second sections of the seventh district. My lot lies over in the fifth district. It's number 47.'

Rhea glanced toward Fears, still seated in the buggy.

'You say, Mr. Fears, these lots are shown on the plat you saw, as a part of the Coventry holding?'

Fears started speaking without moving a muscle preparatory to the act. He spoke with brusque energy. 'That whole part of the county is green on the map. Every lot in the fifth and seventh district's got the Coventry mark—and in the sixth, too.' He stopped abruptly.

Intangible change came over the Corns. Jere, standing close to Micajah, merely tapped his walking-stick on the ground and spat tobacco juice; Jet and Littleton, squatting at the edge of the sawdust hill, looked up briefly and returned their gaze to the ground. Micajah, now standing at the rear and side of the buggy next to Fears, did not move a muscle. Yet hostility stirred in the Corns. Rhea sensed it.

'Mr. Corn, do you-all live on this land?' he asked, maintaining with the exactness of forgery his polite manner.

Micajah's answer was short: 'I a-said the home-place was on Pa's lots. My son, Zeke, lives on 47.'

Rhea's manner relaxed slightly. He became more genial. 'Well, of course it's possible the plat markings may be wrong—and possible, also, that my friend, Mr. Fears, may not have looked closely enough—may not have had his eyes skint.' He smiled briefly. 'Of course, I wouldn't think of making a decision until I have looked into Coventry and Company's claim,' he added.

There was an answering flicker on Micajah's face, then the Corns were as solemn as before. Micajah reached down deliberately and picked up a splinter from a pine board.

29

'I just happened to hear about this, Major Rhea. I heard the Yankees are runnin' out new land lines, too. And I come over here to let 'em know about our holdin'. I always figure the time to stop trouble is before it starts.'

There was a clear, ticking silence. The four Corns, two squatting and two standing, were as still as the big sawdust mound that rose like a blank wall behind them. Only the restless movement of the horse's hoofs was audible. The big animal now pawed the sawdust at his feet and Fears tightened the reins and drew a silver watch from his waistcoat pocket.

'The train's about due here, Major, and I'd like to move my horse on out before it comes. Get in and we'll go over to the courthouse. We can finish this over there.'

He overcame Rhea's protests and drove him away at a trot toward the courthouse grove, a quarter of a mile distant. Major Rhea had insisted that Old Jere take a seat beside Fears and that all of the Corns ride the buggy over to the grove, but they declined. They followed it on foot.

'You are quite right in your attitude about trouble,' the Coventry and Company agent said to Micajah, resuming the conversation after the horse was tied and the Corns had gathered again about the buggy. 'And, I assure you, sir, no one is more anxious to avoid trouble in the matter of these land claims than Coventry and Company.'

As he spoke he fixed his eyes on Micajah, but occasionally shifted his gaze to include Jere. 'I discussed this very question with Mr. Christopher Coventry today. I am most pleased to say that Mr. Coventry's view of the matter coincides with mine exactly—exactly.'

'I tell ye, Mr. Corn, there is no need for ill-feeling, or even controversy—yes, even controversy, sir. Where there is a conflicting claim to any lot of land Mr. Coventry holds title to, it is his wish to settle the question amicably and—if possible—out of court.'

His voice lowered and his manner became more intense. 'Why, he told me, Mr. Corn—sez 'e, "Where there's a family living on the land—where they have held actual possession of it over a period of years—where there's a bona-fide native claimant by possession—I do not wish to contest his right. I am willing to make any agreeable adjustment that will fairly protect the interests of Coventry and Company."

'Sez I, "That policy will save Coventry and Company a world of difficulty—a world of difficulty." '

The monologue was interrupted by a great voice. Towering, one-eyed Calhoun Calebb was approaching. He was still a few paces distant from the group, yet his words, said without effort, could have been heard beyond the borders of the grove.

'I see the Corns have found you, Major. How are you today?' Without pausing for reply he continued: 'We are family friends, and kin. Cousin Jere's wife was related to my mother. If there is anything you want to know about them, I can sure tell you. They live down on Cedar Creek in Telfair County, and nobody ever lived better. They are no volunteer Corn, either— they were planted and planted right. They've been livin' out there since Indian scalps was a-bringin' thirty dollars apiece.' He concluded abruptly, laughing loud.

Micajah did not speak and there was no smile visible on his face, except for the illusion of mild smiling from his curving mustache. Old Jere and the younger corns, however, looked pleased.

There was a flicker of annoyance on Rhea's face before he smiled politely and replied, 'Why, yes, Captain Calebb, Mr. Corn and his family seem to be long-established citizens of Telfair County.' He had been careful to give Calebb his Confederate army rank.

'Cousin Micajah was telling me awhile ago about the information Zenas over there had given him,' Calebb said, explaining his interest. 'He and his father came here to clear up the apparent conflict and I directed them to you—I hope that was the right thing to do?'

Rhea said that it was, thanked Calebb, and turned again to Micajah. 'Of course, Mr. Corn, I alone am not privileged to speak for Coventry and Company. I could not even give any definite opinion until I have investigated all of the facts. As I have said here, I am not even sure that we have a claim on your lots. Moreover, sir, I will have to turn over my findings to the company's law office. Mr. John Casement will have to act with me in the case. You will have to see me again—that is, another meeting between us will be necessary.'

The pat of Jere's walking-stick on the ground could be heard and the white brush of his beard shook. Micajah only shifted his gaze from Rhea's face and permitted it to wander into the recesses of the grove. Finally his eyes returned.

'Major Rhea, I don't know as we got anything to come back to Lancaster for. We a-do our tradin' in Jacksonville. It's a nice little town here, but I don't know as we 'ud ever have a cause to come back here.'

Rhea smiled and nodded his head in a slightly apologetic manner. 'Why, yes, the meeting need not be here, Mr. Corn. In fact, the company's offices are at Pineville, not here. It has numerous land claims to clear up. Since you came here I supposed you wished to work out some definite agreement with the company.' He looked again into Micajah's face.

Micajah's eyes did not meet his, but were wandering through the grove again. 'We just come here to let your company know that it had its lots a-marked wrong—if it had a-marked our'n. And not to send none of its surveyors into our woods. Don't know as it takes any agreement.'

Rhea pulled briefly at his beard and shifted his stance. The visible portion of his cheeks grew more florid and he opened his mouth once without speaking. When he spoke his tone bore its usual modulated politeness, but there was cold rigidity in it. 'Why, yes, Mr. Corn, but an agreement would be to your advantage. From what has been said here about your possession of the land, I would think you have a good claim to it under the law, even if you have no title. Would he not, Captain Calebb?'

Calhoun permitted a pause while eyes were turned in his direction, then he said slowly and sententiously: 'The law of adverse possession is well established in the State. Twenty years' actual possession, even without color of title, gives a man absolute claim, Major.'

No one spoke. After a moment Calhoun added: 'I, of course, am not representing the Corns here—my interest is merely that of a friend in directing them to the proper authorities. But if you want to know the Georgia law, that is it. And,

33

under color of title, the claim becomes absolute after seven years.'

'Why, yes, that is what I thought,' Rhea said, turning back to Micajah. 'If you and your father can establish that you have had actual possession of this land for more than twenty years the title is of no importance. By the law of Georgia it's yours— it is yours by the law. And as you say, we don't want to have any trouble over it.'

There was a pause, and then Old Jere spoke, with a shrill cackle: 'We don't question it a-bein' our'n—it's our'n all right. By the law of Georgie, aer by the law of shotgun.'

5

BY the *law of shotgun*! Micajah mused upon the sharp, quavering dare his father had flung at Coventry and Company on the afternoon before. As they went along past the crooked rail fences of the fields beyond Lancaster's houses, Micajah looked at the fresh-turned earth and away at the distant pines. The horses walked at a steady pace and almost soundlessly on the soft turf between the ruts. He kept thinking about it. He took a twist of tobacco from his pocket and bit off a chew. Deliberately he moved it with his tongue back into his jaw.

They were on the long road back, forty miles through the woods. Micajah was on the driver's seat. Old Jere, with a blanket wrapped about him, sat in the wagon-bed with Jet and Littleton. Once Micajah turned around and regarded the brushy white whiskers and hair that never quite covered the scalp scar on the top of Jere's head. His clear blue eyes glistened with amusement and tenderness as they fastened on the nodding old head. Pa, he thought, would give them a shotgun salute, all right, if the varmints came snooping around his woods. When he came to Cedar Creek that was the only law.

Pa came to Cedar Creek in 1820. He had tried settling on the river first, had set out to clear up a place on the Indian side of the Ocmulgee. He and his four brothers and his father, Jonathan Corn, went over there and cut down seventy trees to make a clearing for the house. They had the walls nearly up when the Indians came. Pa always said that the first token he got that the Indians were near was the crack of their rifles. Then he saw Old Jonathan crumpling down under the log he was holding.

There wasn't nobody there but Pa and Jonathan. Jonathan hadn't hit the ground before Pa felt a stinging in his shoulder and he followed him down. All the time the Indians were whooping and swarming around. He didn't have a chance to get to his gun. He played dead, but it cost him the top of his noggin.

He said he thought the Indian was braining him at first, when the knife blade hit the bone. But he had plenty of time to make a second guess. The hellion's hand slipped on Pa's shock of hair and he took hold again and sawed away till he got the scalp.

Pa said he would have drowned, sure, swimming back across that river if he hadn't been scalped. He was having to take it with his right hand because his left one was no good. The river was up pretty smart, and he said every time the water splashed up on that raw top it put new life in him.

He said he never hated nothing so much in his life as leaving Old Jonathan dead over there with those heathen Indians, but it couldn't be helped. Making his way to the Widow Wilcox's after he got across was worse than the swimming, he was so nigh out. And, by God! If the widow and Araminta both

36

didn't faint when they saw him. If it hadn't been for the widow's daughter, Mary Ann, and old black Rody—Rody's mammy—he'd of laid right there in the dog run where he fell and died.

He and Ma weren't married then—that was in March of 1818—but she nursed him through and married him the next Christmas. It was nigh a year and a half after that before they moved out to Cedar Creek. He already had ten acres of the Sugar Field cleared and the old crib of the house built, right where it stands now. It was more than twelve miles from Old Jonathan's house, the way they came. When Pa and Ma pulled up in the old block-wheeled wagon behind Brandy and Red, the place was all ready for living in. Pa's cows and shoats were in their pens. Ma's old walnut four-poster and its little trundle and house fixings were all in place.

It must have been pretty lonesome for Ma, without her sisters and brothers and all the people along the River Road, though little Jere was six months old then and gave her and her girl Rody plenty to do along with the housework. But there wasn't a neighbor nearer than Jacksonville, excepting Old Joe Wilson, below the trail of Horse Creek, nearly five miles away. And there were Indians straying through the country then, let alone wolves and bear and other varmints. They were supposed to be friendly, but there never was an Indian you could trust. It was Old Jonathan's being friendly with them and trusting them that got him killed and Pa pretty nigh it.

It was more than fifteen years then since they'd been put across the Ocmulgee and there were militiamen in the old blockhouse, too, but it didn't keep them from slipping back. There was an old dance-ground in the forks of the creek up above him, Pa found out, and they kept coming back there. Pa didn't have nothing for an Indian but lead and powder, and Old Joe didn't like 'em any better. He'd come to Telfair before there was any Telfair and he'd been killing 'em all his life. They made that dance hot for those red devils. Micajah remembered hearing about the argument Pa and Old Joe had over killing one of them.

That must have been late in the fall of the first year Pa came to the Creek. There were three of them, but Pa and Old Joe didn't see but two, squatting down over a fire. It wasn't long before dark. Pa and Joe came up into the wind, crawling on their bellies, and got pretty close by before they rose and cracked down. They both saw one of the Indians fall by an old stump and they saw another run through the bushes.

Pa said, 'Joe, ye let your'n get away.'

'Like hell I did,' Old Joe says. 'Mine fell by that there stump.'

'That one's mine, Joe. Your'n was the one to the left,' Pa said.

'We won't have no argument, Jere.' Old Joe says, 'I know my game. Go look at 'im and if he ain't got a hole one inch below his left nipple, I don't claim 'im—he's not mine.'

And sure enough, Pa went there and turned the varmint over and there was the hole just as Old Joe said. But Pa was satisfied before he turned him, because lying just behind him and almost on top was the Indian Pa shot—a hole as big as your thumb in the back of his head.

It surely was rough living on the Creek in those days. And Old Joe and Pa had rough ways. Pa was bad to cuss, too, back there, Ma said—and didn't give a thrip for man nor devil, and not much more about his God. No wonder Ma never got used to it! But Pa was tamed—tamed by his own hand in less than a year after that. Till yet he ain't never said a word to me about it, Micajah thought, and I reckon he won't. I don't blame him. It's God he's got to settle with, and these fifty years since I believe he's done his best to be godly.

Ma said it was disentery little Jere had, but Rody said he'd been marked by God and wouldn't nothing have saved him, and Pa needn't have made that long walk to Hartford. But there—fifty miles away even the way Pa went—was the nearest doctor and Ma had used everything she had, or knew about.

They didn't have no animals, excepting the steers, Brandy and Red. But Pa could make better time on foot than a horse—especially cutting through woods like he did and not hitting the River Road for nearly twenty miles. Two days and nights and till noon another day and he was back at the house with the little vial of doctor's medicine. Pa was a powerful man then and never knew quit.

Ma was twisting in labor when he got there—poor Ma always took it hard, having her babies. And Rody had her hands full with the two of them. But she tried to help Pa give little Jere the dose. Pa, I reckon was a mite shaky after that walk and pretty nigh frailed out by it. The baby looked like he didn't have strength to live, Rody said, but he could still holler, lying there on that trundle. Pa tried to pour it down him out'n a big spoon the first time and spilt it. They wasn't much more'n a dose left when he finally got it down the little un's goozle.

He just stopped hollering while it was going down and gagged once and heaved. Up she come, the whole business. Pa caught it in his hand. Then he slapped it right back down that baby's throat and caught him around the neck to hold it down.

The little un heaved and heaved and Pa kept holding him tight around the neck to keep the medicine down. His face turned red, then blue, and Rody started beating Pa on the arms to make him turn his neck a-loose. Pa did finally, but it was too late. Little Jere was dead.

Ma was out of her head at the time. They never told her no better'n it just died of disentery. Pa took it out behind the cow pen on a little rise and buried it. That night Mark was born and the house had another baby in it.

All Pa said at the time was, 'By Gawd, Rody, it was die anyway, if he didn't keep that damn medicine down!' But it told on him in a little while. He couldn't sleep of a night and he used to get up and go out after the wolves he heard howling. In about six months he broke down and told Ma about it. He'd been trying to pray to God all that time, but he couldn't. It tore Ma up nearly as bad as it had Pa when she heard he'd choked little Jere, but she prayed to God for Pa. That was the beginning of our family altar, Ma said. Pa never could pray, and he counted on Ma till she died—as well as read the Scripture to him.

That was all before I was born, Micajah thought. Pa never used an oath around the house to my knowing. The first thing I recollect—and I was just a nubbin of a shirt-tail boy—was Pa putting Herod in the wolf trap. It wasn't a wolf trap either, but it was dug and covered like one. Anyhow, old man Rives couldn't find him.

I wonder how Herod took up with Rody? He'd hardly had a chance to see her before he came there to the house. It might

40

have been he just ran off to get away from old man Rives and his bull whip. Everybody in the county knew about how that old man treated his niggers, but nobody did anything about it, except Pa with Herod.

The first time Herod came to the house it was near Christmas-time. Rody asked him to let Herod stay, but Pa said he couldn't do a thing like that. He gave the darky two days to go somewhere else, and when he didn't, Pa took him back to old man Rives. Ma felt awful bad about it. She said that old man would near about kill him, but she wouldn't say anything to Pa.

It was along in the first of the year when he came back a second time. It was after breakfast and Pa was off looking after a turkey-pen he'd been baiting. Mark and me were building us a trap to catch partridges—out back of the house by tne old log washbench. Ma and Rody were in the house by the fire, but it wasn't cold much with the sun shining. I was sitting on the log watching Mark. (That old log tub is as good as it ever was, right now.)

'Little Marster, is Rody inside' Herod asks Mark. He was no big fellow, but keen-built and pert. Though he didn't look pert that morning. You could scarcely see his eyes they were so sunk in his head, and he was dragging bad. There was a red streak across his black face that went clean beyond his ear. It had festering in it.

Rody was at the back door before Mark got it out of his mouth to speak. Rody and Ma doctored the darky and put grease on his welts—they were two weeks old then.

When Pa came back he was bringing five turkeys in two bunches with their feet tied together — he got them all out of the pen alive.

Ma says, 'Jere, Herod's here again and he's in bad shape.'

'That nigger's gone crazy,' says Pa. 'Old man Rives'll kill him this time and it won't be no easy death.'

'He's not a-goin' back, Jere,' Ma says.

I had been meddling at one of those turkeys in Pa's hands and the gobbler let me have it with his wing and knocked me down at that point.

Ma and Pa talked about it after he put the turkeys in a pen out back of the house. And I came in with Mark to borrow his knife to cut some triggers for our trap and was listening for all I was worth. She told Pa he oughter try to buy Herod from Rives. He said he didn't have but eight hundred dollars and that wouldn't buy no nigger. And she said it might if he just used his head a little along with it.

Pa did have the money ahead. He had been having the best run of luck with the Sugar Field then he ever had, before or since. Four years straight running had been high and dry and it had really made the cotton. He was cultivating with those old wood plowshares then, too.

He wouldn't let me and Mark go along when he and Herod went out into the woods not far from the sheep-pen and dug the hole and fixed it like a wolf trap. But we slipped out there with Rody some when she went to carry Herod victuals. The pit was covered over with rails, then brambles and pine straw. He couldn't build a fire, but it wasn't cold in there, he said— anyhow he had blankets to wrap up in. It looked just like any other wolf trap. Pa made him stay in there during the day, but at night he let him come out and stay up in the loft with Rody.

It wasn't a week before old man Rives and two of his boys came looking for Herod. Pa told them the darky had been by, but he wouldn't let him stay. Rives grumbled about Pa not holding the nigger for him and Pa said he wasn't holding any creature of any sort for Rives to kill. The old man didn't like that and they all went off still looking for Herod, going clean through to Lumber City before they came back.

Pa told them again he hadn't seen the nigger and Herod had to stay in his hole. The next morning, when they were about to leave, Pa told Rives he would give him two hundred dollars for the nigger loose on the chance that he'd come back to Rody.

The old man shook his head, pulled his long cooter nose and spit a mouthful of juice at the fire. No, he said, it would be worth more'n two hundred dollars to him just to get to kill that damn nigger. Pa juggled with him, though, and finally he agreed to take five hundred. After he and his boys had cleared out of the house and were on their horses, he turned and yelled back at Pa, 'I'll bet ye can whistle right now, Corn, and that black hyenie'll come lopin' out'n the woods.'

Micajah remembered that Herod had helped Pa build a kitchen with a clay floor behind the house soon after he came. Pa and Ma figured when they bought Herod we were fixing to get River-Road rich, he thought. Pa and Herod cleared twenty acres of cotton land and Pa bought Miss Jessie, the little claybank mare. It was the next fall he got the roan gelding and a saddle for Ma to ride, and somewhere in there he got old

43

Cash and Sassy, his bear hounds. The Corns lived sweet out of the Sugar Field for a while.

Then came '33, the year the stars fell. I was scarcely ten years old, but it seems as plain as yesterday. It was a bad dose of medicine! First wolves got the lambs that spring. I reckon they got into the flock six or seven times. There wasn't but three lambs left, and they killed four ewes. And the traps didn't stop 'em. It set in to rain about the first of April and the creek came the highest it's ever been, before and since. Water came clean out of the swamp. It drowned every young thing on the place excepting the geese, and everything in the woods, too, near about it. Pa didn't stick a plow in the ground till May the twenty-ninth. And that was the last drop of rain we had till August the twenty-fourth. Pa put in three acres of corn at the Sugar Field that year along with his cotton, but it didn't even make a nubbin for the coons.

It clouded over a few times in June and early August, but I reckon didn't a dozen drops fall. All through July and most of August the sun just lazed across the sky like a buzzard—only it was white and the ground was black. There were stretches of a half-a-mile in Cedar Creek as dry as a dead cow's bones and its shrively puddles were like horse pee. The wire grass and pal-mettos turned gray and underbrush in the bays parched up. Even the pine tops got a yellowish sickly look. The varmints you killed in the woods weren't fitten to eat and we had to live out of the smokehouse.

By middle of July Pa had done forgot about his crops. He was trying to do something about the dumb creatures, but there wasn't much helping them. It was whether the human could live, or not. He'd hung up snakes all around the place and in the swamp and the old rattler got where he didn't buzz at all before he hit. Old Cash got bit and it killed him straight way.

Pa was after Ma to pray for rain, but she wouldn't—not for a long time. She hadn't liked Pa's bear hunting, or the drinking that went with it. She said God had been good to us and we had tried to forget Him. He was letting us know He was still God. But she finally did pray for some in August.

Then Ma came down with malaria. Mosquitoes were riffling and whining through the air like bees and the woods took fire all about so that it stayed smoky most of the time. But the smoke didn't hinder the mosquitoes. Even the swamp started burning and it got most of the Sugar Field fence—we hadn't secured it.

Pa tried to save a few of his cows, besides the horses and old Brandy—giving them corn and fodder. About time the rain finally came, his corn ran out. I think Pa tried praying a little himself before the rain finally got there. He used to get up during the night and walk out into the woods.

That winter was nearly as tough going as the summer was for us. Pa got a little corn at Jacksonville, but it cost like gold itself. We didn't taste a piece of hot meat, or mutton, or beef that winter. It was all deer and turkey and that was hard to get.

But it wasn't all over yet for Pa. Long close to the break of winter Herod ran off. And Pa never was able to find hair nor hide of him. Rody hadn't had the first child by him, nor hadn't tried, it looked like. That ended Pa's being a planter—and bear hunting, too, for many a year. He killed old Sassy after Herod left, but he kept some of her puppies.

6

THE Corns rode into McRae on the morning after they left Lancaster. The sun, shouldering up over the pine wall, made sharp, shining streaks of the steel rails lining the railroad clearing, as they came in sight of the courthouse. They had camped a few miles above the village to break their long journey with food and sleep, but by the first light of day they were again in the wagon. The halt in the county seat was brief. Micajah had left four bags of wool at McNeal's general merchandise store on the way up to Lancaster. He now stopped to get a half-dozen jug coffee-cups, spices, nutmeg, and a supply of salt.

They did not rest their hats at all. Inside of an hour they were back in the wagon and headed into the piney woods along the old Blackshear Trail. As they passed beyond cleared fields, the morning sunlight quieted into piney-woods twilight. Old Jere, a blanket wrapped around his shoulders, sat in the wagon-bed and nodded. Beyond him, Jet and Littleton lay on their backs looking up into the pine tops and talking now and then about their trip. But Micajah, sentineled in the wagon-seat, looked out over the ears of the horses and along the meandering three-path trail into the years that had passed over his shoulder like turns in the road.

He was trying to recall when it was he first heard about the tax sale. As well as I can recollect it was the day I heard Sheriff Boyd yelling in front of the courthouse door at Jacksonville and wondered what in tarnation was going on, he said to himself. And that was before he got shot in the leg. I ran into him and old man Ashley there in the clerk's office that afternoon. It must have been February, or March, '45. I reckon I never would have thought about getting papers on any land if I hadn't been wanting to move away from the home-place. I had hunted over the hammock on Big Horse and knew it would clear eight or ten acres of good cotton land and it was about ten miles nearer to Civil's folks. That map the sheriff showed me in his office there looked like a crazy-quilt—I couldn't tell a thing about it, with it all listed off in squares you couldn't find on the ground. First time I ever really knew what a land lot was! I finally got old man Ashley located as to where the hammock was on the creek and he told me what land lot it lay in. I could get papers on it for about two dollars, he told me, but I'd have to take the whole two-hundred-acre lot. He said to come back to the sale the next Saturday; he wouldn't give 'em to me then.

Micajah's thoughts went on to the time he had tried to set up his own home. Civil and Ma didn't get along any too well, but it was on account of Rody, he reflected. Civil never was used to niggers and Rody had an idea Corns were better than her folks in those first days after we were married. And Mark was the oldest born and there was little Jonathan coming along. Ma had him after Pa thought she couldn't have another.

47

It seemed for me and Civil to get us a place of our own was the thing to do. Civil was carrying Clute then and Kinch was a baby. She wanted to go home and stay with her ma and let me get the new place ready. It was really crowded at home like it was.

But shot-'n-powder, did Pa blow up! He said—breaking over a little—by God, he'd killed Indians to make a home and place there for Corns to live and they couldn't go traipsing off to settle among Fussells, or Vaughans either for that matter. He said Mark didn't have no woman, let along younguns, and it looked like he wasn't going to get one. He said a lot.

It made me bull-headed. Besides, I wanted to get away and be my own man. They don't make 'em more close-mouthed than Civil, so she didn't say any more to Pa's cane-raising than I did. We just went ahead getting ready to leave. Finally Pa called on Ma to help. She said if he'd build another crib to the house and let me and Civil have it—the whole two rooms and loft space—he might get further'n he could with all his noise making. She had been after him for a bigger house for a long time. I reckon it was Ma and her double-pen house idea that held us there.

I had already got papers on my lot and what old man Ashley told me about a deed fixing a man's land lines made up my mind to get 'em on the home-place. It cost me ten dollars and a half, because the Sugar Field lay in four different squares. It was good money spent, though, because it's a paper that sets out your holding as any man can see and keep off of it. I'd never thought of Coventrys and their maps then, but I knew it was good money spent. It may take those papers to get shed of that Coventry crowd.

But Pa blew up all over again when I brought him the papers on his four lots. And I showed him I'd taken them out in his name. Pa said, by God, what did he want with the damn papers, there wasn't anybody going to move on his land. He'd been living there twenty-five years without anybody's papers. The piney woods wasn't like the river bottoms, he said, there was room in the piney woods for everybody. But he took 'em and we built the other pen.

Clute had been born and it was more'n a year after that before Civil and me clean gave up the idea of settling down below and having our own house. It was an act of Providence that we stayed, because Ma died when Clute was four months old and we hadn't been living in the new part of the house more'n six months. Ma hadn't been strong, never since Jonathan was born five years before. She got to passing blood when she made water and took her to her bed. Then corruption came. Nothing Rody tried did her any good. She died of an early October morning.

Pa looked like he never would get over it—and I reckon he hasn't till yet, in a way. He quit talking and hunting, or going to town. He just worked around the farm and sat in his room by the fireplace, fire or no, for about five years. And he got Civil to read Scripture to him a lot outside of family prayers.

Mark was worse'n Pa. Ma was about the only one he ever talked to around the house. After she went he scarcely came in the house except for sleeping and eating. But he was still a powerful worker and he could tell when rain was coming a week ahead. He pretty near hit it right every time.

Civil was the only woman there, except Rody. She was needed.

Catfish ate the corn off the stalks in the Sugar Field in August of '47. That was the same month Mit was born. It was a high freshet and fast-rising that brought little Mit in—the first Corn girl baby. Cotton in the Sugar Field was already opening and we were going to start picking Monday coming. It was Wednesday when it began to rain and by the next Wednesday everything was covered there and up in the new ground, too. Everything we made that year was in the cow-pen field. We thought Mark was plumb fool for wanting to plant cotton here, but the bale we got off of his four-acre patch was every strand of lint we picked.

That fall old Duncan Cameron—Ben's father—moved over on the ridge and build his blacksmith shop. People had crowded in along the creeks and the Blackshear Trail by then. I reckon there were a half-dozen families in a five-mile range of us and about that many strung out along the sixteen miles to the new Scotch settlement on Gum Swamp, where Macville is. But there was none close enough to give us any trouble except the dang Cones and Fussells. It wasn't the closeness, either. It was their dang thieving ways. Ma didn't have any use for any of the people that moved out around us in the barrens, except Old Trapper Joe Wilson and he was there when we came. She had died before the Camerons moved in. If she could have known a granddaughter of hers married into such cattle as the Cones, she'd break the box she was buried in.

No Cone nor Fussell farmed any. Their women tended just enough of a patch of corn and sugar cane and collards for eating. They spent their time hunting, frolicking, and stealing other folks' stock. It was the fall Camerons put up their shop that our calves and pigs started going amiss. Pa and Mark rode the woods to see if they couldn't come on a carcass, or some sign of the stock. They went out as far as the Fussells' and Mark saw a calf in their cowpen he said was ours, but we didn't do anything about it then. We were all satisfied those rogues had got our stock.

During the winter two heifers went and Mark found part of a cow head with the ears on it close to the Coneses'. The ears had our mark in them: a swallow-fork in the right and an under-bit in the left. Pa wanted to go over and run 'em out of the country, as he put it. I knowed it wouldn't do. There wasn't but three of us, though we could have got plenty of help. The right thing to do was to send 'em a peaceable warning first and tell other folks what they were doing.

I rode by Rufe Cone's house, not carrying a weapon of any sort and spoke to him without any fuss. I told him what Mark had found behind his house. Then I said, 'We are a-goin' to see that our cows don't use around yore place nowhere and you a-better see that their heads ain't a-layin' around yore cowpen.'

Cone clouded up at first and says, 'I don't a-want to have no trouble with ye, Corn.' He was sitting by the door to his shanty picking fleas off of his hound dog.

'We are mighty easy to get along with, Cone,' says I. 'You leave us and our stock alone and we'll give ye plenty of room.'

He denied it, of course, and I didn't push no charge—I just rode on off. But that wouldn't do for those rogues—it was born in 'em to steal, I reckon. We had nearly sixty head of cows that year and we marked all the calves early so we'd know them. It was October when we missed two of the young heifers that had plain marks in their ears.

Mark knew 'em as soon as he saw 'em in Cone's cowpen, but he got down and examined their ears to make sure. The swallow-fork was in the right, but Cone had cut the under-bit out so as to look sort of like a crop. It was plain their left ears had just been cut.

Me and Pa had got off of our horses, too, and Pa walked toward the house to call Cone out. He came cussing and bellering at Mark to get out of his cowpen. Mark went ahead laying down the rails to let the heifers out. I wouldn't've shot Cone if he hadn't raised his gun. In spite of the heifers and what he was calling us—and those four bull-nosed boys of his. I called to him to drop his piece and so did Pa. Then he pulled the hammer back, so I let 'im have it. It was none too soon, because he fired before he fell. Queer thing. It missed Mark wide, but got one of the heifers back of the horns and dropped her.

If I had it to go over with again, though, I'd let him have the cows, I reckon. Rather than killing a man. A man's got to take care of his own, all right, and a rogue ought to be shot, but I've seen too much shooting since then, and lost too much by it. God don't hold with killing—be it armies, or men.

We'd been a sight better off if we'd let the dang Yankees have the niggers and even a foot or two of our land, maybe. I'd sure have done better to let 'em have Rody than get Kinch and Clute killed. They wouldn't have come down here on us then—and us ten years getting them off of our backs!

But it's human to fight. There's things a man can't take. I doubt if God would ask him to—not, and really expect him to do it. And the Yankees were so bullying and rough. As General

Foster said, all we asked was to be let alone—us and our niggers.

If we could just have seen at the upshot how it was coming out! But foresight ain't hindsight. I didn't put no word in his way when Kinch went marching off along with Jonathan in the Telfair Volunteers. I reckon maybe I was sort of proud of it. And Civil saying all the time it was no concern of ours out in the barrens. She never liked Rody anyhow. It would just get her boy killed, she said.

I must have been point-blank crazy to think Kinch couldn't get killed. It was just Ma's River Road ideas in me — and plain fool!

Then look at me when word come that they had killed Kinch up in Maryland! I acted just like a cow smelling blood. Thinking I could take my flint-and-steel and walk up on 'em somewhere and get their scalps! And taking poor Clute with me. I reckon he'd've joined up anyhow, if I'd left him, though. He had the same sort of fool in him. Maryland! I didn't even see it. I didn't even get in the same army. And the first shooting I got into was at a town called Murfreesboro, way over in Tennessee.

There was plenty to shoot at all right, and plenty shooting at ye. I had a pretty good rifle they gave me—for a while. I seen it drop 'em, too. And at first I thought it was pretty fine. But by that time another year I was sick of it. At Dalton and at Resaca, where they winged me. Them poor devils hadn't ever heard of Kinch and didn't know me from Adam's haw steer. They hadn't come to get me, either—just mixed up in it, like I was.

And Clute had done been sent off with another army before that time and killed, poor boy, up there at Chattanooga, but I didn't know anything about it till after the fighting was over and I came back home.

The place had run to weed, near about it, and there wasn't any stock left; but it was home. Them little gourds swinging in the breeze on the martin pole was the first thing I seen through the pines. Me hoofing it and barefoot. Danged if I didn't lope a little.

Things were pretty bad there, but it didn't look like it to me then. Poor Mark had hung himself in the barn the year before. He was off in the head before I left. Pa had let General Foster's men have all the horses, except old gray here and she was just a year-old colt. He and Jet and Zeke were using bull calves; what little plowing they were doing. There wasn't but six cows left — and a lot of Confederate money. And Civil got a letter at Jacksonville awhile after that from Jonathan. He was at some place in Tennessee called LaGrange, or near it. He'd married a widow with a plantation and wasn't coming home, the letter said. Pa took it hard, because he thought the most of Jonathan.

What got under my hide, though, was the morning me and Pa walked down to the Sugar Field. It was the first time I'd ever seen it like that: grown up in weeds and sassafras roots, and pine saplings coming.

I says, 'Pa, I've seen her covered in water, and over yore head, so as to use a dugout to get here. But I never expected to live to see her like this.'

'No,' he says, 'It's the first time since I broke it forty-five years ago, but we didn't have nothing to plow her with and it waunt no use. We couldn't get rid of the cotton if we grew it.'

A long keen bark came from the distance through the pine woods. It was the tenor baying of a hound and ended in a whine.

Jet roused to his feet from the wagon-bed. 'It's Ole Fancy, Pa. She hears us a-comin'!'

Slowly, Micajah stirred from the grip of his thoughts. He slapped the lines over the horses' backs and looked around him. 'If we don't make haste it'll be cold supper—Yankees, aer no,' he said irrelevantly.

7

MAJOR Alan Rhea restored a linen handkerchief to the breast pocket of his gray suit, slipped a trifle forward in his armchair and then leaned back. During the six weeks that had passed since Christopher Coventry's visit to the neighborhood, the courthouse ceremonies at Lancaster and his employment as woodsman-agent, he had been continually busy familiarizing himself with Coventry and Company's landholdings, receiving reports of the surveyor and adjusting complaints. He was now seated in the office provided for him at Pineville. Its walls were ceiled with unpainted pine boards. They were of rich amber color, lighter and deeper shades of wood grain marking them in an irregular pattern. With the exception of a large map, on which Coventry's extensive landholdings were colored green, and a pictured calendar, there were no decorations on the walls.

Rhea glanced at the litter on his roller-top desk and allowed his gaze to rove across the ceiling before looking at the man with whom he was casually conversing. His eyes held their habitual intentness, but there was a covert amusement in his voice when he spoke. 'By the way, Mr. Casement, could you use the professional services of Captain Calebb for the company?'

'Calebb! Is the company hiring Calebb?' John Casement, the local counsel for Coventry and Company, showed surprise which was moderated when he detected Rhea's lack of seriousness.

Casement was a man like a cameo. He was formed with a pretty conformity that brought him into bas-relief in any group. He had long, rather narrow eyes of rich brown color, socketed flush with his face and bearing the look of complete assurance. The lines of his nose and jaw were straight. There was a touch of color in his cheeks. His voice bore cultured modulations and a slight trace of Irish brogue. He had left Ireland when he was nineteen and, like Calebb, had found new enterprise in a new country.

Rhea meditated a moment before replying. He was thinking of the conversation he had had with Calebb in front of the courthouse at Lancaster. Rhea would be in a position to name additional counsel for the company when the time came, Calebb had said. 'We Southerners should stick together here.' This phrasing of Calebb's had offended him. It was more than merely the man's brass. Was it Calebb's physical appearance, his paternity, or the fact that he had been an overseer that prejudiced him against the man? Rhea wasn't sure it was any of these things.

He returned to Casement's question with a smile and replied with simulated seriousness, 'Why, yes, Mr. Casement—if the decision is left up to Calebb.'

Casement divined the extent of Rhea's dislike for Calebb and let himself go. He relaxed in his seat and laughed.

'Calebb might be valuable to the company at that, Major,' he said, matching Rhea's mock seriousness. 'It might use him as a scarecrow to keep squatters off the land and save the tedious travail of the courtroom.' He paused for a moment, then added in an apologetic manner, 'That may not be kind, but he's grotesque! And I'll say for him, he's a lawyer of no mean ability.'

'Of course we can't condemn him for his looks. The poor man had no hand in that.' Rhea sat forward in his chair. His voice grew lower and more intense. 'But for unadulterated brass I have never met his equal. He seems to be without any sense of professional decency. Why, sir, do you know he baldly told me he was seeking a connection with Coventry and Company and wanted me to recommend him. Said his knowledge of the backwoodsmen would be worth it to the company.'

Casement smiled in deprecation. 'He not merely tries to seize Opportunity by the forelock, but to scalp him! I've noticed his presumption, myself.'

Rhea was recounting the story of Calebb's runaway Yankee father when they were interrupted by the entrance of Zenas Fears and Ian McIntosh, the Coventry general superintendent. Rhea and Casement had been awaiting them and turned to the business of the meeting.

Fears, Casement, and Rhea looked toward the superintendent to begin the discussion. McIntosh was a brawny, bolt-upright man, who began speaking with an unhesitating readiness that characterized his whole appearance. His blond hair was streaked with gray, but age had not touched his intense vigor. A graying forelock grew aggressively forward on his low wide forehead and his plum-blue eyes confronted the scene without giving, or asking. He leaned square shoulders forward and put his hands on his knees. There was a Scotch burr in his voice.

'I deed nawt br-ring in the sur-rveyor, Schloss. I theenk Fears here can state the situation better. Schloss has a noggin full of figger-rs, but he knows naught of what goes on about heem.' His tone was a vibrant bass.

Fears bent forward his lean face and close-cropped head. 'Mr. Schloss runs the lines and leaves the arguments to me,' he said with vigorous energy and broke into a sharp, gusty laugh.

'You two know what these squatters are like,' he continued, nodding toward Rhea and Casement. 'Backwoodsmen, narrow between the eyes, and you can't reason with them. They are suspicious of everything and full of prejudice. There is nothing to most of them. They talk loud, but run if you call their bluff. They wouldn't give any trouble at all if the Coventrys waunt Yankees.' He paused, looked quickly at the faces about him, then smiled and went on.

'We are working in Telfair now, in the Sixth District. We have run into some of the more respectable ones who've been living on the land a considerable time and pretend to have some kind of claim to it—some of them have deeds, I think. That's no business of mine, but they don't want any lines run through the land they are claiming.

'I've tried to reason with 'em. I tell 'em it will not have any effect on their claims, that we merely want to run out the lots. I tell 'em it will be as much a benefit for them to know where the lines lie as anybody else. Hamilton down there on Sugar

59

Creek yesterday said he knew where his lines were and didn't need the Coventrys to tell him. He was carryin' an old flint-and-steel on his shoulder. We had the same trouble with Lum Fussell and we'll get over about the Corns next week.

'I know Lum Fussell and Kit Hamilton, but I couldn't do a thing with them. And yet there's nothing to either one of them. They were just bluffing with their guns, but I couldn't get Schloss to go ahead. All these squatters are scalawags and thieves and live like niggers, or worse. Most of them were de-serters during the war—those they were able to catch and con-script!

'I helped round up a passel of 'em over there in Gum Swamp near where Lancaster is now, during the last year of the war. They'd got to be worse than the Yankees, thievin' around at night.

'There was so many of them and they'd got so bold they wanted to put up a fight. I remember my troop—Wheeler's Cavalry—picked up their bivouac before day. At the first shot they ran into an old log church at the edge of the swamp. Most of them had guns of some sort and they kept up a sprinklin' fire.

'Lieutenant Craig, who had charge of the troop, did a fool thing. He didn't want to set fire to the church and he said he didn't want to kill any of 'em if he could help it. We rode out into the clearing yellin' to beat hell and circled the church, firing at the windows. We only lost a horse, for they stopped shootin' after our second round. One of 'em came out of the door a wavin' a white shirt—I don't know where they got that shirt—stole it, I guess.

'They were a sorry-lookin' lot when we lined 'em up. Like so many egg-suckin' hound dogs. Smokehouse thieves! I said to Craig, "Lieutenant, the Confederacy and the community would be better off rid of this trash." There was thirty-one of 'em. I said, "There's a graveyard right behind the church house and it ain't filled up yet."

'He said, "Steady, Sergeant, there's a law to deal with deserters."'

The taut lines about his mouth broke with his quick, gusty laughter. He went on: 'It might not have stopped desertion, but it would have made a few less squatters for us to contend with now.

'But what I want is instructions. What are we goin' to do about these old piney-woods rooters who are bluffing us?' His words had come in a rapid, vigorous flow. Now that he was through, he stopped suddenly and looked about him.

The faces of the other men were in retreat before his grim intimations. Casement smiled with a distant politeness and looked at the map on the wall behind Fears. Rhea's mobile face was stiff and his gray-blue eyes looked gravely through the surveyor's helper. McIntosh blinked. There was a strained pause in the room.

But in another instant the superintendent was smiling. 'The war-r is over, Fears. We want naw shootin'. This is a timber-r business we are aut to oper-rate. We must do it peaceably.'

'Major Rhea,' McIntosh continued, his eyes shifting to confront the woodsman-agent, 'Mr. Coventry, I believe, was most emphatic about a policy of fr-riendliness weeth the people living on the land?'

Rhea took up the conversation in a quiet, thoughtful manner. 'There can be no question on that point, sir. Any other policy would be repugnant'—he hesitated, then quickened his speech—'well, out of the question, out of the question.' He paused and stroked his beard.

Fixing Fears with his grave, formal eyes, he spoke again. 'You were quite right in not attempting to push ahead with the surveying, Mr. Fears.' He smiled gently and bent his head forward. 'The surveying becomes a secondary question when we run into claimants on the land in adverse possession. That, sir, is one of the reasons why Coventry and Company has retained Mr. Casement, here, and myself.'

He turned to the others. 'I think, gentlemen, this is not a question of running land lines, but of peaceably extinguishing adverse claims.'

Both McIntosh and Casement nodded. Rhea said then that he would accompany the surveying party and investigate the claims. 'I might have an opportunity of seeing their deeds, if they have any— which is unlikely. At any rate, I could offer to arbitrate.'

Fears nodded vigorous assent. He rubbed his hand harshly over his jaw for a moment. 'Major,' he said brusquely, 'there's no man living on his land willing to arbitrate away a foot of it.'

8

FREDERICK Schloss's tripod straddled what he confidently contended was an intersection of the district line with the sectional line bordering the Corn land lots. Equidistant from the tripod's three legs and hanging vertically from its line, the motionless plumb-bob pointed to the exact spot at which these imaginary lines crossed. On top of the tripod was his bright brass compass and from an arc above the compass swung its brass-barreled transit.

To an eye untaught in land lines or in surveying, there was no district line, or section line, or intersection. There was only the tall piney woods with everywhere brown round-barreled trees, as like as the hairs on your head and almost as thick. And there seemed to be nothing which would enable a man to tell an acre here from any one of a million acres in the piney woods of the barrens.

Standing close to the tripod, Schloss looked around him. He was a spare man with a chin like a shoe-last and a wedge-shaped nose. He was clean-shaven except for a drooping mustache and his skin was tanned and leathery. He wore an old derby pulled down far on his head. A briar pipe held straight between his teeth jutted from under it. With woods boots and breeches, he wore a white collar and shoestring tie—all so ill-fitting as to give him a scarecrow look.

Taking the pipe from his mouth, he pointed in the direction of two negro helpers leaning against a tree a dozen feet away. 'You boys, get those axes and bush-hooks away—far away.' His voice was harsh, as if it scraped the roof of his mouth, but held an impersonal quality. 'Now, if you fellows will all stand back,' he continued, looking around him at the straggling group staring rather wearily at him. 'Here, Mr. Fears, you take my watch and pocket knife. I want to be dead sure there's no metal of any sort close enough to affect my instrument—then she's got to be right.'

Fears unfolded his arms from across his chest and moved closer to receive the articles extended by Schloss. Leaning against a tree near-by was Jet Corn and a sallow, hump-shouldered young man who assisted Fears with the chaining.

Thirty feet away, with a shotgun across his knees, Micajah watched the proceedings dubiously. At best this was a useless annoyance. He knew where his land lines lay—knew exactly every lot corner and could find most of the old blazes by knocking off the knots that had grown over them. He had had the county surveyor run out the lines after he got the papers to these lots, twenty-four years ago. And they had followed the original lines, finding some of the old overgrown blazes. He could show this crowd his lines if they really needed to know them. He could go to any corner and walk down the line to the next just by the old blazes, and not miss it anywhere three feet.

But Major Rhea had argued him into letting this fool with the compass use it to run down the line to help him find the old blazes and see better where to put new ones. And instead of starting at a lot corner Micajah could show him, he kept coming out here to what he called a district intersection—going to find his way to the corner. Twice he had tried and missed it.

The Major had been very polite in asking him and Pa to let the company run out the outside lines between their land and the company's and to blaze them good and heavy so the company log-choppers wouldn't make any mistake about the timber. The Major had said there was no question about lines except to find where the old ones were. But this butt-headed fellow in the derby hat kept coming back out here. He was either a fool, or maybe he wasn't—but he wasn't going to get away with anything. Micajah wondered where his father and Rhea had got off to.

After much waving of arms to the rodmen and additional tree-cutting, Schloss had finally got his stakes lined up and was moving on down the line with his tripod over his shoulder. Fears and his helper were measuring with the chain. 'Stick,' yelled the hump-backed man holding the rear end of the chain. 'Stuck,' Fears answered, pushing a short stake into the ground. And they moved on the ten chain-lengths of a lot.

Walking at a deliberate swinging stride, Micajah brought up the rear with the shotgun on his shoulder.

When he reached Schloss and his negro helpers, the negroes were driving a large lightwood stake in the ground. Schloss, axe in hand, was preparing to blaze a near-by tree.

Without seeming to change his gait, Micajah quickly drew up beside the surveyor. He spoke with his usual deliberation, but his voice had an edge to it. 'Tell yore niggers to a-stop that. This ain't no corner of mine. It ain't no corner a-tall.'

Schloss looked at Micajah without moving, and pulled at his pipe. 'It's the corner all right, friend. We started at the district line and chained down two lot-lengths. I know I set the instrument right this time and the instrument don't lie.'

The negroes had stopped when Micajah spoke, without awaiting Schloss's order. Schloss now lowered his axe, frowned and took his pipe out of his mouth.

Micajah's face was stiff, except for the seeming smile of his mustache, and the pupils of his eyes were pin-points. 'The corner ye are a-lookin' for,' he said, more slowly than usual, 'is about fifty foot over there to the southeast. Ye've run yore line off in here twice now.'

'The instrument don't lie, friend,' Schloss said, with a gesture of dismissal. He had put the pipe back into his mouth and had raised his axe to blaze the tree when he heard a voice that carried the cut of a cleaver: 'Drop that axe!'

Schloss swung back around quickly. Micajah held his shotgun at the port, but its barrel pointed menacingly in the surveyor's direction. Jet was advancing to his father's side, his gun in front of him, ready to raise. But more startling still to Schloss were Micajah's eyes. They looked black and danced like bubbles on a boiling pot.

The surveyor turned grayish under his leathery bronze. His voice disclosed a touch of anger and fright. 'Great God, put down those guns!'

Fears, who heard Schloss's raised tones from the water jug where he was getting a drink, now hurried up. He wiped his mouth on the back of his hand and looked from the shaken surveyor to the silent, gun-gesturing Corns.

Fears carried a pistol in a holster at his hip, but he made no move to get it. 'Say, what's coming off here! What's the matter, Micajah?' He addressed the elder Corn with blunt familiarity.

Schloss broke forth in choler. 'These *domn* fools want to lynch me because the lot corner is here and not over there where they think it is!'

Fears responded with impatience, 'My God, Schloss can't we ever get together today—we've lost enough time here, getting started, to run out a dozen lots!'

Micajah dropped the butt of his gun to the ground and looked toward Fears. His voice had regained its usual calm, though there was an underlying grimness in it. 'Take yore man out'n here, Mr. Fears. He kain't run no land lines for us. I'm a stoppin' this nonsensible business right now.'

'Let's hold on a bit, Mr. Corn,' Fears began more formally, 'Major Rhea ought to be back here any minute. And he's in charge of the party, not me.'

Micajah began slowly to move off, swinging his gun up on his shoulder and turning to nod at Jet. 'Me and Jet'll get back on t'other side of our line,' he said. 'I'm through a-talkin'.'

He had moved only a few paces when Major Rhea, accompanied by Jere Corn, came up. Fears turned toward them. 'You-all had better help us out here,' he said. Schloss took the pipe out of his mouth and advanced toward Rhea, gesticulating with it. Micajah was unwilling to discuss the difficulty he

67

had had with Schloss, or the question of land lines at all, but Jere joined in. Micajah waited.

Schloss grew voluble. He was saying the point he had reached for the third time through his survey was unquestionably where the lot corner should be. He had as good a transit as money could buy and he would stake his reputation as a surveyor on the correctness of his lot corner.

Old Jere heard Schloss through with patience. Turning to Rhea he commented, 'I don't care a dang about his reputation or his een-stroo-mint, neither.' Jere repeated the latter word with exaggerated imitation. 'The corner is over yonder and them lines as we a-got 'em blazed are the original lines run by General John Coffee when the county was laid out.'

Schloss did not permit Rhea to reply. He had the air of the arguer, oblivious to reality in a fever of infallible logic. 'I don't care who made the original survey. If he got his district line in there right, this is the corner of the third lot up. The lines probably weren't half laid out. All they had fifty years ago was compass and Jacob's staff. And some of those Indian fighters could scarcely read and write. This was all worthless wild land. There just wasn't any good reason why they should do more than a rough job running in the lot lines.'

Rhea's face stiffened. He gazed with grave intensity at the Yankee surveyor. He was exasperated by the man and sincerely aroused by his loose charges. He had done a considerable amount of surveying himself as a young man and had carefully investigated early surveys.

'If you know no more about your work, Mr. Schloss, than you do about the work of those early surveyors—then, sir, I fear the company made a mistake in sending you here at all!'

Rhea spoke acidly and with feeling, and yet at the same time he realized that his attitude toward Schloss was the only one which might serve to compose the difficulty with the Corns.

Schloss was surprised at Rhea's attack, but not subdued. 'You probably don't know, Major, that the Government's publication of magnetic variations were not even available then. Those old fellows probably guessed at the angle of declination—didn't know what magnetic variation was.'

Rhea looked carefully about him to secure his calm before he spoke. Micajah had now returned and stood near him. Rhea felt a common emotion uniting him with the Corns, and even Fears looked hostilely at Schloss. Rhea spoke with steely softness. 'I am familiar with the Government's published reports, Mr. Schloss. The old fellows you refer to—I am persuaded to believe, sir, knew considerably more about their surveying than you do.'

He paused for a moment, then went on. 'The idea of loose work in surveying seems to come easy to you. It did not with them. They were not only well-educated surveyors, but very careful ones, sir.

'Have you ever heard of Burt's solar compass? That is the instrument they used, and, while it was elementary, they secured highly accurate results with it. And they probably knew considerably more about magnetic variation than you do, sir. One thing is certain, they never set about running lines without knowing accurately the magnetic variation for the particular place they were in—at the time they were making it.

'For your information, sir, they made their own observations from the sun. It was customary to begin the survey either at ten o'clock in the morning, or at two o'clock in the afternoon, because at that time they could get their bearings most accurately. Sometimes they made observations at night from the North Star.'

He paused for a moment, but ignored Schloss's effort to respond. He turned to Fears. 'Get your men together—and if Mr. Corn will be kind enough to show us the corner, we will try to walk out the lines with his help and blaze them again.'

It was hard enough to have to deal with these suspicious backwoodsmen, thought Rhea, without having a liability like Schloss on your hands. Why in the world couldn't the company get a surveyor who was a native here!

The Corns had drawn into a clot. Micajah said nothing at the conclusion of Rhea's implied request, but indicated his readiness to accede by tarrying while Fears and the negroes gathered things together. There was something in the Major that held his trust, in spite of himself. He might be in on the plot to defraud them—whatever it was—Micajah thought, but it seemed unlikely. Anyhow, if they took the lines as he cited them, there wasn't much chance for shenanigans. The Major acted like a straight man and a gentleman.

Schloss was now nonplussed. He was shocked at the emotional turn the argument had taken. He felt vaguely that his own group had betrayed him. He began to doubt whether his argument had been wise. When he spoke, his voice was quiet and chastened. He pulled his black pipe out of his angular face and cleared his throat. 'I am under your orders here, Major Rhea. If you want to accept those lines without proving them, that's your business. I'm prepared to work at your direction.'

The surveying moved along more rapidly. Micajah showed Rhea and Fears the lot corner. 'The line a-goes right up the run of that branch for nigh two hundred yards and corners a little beyond a stoopin' magnolia,' he directed. After Rhea's tactful insistence, Micajah agreed to allow Schloss to set up his transit and line up his rodmen and Fears to chain the lot length. But the blazing was to be only at Micajah's direction and Rhea himself was to use one axe, while a darky used another.

Thirty feet from the corner, Micajah borrowed Rhea's axe and struck sharply at a knot on the great gray trunk of a poplar tree. The knot came off and disclosed an old blaze.

'Here's the first one, Major, and there's another t'other side of the line on this side of that white oak. Blaze'er and a-chop 'er right below the old mark.'

Schloss's chainmen came out within two feet of the old corner, which Micajah located. The surveying moved onward around the square-shaped group of Corn lots. When the upper line ran through the swamp and crossed Cedar Creek, Schloss insisted that his negroes cut a wide path. He must be able to see plainly. And he had three trees as large as a man's body cut down. He took no offsets. 'It looks like he's a-clearin' a road,' Micajah said to the others, though he did not oppose it.

But he found Schloss was like a hog. If you let him get his snoot in, he rooted up everything. After they had established the corner beyond the creek and were moving toward the starting corner, Schloss produced a light axe from his belt and joined in the tree-blazing. Micajah watched him without change of expression and said nothing. He would wait until Rhea had seen him blaze a tree. If Rhea did not stop him he would.

The line was not running through the thick piney woods. Trees three and four feet thick centered the line every twenty or thirty yards and lay close to it on the right and left every few feet. The prolific tree growth seemed to inflame Schloss and he slashed nearly every tree he passed. Micajah had it on his lips to speak to Rhea. Jere was behind him pulling his beard and muttering and Jet dropped back to point Schloss out to him.

The derbied surveyor stepped up to a great trunk thirty paces ahead of Micajah and laid his short axe to the smooth brown bark. He had finished the blaze and was striking three chops below it, when he suddenly let out a bellowing shriek. Both his pipe and axe dropped. He ran crazily dodging about among the trees and beating at his legs and back. 'I-God, i-God, i-God—yellow jackets!' he yelled. 'They're down my shirt! In my breeches!'

Fears' loud laugh was the first one heard. Everybody joined in, even Rhea, and Micajah chuckled with silent, easy shaking of his long frame.

9

TELFAIR County's superior court opened quietly in the winter of 1876.

A sagging sky enveloped the world in gray. And there was an interminable February drizzle that penetrated the marrow of one's bones. The belly of the iron courtroom stove was red-hot and a pot steamed from its top, but heat could not banish a tenuous chill from the remoter parts of the hall. The room swelled with a blur of voices; however, its carpet of sawdust muted the rough shoes that clomped so loudly on the stairway ascending from the floor below. The crowd overflowed the plank benches and a tobacco-squirting row of backwoodsmen in the rear of the room leaned against the unpainted pine walls.

There were a few jimswinger coats among the lawyers on the front benches, but the crowd was largely in rusty jeans and a motley of skin and wool jackets and short coats. The room stank of tobacco juice.

Behind a boxlike unpainted desk, elevated above the rest of the room, sat Judge Elisha Cromwell, a spare, rawboned man with gray hair and a drooping gray mustache. There was a wry look about his black eyes and thin lips, as if he tasted vinegar.

Amid the lawyers and court officers lolling and talking about him, he was terse and abstracted. There had been a shooting at the threshold of the courthouse on opening day in McRae the previous October and he felt the affront. His gavel rang out sharply as he nodded to the sheriff to open court.

Bailiffs moved about the room with their arms raised to hush the crowd. They tiptoed awkwardly, as if they feared the floor would break through with them. The Judge continued rapping. Micajah Corn was seated on one of the benches near the front and his father, Jere, sat beside him. They were motionless, except for the palsied shaking of Old Jere's head. Jet, who had come to town with them, leaned against the wall in the rear of the room with other backwoodsmen.

The courtroom audience looked expectantly at Judge Cromwell and the silence lengthened. His acid eyes moved slowly and searchingly over the assemblage—as if he scrutinized all corners, every bench, each face. The threat of discipline hung heavy over the room.

Finally he spoke. 'Gentlemen, I saw a pistol on a man in this room a few minutes ago.' His high-pitched voice had the penetration of a whistle. 'I cannot reconcile it to my sense of duty as a peace officer to let such violation of the law pass unnoticed.'

He paused and looked accusingly over the courtroom again. There was a quick wry twitch about his eyes and mouth, and he went on. 'It may be that it is my duty to go before the grand jury and indict him'—his voice ceased for a moment of suspense—'but if that man will walk up to this stand and lay the pistol and a fine of a dollar down here, I will let him off this time; otherwise, I will go before the grand jury and testify against him.'

His final words seemed almost to echo in the room as he ceased and moved his eyes over the crowd. There was no curious looking-about among the men facing the Judge—each seemed held in a self-conscious strain and the pause lengthened.

Finally a man with ragged gray hair, whose chin whiskers and boiled shirt-front were splotched with ambeer, got up uncertainly from a bench, then walked quickly forward and laid a black-barreled revolver on the Judge's desk. He dropped a silver dollar beside it, saying, in a chalky voice, 'I forgot I had the thing on me, Your Honor.' He smiled feebly and added, 'I apologize—I knew better, of course.'

Judge Cromwell looked at him only a moment, then his eyes continued to rove over the room as he began speaking. 'It is a very bad example for a member of the bar and an officer of this court to be setting—I hope you won't be so forgetful in the future, Mr. Crawley. However, you are not the man with the weapon I saw.'

His voice was swallowed by a threatening silence. A mountainous man standing upright in the middle aisle at the rear of the benches shifted his heavy-booted feet. Above his giant red walrus mustache, small marble-like eyes looked fixedly at the Judge. His feet moved several times before he got into motion, but finally he tramped forward, swinging a black wool hat in one hand. His fat mouth opened and closed giving out a sort of wordless wheeze as he pulled a long, old-fashioned dueling pistol from his shirt bosom and laid it on the desk.

75

'I believe you are a Graham, eh?' said Judge Cromwell, and without waiting for a reply he continued. 'You ought to know better than to bring that gun into this courtroom—and of course you do. The next time you won't get off so easy.' Then he quickly looked up at the courtroom. 'This is not the man, nor the gun,' he announced shortly. His face remained grim and the strain of silence was on again.

A long, rib-shaped man wearing a wool fascinator over his head came forward next to relieve himself of a derringer and a dollar bill, but the Judge's black eyes were not appeased. Others followed, separately, reluctantly. It began to look like a camp-meeting call for repentance.

Micajah, looking placidly on, caught sight of Jet's spotted calfskin jacket swinging down the middle aisle among the others. In the side pocket of his jeans breeches he felt the weight of his own long-barreled pistol, but no muscle moved behind the seeming smile of his curving mustache and he remained fixed in his seat.

Finally Judge Cromwell's eyes mellowed and the lines in his face relaxed. He looked at the pile of weapons on his desk. 'I think now we may be able to settle our differences here in a lawful, orderly way.' He turned to the clerk. 'Call the first case,' he said.

Micajah Corn had no case on the docket, but he was more than a curious listener. He had come in support of his son-in-law, Ardel Cone. Micajah had scarcely spoken to Cone since he married Georgie eight years ago. Fifteen-year-old Georgie Corn had run away with the fiddle-playing scalawag and Micajah had cut her off. No Corn had had traffic with her since, except occasionally her mother. But now the Yankees were trying to take a lot of land away from Ardel through the court and Micajah felt that no kin of his—even if he were a Cone— should be without support against the Yankees. Not that Ardel had called on him, nor did he intend to testify for him. But the Corns were there so people could see they were supporting Cone against Coventry and Company—there just in case he needed them.

Neither Micajah nor Jere had spoken to Ardel since they reached the courtroom, but Jet had taken up with him. There had been no talk about it between Micajah and Jet. The son had merely said when they reached McRae, 'I'll see Ardel, Pa.' He knew that Micajah had expected this of him.

Major Alan Rhea and John Casement were now entering the courtroom and pushing their way through the crowd. Rhea in gray serge and Casement in black frock coat appeared in sharp contrast to the men around them as they paused along the middle aisle to search for a possible seat at the front. A bailiff arose and motioned them forward.

For the previous hour they had been closeted in the clerk's office discussing the ejectment case against Cone. The deed Cone held had been registered only two years before, but it purported to be a conveyance made by the sheriff in 1864 as the result of a tax sale. Casement's search of the records revealed that there had never been such a sale.

'It's plainly a forgery,' Casement had said, rubbing his chin thoughtfully. 'But it gives color of title and he has witnesses who will swear they lived on the land before him. Cone is shrewd and Calebb's his lawyer. His proof will be flimsy, but not too flimsy for one of these Telfair County juries to swallow!'

Major Rhea's formal manners had almost broken with his irritation. 'It's not my fault!' he had exclaimed rather sharply and had then risen and paced the floor.

He had continued, with feeling: 'I can get nothing through to Mr. Coventry any more. Lechleiter has been here from New York—he is insufferable'—He broke off here and, after a pause, continued in more measured manner: 'I told him we should settle this case the best way we could. He would hear to no compromise. His attitude is quite different—quite different!' He ended his complaint by violently poking the logs in the fireplace.

'We'll be lucky if we win it,' Casement had retorted cheerlessly.

But now in the courtroom their faces were bland and confident, as they sat near the Judge's desk in chairs provided by the bailiff.

Calhoun Calebb entered the courtroom through a doorway at the rear of the Judge's stand. His head and shoulders reared above the Judge on the dais as he stood beside it. He looked briefly over the crowd and his cavernous face swung right until its solitary orb sighted the steaming pot on the courtroom stove. He wore a rumpled sack coat and a homespun shirt without a scarf.

As the jury in a case on trial began to file out of the room, Calhoun greeted Judge Cromwell in his resounding bass voice. The clerk announced the case of Coventry and Company against Ardel Cone and Calhoun beckoned to Cone in the back of the room to come forward.

There was a single counsel table, located at the right of the Judge's stand. Casement and Rhea had taken seats at the end near the Judge and Calhoun had seated himself and the defendant adjacent to the courtroom crowd.

Cone had a clownish air. His pale eyes protruded and there was a bare callousness in them. His wide tobacco-stained mouth was habitually in a good-humored smile. Now he grinned broadly and ducked his head at the courtroom and there was an answering titter. Those who knew him—and most of the backwoods men and women in the courtroom did— knew that nothing bothered Ardel.

The sheriff, a wheezy man with wattles depending from his chin, stood up and called to twelve men in the benches to come forward and occupy the jury box across the room from the counsel table. The men got up from their seats deliberately and moved across the parquet in an irregular file. Their dress was uniformly homespun and jeans; their beards and hair grew wild. They sank into reposeful attitudes in the jury chairs.

Judge Cromwell glanced toward the counsel table for approval and quickly Calhoun was on his feet. His mouth, twisted by the lava-like scar on his left cheek, was in a broad smile as he looked into the faces of the recumbent jurors. 'We accept the jury, Your Honor. All we want is twelve honest men and they're a-settin' in the box right now.' The idiom did not sound natural on his lips, but it seemed to pass muster with the crowd.

Casement did not rise, but his eyebrows puckered and his voice rang out sharply. 'Your Honor, the defense counsel knows your question was addressed to me—first. His conduct is not only irregular, but unfair to my client and he knows it.'

Casement knew that one of the jurors had testified against the company in a previous trial and Rhea leaned over to tell him that another was a cousin of a man the company had proceeded against the year before. The Coventry counsel spent the next two hours challenging jurors and seeking acceptable substitutes.

The presentation of proof required less time. Major Rhea took the witness stand to establish Coventry and Company's claim to the lot of land in question, setting up what he called the company's 'short chain of title.'

Against this Cone testified that he had bought the lot from one Lum Bozeman two years previously. Bozeman, so hunchbacked that his long beard brushed his knees as he sat in the witness chair, said he had bought it of Lige Dowdy, who took the stand to testify that he had acquired it from the Widow Fussell. The three men had collectively owned and lived upon the land for more than seven years and their title was a sheriff's deed obtained by the Widow Fussell through a tax sale, according to the proof.

Casement presented court records to show that the lot in question had never been sold for taxes and that, impliedly, Cone's deed was a forgery. A sallow-faced man with squirrel teeth swore Lum Bozeman had pulled turpentine boxes with him up in Coventry County three years before, when he was supposed to have been farming the Telfair land. On cross-examination Calhoun made this man admit that he had once worked for Coventry and Company as a log-chopper.

Calhoun leaned his chair back and looked up at the ceiling in an abstracted fashion while Casement made his argument to the jury. He appeared to be oblivious to the quietly speaking company counsel, but he was listening closely.

Casement's words were as well chosen and correct as his white collar and his buttoned broadcloth coat. He looked frankly into the jurors' faces and spoke in a serious conversational tone. He recognized that Coventry and Company was a corporation that came into this community from another state. It was not natural for the jurors to feel a personal interest in a thing so impersonal as a corporation.

But a corporation, he told them, must have rights in court as well as an individual, and if they would but reflect a moment they would realize that the rights of this corporation were of direct interest to them—protection of these rights was essential to the livelihood of their neighbors and even of themselves.

His tone became confidential as he reviewed the evidence. It was easy, he said, to forge a deed to a lot of land. It merely required a little penmanship. But with such a deed a man must live on that land, must hold that land, hostilely and against the world, for seven years. That was what the Georgia law said. Or, if there were three owners in succession, the three must have held it for seven years.

There could be no doubt that Cone's deed was a forgery. Opposing counsel had admitted it may have been a *coffee-pot deed*—May have been! Cone knew it was—he couldn't afford to deny it was—a coffee-pot deed!

At Casement's use of the term 'coffee-pot deed,' Calhoun eased his chair legs to the floor and released his breath audibly. The phrase had come into common use after disclosure in a trial two years before that a forged deed had been given an aged appearance by soaking it in a pot of coffee.

Casement pointed out that the supposed owners and occupants of the land before Cone had never recorded their deeds at the register's office and had never paid any taxes on the land. The statement that Bozeman had lived in Coventry County when he was supposed to have been living on the land in question had gone unchallenged.

Casement raised his musical voice as he concluded. 'Gentlemen of the jury, you made the land law in Georgia— Coventry and Company had no voice in it. Under the law you made and according to the facts in this case the land belongs to Coventry and Company. They only ask you to give them the protection of your law.'

Calhoun came up from his chair slowly and walked stiffly across the room. Like a tree, he stood towering above the jury for a moment without speaking. His arms hung naturally by his sides, but his hands were clenched. He turned sideways so that the scar on his face was toward the judge and counsel table. His face wore a twisted smile.

'So the laywer for the Yankees says that Ardel ain't got no claim 'cept a coffee-pot deed.' He continued to smile at the jury as he walked back and forth before it. 'Coffee-pot deed!' he repeated after the second round. 'Gentlemen of the jury, I repeat, a coffee-pot deed!' His great voice rose without effort until it rattled the window-panes.

'Do any of you know what a coffee-pot deed is? I betchew do— everlastin' one of you. You don't a-know nothin' else!'

He suddenly swung around and in three giant strides crossed the room to the stove where a big-bottomed coffee-pot steamed noiselessly. He yanked it from the stove and in three strides stood again before the jury.

'Here's the pot! Gentlemen, you know as well as I do. It's as familiar to you as hard work.' He held the pot toward the seated jurors. 'And you know that smell. It's coffee you tell me, and you know. You got a right to know—you've smelled it about daybreak ever' mornin', fur the last fifty years, I'd say, jest a-lookin' at most of ye.

'That's the kinder deed Ardel Cone's got—a coffee-pot! And a skillet, maybe! And you know what that means—don't nobody know no better than you do. You know what it takes to put coffee in that pot and meat in that frying-pan. You know why you smell that coffee-pot mostly before daybreak in the mornin'. The marks are on your hands and on your backs, too. Coventry and Company up in Noo Yark'—he humorously imitated a Northern accent—'Coventry and Company mought not git it, but it's plain as the south end of a mule to you, gentlemen.

'Ardel says he spent two year behind his plow and his hoe tryin' to make that land fill his coffee-pot—and more'n apt it was parched peas half the time. Mr. Coventry and Company didn't come around any durin' those two years to take a-holt of that plow, aer hoe any. Yes, sir, he set right in his cushion chair in Noo Yark and let ole Ardel bust his plow-pints on stumps and his back over a hoe-handle.

'And Mr. Coventry and Company didn't set up none of a night when the ole sow littered to keep her from a-wallowin' on the pigs. He never even prayed for rain when dry weather was a-firin' the corn.

'Ardel waunt there but two years, as he was plain to tell you, but before him Lum Bozeman tried to fill his coffee-pot there and Lige Dowdy afore him. And more'n apt the Widow Fussell did some plowin' there to fill her coffee-pot.

'You may not've hyurd much about it, but if you are a rich Yankee in Noo Yark you can git a deed that don't call for any plowin' aer hoein', aer corn-pullin'. You can just hire a land agent, aer a lawyer to pick up somethin' fur nothin' down heah amongst a lot of ignorant Georgia crackers. I say, you mought not a-hyurd much about the kinder deed he's got, but I don't have to make you acquainted with no coffee-pot deed.'

He stood holding the coffee-pot before him. He lifted the lid so that the aroma might flow from it more freely. He smiled and continued standing silently before them for a time.

Judge Cromwell's charge to the jury was brief and its closeted deliberations briefer. Calhoun had won his ninth consecutive ejectment suit against Coventry and Company.

10

CALHOUN Calebb snorted and subsided into his twisted smile. The warm current of blood through his veins was impervious to the damp February chill. He felt an expansive sense of possession over the small circle of backwoodsmen standing around him in the lower hallway of the courthouse. It extended to backwoodsmen all over Telfair County and dimly to the entire pine barrens. There was something about the cumulative moment that made him feel as if he had successfully defended the county against an attack.

'Well Cal, ye done it to 'em agin!' a goat-bearded old man called from the circle. This was followed by slow, jarring laughter.

'Boys, they just didn't have a case,' Calhoun retorted with mock regret, renewing his twisted smile.

'Naer a coffee-pot!' said a sallow-faced stripling.

Cone, who stood in the center of the circle with Calhoun, spoke with a rueful grin. 'Man, don't talk about that aer coffee! Cal got me so hongry a-messin' with that pot, I'd a-settled the damn case for a cup and saucer full.'

Laughter jarred through the hallway again and Jet, who occupied the center with Cone and Calhoun, tried, 'I'll bet the jury is a-drinkin' it over yander at the dinner-house now,' but it brought only an echo.

Micajah appeared at the doorway looking for Jet. He had fed his horses and was ready for his own meal. Outside the courthouse he had met Major Rhea, whose cordiality showed no strain over the lawsuit. Rhea had told him Coventry and Company should not have gone to trial in the case—the suit was brought over his protest.

Micajah had asked, with a smile not altogether free of irony, 'Major, when's the company a-goin' to law us?' But Rhea had not jested in reply. He said he had already recommended to Lechleiter, the company's general agent, that they set up no claim to the Corn lots.

Micajah now advanced through the circle and shook hands with Calhoun. 'That was the master speech, Calhoun,' he said.

Calhoun observed that Micajah spoke to Cone, but did not shake hands with him.

Micajah did not tarry long, but nodding to Jet turned to go.

Rearing above the crowd like a mastiff in a hound pack, Calhoun strode through the circle and accompanied Micajah to the doorway.

From the courthouse Calhoun walked alone to McNeal's, where visiting lawyers stopped during court week. He had no sense of his solitude. Already, he had in his pocket his fee from the lawsuit. Before the case had come to trial he and Cone had arranged a sale of the timber on the land for five hundred dollars. Calhoun had taken two hundred dollars as his share.

He worked for a fee, but the case meant more than that to him. This was the ninth ejectment suit he had defended and won against Coventry and Company during the past year. He hadn't lost a single ejectment case against them. Of course there had been three squatters who had come to him without any case, he recalled, and he had refused to represent them. But, my God, he had to have some proof of a claim to get by the judge!

Rhea and Casement must have known they were going to lose. Still they looked sick when the jury brought in its verdict. It wasn't just the one case—it was the added dose that made them sick. Calhoun recalled the conversation he had had with Rhea almost two years before. They had just come out of the courthouse at Lancaster where the Major was telling a yarn about the backwoodsman and the one-legged bed. He had slept in a one-legged bed more than once, Calhoun responded, and from that he had spread out to his intimacy with back-woodsmen and the peculiar value his experience might have for Coventry and Company. When he suggested that Rhea might help him and the company, too, Rhea had stopped nodding his head and saying, "Why, yes,' and his Vandyke beard had taken on a stiff, waxy look. He pictured to himself Rhea's regret now: with exaggerated formality the frigid aristocrat was kicking his own backside.

Calculating roughly, Calhoun figured he had made nineteen hundred dollars from the cases he had won against the company. In those early days when he talked about the prosperity Coventry would bring to the pine barrens, he hadn't guessed his would come in such a way. He smiled a little as he thought of this. He should thank Rhea for not employing him. The ejectment suits offered vast possibilities.

When Calhoun reached the boarding-house he went up to his room to wash his hands before dinner, instead of using the basin on the back porch. He wanted more time for his train of thought.

When the Coventrys first came, he had imagined he had something in common with them—a heritage. What rot! He probably had as much in common with the backwoodsmen as anybody. The Coventrys had taken up with the River Road *rooster-crats*. Calhoun snorted. He would certainly make common lot with the squatters as long as he could win their claims in the courts. A sorry pack of hounds, maybe, but they were for him and he was for them. If there must be boot-licking, he preferred to wear the boots. Nine ejectment suits weren't even an eye-opener—Coventry's land claims offered vast possibilities.

'Vast possibilities!' Calhoun said the words half audibly as he poured water from a crockery basin into the slop jar and gazed beyond the muslin-curtained window into the gray. He felt his blood drive harshly from his chest into his veins. There was big money ahead of him—and power. He was anxious to be after it.

Winning a case against John Casement was a pleasure, too. Smug, pretty-faced interloper, Calhoun thought, with feeling. He would make the Coventry pimp eat his own words. *The squatters' scarecrow!* Casement had not intended his epithet for Calhoun's ears, but he had heard Crawley repeating it. Calhoun gave his horse snort that ended in a twisted smile. He was the squatters' scarecrow all right. He could put that pink-cheeked pimp on the run any time they met! And old wax-whiskers Rhea, or any other Coventry-kept crowd!

Squatters' scarecrow—he would use that handle in his next land suit before a backwoods jury. 'The company mouthpiece calls me the squatters' scarecrow!' He tried it out on his own ear. It rang well. He could do a lot with that phrase.

But somehow his reflection ended in a sense of weariness. He sat down heavily on the side of his bed and his weight shook its high carved head. As he leaned back against the bed-stead, he fingered the twisted scar on his cheek. The scar had always brought him names— when he was a boy he had hated it.

It was about all his childhood held—that and taunts about his father. Those days stank of urine and nux vomica. He sup-posed it was because on that flame-blind morning he had wet his shirt-tail. When he fell on the red-hot coffee-pot rack he had been paralyzed except for that. It must have been five or six years before he stopped wetting himself—every time he got in a rage over being teased or slighted, or had nightmares at night. His mother must have given him a peck of nux vomica pills. He wondered if they had really helped.

The burden of his paternity had been equally grievous. He wondered now, as he had wondered many times, why Matthew Calebb had deserted his mother. Was it, after all, essentially as the Calhoun men had said, because he was a *damn Maine Yankee?* What rot! Yet in some way there must be truth in it. And he had never seen the man—except with eyes too inno-cent to know him. He might still be living somewhere in the North—or God alone knows where!

Manifestly his father was the intellectual superior of his mother, or any of the Calhouns. He was a graduate of Amherst College and was considered very learned by everybody in Lumber City, his mother said—but that went with the reputation of any schoolmaster. And he had kept her in after school to court her—she hardly in her first crinoline! She must have been a pretty thing then with her big gray eyes and chestnut-colored hair, and that spontaneous laugh of hers rising like the sound of water filling a pitcher—she still had that.

How could that damn scoundrel have done it! He felt his blood turn poison and light sweat sprang out at his temples and mouth, as it always did when he dwelt upon his mother's mistreatment.

His father had left after the Yankee colony at Lumber City dwindled away and the school there closed. For almost a year, then, he had tried teaching schools at Jacksonville and among the Wilcoxes and Coffees on up the River Road, but he could not bear their high-and-mighty ways and their ignorance, his mother said. Matthew had told his young wife he was in correspondence with the book publishing house of A. Saul and Brother in Boston. If he went there he believed he could secure a position. The Calhouns later established that he did board a vessel at Savannah for New York. Further than that they could learn nothing.

Calhoun's memory of life did not go back behind the morning of the burn in his fifth year. He wondered now if the pain of it had not blotted out all earlier impressions. He could not recall that he was ever happy during the years at his grandmother's and at Old Sodom school. A teacher there once had called him Caliban. The man had a hump-backed nose and was named Bullard. Calhoun didn't know who Caliban was, but he had flushed hot and buried his face in his arms—and wet his seat. The Wyche and Bridges boys used to ask him where his father was. He thought his father was dead and said so, at first. They had called his father a 'damn Yankee runaway!' He could lick the Wyche and Bridges boys, both, but that did not altogether cure the rankle of it. And he used to catch his uncles looking at him sometimes, then they would look quickly away. Their mouths were always drooping when he caught them. They would clear their throats and whistle, or walk off then.

It hadn't been much better after his mother sold her negroes and they moved to Dublin. She had sold the negroes and everything else she could sell and turned it into money. She wanted to get away from Sodom and the Calhouns as much as he did.

At least he had got rid of his uncles' staring. His mother had created more or less of a fairy tale about his father, God bless her! He had been lost at sea on his way to New York, she said, and she talked often about what a fine mind and what great learning he had. Calhoun had always spent a great deal of his time in his mother's company—when he was not reading. The self-conscious kindness of the boys who avoided looking at his face or making any allusion to the disfigurement was as intolerable for him as those who called him *Cut-plug* and *Rawmeat*. He could feel now a breath of the smoldering fury that made him shove Fulmer Grainger, the boatline owner's son who wanted to be kind to him—Fulmer, who was supposed to be his best friend. Even his mother had been mystified and ready to condemn him then.

The poison from Fulmer's ill-concealed pity—for that is what it was—had been accumulating in him for nearly a year. But it probably would never have broken out into passion except for the boat ride. How Fulmer persuaded his father to turn over a steamboat for a picnic, Calhoun never knew, but it seemed too wonderful an outing to turn down. He said the boys of their class at the academy would ride down to Mount Vernon on Saturday morning and come back in the afternoon.

Calhoun's mouth twisted in a smile as he recalled the panic he had felt when, after the gangplank had been drawn, that coopful of ruffly girls had come out of the cabin onto the deck. Fulmer knew about his fright before girls, it had been deliberate concealment. He had picked his sister Nellie—one of those finespun creatures like a Dresden pitcher—as Calhoun's partner. She had a tiny waist, tiny hands and feet, and a tiny voice, and she always lowered it a little when she spoke to him—as if he were sick.

He had thought of diving overboard and swimming back to the bank, but he didn't. Unable to utter a coherent word, he had stood by the railing, watching the tree-walled river banks push by the boat.

The bitter dregs of the draught had been Nellie's trying to teach him to dance when the boat hands made music on the lower deck. He could see now the gentle daintiness with which Nellie had taken him by the hands to draw him out into the circle. He had felt like a gosling trailing a flock of biddies. When the circle had broken, still holding to his sweating hands, she had tried to show him the two-step and a whirl. She had fluttered about him with that sweet-sad look on her face.

When he tried it he tripped over his own toe. He had to run to keep from falling full-length.

His reason kept telling him he could not fight Fulmer, he couldn't fight a fellow who was trying to be nice to him. Nobody would understand. That was the maddening thing about it. He had gone to the back of the boat and watched the big stern wheel churn the muddy water into suds. The water did not churn any more than his insides. Then, unexpectedly, the moment came. He saw Fulmer standing close to the edge of the railless bottom deck looking toward the bank. No one was around. He could not remember what he thought, or that he thought at all, but he could feel now the impact of his shoulder against Fulmer's back. At that moment he had hoped the boy would drown. But he yelled 'Man overboard!' and a great commotion followed.

Evidently one of the boat hands saw him and told Captain Ashworth and Nellie. Then everybody knew it and the pretense of good manners between them fell away. A Clarkson boy had shouted into his face, 'Why, you dirty Yankee runaway half-breed!' Another had yelled, 'You Caliban!'

But he had shouted back—had let loose as much as they did. 'I hate you! I hate you!' he could only shout at first, then he had called them 'hypocrites!' and 'ignoramuses!'

Still sitting on the bed, he concluded his recollection of the episode with a shrug. That had been fourteen, no fifteen years ago. Since then he had acquired an alligator hide. Now he did not mind his disfigurement and nobody cared who his father was—the war had changed a lot of things.

The war! The war! He thought of its foolish beginning. In those early days, when he was still an overseer, Major Rhea had shown him almost open contempt. Later he had enlisted in Brown's militia and had been cited for bravery at Macon and was made captain of his company after he helped General Foster move the documents out of Milledgeville.

But all of that had ended with the war—the ragged, one-eyed war! No more half slave and half free—no more half-breeds! Now a new day and a new country—these pine barrens—with their railroads and sawmills!

11

D AVID McIntosh, the general superintendent's
eleven-year-old son, leaned over the upstairs
banister, straining his neck to bring the front
doorway below within view, and counted twelve weighty feet
and trouser legs as they entered and moved toward the library.
At least eight of those feet were strange to the McIntosh
household, David concluded.

Kathleen, his sister, whose maturity this summer prohibit-
ed her from peeping down the stairway, had been impressed,
too. An hour earlier, her father had crossed the dew-wet lawn
to where she sat on the back porch polishing his tan shoes.
This menial act of devotion had always, before, brought a
small protest from him. But he only asked where her mother
was—had looked at but had not seen the shoe in her hands.

In the somber library the company men were seated about
a long walnut table. Casement, at one end, leaned forward in
his chair. Small rigid lines showed about his mouth and his
usually direct eyes were fixed on the dimness framed by the
opposite window. He cleared his throat and glanced along the

line of faces about him on either side of the table. On his left sat the two Savannah lawyers. The nearer was slab-faced with gray curls, parted in the middle and depending almost to his shoulders. He was expressionless as Casement glanced at him. The man beyond had a square, heavy face. Bulldog wrinkles showed about his nose and mouth as he sat studying the handwriting on a sheet of foolscap paper. The New York lawyer, who had come down with Karl Lechleiter, Coventry general agent, rummaged in his portfolio. His protuberant teeth, usually bared in smiling, were covered by solemn lips.

At Casement's right, Major Rhea leaned back quietly in his seat, his forearms rigid on the chair-rests. Beyond, the gray forelock of Ian McIntosh's head hung almost in his eyes.

Casement's gaze rested on Lechleiter. The general agent seemed remote from the tension in the other men. He was a slight man and looked smaller in the great armchair in which he sat withdrawn a little way from the table.

'When I first ran into squatter claims based on that tax sale of 1845, or supposed sale,' Casement began, adjusting a package of legal papers on the edge of the table, 'I did not dream of its extent. I have made further search of the Telfair County records since I last wrote you about it, Mr. Lechleiter. You know then I thought a hundred lots would cover it.' He paused and opened his mouth for a terse intake of breath. 'That sheriff levied on the whole sixteen-hundred-lot holding. I am now convinced that more than two hundred, probably three hundred lots were sold off to satisfy that one seven-hundred-and-forty-dollar tax claim back there!'

His eyes dropped to the papers before him on the table for an instant, then returned to Lechleiter. 'Most of it went to the two or three land speculators that I have mentioned at around the same figure, about six cents a lot. It was all fraudulent on the face of it.'

The Savannah lawyers nodded eagerly. "Fraud!' one of them echoed.

'I tr-rust the feder-ral judge weel theenk so!' McIntosh, sitting forward with a hand on either of his spread knees, cocked his head to one side and twisted his lips in a tight smile. Rhea added that three hundred lots would mean more than sixty thousand acres.

The Savannah lawyers returned to an examination of papers on the table before them and Casement stared at Rhea with an abstracted look.

Lechleiter now sat up in his chair, bringing his pointed nose and pointed chin onto a perpendicular axis. He rubbed his lean hands together before him as if he were warming them. 'Fraud, eh—fraud?' He spoke in a brisk high-pitched voice. 'Well, I suppose you lawyers have run down the various holders under the tax titles?' Without pausing, he went on, 'How many are there? Who do you propose to proceed against first?'

The Savannah lawyers said they had prepared a list of twenty-six to be named defendants in the first bill. The square-faced man pushed a log paper along the table toward Lechleiter. They would follow the first court petition with others if it turned out well.

'Turn out well!' Casement exclaimed with a show of irritation. He paused to look at the speaker, he smiled wryly. 'Well, at least we'll be in a real court this time. No more squatter juries. No more flimsy evidence.' His voice rose. 'No more loose judges to permit questionable tactics by squatter lawyers!'

Rhea's silent face suddenly crinkled and his beard shook. 'And, no more Squatters' Scarecrow, either—hey, Mr. Casement?' he supplied.

Casement joined in the laughter. 'Calebb probably won't be there —but let him come,' he said, now serious-faced; 'he'll find a judge who sees things our way for a change—and there won't be a damned jury to contend with.'

He got up from his chair and joined the other lawyers at the side of the table in their examination of several abstracts. McIntosh rose abruptly and paced he room looking idly at his bookshelves. Rhea had resumed his silence, sitting as still as statuary. His eyes were upon the bent heads of the murmuring lawyers.

Relaxed in the armchair, Lechleiter put one of his slight legs over an arm, then withdrew it to swing the other over the opposite arm of the chair. He wound and unwound about his finger a gold watch-chain with a Phi Beta Kappa key at its end, looking quizzically at the men about him with pert birdlike eyes.

Finally he interrupted the silence. 'Captain McIntosh, the history of the Coventry holding is astonishing.'

McIntosh halted and faced him. The lawyers raised their heads.

Lechleiter went on, still swinging the watch-chain around his finger. 'I have pieced it together largely from information you lawyers gave me, but I have made further historical study—and it's interesting history.

'To begin at the beginning'—here McIntosh resumed his seat and the lawyers abandoned the court bill—'all of the land lying between the Oconee and Ocmulgee Rivers was purchased by the State of Georgia from Indians in 1805. It was the first land in the State to be disposed of by lottery. Under it every white man, widow, and orphan was entitled to draw and every Revolutionary soldier was entitled to two draws.

'In spite of the simplicity of acquisition—or because of it, maybe' —there was a slightly facetious inflection of his voice— 'it didn't go so fast—most of it. People settled along the two rivers, because there was transportation and rich farming land. The big stretch of pine uplands spreading out between the rivers, which you call the pine barrens, went begging.

'Michael Bloodworth—you know the Milledgeville speculator who was the original grantee—evidently amassed this tract—and he was the first holder of all of it except about twenty thousand acres—for a song. But he got a good price, or what he must have thought a good price, when he sold it to the old Georgia Pine Lumber Company back in 1834.

'Of course you know of the firm of New Englanders who tried to operate the old water sawmill at Lumber City—to their sorrow. But there were some shrewd gentlemen connected with that concern. They shifted the titles about from one pocket to another, through a couple of dummy banks and left them, strangely enough, in the lap of the State of Indiana—and that State minus about two hundred and fifty thousand dollars' worth of its canal bonds.

'I don't think we need to dwell on the period of Indiana's ownership too much in our lawsuit, in spite of the fact that the tax sale took place then. At least we don't need to make any observation on the strangeness of Indiana's holding title.' Here he paused and looked down at the chain-enwrapped finger, smiling momentarily.

He recommenced: 'In about seven years the title went back into individual hands—a man named Joseph Hart. Hart, mute evidence indicates, was as good a politician as he was a land speculator—if you do not insist that those terms are synonymous. He bought a whole lot of titles for a thousand dollars.

'Then the trading grew rapid and intricate. The titles shuffled about in the North through several hands during the next fifteen years. It is a feat in mental gymnastics to follow this jugglery.' Lechleiter moved his pert quick glance over the group of men and smiled. 'But I believe I can do it. Hart divided the holding into sixteenths and sold it piecemeal to six men. McPheters, Sinclair, Olmstead, Jacobs, McInturf, and Jones were their names. Jones acquired McPheters' and Sinclair's titles and sold them all to a man named DePauw. Jacob's title passed to Scheurmann.

'From DePauw the titles passed to Weinberg, from Weinberg to Kreuger, who also acquired Olmstead's titles. Kreuger's titles then passed to Sleeper and later Cadwell. Scheurmann then secured all the titles held by Cadwell and later sold them to Becker-White. It was from Becker-White that Mr. Lancaster first acquired McInturf's titles through the hands of Livingstone and Peyton.

'Soon after the war Lancaster came down here to see what he held title to and you know the story from that point.' Lechleiter stopped abruptly and looked about him.

The New York lawyer laughed, showing his teeth fully. The others chuckled. Their chuckles became smiles. The smiles changed into straight-faced silence and the lawyers, relaxed in their seats, straightened their backs to lean forward at the table again.

Rhea fixed Lechleiter with his grave, large-pupiled eyes. He began speaking slowly: It was not, of course, his function to develop legal theory for the company, but he wondered how the company could maintain its title against some of the squatters.

He asked Casement to hand him the proposed list of defendants, leaning forward in his chair to receive it. Casement shuffled about among the papers in front of him and looked over at the lawyers to the left. They had joined in the search. The slab-faced lawyer found the list and it was passed over to Rhea. The lawyers continued to occupy themselves with their papers.

Rhea went on: He knew of his own knowledge that some of the defendants named had been living on the land through the years of title-jugglery Lechleiter had mentioned, some of them had been there even at the time of Indiana's ownership. Under Georgia law their claim was good, as he understood it, after twenty years of possession even without a deed.

He looked inquiringly at the lawyers across the table, but Lechleiter did not wait for them to answer. He laughed sharply.

'It is up to the lawyers to supply a plausible theory—that's what the company hires them for.' He paused to glance at the chain swinging from his finger.

'And as for the Savannah judge, I will tell you now, I have more than a hope of sympathetic treatment.' He pulled a gold-case watch from his waistcoat pocket and opened it. 'Mr.

Christopher Coventry knew of Judge Illius before he came South; had business dealings with the judge's brother. We know Judge Illius to be alright'—He closed the watch and restored it—'We can't take a chance on losing a quarter of a million dollars' worth of timber!'

12

MICAJAH felt caught up in the scream and throb of Coventry and Company's big sawmill as he walked with more rigidness than was his habit from the company office building on the May morning of his visit to Pineville in 1880. Though a hundred yards distant, the office porch vibrated with the beat of the big fly wheels. The keen saw whine cut through the beat and at one end of the mill shed two stiff plumes of steam spouted alternately in time with the pulse.

It was a rending scene of movement and sound, but the foundation Micajah felt shaking under him was not physical. He had just been told that Major Rhea was no longer woodsman-agent for the company. When he entered the building he had gone to the door of the office that had always been Rhea's and had knocked. When his knocking brought no response, he had tried the knob and found the door locked. The Major had made a practice of being in his office on Saturdays. Micajah had started to look about him when a little glass window in the wall across the hall went up and a man stuck his head out.

He was a beardless, tow-headed, young fellow who looked like a cautious rabbit peeping from his burrow. But his voice hadn't sounded that way. It was cold and through-the-nose, like that of all the Yankees. 'What do you want?' he had said.

Micajah told him and he had answered in his clippity way: 'Rhea's not here any more. You'll have to see Mr. Fears—Zenas Fears.' And he started to duck down again, but Micajah had held him. He wanted to know what had happened to the Major. 'Quit. Month ago. Gone to Florida, I hear,' the young fellow had said, and bobbed back into his burrow.

Micajah stood looking at the square, blank window glass. He stood there several minutes while the words slowly took effect. They had made his ears ring like a whipcracker and his head had buzzed. He was not prepared to believe them and the ringing in his ears had threatened him with confusion. Awkwardly and uncertainly he had walked from the building.

It was not that he had any direct interest in Rhea's employment. Micajah had come to the Major bearing troublous news, to find that the one thing he hadn't figured on had happened—Rhea had quit—had vanished—had pulled up stakes and gone to far Florida a month before. Men like Major Rhea did not pull up stakes and clear out—or they hadn't until now. Rhea's running off—for that was what it amounted to—seemed more disturbing to him at the moment than the ill report he had come to straighten out with him.

On the Sunday previous Micajah had heard over at Cameron Shops that a federal judge down in Savannah had said the deeds he and Jere held to their land were no good. The court of the Yankee Government had said that all of those deeds that the Telfair sheriff and clerk had made up back in '45 were worthless.

Micajah had come to the Major for an explanation and reassurance.

He walked slowly now from the mill toward Pineville's ragged row of wooden stores and went around the covered sidewalks to the rear hitching-racks where he had left his team. Squatting beside a wheel of the wagon, he drew out his knife and whittled at a fragment of cypress shingle.

Major Rhea had said the company didn't want his and Pa's land; had said that under Georgia law it was theirs, deed or no deed; had said the Yankee court, nor the company couldn't change that, but the Major wasn't speaking for the company any more.

Micajah reviewed the conversation he had had with Rhea about the Savannah court business. It was almost four years ago now, late in November, when the word came to him that a marshal from the federal court had a paper for him over in the Telfair county seat. That was a Wednesday. He was still cleaning up his cotton patch and hadn't got to McRae until the Saturday following. They said at the courthouse the man had already gone, but he left a court summons. It said that Coventry and Company had gone into federal court in Savannah and had claimed he didn't have a good title to his land. He could answer if he wanted to.

He heard that about twenty-five or thirty other men had got the same kind of notices, but he did not know who they were. A couple of days later he learned that Dan'l McMillan, Mit's husband, over Macville way was one of them.

Dan'l, Zeke, and Jet all talked about it. They were in favor of hiring Calhoun Calebb and going down to Savannah, to the Yankee court. None of 'em had ever been to Savannah, or knew where it was. None of 'em had anything to put up except advice. It would have taken half the worth of the land to pay the cost—Ardel Cone paid Calebb two hundred dollars just on one land lot right there in McRae.

Micajah had been uncertain. A federal court in Savannah was no place for backwoodsmen to be sticking their heads in-to—they'd better hold to Georgia law. And where could he get any such money as it would take to go all the way to Savannah with a lawyer and law in the Yankee Government courts?

He had gone to Pineville to see Major Rhea, as he had aimed to do from the first. It was slap dark when the Major finally came to his office and they smoked it over.

The Major had sat straight up in his swivel chair, rattling some papers on his roller-top desk with one hand. Micajah had thought then that the company land claims were giving him some unrest.

He would not tell him to stay away from the Savannah court.

'No,' he had said, fixing Micajah with his straight-sighted eyes, 'Mr. Corn, you have a summons from the court—your title will be attacked there—I cannot advise you to ignore it.'

Then he had glanced at his hand on the desk and seemed to mull for a moment, then went on: 'I will say this, sir, Alton Jason, the Savannah lawyer and land speculator, is named as first defendant in the company's bill. He is a man of means and I am sure he will defend his claim. His action might save you the trouble and expense of going into court yourself.'

Then Micajah had reminded him that he had said long ago, and Calhoun Calebb had seconded it, that under Georgia law the Corn land belonged to the Corns, titles or not.

'That is indubitably true, I think, indubitably,' Rhea had put it.

Micajah had recalled at the time that after all he had not paid but twelve dollars and a half for those papers and even if the court said they were no good the loss wouldn't be much. He wasn't much interested in deeds so long as nobody bothered his land.

Now he shifted his weight a little from one leg to the other and spat tobacco juice into a puddle of water ten feet away. Well, even if Rhea had gone and he wasn't speaking for the company now, it didn't change what he had said about the law. Suppose the Yankee Government court had said his and Pa's deeds were no good, the law of Georgia said the land was theirs.

But the reasonableness of his argument did not relieve Micajah of uneasiness. Unthought-of-things had happened— he felt himself on shaky ground. The Yankee Government and the company might not heed Georgia law. And there was no dependence to be put in men who were employed by the company. The Yankee Government didn't care a thrip for Georgia. The South had had a good argument when it fought the Confederate War! He lifted his black wool hat and mopped sweat from his forehead and neck.

He felt a hand on his shoulder and looked up. Thunderation! he had forgot all about Jasmine, poor little chap!

Ten-year-old Jasmine, youngest of Micajah's children, had groped out into the darkness before daybreak with him to come to town. Civil had protested that it was no hour for a little girl to be getting up, but Jasmine had begged and Micajah couldn't deny her. Wrapped in blankets in the wagon, Jasmine had quickly gone back to sleep, not waking in spite of the roughness of the Company Short Road, until they had almost reached Pineville.

She was a delicate child and small for her years. Her tow hair, which curled and escaped plaiting because of Micajah's insistence, hung free down her back and gave an ethereal look to her pale face. She moved as daintily, as timidly as a young she-goat.

She followed Micajah to the sawmill and back to the wagon, walking silently at his heels. And she had joggled quietly on the wagon tongue enjoying the town scene while he whittled, but now hunger hurt her stomach.

Micajah moved to the wagon to get out their basket of victuals. He mustn't make the child suffer with his troubles. Poor she-critter, she would suffer soon enough! He thought of wayward Georgie, running off with Ardel Cone before she had turned fifteen. Georgie had tried to take a part in the free-handed advice about the lawsuit in Savannah four years ago. She had come home for the first time since quitting it—or the first time to his knowing. He had found her there when he got back from Pineville. Civil said she had come to bring word from Ardel. Ardel, Georgie said, had talked with Calhoun Calebb, and Calebb said the Corns should fight the suit in the federal court.

He had been moved to order Georgie out of the house, but he didn't. Now he was glad he had not—after all who was a Corn to be quibbling—and quibbling over what? But he had been pretty short about Ardel's advice then. When he come to need advice from a Cone he'd ask for it, he had said. And he didn't have much more respect for Calebb's. All that half-breed wanted was a fee!

But the word from Ardel was only a cover for the real trouble, Micajah had found out through Civil. Ardel probably hadn't even sent any word. Poor Georgie was no more'n a child, in spite of being eight years married with six living children! She looked old enough: her face as sunk in as a cow's rump, her back already humped and her dugs hanging down to her waist.

He could only turn away and leave the house when he heard what the trouble was. Twenty-three-year-old and she didn't even know her nature! Hell's fire, she hadn't had a chance to find out. She was married before she come to be a woman and started a baby right off. Her monthly flux come on her for the first time alone there with her children. It scared her out of mind. She had put the younguns in the ox cart and come as fast to her ma as a whip could make an ox jog. Poor child, she hadn't given them a chance to learn her any upbringing, scarcely.

Micajah hoped there would be no Ardel Cones in Jasmine's way. He would do his level best to see there were none, God willing! Vaguely, he hoped there would never be a man, so long as he lived, not that he wanted to go against God and nature.

He looked meditatively down at the small tow head at his hip as they entered McClendon's general store. Jasmine wanted a store-bought hat. Micajah had not calculated on its cost, not the one of her choice, and he did not feel in the humor for

109

spending money now. There were hats in piles behind the counter and there were others in boxes on shelves, but the hat that caught Jasmine's eye was with a select few in a glass showcase. These hats sat primly on roosts and looked like gay-feathered birds and bunches of flowers.

The one Jasmine picked out was a gauze affair with lace, pink ribbon, and pink forget-me-nots on it. It was priced at a dollar and a half. Micajah didn't think it helped her looks any—he always thought she looked the prettiest without any-thing on her head. Even pot-bellied Pete McClendon, the storekeeper, agreed with Micajah, but he added he did not pretend to know anything about women's hats.

Their comment passed over Jasmine as if she did not hear their words. She stood there in her droopy homespun dress, holding to the hat on her head with both hands and looking up at Micajah. 'I want this un, Pa,' her quiet voice responded to all persuasion.

Micajah had spoken in a tone of mild disinterestedness and the child's persistence brought no change in his habitual calm, but for a moment he looked off through the back doorway. He had only five dollars and he had planned to buy some webbing and a collar for the gelding. He had not counted on putting out more'n fifty cents for the hat. He wondered fleetingly what Civil would say, spending hard money and the seed not all in the ground yet and nothing coming in till fall—if then! And here the Yankees changing things and taking people's land—and no telling what was coming!

'Wrop it up,' he said finally without looking at Jasmine and moved off toward the front of the store.

Micajah made another trip to the company offices before he left town. He had never liked Zenas Fears' brusque ways, not that Fears had done aught to him. But just at the time he heard that the Major had quit, he hadn't wanted to talk to Fears and he hadn't been sure then just what he wanted to say. Fears was the company man now, however, and he had better talk to him, Micajah decided. He found the office building temporarily deserted with the bookkeepers all out to dinner, but he and Jasmine sat down on the porch and waited. The whining, throbbing mill had quieted now, and men, some greasy and in their undershirts and others with sawdust on their hats and in their eyebrows, were coming out of the place. After a while the bookkeepers came back and the hands lined up before a window at the other end of the building. A man inside the window called out names and handed money out to them. Fears did not show up. Micajah restlessly watched the sun. He was needed at home. Old Jere lay on what Micajah feared was his death-bed and he wanted to get back. His father had taken to his bed a week before and had been growing gradually weaker. Jere was now eighty-two and his time was probably at hand. Micajah had said nothing to his father about his trip to Pineville, nor had he told him of the report from the Savannah court. Jere was in no shape to be worried about land and titles now, Micajah reflected. And Jere must not know he was off in Pineville; that would worry him, too. He must make haste to get back. He had come all the way to Pineville and learned nothing—nothing, except that the Major had quit! But the sun slipped over toward the western horizon and Fears did not come. Micajah decided he would have to give up and go home.

Jere was sleeping quietly when Micajah eased into his room, sock-footed, the next morning, but Civil told him the old man had tossed with fever and talked out-of-his-head most of the night. They agreed that it was time to send word to the family. Another day or two at the hindermost would see him quit this world. It had been years since they had heard from Jonathan, but Civil had written to Tennessee to let him know at least that his father's end approached. Jere's sister, Levedy, had been dead twenty years and the Corns had little intercourse with her Hatton children, but Civil sent word. Jet saddled his claybank mare at daybreak and set out to notify his sisters and brothers.

Micajah took up his place at his father's bedside after breakfast and Civil and Mary Ann busied themselves with housework and preparation for the visiting relatives. Jere lay motionless, his face to the ceiling. He looked shriveled between the dark posts of the big four-poster bed. His tufted hair and beard was thin and dead white and the once florid patches of face and scalp showing through were a pallid purplish gray. There was a nerveless laxity in his body except for the slow, harsh effort of breathing. His pale eyelids were closed like a sealed letter.

There weren't many nights Pa had missed sleeping between those posts during the past sixty years, Micajah reflected, as he shifted his gaze from his father's face to the bed and room surrounding. Shutters closed out the sunlight and a small fire on the hearth gave the room dim illumination. It was little changed since Jere built it there. There was his rifle on the deer-horns over the fireplace, a little dusty now. And his old hickory chair, though new rawhide had been put in the bottom more'n once.

As the sun outside climbed high, Jere stirred and his lips moved. Micajah had drawn close to hear, the words were inaudible. In the afternoon a faint flush suffused his face. Life seemed to come back into his old limbs and he turned restlessly. Micajah could catch his murmurings now. It was the name of Ariminta, his wife, dead these thirty-odd years, Micajah heard most often. Night came on and the fever grew hot and Old Jere struggled in his bed. Micajah marveled at the life left in him, but he knew, too, it was life leaving him. His wandering talk was all of things gone by.

He called his own father's name and called on Joe Wilson to witness he had drawn blood for blood with the Indians. He counted the bales of cotton he had made in the Sugar Field, or was going to make, and the niggers he was going to have—and didn't, Micajah thought as he listened. But more often it was Ariminta he called on to pray for him. The death of little Jere was on him at times—hard. But it was die, anyway! And sometimes he wanted her to pray for rain. Once he called to Micajah and Micajah answered him, but he only muttered about a damn paper claim.

Jere would go without knowing the Yankees were after his land and Micajah was thankful. Jere had not been greatly disturbed when the suit was put in federal court four years before and it soon passed out of his mind, Micajah reflected. He was already sick abed when the news came that the judge said their deeds were no good and Micajah told him nothing about it. It was not right to trouble an old man with so few days left to him in this world. Micajah thought, with a smile that rose only to his eyes, that Jere would have wanted to go to Pineville with him, toting his gun—if he'd known. In the late night a crumbling fire in the big fireplace filled the dim room with wavering shadows. Micajah gazing at the vague, muttering old man nearing death in the white bed had the queer notion that he was carrying away with him the security of the past.

Jere died before breakfast. All of Micajah's children had got there before the end. One of the Hatton boys, Jonathan, had come, and Georgie got there during his last hour.

Jet had stood by the door, just to see that nobody forgot to take off his shoes. A little light had been let into the room which smelled of camphor and sickness. Micajah, grim, but calm, sat at the bed head on one side and Civil at the other. She alone displayed a handkerchief. Zeke, Littleton, Mit, Georgie, Jonathan, and Jet, at the rear, filed in calmly and gravely and stood about the foot. Mary Ann was already there, seated. Zeke's Martha had come with her two children, but she remained in the kitchen, and Jasmine slipped away after Micajah released her hand. Georgie looked around the room and Mary Ann hid her eyes in her hand. The others waited, their heads respectfully bowed, watching the withered gray figure in the bed.

Jere faced his Maker before he went. Micajah had thought he might have to rouse him and let him know he was dying, but he came to before the end. It was just a moment. Micajah raised his head. Jere opened his eyes and looked at them. He spoke of his life. It wasn't all the way it might have been, he said, but he was ready.

13

THE Corns buried Old Jere on the rise behind the cowpen field alongside Ariminta and Little Jere, bringing final silence to his firstborn's cries. Micajah squared a big heart lightwood post and planted it at the head of his father's grave.

Soberly, the Corns went on with their spring plowing. It was a coolish May and wet, so Micajah held off planting his cotton, but his corn, already in the ground, shot up like weeds. He was hopeful the rain would play out by June and the creek would leave his cotton in the Sugar Field alone when he did plant it.

From all that was visible to Micajah and his sons and son-in-law, Coventry and Company was as remote as it had ever been. There was never the echo of an axe nor the rattle of a timber wagon throughout the hot summer that came and went. The logging camps were still far to the north and east of them. Micajah looked up Zenas Fears in June and finally got to talk to him, which had hardly been worth the trouble for all he could learn. But it gave him a chance to set the company right about the Corn lands.

Fears seemed a little gruffer since he had got to be agent, but Micajah hadn't come for courtesy. Fears said he had heard the judge in the Yankee court had knocked out all the deeds of the '45 tax sales and all he knew was what he'd heard. He hadn't heard anything specific about the Corn loss. The company had said nothing to him about them.

Micajah had wound up their talk by recalling that Fears knew, of course, the Corns held title to their land, deed or no deed; and by saying they would never have cause to be unfriendly toward the company so long as this was not forgotten.

Micajah never heard anything more from Fears until after cotton was picked and there had been a snap of hog-killing weather. And then it didn't come direct. Dan'l McMillan told Micajah that Fears met him in McRae and said the two lots Dan'l claimed belonged to the company and he would have to get off. He said the federal court had held that Dan'l's deeds were no good and now it was saying he had to move off and give his land up to the company. Fears showed him a paper supposed to come from the judge and a badge he said made him a deputy marshal of the federal court.

Micajah didn't know much about Dan'l's claim to the land except that he had a tax deed like the Corns' and he had been farming it and living on it since before he married Mit, which was thirteen years ago. That was claim enough. Dan'l had no doubts in his mind. Dan'l had told Fears peaceably but plain that he didn't care what kind of badge he toted, or papers. The land was his, he was satisfied with it, and he aimed to keep on farming and living on it.

It was early afternoon two weeks later that Micajah and Jet set out for Dan'l's in the wagon. Fears had followed up his demand with a threat. He had sent word to Dan'l that he would give him ten days to get his stuff together and get moving. Dan'l had ridden over to tell Micajah the same day he got the word. 'This is an order of the federal court and the court means business.' He had repeated Fears' words. Micajah couldn't say he hadn't calculated its coming, but somehow it was a jolt to him. It had been so slow making up. The court and the company—they seemed to be just about the same thing—had quit talking about papers and were going to try to bully somebody. Dan'l had asked if he reckoned they really did mean business. Micajah did not reply immediately. He looked out across the cowpen field from the corncrib door where they were standing and above the tree-line at the sky. Then he nodded his head slowly and said, 'Me and Jet'll come, Dan'l.'

He told Civil briefly of Fears' threat against Dan'l, adding that he and Jet would be going to stand by him. Civil went a little sallow at his words and her dark eyes clouded as she looked away, but all she said was, 'I knew it was a-comin'.' Micajah said nothing more to fret the womenfolks and Jet followed his lead. The women bore their anxiety in silence.

On the seventh day after Fears' threat, Micajah and Jet made quiet preparations for their journey to Dan'l's. Late in the morning they loaded the wagon at the barn, putting in turning plows, an axe and a saw. At the sound of the bell they came to dinner, pausing in the dog-run to wash their faces and hands and rinse out their mouths as usual. They were talking casually when they entered the kitchen.

Constraint held the movements and closed the mouths of the women. Civil stood behind Micajah's chair and Mary Ann behind Jet's as usual, but it seemed they couldn't say a word.

And once or twice they were slow about passing the victuals and getting them out of the pot. Micajah asked where Jasmine was. Civil said she was croupy as a bullfrog. Civil had dosed her and was keeping her in bed. He put down the piece of backbone he was sucking and was quiet a moment, but he didn't ask any more questions and went on talking about a shed house he was planning to build at the Sugar Field.

'Pa, we can a-get the timber right beyond the cowpen field, there at the back side'—Jet waved his fork in the direction of his left shoulder. 'It looks to me like the next place we oughter cowpen,' he suggested in a thoughtful manner.

Micajah looked meditatively at Jet's fork, then his eyes passed to Jet's face. He watched the motion of his son's thin, reddish beard as his jaws worked heavily. Jet had grown up to be a man, he thought, in the last year or two. He had grown up right before him. Jet had always kept his eyes open. Now he had learned how to keep his mouth shut, had learned to use his head.

Micajah suddenly shifted his gaze to Mary Ann. He gave her an inquiring look. He asked if they hadn't made pot liquor with the greens. Both women jerked up their hands nervously and hurried toward the fireplace.

Micajah told Jet that was the timber to cut, all right, but he was not thinking of the timber. He recalled the way Jet had taken it when he told him about Fears' threat against Dan'l. Jet was counting ears of corn into the gelding's trough. He had kept on counting, but when he came out of the stall he said, 'I reckon we'll have to do something about that, won't we, Pa?' And that had settled the matter for Jet. He hadn't needed to say anything more about it, until Micajah told him the time for action had come, and what to do. Now Jet was handling himself like a man.

It was Littleton, his eyes shining under a loose brush-heap of red hair, who broke over. 'Pa, you-all a-goin' to take all the guns with you, air ye?' he said. If Micajah heard him he gave no sign. He kept up his steady, unhurried talk about building the shed.

'You finish a-puttin' the stuff in the wagon, Jet,' Micajah said when they had done with picking their teeth, 'and I'll join you there.' Everything had been put in except the guns, ammunition, and cleaning tools. The Corn men had not cleaned their rifles, had not taken them from the wall, and weapons had not been mentioned, except for Littleton's blurting. The cleaning and loading could be done at Dan'l's out of the womenfolks' way when the time came, Micajah had said.

Standing at the kitchen doorway, Micajah pulled on his black wool hat, the brim well down, and faced Civil. The pupils of his eyes were barely visible pin-points in the calm blue. 'We a-might be gone as much as a week, Civil,' he said. 'Littleton'll be here close. He's big aplenty. Jest be easy in yore mind.' His gaze had lingered for a moment on the dark eyes, which looked gravely out from Civil's silent brown face. Then he turned and went out.

The women saw their men into the wagon at the smokehouse, where Civil had put in two of her smoked hams for Mit. Earlier Mary Ann had kissed Jet good-bye in their bedroom where he had gone to get his Winchester rifle. Now she was beside Civil at the wagon wheels. Their hands twisting in the folds of their loose homespun dresses, the women looked up silently at the men standing in the vehicle. Micajah clapped the lines together and the fretful claybank mare urged the gelding into motion. Without speaking Civil and Mary Ann walked back into the house and to the dog-run to watch the wagon disappear around the bend of the road.

After supper that evening, the McMillan living quarters took on the appearance of an armed camp. About a lightwood fire crackling in the wide fireplace, Micajah, Jet, and Dan'l sat cleaning their weapons. The black pot, swung from a crane at the fire's edge, boiled noisily, and the men sat back in a wide circle because of the warmth. The blaze cast a brick-red glow on their faces and hands, whitened the sheets of a bed in the corner and sent a flow of light and shadow over the serried log walls. Micajah and Jet were polishing Winchester rifles. Micajah's was new. On the floor beside him was an old Minie musket and between him and Jet lay a long-barreled horse pistol. Dan'l worked over an old Snider breech-loader, the stock of which had been mended with copper wire. On the puncheon floor, glazed in the firelight, lay cartridge-boxes, a powder-horn and shot-pouch. On the outskirts of the male circle, twelve year old D.J., Dan'l's oldest son, sat on a three-legged stool watching the men with glistening eyes. Mit was upstairs in the loft room, putting to bed her other four children.

Micajah's graying hair shook about his neck and shone in the firelight as he swung a gun barrel out before him and squinted through its bore. He spoke intermittently, between puffs at his clay pipe. It was his idea, he told Dan'l, to break all the ground around the house. That was why he had brought along the turning plows. Breaking the ground would do away with most of the cover within a hundred steps and would make bad footing for anybody coming up, to run, or to shoot. There was no tree cover inside the fence, except the water oak by the south chimney and the chinaberry trees at the wash trough. The three of them could break the ground in the morning.

There was a lengthening lapse, and Dan'l spoke, bending his thick body forward and resting his arms on his knees. His purplish-red face was swathed in red beard and hair of a lighter hue. He had small blue eyes, which, like those of an albino, appeared to be perpetually in a twinkle. They twinkled now, in odd contrast to his solemn bearded face and timid manner. 'Do ye a-reckon Fears'll bring a posse with him, Mr. Micajah?' he said slowly.

'I a-don't reckon he aims to pitch yore two hundred pounds out'n here—and Mit and five children with it—by his self,' said Micajah, his eyes twinkling like Dan'l's.

Dan'l subsided. After working the breech lever of his rifle back and forth sharply, Micajah renewed his talk of plans. The McMillan house was a single log pen. The ground floor was divided into two rooms, but the log walls extended beyond the ceiling and furnished space for an unceiled half-story above. The upstairs was a single long room in which the McMillan children were bedded. Micajah said it was his idea to make watching easier and to give a better lookout by cutting a hole in each of the upstairs walls. He had brought along an axe, saw, maul, and chisel for this purpose. A block out of a single log would make a hole big enough to poke your head through and plenty of shooting room. One man could watch the four holes if need be. From the upstairs he could see farther, and shoot farther, too.

Dan'l pulled his beard as Micajah spoke and his small eyes opened in alarm. 'Mr. Micajah, that'll freeze my chillun—danged if it won't. This ole house is a-full enough of holes as it is.' Then he hung his head and looked at the floor embarrassedly, fearing that he had protested too stoutly.

'I counted on a-makin' chocks for the holes, Dan'l,' Micajah replied calmly.

'You a-make this thing the worst again,' Dan'l rejoined with a brief gusty laugh, his eyes twinkling excitedly. After a pause, he continued, looking down at the floor: 'You reckon this Fears is a-comin' way off down here in the piney woods, jest to make trouble for me? Anyhow, he ain't a-goin' to hang around here long when he finds out there's three of us and aplenty of shot and powder. I've heard he run some of the Causeys off'n a lot they were squattin' on and some of the Swilleys, maybe, but he ain't never tampered with anybody who'd put up a real fight.'

Jet, who had just finished assembling his rifle, dropped it across his knees and interposed. 'I heard he killed a sheriff in Tatnall County, once. He's given out to be a dead shot.'

Dan'l rumbled an inarticulate protest, then spoke. 'You know he can't shoot with Mr. Micajah! They ain't a man in the county can.'

Micajah took a chew of tobacco, masticated the quid and spat into the fire, before he joined in the conversation. 'I ain't never shot with Fears, though I ain't tried to avoid it. I hear he's the master shot.

'We can't be shore what he aims to do, Dan'l. He's a daresome fellow and got the company behind him. I've found the best way is to keep yore gun cocked and ready to shoot. Hindsight ain't nigh as helpful as foresight.'

In the two days that followed, the three men turned the log house into a well-defended fort with the aid of Mit and the eldest boy, D.J. A store of meat was brought in from the smokehouse, wood was piled high beside the fireplaces, extra tubs of water were drawn from the well, and on the morning of Fears' expected visit extra corn was given the horses and their ricks were crammed with hay.

On that day—it was cold and the wind blew smoke down the chimneys—the men spent most of their time at the lookouts upstairs and Mit and D.J. gave them a hand now and then. The hours passed slowly, but in uninterrupted calm. Only once did a human figure come into view at the turn of the road, where Dan'l's lane joined it, or at the edge of the pine-tree walls surrounding the field. Dan'l, who first saw the figure, yelled out sharply, but Jet recognized the bobbing spot in the edge of the pines as Aunt Loosh, a negro woman herb doctor. During the day Dan'l had kept rigidly at the front lookout with his rifle in hand, but as dark fell he relaxed. He came down the ladder, his eyes twinkling, and announced that just standing still made him five times hungrier than plowing. He told Mit to cook up a heap of victuals and he got a jug of liquor out from under his bed.

Micajah warned against too many pulls at the jug, and told Mit to put a pot of coffee on after supper for the night watch. He said that Mit and Dan'l might share the fore part of the night and he and Jet would split the late half. Dan'l snorted, a bit resentfully, that Fears was a powerful fool if he came way off down in the piney woods on such a night. The fire burned all night in Mit's kitchen and the watchers drank two pots of coffee, but their vigil was not broken. The only sounds were the pawing of the horses and the occasional whining of the hounds. The watch was not relaxed the next day. Dan'l slipped out and fed the horses before light, but most of the time everybody kept close and the men patrolled their lookouts steadily. As the afternoon wore out, Dan'l came down from upstairs to warm and rest his legs. He sat down by Micajah, who had come down ahead of him, and his eyes twinkled.

'Mr. Micajah, I'm a-gettin' ready to believe you got us all a-worked up for nothin',' he gibed.

Micajah hitched a shoulder and after a moment turned his eyes from the fire blaze to look at Dan'l. His mustache gave its illusion of smiling, but his face was sober. 'I ain't a-got no way of knowin', Dan'l, but don't gobble too soon,' he said.

Late the next afternoon Littleton rode by on the yearling colt. Micajah saw him at the turn of the road and met him on the front steps. He was put out with the boy at first. His eyes showed it and he spoke a little roughly.

'What brought you over here, boy? I thought I a-told you to stay close!'

The gangling sixteen-year-old Littleton swung down from his mount, which he rode bareback, and approached the steps before he spoke. His yellow-brown eyes had flashed for a moment from the horse's back, but he was meek when he spoke to his father standing above him on the steps.

'I come out to a-get Aunt Loosh—Jasmine's mighty sick. I a-thought you'd like to know.'

The pupils in Micajah's eyes swelled and the lines about his mouth softened quickly, but his tone of voice was a gruff compromise. 'It's five mile from here to Loosh's—what ails Jasmine, son?'

Littleton said her croup had grown worse in spite of all his mother's doctoring. Last night she had burned with fever and could hardly breathe. He had already seen Aunt Loosh and had sent her on in Zeke's wagon. Zeke had come by the house and had then driven on over to Aunt Loosh's shanty to meet them and move the herb doctor faster. Mit and Dan'l both came out on the porch and listened as Littleton spoke.

Mit had the dark eyes and brown face of her mother, but the silence was missing. Both her face and her eyes were berry-like: round, unsoft, without line or shadow, except when she smiled or clouded up. She was first to speak when Littleton ceased.

'Pa, we can get along without you—I don't believe there's a-goin' to be any trouble—none big enough that Dan'l and Jet can't handle it.'

And Dan'l added his urging. Jasmine was Micajah's pet and she followed him around like a shadow—just his being there would make her feel better, he said.

But Micajah cut them off. 'It's a doctor she's a-needin' and they've already got Aunt Loosh there—it wouldn't help Jasmine for me to go.'

The following morning after breakfast, however, Micajah set off for home, riding the claybank mare. He had kept the discipline of the fort in force throughout the night, holding the lookout by himself during the last half because he could not sleep. But the night had been as monotonous in its pineywoods calm as those preceding. Mit and Dan'l had continued their urging late and had renewed it in the morning. Jet had joined in, saying he would be there, his help would be enough. Twelve days had now passed and Fears had already failed to carry out his threat.

When Micajah reached home, he was told that Jasmine was greatly improved. She looked very pale and weak lying flat on her back in the bed. Micajah's eyes watered when she put her thin arms around his neck as he bent over her. At the moment he could be nothing but glad he'd come. But Aunt Loosh's brews had cooled her fever and loosened her chest and she was past any serious danger. He had let his thoughts run away with him, Micajah told himself later. Like a woman he had let his imagination take over his reins—it had kept him awake all night and had whipped his mare into a lather over the ten-mile stretch home.

Civil had said little, but there was thankfulness in her eyes, and during the day she had gone up into the loft a minute to kneel and thank God.

The day was raw, and Micajah spent the morning in Jasmine's room by the fire whittling a wooden chain for her and nodding in his chair. Yet he was not easy in his mind. It was womanish to think Fears had dropped his quarrel, as womanish as it had been for him, Micajah, to ride off home at a lope when he knew old Loosh could cure a croupy child if anybody could. Yet, having come home, Civil and Jasmine would not take it easy if he left again. He was still thinking these thoughts when Zeke came by in the afternoon. The elder son, who lived twelve miles away on Big Horse Creek, had been in Lumber City on the afternoon before and the news he brought eased Micajah's anxiety. He had seen Zenas Fears there with the Gray boys and some other men he didn't know, he said. They were all getting ready to go on a bear hunt down in

Tatnall County when he saw them. The Gray boys would not take Fears anywhere except bear hunting!

Micajah was out in front fixing the gate latch when Mit drove up the next afternoon. The marks of trouble were plain, first glimpse. Mit was stiff on the wagon-seat. Her face was a sallow green and her eyes were red with a burnt look around the rims. D.J., his left eye closed and his face puffed, sat beside her, holding the littlest child. The other three stood up behind swinging onto their mother's dress. Their faces were dirt-smeared white. A quilt covered something in the back of the wagon-bed.

Micajah said, 'Mit!' and made haste to open the gate. He led the horses quickly around the house and into the back yard. No word was spoken until they stopped. The children started blubbering, but Mit still sat stiffly in the wagon. 'That's Jet under the quilt, Pa,' she said. 'They taken Dan'l off to jail.'

Micajah and Mit scarcely spoke to each other during the ride to McRae the next day. Micajah looked out over the horses' heads at the Blackshear Trail and Mit kept her eyes on the pine woods. They left Micajah's as the sun got straight over-head, bound for the county jail where Dan'l had been taken by Fears and his posse.

There were folks aplenty at home to take care of Jet, now. Zeke and Jonathan Hatton and Merlin and Jeb West, Mary Ann's brothers, had come over. Crying was a woman's part, anyhow, Micajah considered. He had as well be at tasks for the quick. His head still whirled from it all: the quilt, dead still in the wagon-bed, Civil, black-eyed and white-faced, on the back steps, Mary Ann shrieking and the white flash of her arms as

127

she fell, and flickering into his mind the face of Old Jere muttering out his last gasps. It had staggered him, had sent everything reeling to pieces around him for a moment.

Mit had told him that Fears and his bunch showed up about the middle of the morning. She couldn't tell how long they might have been lying in the woods. She and Jet and the children were in the house, but they weren't keeping watch any longer. Dan'l had gone out to the barn and D.J. had followed him. The first they knew anything was up the men came swarming up out of the barn holding to Dan'l. They'd taken his gun away for him. Jet had shot before Mit knew he was out of his chair. He cracked down with his rifle and a man on the edge of the bunch fell. Then they all ran back to the barn, except Fears.

Fears kept coming. He was holding Dan'l in front of him and pushing him along. Dan'l's hands were locked behind him. Fears was shooting just with a pistol, but Jet didn't keep covered, Mit said. He was rising above the window-sill to take another shot when Fears was almost to the back porch. Fears got him right between the eyes.

'Between the eyes,' Micajah repeated to himself half audibly and he felt the iron lump in his chest swelling. His eyes smarted as he sat motionless in the wagon-seat looking out over the horses' heads. His chest swelled to bursting, but it had not burst. As the pain of it eased off, he felt weakness, as if from loss of blood. He hadn't had that feeling since he heard the Yankees had killed Kinch back in '62. This seemed the hardest take Death had ever made of him.

Poor Jet had gone in his father's stead. Just thirty-one years old and a wife and young one depending on him. If

Death had come for his toll, it should have been him, Micajah. He had run away—had been tricked by woman weakness! The hard lump swelled again until Micajah wheezed as he breathed, but he did not move in his seat or shift his gaze.

Before him, in the white blaze of his mind, he saw two figures advancing across Dan'l's yard in quick, heavy movement—one behind the other, pushing harshly, carefully.

If he had been there, he would have waited until Fears got to the porch. Fears couldn't have kept cover and made the porch, not even if he'd knocked Dan'l in the head. He, Micajah, would have got his shot in then if he'd been there. If he'd been there! Well, Fears hadn't left the country yet.

14

IAN McIntosh looked troubled as he leaned forward in his top buggy and urged his bay mare on with restive pulls at the reins. He had returned from the coast to Pineville the evening before to learn of the shooting affray of the previous morning. Kathleen had been his first informant. As they now rode through the somber November forenoon toward McRae, where Dan'l was a prisoner and the posseman shot by Jet Corn lay seriously wounded, she spoke to him gravely.

'Fears shot the man in his home, Father?' She uttered her words in a low voice. Her mobile, rather wide, mouth became a straight line again after she had spoken and she looked off over the horse's head. The color in her cheeks was fainter than usual today and her fair skin had a bluish tone.

Ian glanced at Kathleen, speaking quickly as he turned his head. 'Twas nawt his home.'

'But that's quibbling—it was *his* family.' Kathleen's eyes met Ian's. They had the same light, the same openness, and were of the same plum-colored blue.

Ian tugged at the horse's reins. 'He had shot one of Fears' men, I hear.'

She continued to look at her father. Her lips tightened. From under her hat a wisp of straw-colored hair blew into her eyes. She shook her head quickly. 'Wouldn't you?'—Her voice grew louder—'In your own back yard—if you thought he was coming to get you?'

'But it wasn't hees back yar-rd—'twas company pr-ro-perty.'

Kathleen confronted him. There was the look in her eyes of a young bull charging in innocent fearlessness. 'Are you going to let the company kill men and take their homes just to get timber?'

He came bolt upright in the buggy and allowed the reins to slide through his fingers, but he held her gaze. The pause grew long. Finally he spoke in a soft voice. 'Is that kind of you, Kit?'

After another pause he added, 'Hadn't we best learn mor-re aboot it befor-re jumping to conclusions?'

Her gaze had lowered when he spoke and a flush came into her cheeks. She looked up again and her lip trembled as she started to speak. 'I wasn't fair to you—I'm sorry, Father—I know better—you had no part in it.' She paused and gave him a quick, crooked smile. 'And there's nothing to be gained by talking like this. But I feel so terrible about it—'

Any event affecting the company concerned Kathleen. She had always been interested in it. She liked the pine wilderness in which she had lived intermittently during the past seven years. The vastness of it, the keen whine of the saws at the Pineville mill and the groan of the slab hog, the pungent smell of pines and raw lumber, the rough-shirted men, black and

131

white, whose work her father directed—all of these things were the stockade, the buckskin, the musket of a lusty adventure that stimulated her. And her stalwart, tireless father was the center of it. Since her childhood he had made her a companion, had talked to her about the mill and the forest, his work. She felt that she shared his responsibility.

Her mother did not take this view and her mother's opinion— since Kathleen's return from the seminary in Savannah three years before—affected her father. Kathleen had come back to the pine wilderness to become a part of it, to become— she had fancied—her father's right hand. But her mother had plans for her that were to leave her in Pineville as little as possible, she had found, and her father, possessed of two sound hands, had made few demands on her. Her role in the adventure was still indefinite, but she lost no opportunity to take part.

Yesterday she had heard that the prisoner's homeless wife and five children were hanging around the jail. Thought of the woman and her brood taken by the law from the security of their backwoods home weighed on Kathleen's conscience. She saw them in draggly backwoods dress with pinching fear and bewilderment on their faces. This was no role for the company, or her father—bullying a poor woman and her children! It was because of them she had insisted on accompanying him. She felt she must do something; she did not know what.

'Too queek to shoot! Too queek to shoot!' Ian repeated abstractedly, breaking the silence that had followed Kathleens' words. He said he had cautioned Fears against using his gun when he put him in as woodsman-agent. He was largely responsible for Fears' appointment. Of course Major Rhea had resigned of his own choice, but he had really been too much of a gentleman for the job.

Fears had seemed like the man for it, Ian said. He looked at Kathleen and then studied the horse's rump as he went on. Fears was without fancy feelings or ideas and believed implicitly in the power and reputation of the company. A little brash, maybe, but he knew no fear and understood the backwoodsman as a mother does her child. There had been need for a stronger policy toward the squatters. The company could not hand over its timber and land to every squatter who chose to steal it. It would stir up local prejudice, which was already strong enough. Fears had really been acting in the capacity of a deputy marshal of the federal court at the time, but few would make the distinction, Ian thought, looking absently off into the pines.

The McIntoshes drove past the ragged row of stores facing the railroad track at McRae and on to its gray-weathered frame courthouse. In the sheriff's office, a bare, lightless room, rank with dirt and the acrid smell of tobacco, they found John Casement waiting for them.

Casement was wearing his usual impeccable frock coat, as he arose to greet them. He was grave, but he smiled fleetingly at the sight of Kathleen's vivid face. The reaction was unconscious and momentary. He thought now with distaste that the business before them was not for ladies, yet he knew that she would want to remain.

Kathleen's eyes brightened and her lips twitched when he first confronted her and she half-turned away and took her father's arm, but as he became impersonally grave again, she released her hold and glanced about the room.

Brushing back his aggressive gray forelock, Ian began without hesitation. 'Now, Jawn, what ees the situation?' His vibrant voice carried a somber note.

Casement dropped his eyes and placed his knuckled hand on the plank table between them. 'I suppose you should know without waiting that Johannes Schumpert, the wounded man, died this morning.'

'Died!' Ian and Kathleen repeated with simultaneous intake of breath and sat down.

Casement continued in deliberate dolorousness: 'Of course, you know he was a rodman on the surveying crew. He came from Reading, Pennsylvania; no family here. His nearest relative is an aunt. I have communicated with her, but haven't heard anything yet.' He paused and smiled wryly. 'Her answer may be notice of a damage suit. He was acting as a federal officer at the time he was shot, but he was still in the company's employ.'

Casement was interrupted by the entrance of the sheriff, whose office they occupied. He was a dark, hard-eyed young man, with an uncertain, lipless smile. A circle of close-cropped fringe around his mouth emphasized its grimness. He kept his dubious smile and nodded briefly when the McIntoshes were introduced. Moving toward his desk across the room, he drawled over his shoulder, 'Guess you-all knowed Dan'l McMillan's house and barn burnt last night?'

He ignored the sharp exclamations behind his back and continued in malicious calm: 'Didn't hear whether Zenas Fears aer any of his possemen did the burning.' He sat down at his desk and turned his back.

Ian looked affronted, but Kathleen smiled fleetingly. After a pause Casement asked if any of the family had been at home.

'Depends on what you mean by home,' the sheriff continued, with his back to his audience, rattling papers on his desk. 'I hear the company has done changed McMillan's residence to the county jail—leastways that's where they all were.'

Casement, leaning across the table to McIntosh, murmured that they might move over into the Ordinary's office, but Ian shook his head. His brow was gathered in a twist and his eyes were frankly pained. 'Jawn, thees thing has nawt come out right at all, at all! McMillan must nawt be per-rsecuted. A harmless family and heem in jail! There's been too much tr-rouble alr-ready. I want heem out—I want heem tur-rned loose today.'

Casement looked off into space reflectively, before he met McIntosh's eyes. 'That's not as easy as it looks, Ian.' He gave a brief, dubious shake of his head. The man was supposed to be carried into federal court, he said. One of the charges against him was contempt of court. Fears had held him there until Ian came, but after all Fears was responsible to the court. If Ian were thinking of dropping the charges, he could not consent to that. 'In fact we cannot do that,' Casement concluded, drawing in his lips tightly.

Ian interrupted him. 'Cannawt! Cannawt! I do nawt want to hear what we cannawt do, Jawn.'

Casement's mouth tightened and he spoke with a hint of sharpness in his voice. 'Suppose we get the charges dropped and your—your beneficiary comes back with a sweet damage suit against the company for false arrest—you don't think he loves us, do you?'

There was belligerence in Ian's bolt-upright back and un-blinking eyes, but it was momentary. He smiled. 'Don't ask me questions, Jawn. It is answers I want. You're the lawyer.'

Casement's tone and manner became judicial. He said that he advised telegraphing the company lawyers in Savannah to take up the case with the judge and arrange bond for McMil-lan—get him out on bond and let the cases lie dormant in the court.

Kathleen, who had been sitting quietly listening to the men, caught her breath and interrupted. 'Papa, what about the family?' Where would they go when the man was released? They had been burned out and probably had nothing but the clothes on their backs. There were five little children.

'I was coming to that—coming to that,' Ian replied, and without further words reached into the breast-pocket of his coat and drew out his wallet. He counted the bills. There was a hundred dollars, he said. 'Will you lend me what cash you've awn ye?' he said, addressing Casement. Kathleen opened her purse and emptied its contents on the table, also.

The money-counting was interrupted by the entrance of Zenas Fears. His clean-shaven face wore a coating of submis-sive calm, but vigor lay in the lines about his mouth and the thrust of his head. His lead-colored eyes were downcast as he shook hands with the group. When he had finished, he stood stiffly, shifting his weight from one foot to the other.

'Well, Zenas, begin at the beginning. I have been waiting to get a full fir-rst hand account from ye,' Ian said, looking up at him.

Fears' discomfiture seemed to increase as he started to reply. 'And I have been waitin' to give it to you, but it is hardly the kind of thing to talk about before Miss Kathleen there.'

Kathleen had seen this coming and had put her hand on her father's knee under the table. Casement was about to join in the Fears protest, but Ian glanced into Kathleen's eyes for reassurance and said, 'Eet's all r-right, Fears. Pull up a chair and sit down.' Miss Kathleen, he added, was as much interested in the thing as himself. She could stand it, he supposed.

Fears' submissive restraint quickly wore off as he sat in a chair with his hands on his knees and addressed his story to Ian. He didn't know what McIntosh had heard, but he wanted him to know that he had done the very best he could to prevent any shooting. He remembered what McIntosh had said and just wanted him to keep in mind it was his—Fears'—hide that was shot at. But he put the man he was going to arrest first. He had meant to take him without gun-play.

He had taken along a posse of six for that reason and they had lain out in those woods all one day and night, before they closed in, waiting for the right sort of chance. He knew that old Micajah Corn and one of his boys had come over to the McMillan's and had learned that the old man had gone back home before he went over there. He knew they were tough people. McMillan wouldn't have given much trouble by himself.

They had crept up to the barn that night and waited until McMillan came out to feed his stock next day and had got the drop on him before they moved. They were all over him before he knew what was happening.

Then this Corn boy in the house had shot Schumpert when they came out of the barn. The posse run back to cover. He knew Corn would plug him, or whoever tried to pick up Schumpert. He had hold of McMillan, who was handcuffed. He tried to use McMillan for a shield, to run him up to the back door and close in on Corn without shooting him. Just as he got to the back porch, McMillan jerked loose. Corn was at the window, his gun already aimed to shoot. Fears' voice was swift but casual. 'I couldn't lose no time. I shot from my hip.'

There was a moment of silence in which the listeners adjusted themselves to the cessation of speech, then Casement said reflectively: 'An eye for an eye, it seems. Corn got Schumpert and you got Corn. I guess the score is even between the squatter and the law.'

The sheriff, who had come back into the room unobserved during Fears' monologue and now sat at his desk, turned about in his chair and drawled, 'You're overlooking something, ain't you, Colonel?' The group at the table looked up. He went on without awaiting a reply, smiling tightly. 'Schumpert's squatter, Corn, is dead, but Corn's deputy marshal is still around here.'

At the sight of the sheriff, Fears' jaw tightened and his head thrust forward. The man's smile became almost a sneer when he looked at Fears, but neither spoke.

After a lengthening pause, Casement said, 'I guess you're right, Sheriff: Fears is here. What do you intend to do about it?'

The smile came back to the man's face. 'I reckon I don't intend to do anything about it, unless Micajah Corn asks me. So far as I know, there ain't been no killin'—it's all jest hearsay. Fears claims he's a Government officer and shot in self-defense. Of course Micajah could prosecute him for murder, but I doubt if he does. I reckon he won't call on me.'

Casement had got up from his chair, as the sheriff spoke. Now he addressed him abruptly. 'You were going to let us see McMillan, I believe, Sheriff?'

McIntosh interrupted to say they hadn't finished counting the money they were making up for the McMillans and asked Fears if he wished to contribute. Fears handed Ian a ten-dollar-bill and left the room.

'Come on,' the sheriff said, 'you can see the prisoner now, if you like.'

The Telfair County jail, which occupied the same building with the sheriff's residence, stood a hundred paces from the courthouse. It was built of hewn logs and had wooden bars in its high small windows. The sheriff led his party to the side door which gave entrance to the jail itself. The room inside was only a wide corridor, with cell doors in one side of it. It was dark and bare except for a few split-bottomed chairs and a plank table. The sheriff flung the door wide open to give the room more light. As Ian, Kathleen, and Casement filed in behind the sheriff, Dan'l McMillan and his wife, who had been sitting down at the back of the room, stood up. Their five children were squatting against the wall or sitting on the floor around them.

The McIntoshes and Casement stood in the semi-darkness blinking in an effort to adjust their eyes to the light as their escort spoke. 'Dan'l, these people come to see you. It's Captain McIntosh, from the company and his daughter and Colonel Casement.' He stood aside.

Ian advanced a step to shake hands, fumbled in the half-light and halted. Kathleen remained a little behind her father and Casement was well in the rear.

The McMillans stood motionless. Dan'l's thick arms were stiff by his sides and his small eyes looked from his bearded face straight in front of him. Two of the smaller children clung to Mit's flowing homespun dress and a third scuttled behind her on his bottom. She gave no evidence that she knew of their existence, but stood beside her husband staring ahead into the same nothingness. In the semi-darkness the two figures looked as if they might have been carved out of one piece of wood.

They had not spoken when the sheriff addressed them and they did not reply to Ian's 'Guid mor-rning!'

Kathleen made no effort to assist her father. She was awed by the McMillan's hostility. She hadn't expected friendliness, but this mute implacability left her with nothing to say.

Ian shrugged his shoulders, took a step forward and began speaking. He sounded like he was making a speech. 'These are nawt the circumstances I would have chosen to meet ye under-r, Mr. McMillan.' He faltered a moment, then went on, his bass voice rising: 'I want to say, speaking for Coventr-ry and Company, that we did nawt direct your-r arrest and would have opposed it had we known. Nawt that we have any doubt aboot our title to the land you're living on, but I deed nawt come to talk aboot that. The company is opposed to violence and it would r-rather've lost the land than to have men killed.'

He paused again. The McMillans did not stir or give any evidence that they heard him.

'I—I,' Ian fumbled a little, but went on: 'The company feels that the feder-ral officers were too hasty in enforcing the law. I want to say for-r myself, I am shocked and ver-ry sad—I wouldna had it happen for-r anything. I am told the char-rges against you cannawt be settled now, but the company will go your-r bond and you can go fr-ree with your-r wife and children. Maybe later-r the case can be fixed. My only interest now is to help you.'

He paused again, feeling the sweat break out around his eyebrows. The going was hard. It was like talking to a blank wall. Kathleen caught the eye of one of the children looking out from behind the mother and smiled at it, but the child only stared at her. Casement turned away and looked out of the door.

Ian went on. 'I know ye don't feel kindly towar-rd me or the company—I can under-rstand that. I bear-r ye naw ill-will though. We have just hear-rd aboot the bur-rning of your-r house. That is a terrible misfortune. Terrible!' He halted again, 'We want to come een weeth your-r neighbor-rs,' he recommenced, 'and help you. Here's a leetle mawney we've got together.' He took a step forward and held out the money toward the silent McMillans.

There was a full pause. Dan'l shifted his weight on his feet and glanced sideways at Mit. Mit's berry-like face was expressionless. Suddenly she tightened her lips and skeeted a stream of tobacco juice full into Ian McIntosh's eyes.

15

ARDEL Cone, squatting against the wall of Calhoun Calebb's law office above the Lancaster Banking Company, shot a stream of ambeer with unerring accuracy at the sand-box across the room and wiped the back of his hand over his loose, stained lips. His skunk cap and cowhide jacket were damp with the misty December drizzle falling outside.

Calhoun stood before an open fire at the back of the room, which had the musty, scuffed anonymity of a church hymn-book. He stood with his coattails lifted, warming his seat. 'Take a chair, Ardel,' he said, as he came forward and sat in the swivel chair at his roller-top desk. But Ardel preferred to squat; his aim was better from that position.

'The company is out to take some more land from me, Colonel,' Cone began, looking at Calhoun callously and grinning. Calhoun turned in his chair to bring his deep-set eye to bear on the squatting figure and drew down the twisted side of his mouth, but said nothing. 'They filed a ejectment suit agin me at the courthouse this week—the clerk says it'll come up the January term,' Cone went on.

Calhoun asked what kind of case Cone could make for his claim. The backwoodsman, never shifting his callous eyes, grinned. 'I put a shack on this piece of land more'n a year and a half ago,' he said, 'and broke up a tater patch then. I actually been a-livin' on it for nigh a year.'

Cone paused, but Calhoun did not smile or speak. The backwoodsman went on: 'I a-had regular crops in this year. I ain't a-goin' to have any trouble a-gettin' my witnesses. And ain't aer one of 'em got witness-chair corns on his ass—I a-guess ain't but one of 'em ever been seen in Coventry County Courthouse. But I a-got to get me a deed.'

He paused again, continuing after another meditative shot at the sand-box. 'I ain't no hand at drawin' up a deed, myself. I thought you might get me one.' The loose grin remained fixed on his face.

Calhoun, who had been leaning back in his chair, sat upright and clamped his jaw shut. 'Say, Cone, what do you think I'm running here! I'm a lawyer and officer of the court.' His deep and usually soft voice sounded harsh.

Corn's grin became a slow, jarring laugh. He spat and wiped his mouth. 'Don't get yore dander up, Calhoun, don't get yore dander up—I was jest a-foolin', of course.' He never took his eyes from Calhoun's face and continued talking 'I can get the deed all right. I can get a plumb good deed—all aged and everything, but the man wants twenty-five dollars. I jest hate to put that money out. Fact is I ain't a-got it right now.'

Calhoun turned in his chair and looked down at the litter of foolscap on his desk and spoke. 'I advise you to get your deed and get you another lawyer while you are getting it,' he said.

Cone's eyes sharpened. He looked at the blind side of Calhoun's face. His grin vanished. 'I would shore a-like to do business with you, Calhoun, a-cause it's going to take a good lawyer and there's a-goin' to be some real money in this un— no chinquapins, backlog stuff. That shack and little patch of mine is a-settin' right square ker-dab on the jining of four lots of land—ye a-get that? Eight hundred acres of good pine timber. With stumpage like it is today and a-comin' up, we could get three thousand dollars aer nigh for that timber. That wouldn't be bad, halvers?'

He looked at Calhoun's profile closely. His tone of voice changed to one of surprise, tinged with injury. 'Colonel, when did you a-go to gettin' chicken-hearted over this passel of Yankee land pirates? You've been a-tellin' me all this time they didn't have no right to our land—they's jest a bunch of big-money land and timber thieves.'

Calhoun did not answer for a moment. When Cone had come in and interrupted him, he had been thinking of this very thing—renewing these opinions. During the past four years he had come more and more to identify himself with the squatters. Not outwardly: his manner of life and social contacts had changed little. Nor did the relationship rest upon any intellectual process. It had grown, like an attachment to a whore. He had not become a squatter; the squatter had become his quarrel. When Coventry and Company filed suit against land claims under the 1845 tax titles four years before, he had not been employed in the case and had been only casually interested. But the federal judge's decision of the previous winter had shocked him. He had visited Savannah to study the record of the case. At every opportunity since he had been avidly searching out its strange ramifications. The history revealed in that lawsuit was more than strange, it was without precedent. In his opinion, the Coventry title was invalid, but how to prove this and give it effect had baffled him.

'They have no right to the land—not an acre of it—just as sure as shooting!' he broke forth suddenly. 'They have no right to it, but what can you do about it with a Yankee court backing them up?'

He went on rapidly to lay down his premises. The old Georgia Pine Lumber Company that bought the three-hundred-thousand-acre tract of Michael Bloodworth had later mortgaged it to the State of Indiana. Calhoun had got a certified copy of the court record of the deal from New York and there were a lot of shenanigans in that, but they weren't important. Indiana had foreclosed and had taken title to five hundred square miles of Georgia soil!—Or had it? Of course it foreclosed the mortgage and took the titles—that was all it could get hold of for the two hundred and fifty thousand dollars it had sunk in them—but Indiana never did record its titles in Georgia and its title wasn't recorded when Sheriff Boyd in Telfair County sold those lots for taxes in '44.

Those titles were never recorded, Calhoun said, until after they had passed back into individual hands—until Joseph Hart had bought them for a thrip. Indiana had only been recorded as a former title-holder when Hart made record of his ownership. And he had bought the whole caboodle for a measly thousand dollars! Titles that Indiana had sunk two hundred and fifty—three hundred, originally—thousand dollars in! What was the deduction? It was so plain that the wayfaring man couldn't miss it. Indiana knew, or believed mighty strongly, that she could sustain no claim to the land—that the title was just so much paper as long as she held it. She had practically given it away.

'If I could have had a hand in that Savannah lawsuit, I believe I could have won it,' Calhoun said regretfully, 'or made that Yankee judge squirm like hell. But of course Alton Jason is a lawyer, or thinks he is. And he and his brother had the only big holding—about sixty lots.' Their mistake had been in taking the lead, he added. They should have advanced the little fellows, the *squatters* who lived on the land. Of course, if they had made the contention that Indiana could not hold title to the land, it would have upset their claim, too. But the little fellows back on the land would have been all right. Not a single one of them had gone into court to answer the company's bill!

Calhoun's words came rapidly. His big voice had risen almost to a platform pitch. His solitary gray eye shone like pit-fire as he spoke to the squatting figure before him. Now he sat silent for a moment with his chin on his chest. Finally he resumed in a quiet, reflective voice: 'If you had got the Corns to let me take their case, I could have saved them—Jet Corn would be alive today!'

Cone shifted his weight from one leg to the other, spat, and twisted his neck to shunt the burden of Calhoun's words. 'You know Micajie, Cal. It kills him to turn aloose a dollar. He waunt a-goin' to spend no money a-goin' into court. He don't believe in courts nohow.

'And, hell's hoecakes! Calhoun, I waunt the man to a-take it to him. He's got more prejudice for me than a moccasin's got pizen.'

146

Calhoun, looking out of the room's single window into the gray mist, scarcely listened to Cone. He broke his silence sententiously: 'When those titles went north to Indiana that land reverted to the State of Georgia.'

'Why didn't the State a-do somethin'—the legislature?' Cone said tentatively, with mild interest.

Calhoun, leaning backward, stopped his chair in mid-air and stared at Cone. He got up suddenly. He put his hand into his hip pocket and took out his pocketbook. 'Here, Ardel, I believe you said you needed twenty-five dollars,' he murmured.

When Cone had taken the money and gone, he stood in the middle of the floor, thinking. Why had he never thought of approaching the question of land reversion through the legislature? If the land really went back to the State, it was the responsibility of the State Government to deal with it. But the land had reverted in 1842 and this was 1880, almost '81. The state had asserted no possession, no claim then—nothing had been done about it. Still the State Government had not known, had had no record of the change from private to public hands—no official notice. And after seven years the title had gone again into private hands without protest. A retroactive law—going back thirty-eight years and dispossessing all the intervening title-holders—that would be unconstitutional, he supposed, but there must be other ways of getting at it.

Calhoun's mind reverted to Cone. He felt uncomfortable over having accepted Cone's land suit. Fifteen hundred dollars was fifteen hundred dollars, however, and he could probably win it—if he couldn't take the land away from them one way he could another! Then his footloose thoughts skipped again to

147

State Government. Why could not he, Calhoun Calebb, go to the legislature? That would be the way really to get something done. By God, there had been many a straight, hardworking backwoodsman done out of land that ought to have been his— besides the riffraff. Such a fight in the legislature would make him with the people of the pine barrens.

Early in February Calhoun confided his ambition to Judge Elisha Cromwell. It was not merely that he was full of the impulse and wanted to talk about it, nor that he sought the judge's political judgment. Judge Cromwell was a political power throughout his circuit and Calhoun's friend and could give him substantial aid if he were minded to.

He had felt out the acid old judge guardedly during court week at Mount Vernon, before he disclosed his aim. He was somewhat disappointed over Cromwell's attitude. Not that the judge discouraged his ambition to run for office. He even agreed that it might be shrewder for him to offer himself for the Senate than the House, when Calhoun explained that his greatest political following was in Telfair County, while he lived in Coventry. 'I reckon you're not too young for the Senate, son. Might as well bang away at a turkey as a partridge,' he had said.

Calhoun had agreed that it was a long time until the next election, but said that he wanted opportunity to look over the district carefully before he made up his mind. The judge said that this was wise. He had said, too, that Calhoun would make a creditable showing in the Senate and, in his offhand judgment, a creditable race. He had warmed up to the point of declaring that, in so far as he could see the situation at a distance, he would be able to give Calhoun a little help.

Calhoun had told the judge that it would be no tobacco-swapping, baby-kissing contest. He had an issue. It would make a real rabble-rousing, gun-toting cause, he had said, his eye beginning to shine. And he had no doubt about the division of sentiment: Telfair and Montgomery would be overwhelmingly with him and he should get an even break in Coventry. He felt sure he could spread the fire from the stump. He believed in it, fully believed in it; it was the real cause of the backwoodsman, he had continued, growing a little declamatory. Judge Cromwell, sitting by the fire with a hearth broom between his knees, had looked at him over his spectacles. Unabashed, Calhoun plunged on, into the history of Coventry land titles, Indiana's titular claim to the great pine barrens tract for seven years, and his conviction that the land had in reality reverted to the State of Georgia at that point. He would reclaim this land for Georgians, he said.

While he spoke, Judge Cromwell had brushed briskly at the hearth, gazing into the fire. When he had done, the spare graying jurist replaced his broom, took out his tobacco, cut himself a chew and offered one to Calhoun before he had replied. 'But the title now lies in Coventry and Company. The State of Indiana hasn't had it in thirty years. Where can you find authority to take it away from its present lawful holder?'

Calhoun had known, in so far as his search of law books revealed, that he was setting forth on an uncharted course. But he had replied without hesitation and with some force: 'The law of possession. I will assume Coventry's title is so much carpetbag counterfeit. I will assume that this is a body of public land belonging to the State of Georgia since 1842—I will

149

propose a new lottery law with pre-emption for tenants in possession—squatters.'

Judge Cromwell had squinted at the glass-encased clock on his mantle and had sent a stream of ambeer into the fire meditatively. 'And kill the sawmill enterprise here?' He had not waited for a reply, but went on: 'What good did the land do these squatters until the Coventrys came in here with their sawmills? The sawmills have brought more cash money into this country than any of 'em ever heard about before. And the land contentions haven't hurt your pocketbook any, Calhoun.

'What 'ud you do for lawsuits if all this land went back to the State?'

For a moment Calhoun had forgotten himself in his heat. 'What it does for me doesn't matter—I am thinking of the people—' He had set off in a stump speech, and then he remembered Judge Cromwell was not a political audience, that Judge Cromwell had known him a long time. He lowered his voice to say he had not overlooked his own interests in the situation—such a future would be speculative, but he was willing to take his chances. Later he wondered about these chances.

The young man who walked beside him in the April sun shower on the way home from the Presbyterian Church touched Calhoun's curiosity. Calhoun had gone alone because his mother was ill of a cold. He had gone less from habit or sense of duty than to bring his mother a report of the sermon and the meeting. Moreover, the April sun had banished the endless winter rain. It was pleasant to walk about.

If Calhoun had ever met the young man, whom he was now regarding from the tail of his eye, he could not recall the meeting. The boy's cheek was white and beardless, except for the barely discernible end of a blond mustache. He appeared to look at the ground ahead of him and his longish neck inclined forward. His shoulders slumped in sleek conformity with his neck and his torso moved along with a smoothness that suggested a mount of wheels. The set of his gray derby, the fit of his four-button gray coat, and the arrangement of his sky-blue scarf were precise. He had said as he brought himself abreast of Calhoun, 'I saw that you were walking alone, Captain Calebb, and I thought you wouldn't mind listening to me.' Somehow the precision and the smoothness of movement seemed to give familiarity to his blond namelessness. Calhoun thought of a weasel.

They walked along in silence for a distance. He considered asking the youth his name, but he did not. Words came from the pensive profile. The young man had heard a great deal of Captain Calebb; he had heard particularly of his winning land suits against Coventry and Company. Captain Calebb had seemed to him a very smart man and one who was going somewhere in the world. One who would be unlikely to overlook an opportunity and one who could take full advantage of it. He had wanted for some time to speak with Captain Calebb.

Calhoun turned his head to see his companion better, but the young man did not look up. His words came with the same smooth stream of his walk. He said that he himself was a clerk. He had been on his job for the past seven years, very regularly; and if he must say so, quite a lot of confidence and responsibility had been reposed in him. But he had got little money for any of it. He had received only a ten-dollar-a-month advance over the whole seven years and now made only fifty dollars a month.

Calhoun had already decided he had a clerkish look. From his brogue he was evidently a Yankee and must work for the company.

The boy said he had finally reached the decision that he could never make his fortune as a clerk; that he would never make enough money to afford even an extra suit of clothes doing other people's pen work.

There was a brief pause after this, and Calhoun thought he caught a side glance from the eye of his sinuously moving companion.

Words came again from the downcast profile. Lately, the boy said, he had been using his head, cautiously, of course, but he hoped to advantage. And he had in mind a hypothetical case he would like to lay before Captain Calebb. Just suppose there were a big landholder, say, for example, in the State of Florida. Now Calhoun observed that tiny terse lines showed at the corner of his mouth. He went on. Suppose, for example, there were three thousand acres in the tract that this party held. Suppose his title was a chain of many links that went all the way back to plats and grants. But suppose, too, the holder had arranged a short chain of title, by getting the heirs of the original owner of the plats and grants to convey directly to him. And suppose he never produced his long chain of title in court, but always used his short chain, claiming that it would be too laborious and take too long to prove his long chain. And suppose the courts and the lawyers, even the good ones, did not suspect anything and let him get away with this.

But the real reason—suppose—here Calhoun heard his companion draw breath audibly—the real reason was because one of the links—a very early link—a deed that had never been legally executed, was *lost*.

Calhoun had felt his own pulse beat as the intense voice reached its climax. He said nothing, and yet in that second he decided what he would do. The voice was concluding: would Captain Calebb think such information valuable?

'I don't believe I recall your name sir, but come with me to my office and let's get better acquainted,' said Calhoun.

The month following the sidewalk revelation Calhoun found exciting with prospects that appeared in his reach, difficult with cross-current of courses, and disturbing with the consequences that threatened all of them. The cautious young man who had approached him on his way from church had not gone that afternoon to his office with him. But he had met him there at night. Calhoun had learned that his name was Simeon Shadrick and that he was, in fact, a clerk in employ of Coventry and Company. He had, with some effort and reassurance, drawn Shadrick away from hypotheses. Shadrick proved more than cautious. The offer of fifty, or even one hundred dollars had not gained his secret. He gave good evidence that he had, as he said, been thinking. He wanted to join Calhoun in a partnership to exploit his discovery. That discovery was no less important than he had intimated. When the land now held by Coventry had been originally purchased from Michael Bloodworth, the buyers were three men from Maine and New Hampshire, Kiger, Kleeman, and Colfax. They had ostensibly conducted the transaction as agents of the old Georgia Pine Lumber Company, back in 1834, but they took it in their names as individuals. Later they had conveyed the holding to their company, or so the theory of the Coventry title maintained. But the Georgia Pine Lumber Company deed from Kiger, Kleeman, and Colfax, according to Shadrick, had not been executed before a court of record and now the deed was lost.

At first Calhoun had proceeded almost as cautiously in weighing the worth of *the secret* as Shadrick had proceeded when he gave it to him. Its possibilities flashed over Calhoun quickly. Yet he had been incredulous. He had not warmed to it. Indeed, it stirred an unreasoning anger in him. None of this, however, reached his lips. He had told Shadrick that his story was startling, important, and opened up amazing possibilities.

But he found himself unwilling to turn away from the course he had already planned. He had gone pretty far with carrying the squatters' land cause to the legislature—in his mind, at least. It had become a conviction with him. He had seen himself astonishing fellow legislators with its revelations about the land titles; he had thought of phrases, whole speeches to fire Georgia tempers against the Yankee land pirates, in behalf of State's rights. He had thought out private hotel-room meetings sharing in profits as well as glory in giving the land back to the backwoodsmen. That sort of thing had to be done. And he could figure himself in on some of it, too. The new course would upset all of that. The Kiger-Kleeman-Colfax deed dated back of the transfer to Indiana. There could be no reversion to the State if their heirs made good this manufactured claim.

And there was Kathleen McIntosh. His small-potatoes cases against the company hadn't made much difference in the past. Everybody took a little from the company. But this would practically wipe it out—might remove the McIntoshes altogether! Of course, his legislative plan would have got about the same result, but his part and responsibility in that would have been different. At least he could have shifted the responsibility to the State of Georgia.

He talked glibly to Shadrick, but he delayed action. He did not even conclude a definite agreement with him. Yet the neat trick of drawing the fearfully secret and lost deed from his vest-pocket fascinated him. And his brain could not leave the plotting alone. The heirs of Kiger, Kleeman, and Colfax—there must be living heirs somewhere—could set up a clear title to the whole tract of land. There was no legal proof, no record that it had ever gone to the old lumber company back in 1834. Of course these heirs, whoever they were, could be induced to join in a deal that would give them a share in five hundred square miles of land. If they did not want to get into it directly, they could convey their claim, their title—legal proof of which he could devise—to him, or to someone.

The thing kept him rocking back and forth in his swivel chair, or striding the floor of his office at late hours of the night; kept him awake after he had kissed his mother, worrying over his hours, good night and had gone to bed. The hurdling of each hazard with which the company might seek to obstruct the plot whetted his appetite. Gradually the blaze of realization drew closer to him. A million dollars' worth of timber! Five hundred square miles of land! The biggest sawmill in the South—railroads—commissaries—timber camps! 'I can take whole damn caboodle away from Coventry and Company—smug, purse-proud Yankees!' he said once aloud when he was alone in his office.

He contrived elaborate plans through which he might conceal his interest and active part in the scheme from the company and Kathleen. He would appear merely as a local attorney for the dummy owner; he might even employ another lawyer as his front and play a silent part. Could there be any guilt, any meanness, any disloyalty in a million dollars? Calhoun could not convince himself of sin. He told himself that the legislative plan was visionary, its achievement improbable. He argued that it would be more practical and safer if title to the land was in him—he could himself take care of every backwoodsman who had an honest claim. But he knew, back of his ears, that this was legalistic word-spinning. During the month he hardly slept at all.

16

MICAJAH Corn clomped down the narrow stairway from Calhoun Calebb's office over the bank in Lancaster. On the sidewalk he stopped to look around him for the land company offices Calhoun had been telling him about. The weather was running dry and hot in the summer of '81. Sweat criss-crossed the lines of Micajah's lean cheeks, although it was only ten o'clock in the morning and the month was yet June. It had been seven years since he first looked upon Lancaster and the town had spread out. If those years had weighed upon Micajah, his calm face and sinewy figure gave little evidence of it. Zeke, who had followed him down the steps, stood at his elbow. Still in his thirty-first year and plump-smooth, he looked like an unfinished copy of his father, except for his reddish hair and mustache.

Micajah gazed at a sign over the sidewalk, swung from a building adjoining the bank. The sign was white with blue-and-red lettering on it. He read out the words slowly: 'Peace and Plenty Land Company. Homes for the Homeless. Dirt-cheap Dirt.' Through a big window in front he could see a slicked-up young man, with glasses on, sitting at a large polished table. Behind him was a tinted map that covered almost half of the wall. The room was light blue and there were white ruffled curtains pulled back from the window.

The words, 'Welcome' and 'Come In,' were painted on the glass in the door Micajah noted as he pushed it open. The young man—Micajah now saw that his hair was parted in the middle and he wore a pale blue scarf—came forward to greet him. Micajah wanted to see a Mr. Lincoln, he said, looking at the name on the long envelope he held in his hand. The smooth young man said Mr. Lincoln was busy; could he do something for the gentlemen?

Calhoun Calebb had told him to see Lincoln. Micajah said that he would wait to see him.

At the mention of Calebb's name the young man murmured, "Oh, Captain Calebb sent you—I'll see if Mr. Lincoln can see you now.' Micajah and Zeke were ushered into a room where the man Lincoln sat in a plush chair at a wide carved table on which a land map was spread out. Just behind him was a roller-top desk of dark polished wood. The man was clean-shaven and had a bluish, stiff-looking face and had a glass eye. He smelled of bay rum and said, 'Captain Calebb sent you—Well?' Micajah thought the nasal harshness of his tone was more Yankee than usual—it grated on him. Beneath his feet he found the long nap of the red carpet as sticky as clay. Without introduction he handed Lincoln the letter.

Micajah and Zeke were seeking new titles to their land. Georgie had brought word, coming through Ardel from Calhoun, that the new land company could give him straight, clear titles, that went back to the plats and grants. Calhoun, who somehow had a hand in it, had fixed up these titles. They were to cost nothing but a little for the expense and trouble. Civil had been anxious to have him get them and Micajah wasn't against it. He'd rather not have Coventry and the Yankee court dropping down on his back; he wanted to settle his score with Zenas Fears in his own fashion.

Calhoun, who looked more prosperous than a possum in persimmon-time when Micajah saw him in his office a few minutes ago, had said that they had found, after all these years of lawing and fighting, that Coventry and Company didn't have a clear title to the land they claimed at all.

Calhoun had said he investigated the claim of the Peace and Plenty Land Company himself—had abstracted their title. He had gone into detail to explain the flaw in the Coventry title and why the new claim superseded it. It all sounded reasonable to Micajah, the way he put it. Micajah had wondered at the time who would vouch for glib-talking Calhoun, however. He didn't have much use for papers and less for courts and lawyers; they all seemed crooked, more or less.

Calhoun had said: 'I don't have any direct connection with this land company, but they will do anything I want them to. First and foremost, I aim to see that they furnish titles to the *bona-fide* settlers in the pine barrens—and for nothing, except the cost.'

It was big talk, Micajah thought. He had asked Calhoun what the cost would be, but Calhoun could only say 'a nominal amount'—the land company would have to fix that. Micajah had put out twelve dollars for papers back in '45 that the Yankee court had said were no good. Still he was willing to throw another twelve after it.

159

But Micajah and Zeke did not get their titles on the visit to the Peace and Plenty Land Company and they quit Lincoln's office in uncommon temper. Calhoun laughed immoderately when the stiff-faced Lincoln recounted the interview to him in his office that evening.

'I didn't think it would take much to impress those bushy-headed squatters,' Lincoln said, with his glass eye fixed on Calhoun, 'but I went through our regular performance.

'When I worked up to the point where it looked like I was handing him the continent of North America, I said: "We have decided to clear your squatter claim, turning the whole thousand acres over to you, with clear title, for the nominal sum—the small fee of two hundred and fifty dollars." Shadrick fixed the amount, but Saint Christopher! it looked little enough to me.

'This sad-looking old sleep-walker was stretched out on his back in a chair with his hands folded in his lap. I wouldn't have known he heard me, except those drooping eyelids came up and his eyes were sharp. "I didn't come here after the land—I got that—I come to get papers on it," he said in that drawling way, putting hinges between his words. Mind you, he thought he was just getting papers on his land, like you register a horse.

'I leaned over the table now and used my confidential manner to impress him. "You don't seem to understand, Mr. Corn," I said. "Peace and Plenty holds the only clear title to that land—the property really belongs to Peace and Plenty."

'I meant to say more, but he cut me off. He didn't uncross his legs, or unfold his hands, or even sit up off his backbone. And that false-face mustache of his kept on smiling at me. His voice was like the mustache. "If Peace and Plenty puts foot on my land, he'll leave there with a piece o' hide and plenty of buckshot in it," he said.'

Calhoun, who had been smiling twistedly during Lincoln's story, gave vent to a whirlwind of laughter that echoed down the stairway beyond the office door. But when he had sobered up, he told Lincoln that he himself would resume dealings with Micajah and would try to satisfy him.

In the summer of '81, Calhoun felt more nearly amicable toward his world than at any moment within his memory. The Peace and Plenty Land Company met his plans and needs even more nicely than he had hoped. He and Shadrick had little difficulty in finding the heirs of Kiger, Kleeman, and Colfax in New England. They had employed Amos Buck, a Portland lawyer, to help them and had later drawn him into the scheme. There were only three heirs: two grandsons of Colfax and an aged stepdaughter of Kleeman. The Colfaxes were in the insurance business, and Calhoun had had no great trouble in getting them, for a consideration, to make over their claim to the land to Rather Lincoln, a clerk in their office. Lincoln, for a salary and a sixteenth part of the profits, was serving as president of the company. Calhoun had arranged salaries and a small share in the profits for Shadrick and Buck. Buck was not only general counsel for the company; Calhoun had used him as his confidential agent and had concealed all of his stock in the company behind Buck's name.

He did not visit the Peace and Plenty offices, but he carefully watched and operated the company from his own. He denied having any interest in the concern, but posed as its moral patron and championed it as a friend and benefactor of the backwoodsman. And to the squatter he had quickly made plain that his influence with the company was all-powerful.

Money and men were coming to him with amazing ease and swiftness. More even than the substance itself, the social reflection of his riches was sweet to him. Already the attitude of the frostiest respectability of Lancaster was thawing. The Misses DeLacy, in their nigger-driven carriage, were now able to see him and nod as they passed; and Doctor Hernandez, the learned Spanish Jew, was not too absent-minded now to speak; and Benton Mills even came out of his office in the Lancaster Banking Company to shake hands. His obvious wealth and his mysterious influence with the land company that in some measure must affect the fortunes of most of the community could not be ignored. Casement, McIntosh, and other Coventry hirelings were keeping closed mouths and showing themselves very little.

Early in September, Calhoun indulged a hankering that had been with him since his overseer days on the Rhea plantation. He had always tried to keep a good buggy animal as a practical need, but now he bought a fine saddle horse. He made a special trip to Lexington, Kentucky, and brought back a great, black, five-gaited stallion named Nigger. Dressed in boots and breeches, he took to riding in the mornings. His acquisitions became more ambitious a little later when he bought Lookaway Hill, gently rising ground on the outskirts of Lancaster, and employed an architect to design and build for him a bigger and more pretentious house than anything the town afforded. His display had an aim beyond the satisfaction of his own taste for parade, or his mother's modest desires.

The time for which he had hoped and contrived during the past year had come; the time to press his suit with Kathleen McIntosh.

Calhoun was now thirty-six years old and he had never proposed marriage to a woman or even declared his love. With a few regrettable and trivial exceptions, his relations with women in his own walk of life had been uniformly formal and casual. There was a Miss Talmadge in Macon, before the war was quite over and he was still in uniform. He had playfully tried to place a kiss on her palm and had felt the hand grow rigid with revulsion. And later in Lancaster, when he had worked himself up to telling the red-haired Noble girl how like his mother he thought she was, she had been moved to tears and flight. The exceptions were regrettable in their conclusion, but trivial, for he had postponed any thought of marriage until he should have achieved substance and position. He had, of course, had relations with women of sorts and colors in a way, but it was an unsatisfying way that did not increase his self-respect.

He had not cared what other men thought of him since he himself had attained manhood. In the presence of women of his own class he still felt sensitive about his facial deformity. His casual conversation and attention to the ladies was fluent enough, but he felt barred from any approach to sentiment. And that bar was himself; his scarred face staring at him.

He had set his sights high enough to seek the hand of the daughter of the Conventry and Company agent. That was not merely ambition. There was something more essential, more important about it. He had always thought Kathleen was different from other girls. When he had taught her as a child of fourteen in his academy, she had never shown any self-consciousness before his deformed face. On the ride back from a picnic of the previous year, he had broken through the barrier, had spoken to Kathleen sentimentally, and she had not repulsed him, by looks, or manner, or voice. There had been no further sentimental passage between them and he had been able to see her seldom during the succeeding months, but this had not discouraged him. He had not been ready; he had not then had much to offer a lady in her position; the security in marriage a lady was entitled to; the security his mother had been denied!

But when Kathleen returned from the East to Pineville late in November, Calhoun was primed for courtship. A month before, in anticipation of this, he had added a blooded team of trotting-horses to his stables and a light racing buggy. The sleek swift grays, moving in machine-like unison, had drawn people to their porches in passing and had brought horsemen from ten miles around to watch and talk.

Calhoun wrote Kathleen asking for an engagement to go riding on the Tuesday after Thanksgiving, if the weather were not unpleasant. She had heard the tales of his fancy team and accepted with interest.

When she presented herself in the parlor, dressed for the ride, she seemed even more vivid, more smartly dressed, than he had remembered her. She wore a rich green coat suit that swept down behind her regally and a small feathered hat of the same color. The pink in her cheek, though subdued, stood out against the whiteness of her skin. But it was the frank friendliness of her eyes that most inspired him.

When he helped her into the buggy as a negro held the horses' heads at the McIntosh front gate, he felt grim and infinitely alert. He handed her up from the right side, taking the reins when he got in at the left. He affected a left-handedness in driving and customarily sat on that side of his driving companion.

Kathleen's mother and brother, David, watched the team off from the library window. And a passer-by in a top buggy pulled out of the road and stopped to look at the team. Calhoun was not unmindful of the spectators, and at another time he might have driven through Pineville's main street for an exhibition, but now he thought swift action would be more impressive, so he turned the team about and headed for the hard stretch on the Lancaster road, saying merely, with a smile, 'I suppose you want to see them show their mettle?'

Beyond the outskirts of the village, the sandy crooked ruts suddenly leveled into a straight clay-hard stretch of road. On the way over, Calhoun had asked Kathleen about her stay in New York and had told her what he knew of Lancaster gossip, but when he reached the hard stretch, he planted his feet solidly against the dashboard and gave his attention to the team. He brought the reins taut and the grays moved off in a smooth trot. Gradually he drew the reins tighter. The horses' loins flattened down and their flanks flew like bodkins. Their hoofs beat a tattoo on the hard road, and there was the sound of only four feet. Telegraph poles sped by. The rail fence on their left seemed to be doing a crooked dance. Calhoun's eye looked straight at the horses and the road with owlish watchfulness, but his cheek creased and colored with the wind and excitement. Kathleen's face glowed, and she smiled tightly as she held to an arm of the buggy. Her green veil swept beyond her neck and waved behind her.

Calhoun brought the team to a walk at the end of the stretch and they relaxed. Kathleen's cheeks and eyes shone. She made him stop the horses that she might get out and look at their faces and pat their heads. They were smoother than a sewing machine, faster than buckshot, she said. Her enthusiasm was childlike, Calhoun thought. It was stirring to see. The value of the horses seemed increased tenfold. He felt vaguely conscious of vast possessions which he would like to roll out prodigally before her. He turned the vehicle about and returned to the stretch. 'Take 'em back over it, Miss Kathleen,' he said casually, handing her the reins.

Her eyes were tense. 'I suppose I can hold them,' she said, a little dubiously. He reassured her recklessly. But the gloved hands she slipped into the holds were dexterous and she drew the reins taut with a sure skill. The grays again beat out their drum roll of sound over the stretch of hard road.

Kathleen was interested, Calhoun decided, as they idled back toward home. Her interest was in his horses now, but that was as much as he could expect to begin with. She continued to talk warmly about them. He told her half-seriously that her love of horses was the most convincing emotion he had ever seen her display, and added with his twisted smile it was the first emotion in a young lady he had ever seen that appealed to him. He talked about 'our love of horses,' and he was heartened and warmly hopeful as he walked his team through the night back to Lancaster. The campaign had met fair weather.

Kathleen confessed to herself, after Calhoun left, that she had a feeling she was going to drive those grays a lot that winter—if she wanted to. And she did. She also went with Calhoun to a Christmas ball at the Pine Forest Hotel in Lancaster. For this an orchestra and refreshments had been brought all the way from Macon. The Pettigrews gave the ball in Kathleen's honor—to please Calhoun. Kathleen went with him on a January houseparty at Magnolia, a plantation home, and a game supper in Lumber City. He asked her to help him select a tapestry for the parlor walls of his new house on Lookaway Hill, now nearing completion, and she, covering her diffidence with laughter, agreed. And with the approach of spring, she and her friend, Pegota Raffe, rode up behind the grays from Pineville several times to make suggestions about the planting of his gardens.

Calhoun found Kathleen the most agreeable companion he had ever known, except his mother. There had been no moment when he felt that he was repulsive to her. She seemed more desirable every day.

Once, when she had been talking extravagantly about his team, he had said, 'Would the DeLacy girls sniff at you—riding by in it?' He did not know quite how he happened to say that, except that he had always had that fear about any woman who might be his. She had started off saying that the DeLacy girls didn't sniff at her, then stopped. She had taken his hand and had held it a moment, silently looking into his face. But there was pity in her eyes, too. He could not go on.

Calhoun knew he had not yet stirred Kathleen's love. His attentions might be pleasant, but they were still trifling in her measure of devotion, he decided. He must devise a more extravagant gesture. He must convince her that his passion was prodigal, importunate. And more, he must give only gifts Kathleen might think precious. The opportunity presented itself while he was with her at a showing of fine horses in Macon near the end of May. In the lot was a small silver-colored Arabian mare. Kathleen had cried out involuntarily when the mare came into the ring, and had fallen silent after that. Evidently she admired the creature so much she could not talk about her. Calhoun said nothing to her, but before he left the city he arranged to buy the mare. He had the animal shipped down and led to the McIntosh home with a note pinned to the halter.

He had felt a little shaky about it, but he was not quite prepared for her reply. Her letter reached him, almost before the horse could have reached her, he thought. She appreciated his generosity and thoughtfulness fully as much as she had appreciated the mare's beauty, but she could not accept it, she said. Calhoun bolted from his office at Lancaster leaving a client waiting, though he managed a more casual air when he greeted Kathleen in her parlor. He spread his legs apart and put his hands in his pockets as he told her that he had won the horse in a poker game and he had the Arab's burnoose, too, though he had forgot to bring it along. He had tried a grin. It was merely a matter of getting rid of the horse, he said. He had no place to keep her and couldn't explain how he got her. Kathleen laughed at his heavy attempt at humor, but she remained seriously insistent that he take the mare back with him.

He managed to keep up his bantering on the way from the library to the barn. Here Kathleen, colorless and taut, beat on the barn wall with a hammer, and the McIntosh deaf-mute stableman came out. She made signs with her fingers and in a moment the negro reappeared leading the haltered mare. As he approached, she said, "Dummy, hand the halter to Captain Calebb,' motioning with her arm.

Calhoun could no longer maintain the smile on his face. His lips twitched and his deep-set gray eye glittered. He did not move to take the outstretched rope, but stared fixedly at Kathleen. She lowered her eyes in a brief glance at the mare, but looked away quickly as if she didn't dare gaze longer. 'No, I won't take her, Kathleen—that won't do!' Calhoun said in a flat, stubborn tone.

Kathleen turned away and started toward the house.

Calhoun followed, speaking in a jerky, torrential voice. 'Here I go get you the horse you want and now you say you don't want it—can't take it from me—I think—'

She cut him off. 'You think very oddly, if you think I can accept the mare! I am sure I have given you no reason to think that.'

17

LANCASTER was taken unprepared. Eb Swilley, who boasted of being the best weather prophet in Coventry County, said later he knew something was coming. June and July had been so dry and blazing. But he had looked for a cloudburst, or a tornado. He'd never thought of nigger trouble.

It came on Sunday, August sixth. The railroad had an unwitting hand in it, advertising the camp meeting and running excursions. Mother Call, known to the hierarchy of her church as Sister Mary Magdalene, had come on Saturday, wearing the black dress and hat of her churchly office, and the long black veil that trailed to the ground. She was met by her bishops and went quietly on to Samson's Grove, so that her arrival was scarcely noticed uptown. The bishops and the deacons, with the help of the faithful in the neighborhood, had been building a camp meeting arbor for several days. They had cut saplings and blackjacks for a mile around and had set up the biggest brush tent ever in the grove.

The meeting began on Saturday night, though few white people in Lancaster heard it or gave it any thought. Samson's Grove was two miles south of town, and residents on that side caught the beating of Mother Call's bass drum along into the still hours. It sounded wild enough, thudding at that slow, steady pace, with occasionally the top of a shoulder's shriek coming through between beats. But no one in Lancaster would be disturbed over the religious doings of the darkies.

The excursion trains jolted into town during the dark early morning hours. When white Lancaster awoke and looked out that Sunday, a black snow had fallen. Negroes swarmed the uptown streets from the depot and spread out in a long snake to Samson's Grove. The white men who came down for shaves and shoe-shines, to open dinner-houses and the whiskey-selling drugstores, were surprised. No one had ever seen such a crowd of niggers in the town before and most of them looked at the swarm with a greedy expectation of big sales of food and drink. Some kicked themselves for not having joined the fore-sighted who had put up eating and grocery stands outside the corporation limits near the grove.

Sitting, squatting, and jostling each other, the negroes kept up a buzz of talk, broken by slow, good-humored laughter. Most of them had brought baskets, or lunches wrapped in meal sacks. Many of them ate and strewed the potato-peelings, eggshells, and melon-rinds about the streets. They were dressed in their Sunday-go-to-meeting best, an occasional shabby black frock coat, or sagging satin dress, mingled with wash-whitened and starched jeans and homespun. Some of the men in jeans breeches wore patched alpaca coats or linen dusters. There were a few store-bought hats, but most of them

171

wore hats of shuck or palmetto weave. There were long sun-bonnets and white and red head-rags. Snuff-brushes stuck from the mouths of many of the women. Some wore shoes, but most of those bound for the grove carried their leather in their hands or swung it over their shoulders. Many, making no apology for shoes, pranced along on their rusty, yellow-bottomed feet.

Hundreds took foot in hand and went on out to the grove early, but a sprawling black litter of them covered the sidewalk and most of the street, negroes hanging about waiting for Lancaster's nine whiskey dispensaries to open. The older people coming out to Sunday school did not like the look of the streets and said so, but they went on to their meeting-houses and let their children go with them. The drugstores had laid in a supply of cheap 'red-eye' and 'bustskull,' in half-pints, pints, and quarts. When they opened up at ten o'clock it went as fast as they could hand it out and take the money.

By the time people started coming home from church, negroes on the uptown streets around the drugstores were getting rowdy with talk, guffaw, and swaggering. Stuckey, the town marshal, and his two deputies tried to keep the crowd moving toward the grove. It was all three men could do. Negroes kept coming back to the drugstores and some were already drunk. By early afternoon prudent people had called their children indoors and most of them stayed on their porches themselves.

It was almost three o'clock when the trouble broke. It began—the trial later brought out—with a game of 'Skin' out back of an eating-place near the grove. One negro won another's watch. When the second negro got ahead of the game and wanted to buy his watch back, the first negro wouldn't sell it to him. He called Marshal Stuckey, who arrested the negro with the watch and started for the jail with him. On the way, the buck tripped him as they went to step a ditch, got loose and ran. Stuckey said later that both he and the deputy with him shot up in the air to make the negro stop running, but there were so many negroes all about that there was confusion. A shot from *somewhere* killed the darky.

The negroes looked scared at first. Then a squat, thickset fellow, hammer-headed and blue-black, dropped his chin and started walking around in a circle. 'They kill my podner—them town marshals—they kill him!' he yelled out in a voice that was a mixture of a bellow and a moan. A high-pocketed, yellow negro with a gaunt muzzle shrilled, 'Them white mens done it!' Things happened fast after that. The negroes closed in about the squat fellow and the yellow negro and lock-stepped on toward Stuckey and his deputy. A half-dozen pistols were showing as well as knives and razors and brickbats. Some of the negroes were picking up pine knots.

Stuckey had his gun in his hand. He yelled to them to stop where they were. He hadn't killed the nigger, he said, but somebody was going to get killed if they didn't stop. He didn't have time to say more. They were at close range. He shot over them once and so did his deputy. But the black drove had swung around his flank and he saw he was being surrounded. The deputy broke into a run and Stuckey followed, cracking black heads with his pistol barrel as he pulled away from the mob. The marshals headed back for the town fast, just breaking their lope enough to dodge behind trees and palmetto clumps. The negroes were shooting at them.

Eb Swilley said later he was around the hitching-racks back of the stores when he first heard the noise. It sounded like a cattle herd and a beehive combined. He was talking to Sam, his boy about the cowpen and barn. Sam was a stringy, blue-gummed nigger who never got his eyes more than half open, nor his mouth half shut. He was lazy, but good-natured enough. Sam was yessuh-ing Eb and claiming he'd be in by dark to milk and Eb was warning him. The first sound that came to them distinctly was the high, wildcat scream of a nigger woman. Following it came a dull blowing of sound and a garboil of voices.

Sam's eyes came all the way open and the whites skittered. His wide mouth closed and one cheek began to pucker and jerk. His nose spread. He came to his feet as if he had been yanked up and began to edge off sideways. Eb yelled at him 'That sounds like niggers on the rut—don't you go get mixed up in that!' Sam broke and ran away.

When David McIntosh, now eighteen, got off the north-bound local at twenty minutes past three, he did not notice the crowd of negroes about the depot. In his gray, tight-legged trousers, buttoned-up coat and low-crowned derby, he was dressed in the height of summer fashion. Moreover, he wore a new pale blue scarf and standing collar. He was conscious of his clothes. The sawmiller's son had ridden up from Pineville to attend the Presbyterian young people's Sunday evening meeting and to be seen about Lancaster's main street before-hand. He had also heard that electric lights were being dis-played every night in the show window of McAlister's hard-ware store and planned to look at them, though he had seen electric lights before. He now picked his way diffidently through the smelly black welter and set off in the direction of the Pine Forest Hotel.

He crossed the main street, which the railroad split in two, and turned down the intersecting route to the hotel. He halted. There were pistol shots and howls. David looked back toward the clot of people at the station. They had heard it, too, and were spreading out and moving in his direction. He took a dozen quick steps onward and came to a cold stop.

A running, reeling, arm-slinging herd of negroes rounded the corner fifty yards away. The mob had lost its quarry and its head was aimless. A giant, double-jointed, coffee-colored man in front reared back on his flat bare feet and spread his arms. A stringy woman at his side fell down and two following fell over her. Others in front tried to stop, spreading their arms and yelling. 'Hold up, mens!' Heads bent, bodies weaving, feet tramping heavily, the negroes continued to pour around the corner, pushing the front forward, spreading out around it into the street, staggering and falling as they came.

The front of the mass paused for a moment. David looked at them hesitantly. The negroes stood with their heads down like bulls, their noses spread, their faces twisted with panting and crying. The black bulging stream spread toward him. He raised his hand and tried to speak, but his voice broke like a gosling's and he could scarcely hear it himself. Over his shoulder he saw other blacks running toward him from the railroad track. In another moment the spreading mass would trap him. He broke and ran.

The mob was after him. It had game in sight again. David had no aim except to gain cover. Vaulting a board fence and a hedge, he came to a tall white house with the doors and win-

175

dow-blinds closed. The house was latticed between its sleepers and the ground, but he found an opening and scrambled under it.

The thudding, stumbling, panting mob came on, spread around the house. The uproar, punctuated by pistol shots, brought Mrs. Flournoy, sitting by the sick-bed of her son in a downstairs room, to the window blinds. Through the cracks she saw the trampling herd breaking down her hedge, heaving bricks and iron taps at the house. She called to the men upstairs, but they were already on their way down.

The men, her husband and her father, stood a moment in the hallway and took counsel. A mob seemed to be storming the house; what could it be after? They composed the disagreement between themselves by both going out on the porch together.

Negroes were already at the front door. Flournoy and his father-in-law, armed only with their pocket-knives, pushed them back down the steps and demanded to know the trouble. In the yard negroes yelled brokenly, not speaking to the white men on the porch or anyone in particular. 'They kilt a colored fellow!' 'They shot him down!' 'He in de house!' And from remoter parts came, 'White bastards!'

The coffee-colored giant appeared and the elder white man, who had a long streaked beard, addressed him. 'Big Boy, what is the trouble here—what do you want?' The big negro said they were after the white man who had run in the house. He had killed a colored fellow. Both white men said immediately that no one had run in the house—no one they wanted was there. The herd pressed in close around the steps, pushed the big negro forward. The white men threatened, then argued. There were cries of 'Burn de house down!' from the crowd. This kept up until the white men saw negroes coming up with an oil can. They decided to permit a search of the house. It seemed like the less harmful way out.

Let three of their number come forward, the long-bearded man said. He would conduct them through the building. They could see for themselves there was no one they wanted there.

The big negro conferred with two other men and an obese black woman. A reeling, wiry, slavering woman grabbed him by the arm. 'They'll git yuh in there and kill yuh!' she shrieked. The leaders were not willing for three to go in and the white men agreed on eight. The elder man led them in and the younger came after them closing the door, but they would not let him lock it. The white men took them first through the sick-room where Mrs. Flournoy sat fanning her son. They hunted about the downstairs rooms, then made a trail through the upper bedrooms and came back. The elder man tried to lead them toward the front door, but a woman in the crowd cried out, 'De clausits —de clausit under de stairs!'

The younger man stepped quickly back to it, the wench following. He swung the door open and she poked in her bobbing head. She uttered a shriek, pounced with her scrawny hands spread, and dragged from the closet a limp, unresisting figure. The negroes shook David McIntosh, white and paralyzed him with fright, and stood him on his feet, shouting and grabbing at him. They sounded like dogs around a house cat.

At the shouting, the front door broke open and black men and women poured into the hallway. Many of them carried pickets from the Flournoy front fence. The negro searchers pushed David forward and the oncoming group struck at him with the palings. A short, crippled negro man worked his way to the front. He was old and swung a walking-stick. When he saw David, he dropped his stick and threw up his long, rope-like arms, making a whinnying, muttering sound. David recognized his father's deaf-mute stableman and murmured, 'Dummy!' in a half-audible, crumbly voice. The old negro reached toward him and some of the hands holding David turned loose. The negroes hesitated a moment, held by their superstition, and the old negro threw his arms about David. But the crowd from the door trampled onward. They choked the hallway, were jammed into the surrounding mass. In the smother of sweat and smell a shot sounded. A jet of flame blazed and David slumped in the old negro's arms.

The crowd inside now pushed back toward the door. The crippled stableman held David's limp body to him, half-carried, half-dragged him through the doorway, out of the house, into the yard. His eyes streamed and he whinnied as he went.

Outside, the yard and the street for a block around was black with faces. Negroes staggered into each other, fell over the broken fence, ran into trees, and knocked themselves down. Wenches with brush-heaps of wire hair shook crooked arms like the claws of praying mantises above their heads. They shrieked like rutting cats. "Kill white man!' The mass moved in about the walkway where the crippled deaf-mute muttered and fumbled over David's limp form. The black faces knotted, twisted, and eye-whites flickered through them like dog slobber.

A drink-crazed, weaving wench broke from the inner fringe of the crowd, screaming, 'You killed my sister's child!' She seized David's lifeless head by the hair and swung a glinting razor in the air. Blood spurted into the deaf-mute's face. Meanwhile, the mad screaming went on, 'Kill any white man, but don't kill Yankee!' 'Don't kill Yankee!'

18

CALHOUN met the Pineville telegraph operator with the yellow envelope bringing word from Lancaster of David's death, as he descended the McIntosh front steps. Kathleen, opening the screen door quickly, read the message on the porch by fading daylight. She stood there staring at it. Calhoun glanced hurriedly at the yellow sheet and then at her face. It was as expressionless as if she were asleep. Her lips were blue. But it was her eyes that unnerved him. He had never seen fear in Kathleen's eyes before.

David's catastrophic death gave him a jolt. Still it was more than shock that made him reach out and hold on to a post unsteadily. He had never before seen anyone so near to him as Kathleen defenselessly struck down by emotion. He couldn't stand it, he thought. He had a wild impulse to run away. He said half audibly, 'Sit down, Kathleen!'

She did not change her pose. She spoke in a voice as blank as her face. 'I must go now.' Then as she moved a cry jerked from her throat, 'Oh, Mama!' It ended in a gulp. There was no sob.

Her words steadied Calhoun. His head began to clear. He put an arm about her shoulders and walked to the door with her. 'Kathleen, get your hat and a duster,' he said firmly, the bass resonance coming back into his voice. 'I'll send word to Lancaster we're coming and a message to your mother.' As he turned back to the porch, thought was ablaze in him. It was not sympathy that blew this flame. A voice spoke from some cold recess of his mind. Here was the chance he had been seeking, the drama he himself could not devise. Fate had broken down another barrier for him. He would bury David McIntosh and prosecute his murderers, or his name wasn't Calebb.

Captain and Mrs. McIntosh, Kathleen had said, were still in Montreal on their summer visit. Calhoun was now in complete control of himself, keyed up as a marksman drawing his bead. 'David seriously injured. When may we expect you?' he scrawled on a blank and signed Kathleen's name. He wrote the Lancaster mayor that they would be there in an hour and a half, and gave the messages to the awkwardly waiting operator.

There was no train northbound from Pineville before midnight. They rode in Calhoun's team that had been all this time tied at the gate. The grays were hitched to the racing buggy and the earlier action of the day did not seem to have taken any of their spirit or endurance. They had not gone a hundred yards before their loins flattened in an incessant, unflagging trot that sent the soft objects of twilight skimming by. Calhoun skillfully held them at a little under their fastest pace, but he never let them relax. Nor did he himself relax. He kept his deep-set eye fixed on the road and on his horses. Yet he spoke intermittently, raising his voice above the noise of hoofs effort-lessly, without destroying the quiet. It was as if he were think-ing aloud, or echoing Kathleen's thoughts without expecting or awaiting an answer. It was possible, he said, that there had been a mistake in identification. That often happened in such disturbances. In fact, exaggeration always accompanied such disturbances. David might not really be dead—only injured. There was nothing more unlikely than that the negroes had attacked him—no negro would raise his hand against the son of *Captain Iron.*

Over the last miles, Kathleen spoke to him. He must not kill his horses, she said. At the moment foam from their muz-zles and flanks was flicking in the wind. They were dark with sweat and blowing stertorously. Calhoun said only, 'They can make it,' and never relaxed his hold or rigid position in the buggy.

Kathleen and Calhoun found Lancaster in order and quiet, if badly shaken. Not a black face appeared within the limits of the town: the camp meeting was already history. When the identity of their victim had become known to the mass-mad negroes, stumbling and screaming around the Flournoy home, they began to scatter. An emergency deputation of almost a hundred white men, led by the mayor, moved in, surrounding the house and taking custody of David's body. Following the disintegration of the mob, the white men arrested some seven-ty of its members and jailed them in the county courtroom under guard for the night. Calhoun learned this by the way as he moved sympathetically and thoughtfully at Kathleen's side.

There was no undertaker in Lancaster and David's body had been held at the doctor's office. Its door was guarded, but a gabbling, curious street crowd jostled about outside. The thought had presented itself to Calhoun on the way over, now he wondered that he had not foreseen this more fully. Why should Kathleen have come to Lancaster at all? Still their information had been meager and it had been her single desire to come. He would not have tried to dissuade her at the time, though he felt the situation unnecessarily trying for her.

But if Kathleen reacted to the coarse show of sympathy, the callousness or curiosity, she gave no sign. She was silent and self-contained, moving like a sleeper. The doctor had stitched David's slashed throat and fixed the bullet exit in his temple so that it barely showed. She only looked at the corpse once briefly and without change in her face—it was almost as if she had seen nothing under the lifted sheet. She remained in the office with the doctor and Mrs. Pettigrew, while Calhoun arranged to have the body shipped to Pineville on the evening train. He collected a small guard of David's friends to accompany the sheet-covered corpse on the doctor's cot aboard the baggage coach. Without bothering her, he also arranged to have the undertaker come down from Macon, so that it might be embalmed to hold until the McIntoshes could arrive.

Calhoun accompanied her back to Pineville, saw the corpse established in the house, and saw to it that Kathleen was well attended by servants, intimates, and a physician, then at three o'clock he caught the morning train back to Lancaster. He had said nothing to Kathleen yet, but he planned to be on hand to aid the solicitor in the investigation and preparation of the murder case. The sheriff, with his swarm of negroes in the courthouse, was awaiting the state prosecutor's arrival before doing more.

Calhoun realized that Ian McIntosh must not relish his interest in behalf of Kathleen and the McIntosh family. He did not know that Ian had made bitter protest to his wife, but the information would not have surprised him, or even have offended him. Ian had felt resentment when he reached home to find Calhoun taking part in the funeral arrangements and comforting his daughter, but he was too grief-stricken then to consider it or give voice to the emotion. However, he burst forth a week later when twenty-five of the negroes were indicted. His wife told him that Kathleen had asked Calhoun to take part in the prosecution. Calhoun had, in effect, asked to be asked—he wanted the privilege of representing her, and the privilege of acting in behalf of order and society. Without cost, of course, he had explained a little crudely.

Ian had wanted to storm at Kathleen and insult Calhoun—if that were possible. Mrs. McIntosh stayed him. She said she feared that Kathleen was in love with Calhoun, or thought she was. She added that he had been a great comfort to Kathleen at the time of the riot while they were in Canada. Kathleen was deeply grateful and so was she. She said that her daughter had told her that she had already accepted Calhoun's offer. If Ian wanted to estrange his daughter and throw her into the arms of that one-eyed Gargantua, he could pick no better course. Ian listened to the voice of caution and stewed in his own juices.

Calhoun discreetly avoided him. But his attentions to Kathleen were constant and inspired. Every morning he dispatched a boy on a horse to carry her a basket of flowers from his gardens. Every afternoon the boy went back with a book, a magazine, a ballad for the piano, or a letter from him, in which he tried to review amusingly current news and gossip. He came down himself as often as he thought it was wise to take her for a drive.

Ian had been awkward and reserved before her since David's death; he seemed unable to talk about him or let her see his grief. He obviously avoided mentioning Calhoun's name. Her mother had almost been hysterical, sinking into melancholia. Kathleen felt she must show cheerfulness and strength before her. During the days of the family mourning and waiting for the trial of the negroes, Kathleen came more and more to depend on Calhoun's attentions and company. He was kind in a brotherly way. This big, one-eyed giant had an astonishing gentleness and thoughtfulness, she found. His occasional display of crudeness did not shock her now. She looked upon him almost as if he had been her brother.

On an afternoon in early September just before the trial, Kathleen first spoke of her feelings for the unwitting black slayers of her brother. She and Calhoun were seated in a chair swing on the lawn. The twilight had come, lifting the sultry heat a little. Calhoun had just said dispassionately he expected that these slayers would get grim justice.

After his voice had quite died out, she spoke hesitantly looking off into the dusk. 'I don't know—I don't know that I should say it, but I hate to think of them being hung. David is dead and that can't do anything for him. They weren't responsible—just blind maniacs!' Here she paused again and her shoulders jerked in a shudder. She continued in a lowered faltering voice: 'Sometimes I think they were an instrument against us—an instrument—God alone knows why! The South is strange—terrifying to me sometimes, now. I have always felt

185

kindly toward the negroes—they seemed simple and friendly. Now I can scarcely bear the sight of Mincy in the kitchen—and Dummy, poor Dummy! If there's anyone I am grateful to, should be devoted to! But sometimes I look at him and wonder.'

Calhoun in the seat facing her had leaned forward a little to catch her low words. He felt the contagion of her emotion. It held him back a moment, then he spoke deliberately, his vibrant voice as pervasive as the twilight. 'Yes, the South is sometimes terrifying and strange, I suppose. Life here calls for its own peculiar kind of justice—law—protection.' He finally decided upon the word. 'The negroes are as simple and kindly as they seem, in a way—even those who killed David. But they are unreasoning brutes, too—they can kill as simply as they sing. It isn't David we must think of now—it is you—your mother—every white woman—every white man or woman down here. Law must be kept plain and sure and inevitable for the negroes. David's killers must swing, for protection of white society.'

Kathleen was impressed. She shook off her misgivings as sentimentality and spoke more firmly. She had never before thought of the negroes as a menace, but she supposed it must be true. There were so many of them. White society must be stern to preserve itself—to preserve order and the negroes, too. In a way it was a bigger thing than she had thought—and not personal: she did not want it to seem personal—the trial.

As he prepared his case, Calhoun thought less of the necessity of convicting the defendants than he did of Kathleen. Their conviction was as sure as their trial, he need not strain himself to secure that, and the punishment would not be half-hearted. Pondering her words in his law office in Lancaster, he calculated carefully and shrewdly on what he thought would strike her sympathy and stir her admiration.

Kathleen later believed that she could not have endured the thirty days of the trial, without Calhoun: the smell of it, the heat, the grind and tedium, the frequent bickering of the lawyers, the coarse laughter and comment of the spectators, even though they were sympathetic. The courtroom was heavily guarded during the trial. The crowd was kept away from the windows and doors, and fans were supplied. The McIntoshes did not sit at the counsel table, but near-by on a bench in the front row of the courtroom. The only negroes allowed within the chamber were the defendants and their relatives, but the body smell of these negroes was clearly perceptible in the humid air.

Ian had employed an additional lawyer, a man named Graham; but Calhoun succeeded in dominating the prosecution counsel. In the courtroom his politeness and agreeability were unfailing, yet he somehow managed to have his way most of the time. Kathleen never suspected the contention he had with Graham on the outside. The white witnesses were few, but a stream of shabby negroes continued its course to the witness chair for days on days. Calhoun relentlessly covered every phase of the riot. Most of the witnesses were ignorant, many were unwilling. The negroes were intuitively and sometimes humorously ignorant of names and forgetful of faces and incidents. Calhoun was good-humored and tolerant in questioning them. Even in the rare case of a biggity nigger, he was civil in his manner. Kathleen was impressed by his endurance, his infallible memory for every detail—he could quickly give any statement called into question of any witness, repeating even the manner and tone of voice. If a witness's testimony were particularly pertinent, or if one were obviously lying, Calhoun had a way of pretending deafness, asking for a repetition.

When the defense presented its case, he cross-examined four of the negroes charged with the murder. His manner was tolerant and dispassionate. He never yelled at them, or charged them with malice against their victim. This was in eloquent contrast to the tactics of Graham, who bullied every negro who denied an accusation. Even the solicitor was prone to bully them at times. More and more Kathleen came to identify herself with Calhoun as the examinations progressed. She came to feel that he was speaking for her, in almost the manner she would have used. He never attributed cruelty to the defendants. When they denied some act, he repeated his question in another way. 'Now didn't Redeye and the Devil make you do that?' he asked again and again. He treated them rather like children, but he was relentless in his examination. Once when he trapped one of the defendants into admitting on the stand that she had just lied, he said gravely, 'Here you've let the Devil trick you again—Nigger, you need to pray.' Before a defense attorney could make his objection heard, the woman defendant replied with feeling, 'Yessuh, white folks! Kaint you pray foh me, too?' Kathleen had laughed with everybody else. Afterwards she found that there were tears in her eyes.

Finally Calhoun stood before the jury box for his plea. Sweating body pressed against sweating body all over the courtroom and the air was electrical with emotion. The only unfilled space in the room was the small clearing in front of the jury box where he stood alone. He had dressed formally in black frock coat throughout the trial. Now he wore a white flower in his coat lapel. He seemed giant-like and his deliberateness was a little theatrical, but four weeks' absorption in the case had robbed Kathleen of perspective. His dramatic pause now tightened her nerves, made her tingle all over.

Calhoun addressed the judge, looked sweepingly around the courtroom, and his eye came to rest on her for a moment, then he deliberately turned his back and faced the jury. He spoke of the patience of the jurors and said that he would not tax it further with a detailed review of the evidence. But he did not omit the review merely because he did not wish to try their patience. He would not tear their heartstrings with a picture of the bludgeoned affections and overwhelming sorrow of the family of the deceased. Nor would he fire the jurors' passions with a portrayal of the incredibly hideous tragedy that had bowed these heads in grief. David McIntosh's sorrowing family, he went on, had not come into Coventry County's superior court to seek vengeance nor requital for their terrible loss. Their loss could not be assuaged, could not be repaired by human aid. They came out of a sense of duty, of citizenship—they came as responsible members to carry out their obligation to Southern white society.

In her seat between her father and mother Kathleen leaned forward. She realized that at another time she might have thought his words ponderous and oratorical, but somehow their ring caught her up. They were solemn, eloquent, and stirring; they were hers!

Calhoun slowly turned about to include the whole courtroom in his final plea. His masked eye and twisted scar somehow added to his giant figure. He spoke in a calm, vibrant voice. 'I want you to dwell, not on the brutality—the hideous brutality of the acts of these defendants. . .'

Kathleen, watching him, felt that his face was heroic by virtue of its very deformity.

'White society in the South is at stake. . . rests upon the justice you may apply here today, the law you may sustain.'

The voice gathered ponderous depth. Kathleen's pulse synchronized with its vibrance. She felt herself a part of it.

When the voice ceased speaking, she knew that this emotion—their emotion—was the most important thing in her life.

Three days later Calhoun and Kathleen became informally engaged. There was no date set for the wedding, it was not even mentioned. But he asked if she did not know he was in love with her; if she would not consent to marry him, and she had said she would marry him.

Now on the evening following, as he sat rocking a little in his swivel chair in his law office, Calhoun thought about this engagement with mixed emotions. She had been talking in a veiled way about her uncertainty of the future when he spoke out. She was very white and quiet, sitting there on the parlor sofa with her yellow hair piled high and her bosom molded into her black gown. She had answered that she believed that he loved her. She hoped that he did. And she had been willing in his arms and had kissed him. There had been her fingers about his neck, and her lips had been moist and pliant.

He stopped his chair and leaned forward, slowly recovering the sensation of that moment. The lips had been only moist and pliant, he decided. Even at the moment he had felt that the embrace was not all that he had wanted, had hoped for—

even then he knew that something was absent. He understood now why he had not pressed for a definite engagement, why he had been disturbed by uncertainty.

He was sure his sensitiveness had not misled him. Kathleen had been sincere—sincere in her effort—but she was not in love with him—yet.

'Not yet, not yet!' He repeated the phrase to himself as his thoughts moved on. But she would be willing to marry him. Even now she would consent to a public announcement of their engagement. Why not marry her, now, while he was riding the freshet of Fate's favor? No destiny was always secure.

He walked to his office window and stared out into the unlighted street. He might marry Kathleen now, but somehow he knew that he would wait—wait for the response that would not humble him.

19

CALHOUN Calebb pulled the stable gate shut in the darkness. Nigger, the big stallion, swung his hindquarters sideways to straighten his long body in the close turn about his master and nuzzled Calhoun's coat-pocket while he fumbled with the latch. The horse and man were vague shadows in the darkness of the overspreading water oaks beside the lane. Without pausing to look about him, Calhoun threw the reins over the horse's head, grasped the pommel of the saddle, and swung his great frame into it.

The horse carried the man to the mouth of the lane at a walk. Here Calhoun reined in his mount and lifted his chin. He sniffed the light October air and looked at the moon, almost full, and now in plain view beyond the edge of the trees. The animal skittered about in a half-circle, bringing the high house on Lookaway Hill before Calhoun's eyes. Lights from a remote interior glowed through its tall windows. He had quit it a few moments before, telling his mother he was going out for exercise. He had not told her he intended to ride, nor had he roused any of the hands to saddle the horse.

The animal wheeled again and threw his head up and down restively. Finally he moved off up the road toward Lancaster at a quick walk, but after he had gone a little way Calhoun turned him about in the direction of Pineville.

The road ahead was a soft, sinuous strand in the moonlight. On either hand grayish fields spread out to the dark pine walls. The night was warm, but slowly growing cooler.

Calhoun did not think of the weather, nor of the scene before his eyes. He saw again the pointed japonica bush on the lawn at Magnolia and Kathleen and Casement seated beside it. It had been an uneventful houseparty and the incident now so vividly before him could not, he had told himself afterward, have all the significance he felt impelled to give it. But now he retraced in memory his walk to the end of the front porch. It had been idle walking and he had intended hailing them with 'You ought to get on the other side of the bush for that!' (He had no other thought than that they were in trivial conversation.)

They were seated on sofa cushions, almost facing each other, and he could only see Casement's profile. But the look on Kathleen's face had halted him, had kept the words hung in his mouth. Her bright, parted lips. Her deep, fixed eyes—gazing into Casement's. She had never looked at him like that, but he could not mistake the look. He turned away quickly, feeling incredulous of what he had seen. He had almost turned to look again, to be sure. But the sharp pain within him held him back and he felt confusion, too.

Casement! It did not seem possible that she could be in love with Casement. It did not seem that she could be in love with anyone—until some day, some day with him. He had felt that as he walked back along the porch, his feet sounding loudly on the dry boards.

He checked Nigger's effort to trot as they came to a hard stretch of road. 'Slow, Boy, slow!' he said abstractedly, as the animal resumed walking.

He went on with his thoughts. During the two weeks since he had come to mistrust his eyes, he had told himself he was an imaginative fool, touched in the head with morbid fears. Then this morning, the note came from Kathleen saying that she could not see him in the evening, that her mother was not well.

Calhoun pulled his hat more firmly on his head and fingered the strings to his eye-shield, leaning forward a little in his saddle to lessen the jar of the horse's motion. It was not the first time she had broken an engagement thus, he recalled. Her mother's health had been a convenience to her before, perhaps—a convenience. She had written that her mother was not well and that was all he had to go on, but it made the look on Kathleen's face, beside the japonica bush, come back to him vividly.

Suddenly he lifted his head and drew in his lips. He put his horse into a 'rack.' He was out for exercise, he said to himself with force.

The big animal moved swiftly and noiselessly in the sand. The man and mount made a single dark silhouette under the moon. Their bodies swayed in unison.

He was acting like a boy with yellow-eye—a horn-mad old man, Calhoun said between his teeth. He had no time for such mawkish mooning! He was out for a ride.

And where did he think he was riding to? he asked himself. He was not headed to Pineville, he said—he was going to Murdock's old mill—the turn-off was down the road a piece.

Casement had known Kathleen since childhood—how long could this thing have been going on? The question came into his head—shot from one temple to the other—above the soft thud of the horse's feet. His hands, resting on his thighs, slowly reined in the animal, brought him to a walk.

He recalled Kathleen's departure for Montreal during the preceding winter, not two months after their engagement. It had mystified him at the time—to Montreal in the dead of winter! He had used those exact words when she told him she was going. They were sitting then by a lightwood fire in the McIntosh parlor. Staring at the blaze, she had not lifted her eyes or smiled at his exclamation. She seemed to be under some strange compulsion.

He had wondered many times since their engagement if she knew that she really did not love him—he had wondered then what she must feel. But she said nothing, nothing about them, or herself—only that she must go. Her face looked like old parchment in the firelight, her eyelashes the shading of some Latin penman. He had felt like a shirt-tail boy.

Had she been going merely to join Casement? Calhoun considered it. Casement, he recalled, had returned to Lancaster—from a supposed visit to New York—almost before she could have time to get there.

Besides their letters during the winter had brought them closer together, it had seemed, than they had ever been—before or since. When she came home in April, he thought that *the moment*, finally, had arrived. She had greeted him alone in the twilight, behind the ivy on her porch. Her eyes were clear and shining even in the gloom. He had lifted her off her feet in his embrace and her arms had drawn about his neck vehemently.

Nigger, answering to the rein, came to a halt before a dim crooked road branching to the left. He walked toward it and then, moving in an arc, came back into the middle of the Pineville road. The horse carried his rider on.

Calhoun told himself that Kathleen had withdrawn a little after her first week home. She had put him off when he wanted to announce their engagement. And two weeks later she had gone away again—this time to St. Simon's Island. He had been to visit her there, however, going by train to Brunswick. On one trip he encountered Casement in Brunswick at the depot, he remembered—he remembered it now, though he had not thought of it before.

And in July it had been her mother's health, and they had gone to Canada. This time there had been no mention in her letters of their racing his team against the train when she got back, no word of lonesomeness for Lancaster things that were close to him, no personal problems for his advice. She had written about her mother's health, about the village out of Montreal in which they stayed, about the weather.

But he had not thought of Casement. He had only asked himself if she could stand *his* face—his one-eyed ugliness. God, he'd gone over that often enough! He had thought of many things, but not of Casement.

Nigger lifted his muzzle and broke into a trot. Calhoun's thighs gripped the horse's barrel and he looked up. Pineville! They were passing the last woods thicket—Kathleen's was the first house beyond it. He pulled hard on the reins, brought the horse up on his haunches and to a halt. The animal made a circle in the road and Calhoun looked in both directions. He sat his horse for a time and continued to peer into the shadowed emptiness about him and at the moonlit stretch of road beyond. Finally the mount and rider moved off into the pine woods to the right.

From the edge of the trees Calhoun saw, a hundred yards distant, a picket fence, wet-looking in the night-light. The broad lawn within it was dimly gray. The tall gables of the house on the lawn were silvered and shadows dropped from its eaves. The framework of a swing was a dim mound in the distance of the lawn. Soft light from the hallway shone through the glassed front door of the house, making a pale yellow pathway across the porch.

Standing in his stirrups, Calhoun gazed fixedly at the house. He pulled his hatbrim farther over his eyes and dropped Nigger's reins over the saddle pommel, permitting him to browse on the low bushes. Then he took his hat off and continued staring.

There seemed to be a faint glow of light from the parlor window beyond the doorway. The wall receded at the parlor and ivy curtained the porch. He could not be sure. Suddenly he put his hat on his head, jerking it down. He snorted, and taking hold of the reins, turned the horse about. The animal picked his way through the pine trees and back to the road, slowly, then came into the highway headed homeward, but here Calhoun halted him and after a pause turned him again toward Pineville.

When they had come abreast of the picket fence, Calhoun pulled his horse out of the road to the opposite side. He guided him toward the railroad embankment which lay beyond, then turned him parallel to the road. He loosed the reins and leaning forward placed his left hand on Nigger's shoulder. Not looking at him, he spoke in a low, half-whisper, 'Easy, Boy, easy!' The horse sniffed at the wiregrass and moved slowly forward. Calhoun's eyes were on the dim-lighted house.

From the lawn nearer by came the low, half-smothered laughter of a woman. The horse and rider trembled and grew rigid and the horse threw up his head. Both of them had recognized Kathleen's voice—from the chair swing. As the horse wheeled, Calhoun heard John Casement laugh.

Calhoun rammed his spurs into Nigger's flanks with reflex action. The horse reared upon his haunches. There seemed to him to be a suspension of time while Nigger's forefeet hung there in the air, while he wondered if Kathleen were in Casement's arms, if they had seen him, while he choked with the swelling pulse in his throat. The horse's feet came down. Calhoun drove spurs into his flanks again.

20

WHEN Calhoun emerged from the green biliousness and headaches from hating Kathleen during the next two weeks, he felt almost cheerful. He had even forgiven himself (and Kathleen) for having broken Nigger's wind in his berserk ride back from Pineville, now that he had sold the horse. He had cursed Kathleen for a traitor, a cheat, a harpy. He had convinced himself, for a few days, that she was not a virtuous woman. But that, he knew, was merely the hollering of a hound with a load of shot in his hide. And, with the discovery of Casement as his competitor, he had found sounder ground. He wondered uneasily on occasion what it was that Casement had, but now, he knew, he was no longer fighting his own shadow—here was something he could see and strike at—a man whose guts growled, whose temper changed with the weather, who had three dimensions, like other men.

He wondered, too, what Casement might have told Kathleen about him. Casement suspected his, Calhoun's, connection with the Peace and Plenty Land Company—and of course, for Casement, the land company must be a fraud. But he had no proof. Calhoun reflected that he had long ago settled Kathleen's mind about the land company. It would require proof to change her view.

He wondered, but Calhoun would not give way to confusion before a man. Attack must meet attack. The question of Casement's dimensions absorbed him. A man must have thickness, he told Simeon Shadrick, one day in his office. Casement had moved into their scene like a photograph, a magic-lantern picture and for ten years he had remained so. 'There is something behind the picture,' Calhoun commented, stroking his nose. 'And it must be pretty bad—the care with which he has cut himself off.' He meant to see behind that pretty face and frock coat—men who didn't talk about their pasts had good reasons. But all that Shadrick could contribute was the report of an uncle. He had heard when he worked for Coventry and Company, that Casement bore this uncle's name. The uncle, he believed, was in the shipping business in New York, or had been.

It was a slender thread, leading nowhere in particular, but Calhoun pursued it. And when he had returned from New York near Christmas-time, he felt unconvinced and a little chagrined, though he intended to make the most of the findings for which he had spent a month in search. The uncle had been dead five years, but at first Calhoun believed this to be a piece of luck, for his will led to an exciting discovery: Casement's surname had been originally O'Toole; it had been changed in 1869.

However, Calhoun could find no satisfying explanation for this act, though he spent three weeks in the search. Casement got no inheritance from his uncle that was worthy of the word.

He did find that Casement had served in the Union Army during the war—an Irish mercenary. He might have changed his name to bury this past before coming to Georgia to practice law. But this was hardly a full-grown skeleton: Kathleen would care little whether he had been a 'Yankee' or a 'Reb.'

Pondering over the bones of his digging, as he lounged in his car chair coming back, Calhoun decided he might use Casement's secret—the desperate cause which he, Calhoun, still hoped existed—he might use it without knowing what it was. Or if there were no worthy cause, he might create one.

When he walked toward Kathleen and Casement, standing with their glasses a little way from the punchbowl in the dining-room at Lookaway Hill on Christmas Eve, he had followed his plan to the striking point, Calhoun believed. Kathleen's blue gown rustled as she looked up and she smiled cordially at Calhoun.

'Tell us about your New York trip,' she said.

Casement glanced at Kathleen and nodded. His shapely mouth creased in a polite smile as he met Calhoun's gaze. 'Do!' he added.

Calhoun had expected to be asked to tell about his trip, but the cue had come quickly. He turned his scarred cheek toward Kathleen to look more directly at Casement. The smile on Calhoun's face lit up his solitary eye and he bent his head a little to one side. He did not speak at once, but shifted his big frame to look again at Kathleen.

'I'm afraid I can't make it sound exciting. I was too busy for dissipation. One thing that ought to interest you, though'—still smiling, he looked back at Casement—'I met some of your old friends, old friends who knew all about you—who knew you as O'Toole.'

Calhoun's gray eye glittered as he continued looking at Casement. He had seen the smile on Casement's face set like mortar and the color in his cheek seep out. He had never seen Casement take so long to reply, or stutter, before.

He had guessed right, there was some real ghost, Calhoun decided. Still smiling, he turned quickly to look at Kathleen. The smile faded from his face and he blinked.

Her eyes looked black. She was staring at him as if she did not have the power to look away.

Calhoun puzzled over the look on Kathleen's face during the remainder of the winter. He had hoped to confuse Casement. He found that he had done more than that. It was as if, he told himself later in reflection, he had stepped into the stable with his grays and had suddenly and innocently spoken to them in horse language—sounds that meant little to him, but were of powerful meaning to them. Evidently, Kathleen knew of Casement's former name and his past, far more of his past than he, Calhoun, could discover. He had hesitated during the Christmas holidays to ask her for an engagement. She gave it readily when he asked, but he found her changed. Not in the words she used or the gestures that went with them. But she was too gay and talked a little frantically, Calhoun thought. The change in Kathleen grew, he found, as he continued seeing her. They must always go somewhere, or do something, and she seemed to talk incessantly—she permitted no moment's silence for intimacy. He had in the first evenings tried to get at what was the matter with her, but she denied there was anything.

202

As spring approached, Calhoun wondered about himself. Formerly he had felt, without quite realizing it, that he and Kathleen sat upon the same sofa and looked out upon the scene. The fact that she received attentions from other men had never disturbed him. He had not even been jealous of her father or her mother—they, too, were outside the circle of the sofa. But now it was he that was on the outside. He was fearful of any boy who looked at Kathleen; he was more fearful of her father, who had sound reason to dislike him. The change went further, he was less sure of many things.

He had long planned that the Peace and Plenty Land Company should abandon its early policy of caution and take action against the Coventry crowd. He had fixed March as the month in which to file an injunction suit to stop their timber-cutting. He had planned to follow this rapidly with increasing drastic measures. He had given detailed directions to his company's dummy heads. But March arrived and the injunction suit was not filed.

When Kathleen returned in the early fall, after having spent most of the summer away without writing him, she seemed astonishingly cordial. He could understand this change of manner as little as he had understood her strange withdrawal. One evening, when they had had wine at Mrs. Pettigrew's and sat upon the stairhead in the shadow while a game was being played, he pinioned Kathleen's arms against the wall. Their faces coming close, he had looked into her eyes and asked if she remembered the April afternoon of her return from Montreal, behind the ivy on her porch. She had smiled, but in the fragment of time before she smiled, her eyes had strained in panic. Her smiling became laughter; he might have kissed her, but he could not do it. He and she were like two pomegranates on a limb, he thought, pomegranates, with their polished skins tightly covering the red pulp, the brittle seeds.

One night he sat alone in his office. A white sheet of writing paper lay on his roller-top desk beside a shaded lamp. It was blank except for the superscription:

Lancaster, Ga.
February 20th, 1884.

    My dear Kathleen—

He sat before it in his swivel chair. His face was tense, and he began to write rigidly, with great care:

    It seems a bitter fate pursues us and that one or
    the other of us must ever be harassed...

He withdrew his pen from the paper and relaxed as if he could no longer endure the strain of the effort. Staring at the page before him, he twisted his mouth and chewed his lower lip.

A small red beetle scurried onto the writing paper, paused a moment, and confronted him. Calhoun's nostrils slowly dilated, and he reached for the pen he had laid on an iron inkstand. The beetle had turned and was scurrying from the page, but he pursued it with the pen-point and jabbed it through, then scribbled on the paper in its blood.

The twisted scar on his cheek grew purple as he stared at the beetle's remains, and he suddenly leaped up, throwing his chair over backward. He turned without picking it up and moved the length of his office in great strides. His striding finally brought him to a window and he stood a moment staring out into the darkness.

Then he returned to his desk and wrote again. After a few slowly inscribed lines, he leaned back and gazed at the ceiling. He spoke in a half-audible monotone, beating the words off on his fingers.

'This bond between us—in a sense, born of tragedy'—He paused and was silent a moment—*'has ever since been put to bitter test.'* He beat off the remaining words rapidly, then set the sentence down.

After reflection, he added slowly:

> *When, late last year, our misapprehensions were dissolved and our relationship permitted to grow green again, I had hoped (and trusted) that our trials were behind us.*

When he had ceased, he picked up the copy of the injunction petition addressed to the federal court and wheeled his chair around so that the lamplight came over his shoulder. He turned several pages of the bill before he began reading. He read hurriedly for several minutes, then he stopped, sat forward in his chair, and stared at a paragraph. His eye, in its hollow socket, had a feverish look and his scarred cheek creased in livid and purple ridges. He threw the bill across the room. 'Why, the son-of-a-bitch!' he said half-aloud. Then, on his feet walking, he repeated in a loud voice, 'Smart son-of-a-bitch, he thinks he is!'

But in time he returned to his letter and scratched again with his pen:

I would hesitate to write you even this, if I did not believe you would guess without my having told you who the source of this attack upon me is.

He read aloud the sentence he had written, then resumed writing. He scratched out a line at the top of a new page and got up from his chair. Walking to the back of the room, he drew aside a curtain, exposing a washstand on which sat a bucket and basin. He put the bucket to his lips and swallowed hugely, then poured water into the basin. He soaked a towel in the basin and held it to his forehead, staring off toward the blackness framed in the window. 'They'll play hell—' he muttered aloud, but his comment went unfinished and he went back to the letter on his desk.

The idea that I could have forged a deed and brought together the diverse parties of the land company (largely of New England where I am unacquainted) or—

He laid down the pen without finishing the sentence. He plundered through a drawer of his desk and then another, finally drawing forth a cabinet-size photograph. It was of a smooth-faced young man, with hair parted in the middle and a derby held on his arm. Calhoun tore it in two with a giant jerk, and tore the fragments again and again. He walked to the hearth and threw them on the embers, then stirred the coals until the pasteboard burned.

He resumed writing where he had left off:

> *that I would have entered into a conspiracy with such a person as Simeon Shadrick (mentioned in the suit) is an equal indictment of my intelligence and my character.*

He wrote on, coming to his concluding sentence. He laid down a fresh sheet of paper and, holding his arms rigidly before him on the desk, stared at the blank page for a time. A tic seized the muscles at his cheekbone. He wiped the sweat from his hands and began writing:

> *In view of the nature of the drastic charges hurled at me and the peculiar complication of their source, I think it the part of a gentleman that I release you from any obligations of our relationship until my name shall have been fully cleared.*

He added below rapidly, *I beg to remain ever,* then, leaving the letter unsigned on his desk, wheeled his chair about and stared at the long broken shadow the lamp at his back cast upon the wall.

21

ON a late May evening in '86, Micajah Corn walked along the back road to Cameron Shops in answer to a summons. Land troubles had come again.

A dry moon spread soft tinsel over the brush foliage and the bough tips of the tall pines. The grayish sand in the ruts of the three-path road was a misty white. Except for a far-off swish in the tops of the pines the night was still. Micajah moved along the meandering trail at an easy, loping gait. He was in his shirt-sleeves and carried a shotgun over his shoulder. The shadow of his black wool hat hid his face, but it bore its usual melancholy calm. Micajah was now in his sixty-third year. The hair under his hat was more white than gray, but there was little change in his lean, sinewy frame. His hand, maybe, was not quite as steady as when the war ended and his aim beyond two hundred yards not quite as true, though he would have been unwilling to admit the latter.

But it was not of his age or aim that Micajah was thinking as a shadowy smile touched is face. It was a dry harsh smile and a little weary. Civil did beat the goats for contrariness. She had wanted Littleton to stay at home with her all the time. Her

'Well, is Littleton a-goin' along too?' when he announced his departure at the supper table, had shown that plainly. Yet when he told Lit that he could not go, that he must stay with his mother, she had got her back up. She wouldn't side with him, Micajah, if it killed her. It was only when he had said that he, Micajah, must stay in that case that he had been able to carry his point. She had retorted that she had rather be left alone than have him around.

It had troubled Micajah, but he still thought that it was too bad that Civil took things the way she did—too bad for her. It was part of the cost of Jet's killing, he told himself, and he reckoned he was able to bear it. He wasn't complaining about the justice of God's acts; he just wasn't waiting on God anymore, for justice or anything else. Jet's killing had been one too many. He had never yet answered Civil anything about it, but she had taken exceptions when he quit kneeling in prayer and going to Sunday meeting. She had only tried to talk to him about it a few times, but she never forgot it.

And she had got worse after he took that shot at Fears; that was nearly four years ago now. If he'd only got Fears! That would have quieted everything and put him straight. If he ever had any luck—if he hadn't acted simple again! He had spent two years waiting for the right time and place only to let that son-of-a-bitching hellion trick him.

Micajah thought again, in the rote of recollection that always caught him up when the incident came to him, if he had only left that pistol in his jeans and had used his Winchester. He had tied his horse to a bush behind the big magnolia on the swamp road from Coventry Boom. That magnolia pointed the turn, and from it back toward the river was a straight stretch of more than a hundred paces. He had figured the stretch would give him a fair shot and give Fears fair warning that he was a-shooting. But Fears had come at a faster clip than he was expecting on that crooked swamp road and he had leaned his Winchester against the tree and had used his Colt.

He had stepped almost out into the middle of the road before he yelled: "Fears, I come to get ye!' He had thought that Fears might get off his horse, but he was prepared when the slick son-of-hell tried to duck behind the beast's neck. He had fired quick enough, all right. He was sure it took him right in the chest, for it carried him off the horse. The creature had wheeled and had dragged Fears out of sight, one foot in the stirrup. He had never the least thought of following it up at that time, he was so sure he'd got him.

It wasn't till two days later that he learned that Fears was wearing one of those coats-of-mail. He didn't know as he'd ever heard of one before. But just the same, if he had used his Winchester, he believed the bullet would have gone through it.

It had unhinged him pretty bad when he got word of it. Somehow he got so worked up, he suspected at the moment that God had a hand in it. He had cursed Him for it; out loud—loud enough for Civil to hear. Then she had quit sleeping with him, or had made it so as to be more peaceable for him to sleep by himself in Pa's old four-poster. Civil had got just like a cucumber—a deaf and dumb cucumber. But he reckoned he could do without a woman at his age. It gave him more time to lay there quiet, thinking about Jet and hating Fears. He shifted his gun and wiped his hand on his breeches.

Things had sure changed since Pa died, since the last time the Yankee Government court had knocked out the deeds to their land. Mary Ann was married again and gone. He hadn't liked her marrying again, but he hadn't said anything except to try to keep her boy, but Civil, Zeke, the whole passel, had been against him. And Jasmine a-growing up; almost a woman already and the prettiest one he believed he'd ever seen. Her hair shone like a brass fender sometimes. He still had some hold on her, but he reckoned it wouldn't be for much longer. Lit was still at home, but how much good was he? His ma had spoiled him. And he was different from the other boys anyhow. Had timber-running in his head from the time he was sixteen. Get that river in a man's blood and he ain't any more good for farming! For the last three seasons Micajah had had to hire a nigger to help him.

The nigger was trifling, but they had made the cotton. At least the old Sugar Field hadn't changed. The ground was just as dark to the turn of a plow and just as rich. He hadn't made less than six bales any crop since Pa died, and last year he had made twelve. He lowered his gun and paused to look around him as he enjoyed the warm glow inside, thinking gratefully of the last year's cotton crop, as white in the field as a Tennessee snowfall.

He could see a crack of light in the distance. He was drawing near the shops. And now war with the company was starting all over again, he told himself. That God-danged Calebb had his hundred dollars and the Yankee Government court had knocked out the deed that he had sold him. This time it had knocked out a passel of 'em; and this time the company was biggitier and more bulldozing about putting people off their land than ever. And it was fight for the backwoods people now. He was about to believe he didn't care. He had done no good in getting Fears—had almost been on the point of weak-ening two or three times in the last year and a half. This might deliver that slippery copperhead into his hands. Micajah paused a moment before a long, high-roofed building, softly outlined in the moonlight, and took his gun off his shoulder. He entered it through a yellow oblong of light.

Lightwood blaze gave the high-raftered shop its wavering illumination. At one end of the weathered building, built of deals, a fire on top of a forge leaped toward a black suspended plowshare, swinging from a smoke-stained rafter. Midway the shop, on either wall, torches burned. A group of men stood in a semi-circle at a short distance from the forge and others squatted or stood beneath each of the torches. They were men of bushy beards and hair, most of them, and with cheekbones sharpened and eyes glinted by the firelight. They quietly swapped chews of tobacco and talked two or three in a group.

Soon after Micajah arrived, Ben Cameron, his jowls as clean-shaven as a town man's, stood up from the anvil against which he had been leaning and said, 'Men I reckon we'd better start this thing.' Those about the forge backed off a little and many of them squatted down. 'I'll get the talking started,' he continued, 'and we'll hear from everybody who's got anything to say. There seems to be most of the Alliance of Deacon's Courtyard here, but ye are all men with land Coventry is tak-ing too, I reckon. We want to hear about what they are doing—though most of us know something about that—and we want to talk about what we ought to do.'

Cameron had shaken hands with Micajah when he came in and now with a glance to his right where Micajah squatted against the wall, he called on him. But Micajah did not get to his feet, he merely said he wasn't sure he had anything to say; he'd come to listen, mostly.

Cameron then called out the name of Merlin, and a thick-set, swart man with heavy black hair and beard, stood up. He spoke in a booming voice. 'Men, have you a-heard this un?' he began, and then he said Zenas Fears had run Rube Faulk and the Dopson boys off their land that morning. Rube and the Dopsons had stopped a crew of Coventry's niggers come out to cut their timber. The niggers had stopped, but in a little while Fears had come up with two henchmen. Fears had told them, the way Merlin heard it, to go get a court paper if they wanted to stop the choppers. And Rube had 'lowed he'd shoot any man who put an axe in his timber. Then Fears and his men had pulled their guns and bluffed Rube and the Dopsons off.

The black-bearded man sat down and an old hunchback, with hair growing out of his ears and a goat-like beard, said shrilly: 'That un makes the twelfth—he's put twelve families off'n their land around here in Telfair County since April. Men, Coventry don't aim to stop nowhere this time—he'll cut any-body's timber—anywhere now!' There was widespread shifting of feet among the men standing and spitting, and many of the listeners nodded at each other. He went on to say the Pineville sawmill was running now at full tilt and he had heard the company had doubled its logging operations.

A beardless man rose in the rear beyond the torches to ask if the group had heard about the McCrackens in Montgomery County. He said Fears had come down on them with a posse of twelve men, had made them pack their household goods and what little corn they could take and get out. They even had to leave hay and fodder in their barn, he had heard.

A slender, youngish tow-headed fellow, whose lightly bearded cheeks still had a smooth look, stood up almost beneath a torch. He said he didn't have anything to tell them, but he just wanted to ask them all, what kind of law was it that let such things go on? His eyes glistened in the yellow light. There was a startled look on his face.

An old man, who had sat close to the forge with his ear cupped and who had asked his neighbors to repeat things, rose slowly. He had a long nose and long cotton-white hair and beard. He stood straighter than most of the young men and he spoke in the loud monotone of the deaf. 'It's Yankee law,' he shouted; 'the war ain't over yet! They a-call it court law, but it's all the same. A backwoodsman, a Southern man, ain't got no more chance than a jaybird in the Yankee court—nobody has except the damn Yankees and niggers!' He paused a moment for breath, then went on. 'The court crowd's worse than the carpetbaggers was, aer the Sherman army.'

There was more nodding and spitting from the crowd.

The next to get to his feet was a loose-jointed, slouching man, who rubbed his hand over the thin mesh of wiry hair on his head. His cooter nose was red at the end. Spout-like mustaches drooped down his face. He spoke in a loose, muffled sing-song. 'It's a-worse than the Yankee army, aer the Confederate, either. I never a-fit against naer one of 'em, but that a-don't holp none. I a-stayed up in a tree in Gum Swamp most of the time, in-durin' the war—from the conscripters. But they done took my land. Been a-livin' there eleven year and had papers on it, too!'

The cooter-nosed man was followed by a squat fellow, whose skin had the look of fire-shrunk leather. His dark eyes were as unblinking as a chipmunk's. He spoke in a thick, even voice. He said that a man with a Peace and Plenty deed to his land was in no better fix than Zeb Fussell, who had just been put off. All of them were going to be put off their land, the way things were moving. He said that it was foolish for a backwoodsman even to think of going into the Yankee court—or into any court against Coventry, for that matter.

The company owned *other* courthouses besides the one up in Coventry County! He closed his fist and rubbed his other hand over it. The courthouse was just a Coventry deadfall, rabbit trap. He came to his conclusion without raising his voice: 'Shore thing, if we a-let 'em do it their way, they'll a-beat us every time. We a-got to fit 'em our way. And I'm a-thinkin' our way is a long way from the courthouse. You a-can't try a spike in a sawlog. There ain't no way to arrest a loose rail on a tramroad. A pile of ashes a-don't ask no judgment from nobody.' He was still rubbing his fist. Now he released the fist and shook it. 'We don't a-want no court—we don't need no court!'

There were deliberate approving squirts of ambeer from older men and many heads nodded. Two or three men spoke in the same vein. They thought a few dead nigger log-choppers in the woods and beside the tramroad would put the fear of God into the Coventry help.

Cameron did not oppose this course, but he raised his mild voice in behalf of more lawful methods. He called attention to the fact that every man there had a right to vote. The Alliance, he said, was strong in the county. Most of the Alliance men were like themselves, in the same jeopardy or in sympathy with their cause. He stood by the anvil as he spoke and toyed

215

with the handle of a sledgehammer, speaking in a thoughtful manner. They should be active in the Alliance and should make the Alliance strong in the county. There was no reason why they, with the right kind of help, could not elect a sheriff and other county officials. There was no reason why they could not make the judge and solicitor stand in awe of the Alliance. He raised the sledge in his powerful arm. 'We can still get what we want through the law!'—his voice was sharp, and he pointed his statement with a jerk of the hammer—'Georgia government and courts.'

There were two or three faces that rose in the wavering flare of the lightwood to support Cameron, but the bulk of the crowd was lukewarm. Finally Micajah stood up unhurriedly. He got a respectful silence. Any man who had shot Zenas Fears, even if he hadn't killed him, was entitled to a respectful hearing. Micajah had taken his hat off as he rose and he held it before him. He was a little stooped, but he still looked tall, and the blaze from the forge burnished the gray-white hair that brushed his shoulders. His voice was deliberate and so mild that it would not have carried across the room except for its peculiar penetration.

'Ben, here, talks about law,' he began. 'Me and Ben have always agreed, mostly. I a-been for law, too—the kind of law we a-lay upon ourselves.

'It's all right to a-talk about voting and electing us a sheriff and the like. But what good is a sheriff a-goin' to do us in the Macon court? That's where they a-knocked yore deeds out.'

He allowed his voice to fall for an instant, then went on: 'Ben's ideas are good as far as they go. I'm for 'em, but they ain't enough. Coventry is in the saddle here now. And the horse he's a-ridin' is the Yankee Government court—he ain't a-comin' into aer Georgia court agin. If the court's his horse, it's pretty fair sense that we can't a-ride 'im, too.

'Milt Hatton was a-talkin' common sense about gettin' on ground where Coventry can't meet ye. It's Zenas Fears and his posse and the log-choppers and their bosses that's a-takin' our timber and a-puttin' us off'n our land. Without Fears and his egg-suckers and the woods crews they a-can't touch us. We got to put the fear of God in 'em—Fears—the choppers—Coventry and Company. And a-put 'em out'n Telfair County.'

He put on his hat and turned away toward the forge. After a momentary pause, low murmuring began that grew into a loud hum. The men around the forge and under the torches were talking among themselves. A voice spoke out, 'Who's a-goin' to handle the crowd? How we a-goin' about it, Micajie?'

Micajah turned back from the forge and, pausing, took off his hat. The fire threw his long wavering shadow before him. 'It don't need no crowd,' he said. 'Idees can be passed back'ards and fo'ards through the shops here. Every man can work with his own crowd. Any crowd knows its men. What they do they can a-keep close. We'll all a-know what's goin' on after it happens.' Here he paused and looked deliberately from side to side and out to the edge of the group. 'There won't be any stray ears to a-hear things, near stray mouths to a-spread talk about it.'

He turned again to the firelight. The crowd broke into small clots. The men of each group talked quietly among themselves. Micajah told Cameron he guessed he'd be going. A gruff voice at his elbow spoke up a little louder than the level of the conversation, 'Who air ye a-goin' to work with, Micajie?'

217

Micajah looked sharply at the man. After a pause he turned back toward the fire as if he did not intend to reply, but he spoke to the flames. 'There's still enough Corns left to be heard from.'

22

AFTER the meeting at Cameron Shops, the pine barrens turned to action in its own way on its own ground. Five times wooden rails of the Coventry tramroads were fired. Three times trains were derailed from the steel tracks. The big saw at the Pineville mill was broken by a hidden spike in a sawlog. Six times the negro log-choppers were run out of timber they had been sent to cut. These things happened before June had spent itself, and the word of them had spread throughout the piney woods, yet Micajah continued to side his cotton and plant late corn. He was more silent that he had ever been, spent more time about the barn and cowpen than the house, was shut off to himself and moved about with an abstracted air.

Littleton was teased by this and puzzled. He was not surprised at his father's silence, but he was harassed by curiosity. He had asked his father about the meeting on the morning following it. Micajah told him the men at the courtyard had decided to fight, but he did not amplify that statement, merely said he would tell him what he was to do when the time came. Littleton had found out more about the meeting by hanging around Cameron Shops, and had gleaned all he could about the raids. Twice since his first effort, he had tried to draw his father out about their part in the fight, about his thoughts and plans, but without avail.

Laying-by time was almost at hand when Micajah finally sent for Zeke. He told Littleton on Saturday to come back by Zeke's, if he failed to see him in Jacksonville, and tell him to drive over home on Sunday morning. Zeke came early bringing his wife and five children. Soon after they had rested their hats and swapped a little tobacco in the dog-run, Micajah motioned to Zeke—Littleton was already at the well waiting—and they set off toward the Sugar Field. Micajah carried his rifle.

As they climbed over the rails near the toolhouse, he tried it at a fish-hawk. The hawk was in a dead pine across the field and, when they got over the fence, it lifted off its perch into the air. Micajah came up with his gun, easy and quick, and dropped the bird. They circled around the cotton rows and found the hawk at the foot of the blackened tree. It was not yet dead, and Micajah put it out of its agony. He leaned his weapon against the burnt trunk and stretched out the hawk's wings.

'A big un,' he said, 'and a smart un.' There was no suspense in the melancholy calm of his face and he spoke casually. He stood a moment looking sadly at the outstretched bird in his hands, before he added, 'But he ain't no match for a Winchester bullet.'

Zeke and Littleton both knew that Micajah had finally got ready to talk and they squatted on their haunches.

'Corns ain't never believed in a-waylayin' a man, naer a-burnin' people out,' he said. 'But fight can't a-know no shore rules. Some of these piney-woods folks a-come to it easy. This time it's the onliest way.'

He paused as if he were at an end and punched the dead hawk with the toe of his shoe. His face hardened about the mouth and eyes and his pupils shriveled.

'We a-got a reason in this quarrel and we got a enemy. He's done made it a no-rules fight. Our task is laid out. It'll be a bigger thing for the barrens than aught else we could a-do.'

He put his gun on his shoulder and they all walked back toward the toolhouse, bringing the hawk with them for his wing feathers. But Micajah talked more during the day. He talked in fragments, yet he set forth their task clearly.

Fears had nerve and Fears was a dead shot and Fears took no chances. It was going to be a big job to out-smart him. Micajah had no ready-made plan to offer. Fears wore a bullet-proof shirt and never traveled alone now. He would shoot any of them without warning if he got a chance. Micajah believed there might be a way to get him at home at night, from the dark. Yet he had heard that Fears had his house fixed up like a stockade. His place was just beyond town on the other side of McRae, sixteen miles as the crow flies. One night, as soon as they had laid by, they would go scour around the place to see what they could find out about it and about his movements.

The Corns made their journey on the second Sunday night in July. They went on Sunday night, because Micajah thought it most likely Fears would be at home on that night. They kept to back trails and the woods itself at times and it took them more than four hours to reach McRae, horseback. Here they skirted the town and cut into the road to Fears' house a quarter of a mile from his front gate. They tied their horses and continued on foot. Micajah had decided they should stay together on this first night and only make a general survey of the place. He had, however, chosen a hound's night howl as their signal. They had practiced it carefully so that each one could readily identify it.

The Fears place was off the McRae road about a quarter of a mile. On one side of it a field stretched out for a mile's length, on the other a woods lot lay adjoining it, and beyond was the pine forest, which circled and came close to a cane mill in the rear. It was an old dwelling, built in the usual double-pen style with a shed room at the rear.

The night was moonless, but starlit and clear and the Corn men could identify shapes at a distance. The dim, dark silhouette of a spreading tree and the house behind it rose above the serried line of a tall fence. Walled in by the fence, which looked faintly gray from the dirt-white yard, shielded by the black tree that pointed above it, and watched by a gripping stillness, Fears' home seemed formidable.

They approached by the woods lot, since the wind was from the field. Tales about the place had not exaggerated its defenses. Around the house, and almost a hundred and fifty paces from it, was a high paling fence. Micajah found that the palings were almost as high as he could reach when he let himself up off his belly. They were made of scantlings sharpened at the end. Within the first fence, at fifty paces from the house, was another lower fence of pickets. The space between the fences made a free range around the dwelling and loomed in bare gray whiteness, like the field of a target, menaced by the invisible depths beyond. The Corns found that the high paling fence extended beyond the house and enclosed the barn also. Micajah heard the whine of dogs in the outer yard. As they eased around the paling fence, he counted ten of them, ranging about or lying down near a low shed. They were heavier and had longer ears than fox dogs. Micajah identified them as bloodhounds. He had heard that Fears kept them close to the starving point and he concluded that the inner fence was a protection against them for his family. Micajah had expected to find the house dark at the hour, but he had heard that Fears never burned a light at night except behind closed shutters.

The Corns crawled as far down the enclosure toward the windward as they dared, both front and rear, and Micajah could discover no building or other object in the outer yard, except the dog-house. The front gate had a lock and chain on it. In the inner yard he could discern a wellsweep and another in the barn lot. He identified also two trees near the yard well and a smokehouse close to the rear of the dwelling. He suspected that there were guineas roosting in the trees.

The three men scattered out along the paling fence in the woods lot and lay quiet for more than an hour. Micajah held his breath at intervals. He was not sure, but he believed that he could detect snoring in the front room on the near side of the house. Littleton's acute ears verified this. The silence was wearing, but the dogs occasionally broke it with their whining and walking about. Once they barked, shattering the stillness, but they were on the other side of the run and did not come near the Corns.

Finally Micajah led the way back across the woods lot and the men circled around to their horses. It was a stockade all right, stout enough to hold against Indians, Micajah thought. The tales about it had come pretty straight. None of them spoke until after they had mounted their horses and started to move off among the pines beyond the roadway. Then Littleton hoarsely asked if they would have to give up their idea of getting Fears at home. Micajah turned his head sharply to look at him, but moved off without response.

He returned three times during the month of July to reexamine the Fears place. Once by himself during daylight, when he viewed it at a distance. Again, when a strong wind blew from the south and the sky was overcast, he went with Zeke, who had come over to use Micajah's drawknife. He left Littleton, choosing Zeke because he had better cat's eyes and could lie still longer. The wind enabled them to move about more freely to study the dogs. As an additional precaution Micajah and Zeke put turpentine on their feet and clothes. He lay sometime abreast of the dog-house and once one of the hounds came within a few feet of him on the other side of the paling. There were guineas, he found, in the chinaberry trees by the yard well. On the third visit, when he carried Zeke along again, Micajah brought also a 'possum in a sack. He wanted to see if he could interest the hound pack in a 'possum. He approached the dog-house as near as he could go with safety. Holding the animal by the nap of the neck and the tail, he tossed it over the fence and moved back quickly.

Two hounds found the 'possum within a few seconds after it thudded upon the ground. Most of the pack came to the dogs, after they had closed in on their prey. Zeke and Micajah wormed their way around the paling fence to see if any dog remained uninterested, to patrol the yard. They found none. After the growling and scrambling among the dogs had grown loud, Micajah heard a stir of feet in the dwelling. The feet approached a window, but no shutter opened, no light lit, and no voice spoke out. Fears probably had peepholes around, Micajah reflected.

It was mid-August before Micajah found the night he wanted. A stiff ground wind blew from the south and the sky was overcast with high clouds. The darkness was almost impenetrable, even for Zeke's cat eyes. All of them wore homespun shirts and jeans. Micajah figured the gray brownish color would be the least visible against the dirt-white of the yard. Zeke carried a light short ladder strapped against his horse's side. Littleton bore a 'possum in a sack and Micajah made saddle-bags of two bundles of lightwood. In addition to their rifles, Micajah carried a revolver and an axe.

When they had reached their hitching-place in the pines beyond the woods lot and had secured their horses, Micajah left his black hat tied to his saddle. They separated at the woods lot and approached the place on three sides for a look-around before they closed in. When they had drawn together at the paling fence on the north side, Micajah made them all lie low for a time. The hour was near one in the morning. The clouds had lifted a little, but the night was still so dark that Micajah could only make out the dwelling and tree in front as a single dim lump. The blackness was comforting; they could concentrate on covering their sound and smell. That lump of blackness might spit forth flame and lead without warning, Micajah knew, but he believed that the shot would give them more to shoot at than those inside could have. As they lay alongside, he could detect snoring in the front of the house. He could hear, too, along the paling fence, the breathing of both Zeke and Littleton, but he could scarcely feel his own, it came and went with such constraint. His hands felt steadier than they had felt in years. His legs were steel springs and there was a kind of singing in his chest.

Littleton had been told to drop the 'possum over the back fence, close by the corner where the fence extended toward the barn and abreast of the dog-house. Micajah was a little leary of Littleton, but he had gone over the business with him in detail and had impressed its importance upon him. Littleton was to wait five minutes after Micajah and Zeke had moved off around to the front of the enclosure, before he should budge. As Micajah prepared to leave, the thought came to him that Littleton seemed a little free in his movements. He did not speak, but he put his hand on the boy's arm and held it firmly for a moment, before he moved off.

With Zeke at his heels, he wormed along the paling fence as far as he dared go until he could know the dogs had been drawn away. He sat up then and looked through the palings across the shadowy grayness of the run between the fences. The inner fence was lost in blackness. He did not know whether its gate was locked, too. He would have to climb over if it was. With the lightwood saddled around his body, it would take him more than a minute to cross the run. He would wait until both he and Zeke were sure all of the dogs had gone around to the 'possum. He would wait until they stirred in the house, if they did stir. They might hear the fire above the wind, but a small fire would bring them out just like a big one and there would be light enough to shoot by. Micajah lay down and awaited the thud of the 'possum on the ground and the growling of the dogs.

Littleton felt his way down to the corner of the fence without difficulty. When he had halted, he spent some time staring into the darkness within the palings, before he stirred the 'possum in the sack. He could make out the low dog-house and a lump of dogs lying near it. He detected a dog with a white spot on his breast moving in his direction across the yard. He thought once of tossing the 'possum over quickly, but the dog did not get wind of him. Littleton felt about the corner to see how it joined. He found that an inner fence cut off the barn lot from the yard. The discovery excited him.

He laid the 'possum sack on the ground and wiped away the sweat that trickled from his thin mustache into his mouth. He sat up to stop the pounding of his heart against the ground. The idea of his father trying to cross the wide run between the fences to fire the house had put him under an aching, pounding strain. The strain had been in him since he first learned about it and he had protested to the plan, to Zeke. Neither of them dared to try to dissuade Micajah.

Littleton decided that his father had never discovered the inner fence. It would be so much simpler to fire the barn. There would be no dogs, no exposure, it would be safer shooting. He left the 'possum sack where it lay and inspected the barnlot fence, looked through the palings at the dark, still interior. He decided to tell Zeke and his father at the front fence about his discovery, before anything was done. But he paused before he moved off and after a few moments crawled alongside the palings of the lot toward the barn. Just outside the barn he mounted the fence and eased himself inside. He had determined to know what he was talking about before going to report. He stood for a few moments staring into the darkness

227

about him, but he could see nothing except the dim lump of the barn and blackness across the lot. He moved slowly along the wall until he came to its gaping entrance. It was without a floor and he could feel wisps of hay under his feet. The smell of manure and feed was strong. He could hear a horse move in his stable down the way. He turned carefully about to look back toward the lot.

There was a small crunching sound behind him, but before his ears had quite caught it, he was lifted from his feet by a neck-cracking blow. A flash of light, quicker than time itself, blazed before him, there was a stunning impact against his backside, his spine strained, and he went to the ground amid a detonation of sounds. The sounds resolved themselves into bleats. On his knees, even in darkness, Littleton realized that he had been butted by a goat. He did not have long to conjecture. The goat was on him again, striking him full between the shoulder blades and sending him down again. Again the bleating sound blasted the stillness, and now came an answering clamor from the hounds in the main yard. Littleton scrambled to his feet quick enough to lead the goat to the fence and mounted it in time to let the palings catch the force of the final butting. As he paused for the fragment of a second on top of the fence, the whole place seemed to be a riot of alarms. The hound pack was now in full voice. The guineas in the chinaberry trees potracked frenziedly. The goat behind him bleated and the horses kicked in their stalls and one of them whinnied.

23

THEY reached home soon after daylight. Micajah's eyes were black as molten tar, his face was a reddish-gray color. He did not address Littleton, but spoke to Zeke at the turn of the lane. 'Keep a-goin', Zeke, and take that boy with ye,' he said. 'Get him out of my sight before I kill him!'

Littleton went on home with Zeke.

Micajah could not touch food for three days, and finally on the third day—under a load of whiskey toddies and weakness—went to bed. He remained flat of his back for a week. It was the longest illness Civil could remember his ever having suffered.

His interest in the backwoodsmen's quarrel with the company revived slowly. When he got up, he found his cotton falling out of the boll and cotton-picking absorbed him for a time. Early in September he sent for Littleton to give a hand. Civil and Jasmine spent every day in the field and Micajah hired Nancy Swilley and her crowd.

It was the company's mistreatment of Nancy that kindled Micajah's rage again. Civil had not liked his hiring the Swilleys even to pick cotton, but she was full of sympathy for them when they turned up in October seeking shelter. Civil did not approve of Nancy because of her ways, though it was plain she wasn't like other women and maybe wasn't intended to be. Nancy was over six feet tall and stouter than most men her size. She was rough to look at and rough to talk. She plowed and worked in the field like a man, and more than most of them. She worked with them and rutted around with them, those who'd have anything to do with her. And, of course, Nancy couldn't just find one woods colt, in a quiet way, where the family might hide it among the passel of children. She had twins. Twin yard-children offended the sensibilities of the women of the neighborhood. They suspected that each one of them had a different father—Nancy wouldn't know.

But Nancy's capable back had made bread for her family, too. Now her old father was stone blind, and Nancy had made the living for him and her mother for years. Nancy was steady to work and kind.

They had lived in the little pole shanty and she had tended the patch around it for ten years to Micajah's knowing. He didn't know what kind of paper claim they had to it, but he was riled when Fears' men put them out. A manless woman with younguns and blind old pa! It couldn't mean much to the company to have the little piece of land she was using.

Micajah let them stay in Rody's old house. It was a real pity to see Nancy's gratefulness.

About the same time Fears and his crowd ran the Tompkins boys off their land, winging one of them. The Tompkinses had stopped the log-choppers when Fears came along. He told them to put up their guns and clear out. There were only three of the Tompkinses, to Fears' six, but when one of the boys checked his piece as they were backing off, Fears let him have it in the arm.

Fears seemed more nervous to shoot and reckless than ever before. Backwoodsmen were still giving the company a lot of trouble with spikes in sawlogs and damage to the tramroads, but Fears was using about twenty men to help him and he made it hard to hold up the choppers long at any one place. Fears always picked a place where there was nobody much to oppose him. Then two Alliance men over about Macville got caught and indicted for killing a negro turpentine hand. It had put a damper on the backwoodsmen's war in the late summer.

The company's putting Nancy Swilley and her blind father out in the woods seemed to stir more heat at the first October meeting at Deacon's courtyard than anything that had happened in a long time. Still nobody had a plan to suggest, and Micajah only squinted his eyes when Ben Cameron asked him and said it wasn't his part to tell the Alliance what to do.

He didn't say anything in particular to anybody about what was on his mind, but during October he sent Littleton up to the commissary at Camp Number Six twice to buy things and he went once himself to get some trace chains. Number Six was the closest approach the company had made to him. It was about four and a half miles above the Corn place up Cedar Creek. The company had first put a turpentine still there, and two years before had added the timber camp. It had become the main tramroad junction in the county.

Littleton didn't suspect anything until his father took him to the camps one afternoon and told him to keep his eyes skinned. They took their time in buying some cheese and hamstrings, and Micajah learned, without directly asking, that no-body slept in the building. They came back by the turpentine still to get rosin, Micajah saying he wanted to caulk a well bucket. They made a round of the storehouse while they were getting it, and found that the outer door of the storehouse was secured with only a lock and a chain through a hole in the door. An inner room where the office was located and the tur-pentine was stored had a heavy lock in the door, but there was a little glassed office window near it.

The hands kept plenty of lightwood around the retort and the worm was set in a big wooden water tank. The only dwell-ing near the still was the home of the old negro joiner, who made the barrels. It was about fifty paces from the still. Micajah and Littleton found that they kept a pretty daresome dog—he looked like part hound and part cur—chained to a shed in the daytime.

Micajah pointed out several things to Littleton after the visit. The commissary was about two feet off the ground. The coal-oil barrels were sitting twenty feet from the front door and eleven feet from the northwest wall. (Littleton hadn't even seen the barrels.) There were lightwood butts to the floor boards about three feet away. The commissary was a hundred and eight steps from the still.

Little more than a week later, Micajah made another trip to the commissary, taking Zeke along. On the next day the three made a night scour of the camps, about midnight, walking their horses in the creek-bed all the way up and back. They knew every foot of the creek-bed, but Micajah said the trip would give them a chance to test it out for night-riding and give them a look at the camps when they wouldn't be able to see much of it.

They set out for the task on Monday night. (The still had been running for two weeks steadily.) Micajah said Monday was a good night to find the camps quiet and nobody—not even the niggers—doing any late walking. He made them soak their shoes in turpentine early in the evening. A few days before, Littleton had trapped a polecat and Civil had made a canvas bag to put it in. Micajah told Littleton to get the skunk ready. Zeke had thought they ought to kill the joiner's dog, but Micajah said that might raise suspicions. He hit on the idea of a polecat. Before they set off, Micajah got a bundle of lightwood splinters and a short auger ready to go. The night was coolish and foggy. Even Zeke couldn't see a dozen steps ahead of him, though sound carried clear. They napped after supper, but Micajah was wide awake by nine o'clock. He seemed quieter than usual and still as a curlew. His voice was easy as if it had been oiled. Only his black-looking eyes told that he was keyed up.

They put their horses into the creek just above the Sugar Field. Zeke could barely tell the break in the mist around the rails of the fence. And they could make out the open field beyond only by the color of the fog. They took the cowpath into the water, which wasn't deep enough anywhere to swim a horse, and went nose-to-tail up it. Micajah led the way, turning by memory and by the sound of the water sloshing under the horse's feet. They all rode close in their saddles, keeping behind the horses' heads. It seemed to Littleton that his father could smell a low limb; he eased down for one every time. They took it slow, but they already knew how long the trip would require. Only once did they hear a sound, except the hooting of owls and the soft splash of their own horses' feet. They were a little over halfway then, close to the Bercham place. There was a sudden break in the bushes and a sloshing through water, but Micajah did not even stop. He said they had scared a cow coming down to drink.

They got to where the creek turned toward the still and were about a quarter of a mile from it, before they got down. There was a grassy bank and a sand shoal there, about a foot under water. Tupelo trees hung over it. The horses were tied to this shoal where they could reach the grass, but would be mostly in the water.

They came out of the woods a little below the joiner's house. The fog seemed grayer out in front and to their right. They knew it was the settlement, but they couldn't see anything. For a while they sat close together, Micajah pointing out the direction of the joiner's house, the still, the tramroad, the logpile, the commissary, and the double row of loggers' shanties. Then they circled around at a slow walk between the shanties and the commissary, going all the way to the tramroad and coming back on the other side of the commissary, but keeping away from the joiner's place. It was like pushing through lint cotton, held there by a draft too weak to draw it away. There was no light anywhere to be seen and no sight or sound of anybody about. Micajah tried the wind, but there didn't seem to be any. What was stirring was from the north. He cut a stick and split the end to get the polecat out of the sack and drop him over by the dog's shed. Then he went along to the fence. He heard the dog come out of his house, but the brute only gave one low growl before Micajah plunked the polecat over to him. Then there was considerable more noise and more smell. Micajah didn't wait long, but he heard no stirring in the shanty before he left.

They moved on toward the still with Micajah in the lead, single file and close together. The camps seemed like a place of the dead, except for the noise of the dog behind them. And the world, a great gray felt coffin. The fog blanket made it unnecessary to find cover. Sound and smell were the only things to watch and it took a dog to do the smelling. The file quickened its pace.

Suddenly Micajah stopped, stock-still, and listened for the fraction of a second, before he turned. There was a light patting sound on the ground in front of them only a little way off. Micajah turned around and faced his two sons and motioned with his arm. They all fell back below the path toward the creek, feeling their way, but moving swiftly. They were on their bellies by the time the noise came abreast of them. Micajah had drawn a short-handled axe from his belt. The noise ceased. The Corns could see nothing but the fog and hear nothing save their own breathing, though Micajah thought he could detect a nigger smell. The pause lengthened, then the patting started in their direction. A nigger with a walking-stick, probably the old joiner, Micajah thought, as he eased up to a crouch and got his axe ready. The patting came close. A man's head loomed up, but it went by to the right of them and swerved back to the path. They did not move for several moments. Finally they heard a negro's voice back at the joiner's shanty. He was railing at the dog for having killed the polecat and getting the place stunk up.

They were within a few paces of the still house. Micajah found the front door and set to work with his jackknife to cut out the hole in the door to release the chain. He sent Littleton over to the retort to get lightwood and he posted Zeke to watch and listen. He told Littleton to let the water out of the condenser tank on his way back, so there wouldn't be any handy to use on the fire.

With the front door open, they moved cautiously in to the inner room. They found the small window and Micajah put the polecat's canvas bag over the glass when he broke it. He squirmed in first through the small window and Littleton and Zeke followed. Inside, Micajah felt his way through the darkness to the stack of turpentine barrels. He eased one out of the stack and put a hole in its side with his auger and the liquid spurted on the floor. Each of the Corns soaked his feet in it and Micajah caught some in his canvas bag.

Zeke and Littleton began laying a lightwood fire, but Micajah cautioned them not to light it until he should have returned. Then he squirmed back through the window.

Outside, the fog was still thick, but he eased along through it with his sack of turpentine, auger, and armful of lightwood. He paused three times on the way over to the commissary to listen, but he heard no sound. He knew that he must be pyeart. A fog was never dependable. He sniffed the air suspiciously. He wondered if the wind from the north wasn't getting up a little. But he did not tarry for reflection.

He felt his distance along the side of the building and got down on his belly. Carrying his bag of turpentine and the auger in his belt, he wormed his way to the chosen spot. Here he doused the floor above with the liquid, then dug a hole in the ground with his knife and hands. It gave plenty of room to use his auger and he set to work without delay. He put three holes in the floor before he stopped. Then he wormed his way back and got the wood. When he had returned with it, he made a pen of kindling and chunks over the hole in the ground until the wood touched the floor above. He stacked the lightwood knots about it. Then he struck a match to the canvas bag, which he had stuffed in the hole and moved back. He waited until he saw the fire licking up through the auger holes above it, before he backed out to the edge of the building. Cautiously, he put his head out, staring into the slit along the wall where there was no fog, then drew himself and his auger from under the commissary.

Micajah did not pause until he was on the lower side of the building, and then only long enough to wet his finger and hold it up in the air. His suspicion was right, the wind was rising. The fog would be moving off in no time. He strode on to the still swiftly, but paused a moment at the still-house door to look back toward the commissary. Already he could see a dim yellowish glow under the building. He signaled Zeke at the door and Littleton lit the fire inside. Both of the boys were out of the building in three shakes of a sheep's tail, but Micajah held them until he was sure the fire had a good start, even going inside the storehouse to look at their job. He paused on the platform outside to glance toward the commissary and stood there a moment, a tall silhouette framed in soft golden vapor. Then they moved off to the creek.

They had got among the trees when Micajah asked Zeke about the short-handled axe he had left with him. Zeke had forgotten it and Micajah made him return to the still house to fetch it. He wasn't near enough to keep Zeke from pounding the ground getting back to the woods.

They crossed the creek and walked along the lower bank, moving swiftly and without looking back until they came to their horses. They paused after they had untied the animals. It had taken them scarcely more than five minutes to cover the distance along the creek-bank, yet already they could see the outline of a great bronze billow, the fire rising through the fog. As they mounted, they heard pistol shots, from one gun, then a half-dozen. The first wakers at the camp were giving the alarm. They sat their horses a minute watching the cracks of glowing, swirling fog through the trees and listening to the soft roar of the flames. Now they could hear the shouting of voices about it. They could hear the heavy pounding of feet. A muffled, spreading explosion jarred the earth and shook the trees.

'This fog's a-liftin', boys,' Micajah said, and turned his horse's head downstream.

Wind rose before the fire was over and it also took the stables and ten head of mules, nine loggers' shanties, a shop car and wood stack on the tramroad, the old joiner's shack and a negro church. The burning out of Camp Number Six disturbed Coventry and Company all the way to New York. It was plain to everybody that the still and commissary had been set afire. Uncle Lump, the old joiner, said he heard a man running from the still house toward the creek when he woke up and saw the blaze. Somebody must have started the fire. Two fires in two separate places at the same time wouldn't just happen.

Fears got to the camps with his hounds soon after sunup. And more dogs were brought down from Lancaster. But the

238

dogs didn't do any good. Once they took off from the commissary and trailed through the settlement, beyond the stables about a mile to a negro's house. The darky was a turpentine hand working for the company and had been seen at the fire. Fears admitted the dogs just back-tracked him. The creek beyond the still was scoured and beat over, but the dogs couldn't pick up any trail, and it was hard to tell what marks the arsonists left because of people running through to the fire or beating the bushes later. Captain McIntosh, who came down on the train from Pineville, decided it was a waste of time to try to use dogs and Fears agreed with him. Fears bragged, before he left, that he would find out who did it soon enough through the grapevine.

Micajah heard all of the news of it at Cameron Shops without so much as a smile. He didn't let Littleton or Zeke go about the place for some time. He knew that Fears' bragging was bigger than his britches. The burning of the camps calmed that bully down, or perhaps the company bosses did it. That fall and on through the next winter company log choppers stayed on undisputed ground and Fears did not run any more men out of their timber.

24

THE backwoodsmen's quarrel with the company did not grow bitter again until July of '87, when Jock Ruskin was killed.

Micajah knew Jock Ruskin just to speak to. He lived in the lower side of the county and was never up to Cameron Shops, to Micajah's knowing. But he had heard more than once about the part he was taking against the company down in the Coventry Boom neighborhood. Jock was a fleshy, red-faced, Irish kind of fellow, who talked faster than common and was always ready to fight—and he had plenty of nerve, but was a little apt to bulldoze. His three boys—those that were his by blood—were pretty much like him. Jock and his boys had headed up most of the fight against the company from Coventry Boom to Jacksonville. They had led the band to burn tramroads, to loose the rails, to burn turpentine boxes, to drive spikes into sawlogs, and they were always ready to give a hand in running log-choppers off of anybody's land.

Those who talked to Micajah about it around Cameron Shops agreed that Fears had been out to get Jock a long time. But it was the way he got him that raised everybody's fur, though it wasn't Fears they were hating so much as that Deacon boy.

What brought it on was the shooting affray on Peter Swilley's place, or in what Peter claimed was his timber—about a mile from his house on the edge of the river swamp. It was late in May. The Swilleys had stopped some company logchoppers. Then Fears and three of his men came and were running the Swilleys off. They hadn't offered to raise their guns at Fears and were backing toward the brow of the swamp hill, when Jock and his three boys suddenly came up over it and cut down on the posse. They brought one of the possemen to the ground and winged Fears. The bullet took him in his right arm and he dropped his gun and turned tail. Of course the Ruskins had taken trees on them and they had to get cover, too, but it was the first time anybody could recollect Fears running.

Fears went to town and swore out a warrant against Jock for murder, on account of the posseman who was killed. He knew that it was one of the Ruskin boys who killed the posseman; it was Jock who had winged *him*. He said he was going to arrest Jock, though nobody believed he ever intended to take him. But the sheriff didn't want to serve the papers and Fears said he was going to.

Fears went with a dozen men three times to Jock's place during June, but Jock wasn't there. They tried to catch him in Jacksonville and at old Blockhouse Church. They even tried to waylay him coming home, hiding under the Horse Creek Bridge, but every time Jock knew where they were as soon as they had left McRae headed in his direction, and he knew every move they made afterward.

They would have been cold-trailing Jock till yet if it hadn't been for that Deacon boy. Tump Deacon was a woods colt, according to those who talked to Micajah, and no blood kin of Jock. Jock had taken him when his ma died, in a pole shack out in the pine wilds. He wasn't bigger than a lightwood knot then, and Jock raised him along with his youngest boy. He was close to Jock and stayed there on the place with him, after the other boys branched off. There were some who said the Deacon boy was a trap-robber and a cattle-thief and that they knew he was no good before anything happened, but the reputation had never got out on him.

Anyhow, it was the Deacon boy who led Fears and his posse to Jock. A turpentine cropper in Jacksonville told Micajah that Deacon met them out beyond Shelton's Chapel in the afternoon—Fears and eight men—and slipped them up through the pine woods so that none of Jock's neighbors and watchers saw them. And this Deacon boy was supposed to be keeping a lookout on the River Road at the end of the lane himself. They came to the field horseback and stopped back of the barn. They were running out from behind it before even Jock's wife saw them. He was lying there asleep on a bench on his front piazza. They drilled him between the ears before he could rise up hardly, though, of course, Fears told around McRae that he resisted arrest.

The thought of Fears shooting Ruskin lying down made Micajah fester and ache inside like there was a boil in his chest. Still he told himself that it wasn't his pa, nor his quarrel. It was for the Ruskin boys to settle. There was a report that the company gave the Deacon boy a farm back from the River Road up above Blockhouse Church. He left the country after the shooting, though he came back around about Christmas-time. There was a Swilley girl he had been going with. She was in a family way when he left. He came back and married her and they settled on this place, though it wasn't much of a farm to turn-up a man over, those who knew it said.

The death of Jock Ruskin had put a damper on the people on the lower side of the county, the way it all came about and everything. And the Ruskin boys, while they weren't afraid of the company, had the score with Deacon to settle first. They spent most of their time, summer and fall, trying to find him. They didn't try to take the lead in anything against the company and the fight never came on. But after Tump Deacon showed up out beyond Blockhouse Church, it looked like the Ruskin boys couldn't get him. The talk about it was all around the county. This slick polecat got him a gopher hole which he could carry around with him. He didn't show himself much off of that farm the company had given him, nor out of its pole shack. But when he did come, this Swilley girl he'd married and the baby she'd throwed him in the fall were with him. She wasn't ever suckling the youngun; he was the one always carrying it when they got out as far as the River Road. There was no way to get a shot at him, for he never put it down.

Things were quiet around Cameron Shops and practically all over the county until Fears started trouble with the Hurd boys. Micajah knew Mathias Hurd, who served a term as sheriff back in '80 when Jet was killed and Dan'l was taken, and he knew the Hurd boys never had any use for Fears or the company. Ben Cameron, telling him about it on the day after the killing, said the three younger boys had been running a pepperbox sawmill close by their home place on Sugar Creek.

Careful as Ben always was, he said he didn't know what right they had to the timber, but they claimed to be cutting it under a lease.

They had been running there about five months when Fears came down early in March, Ben said. Fears had seven men with him, and he stopped the Hurd boys and their log-cutters in the woods and nailed a claim against their sawmill for timber they'd cut. The Hurds were outnumbered, so they took it from him. But it wasn't a week before they came to McRae looking for Fears. They ran into him by himself, coming away from the depot in the afternoon, leading a new bloodhound puppy that he'd got shipped in. There was nobody close enough to tell who shot first, but it was the oldest boy, next to Mathias, who ran into Fears. The other two came up from behind the depot after the firing began.

There were no close witnesses, Ben said, and those watching were thinking mostly of themselves. But the oldest Hurd boy was the first one seen to go down. Then it looked like Fears fell to his knees, but scrambled around and got behind a telegraph pole. The other two Hurds were coming up on his side and behind him, where he first stood. He turned the puppy loose when he went down and it came a-hollering down the street. A stray bullet had clipped it on the ear. The shooting didn't last long after Fears made the cover. He sent another one of the boys down with bullet holes through his shoulder and in his leg. The youngest Hurd boy cleared out then. Fears came through without a mark on him that anybody could tell.

The first Hurd shot was dead when they got to him. After Mathias learned about it and came to town with a crowd from Sugar Creek, they got a mob together that night to lynch Fears,

244

but he had left town and gone to Lancaster. Some said he found that puppy and had its ear patched and took it with him when he went.

Micajah felt sorry for the Hurds—powerful sorry, as he sat on Ben Cameron's worktable meditating about the shooting. They weren't short on nerve. Not many men around the county would offer to swap shots with Fears. But they just rushed in like the boys they were. It took thinking, still thinking, and a lot of it to tie-into that copperhead.

But reaction in the county took a helpful turn for the backwoodsmen and a peaceful one. Ben Cameron called a meeting of the Deacon's Courtyard Alliance two weeks after the fight, in spite of the fact that almost everybody was busy breaking ground. Micajah came, bringing Littleton and Zeke with him. Zeke had brought his passel over to Micajah's and left them with Civil and Jasmine. Some of the people around McRae were talking about running Mathias Hurd for sheriff again and Ben wanted to get the Alliance behind him.

Micajah was for it, though he didn't say much at the meeting. He just agreed with Ben that they would have a job to put Mathias in over the opposition of the people at McRae and Lumber City, but he'd give what help he could. However, he got worked up during April and May. He let his planting go, with just Littleton to tend to it most of the time. The county committee had fixed June third for the election. First Micajah rode around the district with Ben telling the folks about it and telling them to be sure to get over to the courtyard to vote for Mathias. Later he made a trip beyond Jacksonville along the River Road to talk with some of the Corns and Wilcoxes. Once he went nearly to Lumber City to see some of the Vaughans and Hattons. He made it personal with them. He told them, when they went to vote, to think of Jet Corn and the way Fears killed him.

Along about the same time he went above Macville to see Dan'l, where he was tending a turpentine crop. He had sent word a week before that he was coming, but when he got there he found Dan'l gone. He was surprised and more surprised at the way Mit took it. She said they didn't want to get into any more fighting with the company; they'd had enough. And they were getting along peaceable where they were. Micajah could hardly believe he was talking to a daughter of his. Still he knew he was warmed up over the campaign; and they had had grievous trouble. He wondered if the company owned the timber Dan'l was boxing, but didn't have the commonness to ask her. They had given it out to Civil they'd leased from a Clements.

Mathias Hurd won the election against the man who was in office by a sizable vote and there wasn't much shooting. The Alliance put watchers at every box in the county, but they tried to use sober ones and men with cool heads. Micajah stayed about the Deacon's courtyard box most of the day. There wasn't a rough word spoken at the courtyard. The vote there was all one way. There was shooting at Macville, but they were Macville men and drunk. Micajah said it was the first sheriff's election he ever gave a damn which way it went. When he rode into McRae with the box on Monday and got it official, he took a dram to celebrate.

With Hurd as sheriff things looked up for the backwoodsmen. It had been a hard blow to Fears, who had campaigned against him openly. Now Hurd would have his own organized band, clothed with the law and paid by the people to oppose the company—and him! During July and August, Fears hardly came into Telfair County, and when he did it was to go straight to his home. He never went near the courthouse, nor loitered about the street. He never tried to serve a single eviction paper and there wasn't any logging going on in the county, except at Coventry Boom, down toward Lumber City, and at Temperance on the Coventry County line.

Then three fool boys tried to burn the big mill at Pineville and got caught. Micajah was put out. It seemed that his crowd never could let well-enough alone or be cautious about a thing. But it cut both ways, he decided after a time. One of the boys was Mathias Hurd's youngest brother, who had been in the shooting with Fears. He and a cousin of his living up in Coventry County and a fellow working there at the mill did the firing. It was night, but they just came up in the open with night-watchmen on the ground and set fire under the mill shed. The night crew caught them before they got out and they put out the fire, but not until after the whistle blew up a crowd.

It had given Fears and the company a hold over Mathias Hurd: a charge of arson against his brother. Calhoun Calebb took the case for all three of them, though it was a hard one. Micajah wondered if Calebb was the best man to handle the lawsuit, anyhow.

On the other hand, Micajah suspected that the damage to the mill was more than the bosses let out. September came and went and they were still shut down fixing it. The mill-hands around Pineville were put out, but it practically dried up the company in Telfair County.

Poplar leaves were just beginning to turn when Micajah got a token. A strange mixed thing it was, but he felt later that it was more sweet than bitter. It came to him just like the time he had the Rowan girl by the swamp lake on Horse Creek. A green young buck, he was then. He had left his fishing poles in the bank and was trotting out to the hill to get some lightwood while it was still good daylight. He was just about to cut into the cowpath below the hillside brush when he heard her steps, quick and barefoot, in the leaves. He knew it was a woman. And he knew—he could never tell how—that she was coming to give herself to him. It came to him as sure as shouting as quick as he heard the rusty clip of her feet; although, when he looked down the path, before he stepped out to block her way, he saw it was the Rowan girl whom he had never said a dozen words to in his life. That was more'n forty years ago.

This time Micajah was hunting squirrels down Cedar Creek, almost where it runs into Horse, and he had no more idea than he had the other time what lay in his way. He later puzzled on how he came to wander off so far from home, almost to Zeke's place, just to shoot at squirrels. He couldn't have had any notion, because the path across the creek was only a settlement trace and didn't lead anywhere directly.

The pines on the hill alongside the swamp were big-barreled as washtubs and thick as an oat patch. He had been walking along the edge thinking how much more alike pines were than anything else in creation and how there was no beginning nor end to them when he heard a squirrel bark in the edge of the swamp pretty close to the trace. He had spotted him, a big old fox, up a tall whiteoak, and was raising his shotgun to catch him when he came around the trunk. That was how he was when he heard the quick clip of horses' feet on the trace coming toward the ford.

He brought his gun down without firing and, as he withdrew it, the token came to him. He knew, with the same certainty with which he had divined the steps of the Rowan girl, that Fears rode one of those horses. It was the same strange knowing, the same sweet cool sureness in the marrow of his bones.

There was a difference, though. He had come a-planning no such thing, in the least, nor ever thinking about it this time. Still he always carried buckshot in his choked barrel. He ran toward the ford, moving easily between the trees. It was a sure-footed, swift stride, but the horses were moving fast and they seemed to stretch their lope at the creek. They jumped the shriveled stream, because Micajah could not hear them slosh the water. When he got to the crossing and glimpsed them, they were almost a hundred paces past it. He had to leave his cover and step out into the ford to get a shot. There were three of them and Fears was on the left. They were practically out of range and swinging around a turn; but Micajah was cut down, leading Fears to the left by two feet.

They disappeared around the curve before the smoke cleared, but he heard them check their horses and he heard the beasts trampling around excitedly. It was no time to go turkey-necking. He disappeared into the dim brown depths behind the gray, twisting trees of Cedar Creek.

He later learned that his hurried shot did Fears no great damage. A ball nicked his left ear, another cut his hat brim, and a third parted his hair on the left side, taking some scalp with it. Micajah had led too much to the left but Fears had

249

been too far for buckshot to go through that skull of his anyhow.

Thinking it over, Micajah wondered about the incident. The token had been the same each time, but things hadn't turned out the same. It was the buckshot. He had been better loaded for the Rowan girl.

Yet somehow the thing he minded most about it all was that Fears had the idea that it was Zeke or Ardel Cone who did the shooting.

One of the Ruskin boys had better luck a Sunday night later that fall. Deacon and his wife and baby had come out of Blockhouse Church after the evening meeting and were standing on the steps. There were church-goers ahead of them leaving, but no one in sight to be suspicious of. Deacon had filled his pipe in church and he handed his wife the baby so he could light it. He struck the match, but never got it lit.

25

UNMINDFUL of the January wind and water, Micajah stood on the boom he and Littleton had constructed at the mouth of the swamp lake on Horse Creek. He held a long pike-pole, with which he had been pushing pine logs into place in the raft they were assembling. A freshet in the Ocmulgee had the creek backed up and it was clouded with yellowish mud. The swamp trees that walled the creek and swung out around the lake in somber distance were leafless and gray with thick drapery of Spanish moss. The sky above was slate-colored. It dulled the water's surface and dimmed the distances with formless swamp haze.

The nose of a dugout slid over the boom log above Micajah and the boat came to a halt. He had seen Zeke paddling across the creek, but he offered no greeting until his son spoke. Zeke sat in the stern of the canoe. A negro, who had been sitting in front, now stepped forward to secure the boat to the log.

It was the presence of the negro that restrained Micajah, though he gave no evidence of it except his silence.

Zeke's howdy had more gusto than normal and he hastened on. 'Pa, this is King Charles, one of old Herrod's boys—

the one I told you about. He's all right, Pa. He's been working with me off and on for over a year.' Zeke still held his paddle suspended. 'And he can shoulder a bow oar with any un that runs the river. Ask Lit. He knows him plenty.' Here Zeke laid down the paddle, but did not stir from his seat and still looked at his father. 'Seein' as how me and you is kind of green at a-driftin', I thought it would be all right to bring him along.'

The negro, with his shuck hat in his hand, stood up on the boom log. He was a blue-black, thick, square-cut negro whose nostrils and lips flared out like the edge of a turtle's shell.

Micajah had walked toward the boat, still looking at the corduroy of floating logs between the boom and the bank, while Zeke spoke. Now he looked up briefly at the negro and said, 'Howdy,' then, without another word, he went on with moving the logs.

King Charles agilely crossed the floating timber to the bank, where he spoke to Littleton and secured a pike-pole. The bow and hips of the raft had been laid. And Littleton now moved out on the raft to begin fastening the front binder. The negro worked silently for a quarter of an hour, then, as he skillfully rode a log in from above the boom to its place along the outside of the mid-section, he spoke to Micajah.

'Boss, Mist Lit, dere, can vouch for me—he knows what kind of nigger I is—and raf' han', too. I'se de pullin'est oa'sman on dis river. I'se one of old Herrod's boys, whut belonged to yoh pa. I'se heerd him talk 'bout you and I sho is been a'wantin' to meet you a long time.'

Micajah paused after he pushed another log into place with his pole and looked at the negro. His eyes drew into a smile.

'Bein' one of Herrod's boys ain't no recommendation to me,' he said, 'that rapscallion runaway.'

'I'se hearn that, Boss.' King Charles' fluently flaring nostrils and lips seemed to preface an outburst of passion, but they swept into a broad white grin. 'That was 'fore I was born—and probably how come me to be borned,' he said, pausing to laugh. 'Pa couldn't get no chillun with Rody and moved off where he could. Then he got 'em all around down in Tattnall County.'

Micajah tarried a moment in casual interest. 'How come you call yoreself King Charles—Herrod was a Rives nigger?'

The negro uncurtained his white grin. 'I'se a Charles on do sho' side of de family. Herrod never lived none wid my ma.'

The Corns made camp on the high side of the creek when they knocked off work that afternoon. Micajah and Zeke prepared side meat, hoecakes, and coffee, while Littleton gathered wood for the fire. Micajah sent the negro out to the hill spring for water and, as he squatted over a greasy spider scouring its inside with charcoal, he took Zeke to task. 'What in the name of God ails you, Zeke, a-bringin' that loud-mouthed nigger down here?' Micajah's voice showed more surface heat than usual.

'Pa, his mouth a-don't mean nothin'. You can depend on him about anything, and he's one of the best raft hands on the river.' Zeke had been preparing his defense.

Micajah's voice rose in irritation. 'Haven't you got any gumption at all, Zeke? Yore wit must be the master weak! Bringin' any nigger—aer anybody else along on a trip like this un.'

The Corns' log-rafting was a secondary aim; a means to an end. The big mill at Pineville, after five months, had not resumed operations, though the company continued its logging in Telfair County. In December, Micajah learned through Littleton that it had doubled its timber drifting to Darien for the St. Simon's mill. To press their advantage against the company effectively, Micajah reasoned, they must fight this. They were loading their guns with a new wadding. The company did not drift single rafts, like other people, it sent them down in trains, chained together. Littleton had suggested they loose the chains and the rafts, en route, to harass and gum up the business. It required high water to drift the trains and high water was also best for tearing them up and sending the loosed logs out into the swamp. Micajah believed that the backwoodsmen were near to winning their fight with the company. There must be caution, clear-headedness and sure action.

He told Zeke that he must send King Charles back as soon as they finished rafting the timber. There was a five-raft company train ready to leave the Temperance Boom above them then; would probably be adrift on the morrow. Their raft must drop in behind it by the following night or morning.

Zeke was reluctant to send his negro home; he had promised him the trip; he had no ready excuse. Micajah said he didn't give a damn for excuses; the nigger must clear out.

He was even more certain that King Charles must not go with them after he had listened to him that night. Indeed, he was troubled to think that the negro had been there at all. The ominous-looking black, who seldom appeared ominous because of his continuous grin and laughter, recommended himself loudly during the meal, but he was even more enthusiastic about Mister Lit. When Littleton and Zeke had set out in the canoe across the lake to fish trotlines, he grew confidential with Micajah, apparently unmindful of his lack of sympathy.

'They ain't another un like Mist Lit an' they never wuz,' King Charles began, lying on the ground and grinning across the fire at Micajah.

'He come to my place another year past when I wuz a-croppin' on Mist Bob Vaughan's and a-tryin' to get my cotton planted. He say, "King, I got to have you—got a raft down heah in the mouf of de creek—we got to ride dis rise comin."

'I tell 'im I can't go, but he won't take no. He finally offers me two dollars a day till I get clean back dere, aer to go havers on de timber. I takes de two dollars, 'cause I knows Mist Lit's rafts.

'We gets down dere at the mouf of Horse Creek an' he ain't got but seven logs—jus' seven. I say, "Dis ain't gwine hold us up, Mist Lit." He say, "I got five more 'round de bend heah and I got a boat, anyhow."

'I knowed he didn't have no more logs—he aimed to pick up one on de way down. I wuz sorry then I 'greed to go wid him. We pick up all de way. Time we got to Alligator Lake we'd been more'n two weeks on de river an' had more'n a hundred logs in dat raft. An' I kept greebin' at him all de time 'bout stoppin' so much an' me not planted my cotton yet. At Buckhorn Bluff I say I'm gwine get off an' walk back home, but he promise me he ain't gwine stop near nuther time.

'But he did an' I swore den I'se gwine quit. He talk jus' as independent. He say he gwine keep goin', not even goin' to stop to let me get off—he gwine to run night an' day. Long late in de afternoon, we come out'n a reach and they wuz some logs

255

caught up under a clay root in a little eddy at de turn. I seen 'im cut he eyes day way, but he never said nothin'.

'We passed 'em, but before dark, he started pullin' de raft into de bank. I tell 'im I thought he say he wuz goin' to run all night. But he say he don't think we better go though the Narrers by night.

'We had tied up an' I wuz gettin' some supper cooked when he put his canthook and some dogs in de boat an' got in. 'I say, "Where you gwine?" He say, "To get dem logs." I 'greed to paddle 'im up dere.

' 'Fore we got even close, we seen another boat come out'n de swamp wid three mens in it an' dey all had gun barrels a-stickin' over the side of the boat. I seen dem gun barrels right off. An' dey push right onto dem logs an' started to doggin' 'em.

'I tried to back up, but Mist Lit said, "Keep a-paddlin', Nigger," and we come on. We push de nose of our boat up on de other side.

'Dese mens looks at him hard, but finally one of dem said howdy. Mist Lit jus' a-sittin' dere cool an' smilin' like a 'possum.

'He say, "I feels damn good now. I lef' dese logs heah eight days ago an' I never 'spect to seen 'em ag'in." Den he don't even look at de mens any mo'. He jus' shif's 'round to me an' say, "King, gimme some of dem dogs dere." An' he starts drivin' one in to pull de logs out'n dere.

'In a minute de mens back off widout openin' dere traps.

'Next mornin' we come through de Narrers. Jus' as we come on to Phinholloway, we seen a big long cant log a-lyin' on de bank, overhangin' de river. It must of run close to sixty

256

foot. I seen 'im studyin' it as we come on, but I didn't have no idée what he aim to do.

'We wuz nigh abreast of it, when he say to me, "Hold de bow up jus' a little." An' I say, "For Gawd's sake, Miss Lit, you gonna break up dis raft!"

'He say, "Hold 'er up!" An' 'fore I knowed what wuz happenin', he up in de bow wid me, done take a canthook and yanked top end of dat log onto de raft. Den he run back an' yank 'er ag'in an' it bounce right onto de raft, clean.

'Den he crack he heels and holler an' sing:

> ' "Some shine like silver, sometimes like gold,
>   Maybe be branded, but gonna be sold." '

When King Charles' laughter had died out and he had borrowed a chew of tobacco from Micajah and spit into the fire, he resumed.

'We didn't have no mo' trouble then until after we'd got to Darien an' got paid off. He give me forty-two dollars and my railroad fare back from Brunswick. But he wants to play a little poker dere at de Wilcox House, he say.

'He promise me he ain't gonna play much. He gimme most of his money—nigh two hundred dollars—to keep for 'im. An' he tell me, "You keep comin' in dere while I play. An' if I wink my eye at you, you tell me de man I got business wid done come an' waitin' for me."

'I kep' a-comin', but he didn't wink. Finally I say to 'im, "'Bout time fer de boat to Brunswick." Den he come out'n dere and he say, "Dey's takin' my money, King Charles. Lemme have fifty of dat I lef' wid you." Den it did get time fer de boat an' I tried to get 'im out, but I couldn't do a thing wid 'im. He stayed rat deah ontil he lose ever' cent he had an' ever' cent I had, too. We had to walk back!'

But Zeke did not have to think up an excuse for sending King Charles home. When the Corns had completed their raft the following afternoon, they decided to let it down through the mouth of the creek and tie it up below. Then they would hunt squirrels and turkey until after dark to add to their supplies. When the moon rose, they would drop on down the river. They were in no hurry to overtake the company raft train.

Getting the raft off took longer than it should. When it swung out of the creek mouth down the swift-moving river current, the swamp haze was already thickening. Littleton was at the pilot oar in the stern and Micajah and Zeke manned the bow oar in the front. As they swung it in toward the bank Littleton told King Charles, who had been allowed to help tie up the raft, to jump ashore with the rope to snub it. The negro leaped to the bank clean as a goat and had his rope ready to loop around a cypress stump. But as he ran on the slippery mud, his feet tangled in a dead brush-top too dim to see. He slid forward. Struggling for his balance, he threw the rope loop at the top of the stump. It went over, a kink in it catching the mid-finger of his hand beyond the stump. The heavy raft, driven by the swift current, snapped the rope taut with tremendous crackling force. Reared back on his heels for the snub, the negro's face was suddenly contorted with pain. He let out a gunshot blast from his backside. The finger had been jerked from his hand. But he uttered no other sound and swung onto the rope and looped it until the raft was secure.

It was nearing four o'clock in the morning when the Corns finally loosed the raft and it swung out into the black current, running smooth under hovering gray mist. They had not slept, having to doctor the negro and take him back to Zeke's. The raft straightened out on the broad back of the flooding river that spread off into the invisible distance of gray dawn toward dimly looming swamps. The morning was still, but bitter cold. A small fire burned at the mouth of the lean-to of pine boughs, erected close to the bow-oar walk, though none of the men left his place to warm.

They had turned into the reach above McRae's landing when day broke. Suddenly the gray mist slunk into the dark of the swamps on either hand, the air cleared, and an azure and opalescent eastern sky announced the coming of the sun. Its approach was calm and steady and limitlessly outspreading. The surface of the river grew muddy-brown with glinted facets on it. Trees in the texture of the swamp walls became clearly etched in trunk and bough. And the sky above the eastern wall grew richer in ocher, rose and blue—as an organ swells. Suddenly the red sun-rim rose above the tree-line at the end of the reach and a million suns sparkled from the ripples of the river.

Drifting almost straight down the reach, the three Corns—Micajah and Zeke before the fire and Littleton at the stern oar—had stood motionless to watch the sun rise. As they approached the river's turn, the two at the fire returned to the bow oar.

Littleton's sharp-edged baritone voice cut through the cold morning air. 'Bow, White!' he cried, directing the bow-oarsmen to dip the long blade of their oar to the left and pull the point of the raft toward that bank. In his twenty-fifth year now, Littleton looked a man, confident and commanding in the morning sunlight at the pilot's place. He was not quite so tall as Zeke, but the breadth of his shoulders, the depth of his chest, the trunk-like mold of his neck and the upward point of his chin, distinguished him for the symmetry of his figure and his fine bearing in any company. He looked less like the Corns than any of Micajah's sons. The nostrils of his straight nose flared emotionally and added to his calm Corn mouth and chin were full lips. More exceptional still were his eyes. Hazel-brown with large pupils, they gazed with hard directness, and rebellion lurked in their depths. The black wool hat he had put back on his head when they reached the turn covered copperish-bronze curly hair.

'Bow, Injun!' he now sung out. And when Micajah offered, 'Looks like a clay root under the water to the right, there,' he replied, 'That's nothing but wind riffles—keep a-pullin'!' He spoke in the same tone of command.

Micajah accepted the direction of his son with evenness and grace. The pilot, he knew, must command the raft; the main thing was to work together. Littleton did know timber-drifting and he was rather proud of him now. He himself had never had time from farming to learn it—had never made but five trips, all told, and they were years apart. In some ways, Littleton was the smartest of his boys, Micajah reflected. He could calculate all right, quick and far ahead. He would never have made the mistake that Zeke made in bringing the nigger along; Zeke hadn't seasoned into a man like Micajah had hoped he would ten years before. But Littleton didn't have a man's patience and grip on himself. And no hand could hold

260

him, unless it was the wishy-washy pleading of his ma, sometimes.

Before noon they reached the forks, where the Oconee ran in and their waterway spread out into the broad Altamaha. Close to dusk they passed a sinking raft, piloted by a giant of a man, with two hunched darkies at the bow oar. It was a pickup raft and even the walk-way at the bow was under water. About the only dry parts on it were the oar benches and a lean-to. The hands looked cold and the pilot hollered to ask them for a chunk of fire. Littleton knew him, but didn't speak. Micajah threw them a chunk. At dark, Littleton moved up to the bow oar and sent Micajah back to the stern. He kept a sharp lookout into the dimness ahead, hollered quick calls back to Micajah, and made Zeke step lively to give him a hand with the long oar.

Littleton gauged his time and distance well in the pursuit. They were approaching the Narrows at sundown when they passed the long company raft train. Already the negro hands had pulled in to the bank and tied up. Littleton drew close to the clay roots on the far side of the river, while all of them—Zeke at the bow oar and Micajah in the lean-to—gave it a sharp inspection. Two of the darkies were squatting by a fire on the bank, another was at work on a lightwood stump with an axe. A fourth was walking along the bank from the tail end of the train. The Corns drifted on. At dark Littleton took the bow oar again and put their raft safely through the Narrows. They tied just below Phinholloway.

They had eaten a snack aboard the raft before they stopped and went immediately, if deliberately, into preparation for their boat trip back up the river. Into the dugout they put their rifles, three paddles, pike-poles, an axe, and a pair of wire-cutters. It was a muscle-stretching pull back up the big river and sweat dribbled from them in spite of the cold. It was around eleven o'clock, Micajah figured, when they reached the camp by the company raft train. They could barely see a glow of the campfire embers on the bank as they pulled by the train. They did not cross the river until they were above it. After they had tied up, Micajah and Littleton left Zeke at the boat and crept into the camp to see that the niggers were sleeping soundly. They returned and picked up Zeke. They moved along the vine-tangled bank toward the rafts with a deliberate swift-ness. Littleton had close-looked company raft trains and knew that the coupling chains between them were simply knotted together and that the knots were secured with wire, some-times. They would not be hard to uncouple. And it was easy to loose hemp rope.

They paused a moment as they reached the upper end of the long bed of rafts. At their outer edge the dark current bur-bled by. The moon was still up and the dim broken reach of pine logs was sleeked with silver. There were black patches of water between the rafts and on the farthermost raft, barely visible, was a shadowy lean-to. But the scene was still. Micajah was thankful there were no dogs here to bother them—or goats! They must be more'n careful not to let one raft snub another, he told Littleton, who motioned to Zeke without re-ply.

Micajah remained on the bank at the tie-rope of the up-permost raft and Littleton and Zeke went aboard. They first secured the pike-poles before Littleton cut the wire and un-coupled the chain. After he had risen, Micajah untied the rope around a cypress trunk and eased it off slowly. He stopped it when the raft was close enough to the one below for Littleton and Zeke to jump across. They fixed their pike-poles firmly into logs of the upper raft and Micajah eased off again on the rope. The stern end of the raft swung slowly out into the current. Gradually its motion became swifter. Then Micajah let the rope go and the raft stern swept out into the stream. Littleton and Zeke held the bow free of their raft until it pulled away out into the river. Stern-first it drifted off and became a shadowy patch of flotsam in the distance.

Then methodically and deliberately, the Corns set about loosing the four successive rafts below. In less than an hour their slow, soundless job was done. Five company rafts, stern-end foremost and manless, were adrift on the dark swollen waters of the big Altamaha—headed into the Narrows. They would be sure to smash up—every one of them—and the loosened logs would drift out into the swamps from there to Darien. But the Corns got into their dugout without pausing to reflect on this. They must get around these wild rafts and through the Narrows themselves to their own timber and cut loose before they got caught in the jam.

Micajah and his sons had returned home before word of the loss of the rafts got back. The negro raft hands had not reported it and they had not returned to company precincts. Captain McIntosh learned little except that the rafts had smashed up above Darien, some of the branded logs floating into the timber port, and the hands had run off. But the Corns did not long leave room for doubt. During the high water of that winter they broke up seven more raft trains. Littleton continued to direct the action on the river, but Micajah planned

263

the campaign. He took care that they should never repeat themselves in just the same way. Instead of dropping below the next raft train, they held their raft behind it. Micajah scouted ahead along the swamp edge in a dugout to locate the camping place of the company raftsmen. And they tied up ten miles above it. To make themselves inconspicuous on the river, once Micajah remained in the lean-to when their raft came in sight of anyone on the banks or adrift; another time Littleton and Zeke smutted their faces and hands. They exchanged casual river greetings, but they kept to themselves and were closemouthed. When they found a white guard keeping all-night vigil at the rafts, they slugged him, Micajah remaining in the boat to decoy him to the water's edge while Littleton and Zeke slipped up on him from behind. Once they ran the whole crew of negro hands off from their camp, dressing up like Ku Kluxers and using gunpowder bombs Micajah had devised to throw into their fire. When the company welded and locked the chain couplings on the raft trains, Littleton got hacksaws from Savannah to cut them.

Micajah felt that they had out-calculated the company on every turn. He believed that they were twisting its neck until the wind was pretty near cut off. He took out a little time to plant early corn, but they carried on their war as long as there was rafting water in the river. Late in May, they wound it up by cutting loose the company booms both at Coventry Boom and Temperance on the same night. It turned the Ocmulgee into a log jam and tied up raft and steamboat traffic for days.

June had come before Micajah got his cotton into the ground. There seemed to be peace and quiet in Telfair County, but that month a thing happened which confused him and weighed upon him. Fears moved up to Pineville, leaving the county and putting another agent for the company at McRae. This agent was under Fears, but Fears would now visit Telfair seldom if at all, Micajah heard. Ever since he had got the shot at Fears on Cedar Creek, Micajah had felt assured, without reasoning about it, that he would get another token—a token that would give him the one shot too many for Fears. This raised doubts. Too, Micajah now paused to look back. There had been Rhea—gone nine years—Fears, and now another man whose name he was not even sure of!

It was late in September before another freshet spread the Ocmulgee out of its banks and sent swift current along its crooked course. There had been two weeks of general rains beforehand, but even after the high water came Micajah did not stir. Littleton grew impatient. Pa always took his time, but there was something queer about his delay. He had talked about the stage of the river and the company's rafting preparations and Micajah had only looked off without speaking, or talked about his cotton crop, or walked away.

When Littleton learned of another five-raft train in the making at Temperance Boom, he decided to have it out with his father. They were fixing sacks for cotton-picking at the Sugar Field shed house. He studied Micajah's silent face as he tied a rag strip to a long croker sack. Pa looked older, Littleton reflected, but he banished the thought. It hadn't been four months since he was outpulling Zeke on a bow oar, or nigh it. He spoke. 'Pa, if we don't start a-cuttin' timber by mornin' we can't get in behind that big company raft train with even a pick-up.'

Micajah looked up briefly, dropping his eyes again to the cotton sack before he replied. 'Can't a-do it nohow.'

Littleton shifted to the wind. 'Oh, shore we can get a starter—we can cut enough ash in the creek swamp and throw it right in, to a-get on the river with a skiff.'

'We don't need to a-get this un—I got cotton-picking to look after,' Micajah responded, gazing mildly into the distance through the crib doorway.

Littleton looked harassed. They needed to get that one as much as any they had smashed up the winter before, he said almost violently. What was the difference now and then?

Micajah cleared his throat and looked directly at his son. 'There is a difference, Littleton. Now we've got cotton-picking to do. And it's about time you was a-comin' to yore senses and a-takin' yoreself in hand!' He added that the company wasn't bothering anybody around the county now—they had a new man and nobody had been run out of his timber that summer.

Littleton got a bigger shock a week later when he rode his horse, suddy with lather, in from McRae and called his father out on the dog-run to tell him about Fears. Fears was in McRae. He was alone, and Littleton had learned he was on his way to Lumber City and Coventry Boom.

At the mention of Fears' name Micajah's face grew still and tense and he looked steadily at Littleton for a moment. But as his son continued talking, he looked away. He swayed a little as he shifted his stance. There was a pause after Littleton stopped talking before she spoke.

'You sound like a boy with a buck ague—a shootin' with yore eyes shet,' he said dryly. 'You can't get a man that way.'

Micajah wondered about it himself as he walked out to the well for a fresh drink. Six months before he would have taken such a wild chance—relying on a token, or any fool thing—it was a fool thing!

Fears wasn't bothering Corns now, nor Corns' land!

Dan'l McMillan was killed in the big mill at Pineville late in September. When he heard about how it happened, Micajah couldn't feel sorry, except for Mit and her passel having no man to make for them. Even before he and Civil went up to the funeral and Mit told them about it. He didn't offer and Mit didn't ask to bury Dan'l at home. It was Civil who arranged that.

After the rites he and Civil sat stiffly in the varnished rocking-chair of Mit's front bedroom while she talked. Micajah did not like the thin, board mill houses, built so close together you couldn't spit out of one window without spitting into another. He would never have thought he'd be sitting in one.

Mit looked a little shrunken about the cheekbones, but her face was still round and her berry eyes let out as little of her feelings as ever. She spoke in an even, flat voice with a grim resignation.

'It happened right before my eyes, Pa. I had come to the mill to bring the dinners, because the younguns was sick. And I left Dan'l's till last.

'Jest the day before they had a-moved him up in the mill shed. He'd been a-workin' out on the yard. They had him on a button saw about ten feet away from the log carriage.

'I come up a little before the whistles blew. The place was a-jarrin' with the run of machinery. The big circle saw was ascreamin' through the logs an' the niggers on the carriage was whippin' the logs over for the carriage to shoot 'em back acrost them teeth you couldn't see. And the boards were a-runnin' down the roller bed and, below, the slab hog was a-grindin' as a fellow dropped slabs into it. Things was movin' so fast and there was so much noise an' clatter a body couldn't hardly keep her head, a-let alone tell what was happening.

'It look like there was a shot, and it waunt no shot neither. I was standin' a little out of the way in the saw filer's corner and Dan'l had just come out around in front of where the button saw was. There was a sort of flash-out from where the big saw was spinnin' and the log and carriage come to a quick stop. And I looked over and Dan'l was done cut half in two, Pa. Blood a-spurtin' from his face and front and he was a-fallin' back against the button saw frame.

'Jest two minutes more and it wouldn't a-happened, Pa.' A tear slowly slid down Mit's cheek and she paused, then went on, 'The whistle was jest about to blow!'

Civil had raised a handkerchief to her face, but Micajah continued to sit regarding Mit. His almost pupilless eyes were kindly, but not moist. Behind his smiling mustache, his mouth was still with constraint. It was all right for poor Mit to believe that, if she wanted to, he thought, but it wasn't so. Dan'l had it coming to him—leaving the barrens and going to work for the company after what it had done to him, to his folks in the piney woods! Just as well it was a squatter's spike!

He asked Mit to come back home to live, but she declined. She had put by a little money, furnishing dinners to men who worked at the mill, and her son, D. J., was now working in the mill. She believed she could make a go in Pineville. Living in the country didn't appeal to her after knowing so many people and having so much to do in town.

But Micajah was puzzled by the swift and inscrutable hand of Death. It was a hard thing to see into. On the way back home Civil asked him again when he was going to make his peace with God. He wondered.

26

CALHOUN Calebb moved swiftly down the steps of the Coventry County Courthouse. He was in no haste to get anywhere. His stride was a part of his bitter determination to ignore a hostile pity—pity he suspiciously attributed to a widening circle of people. He did not note that the steps were new or that the old building had been freshly painted. The park of pine trees that once surrounded it had long been gone. Now a colonnade of Spanish bayonets bordered its wide walk to the street. And a row of tall elms shaded the thoroughfare crossing what was once the outer edge of the park. He was not conscious of them. They marked no change for him.

Calhoun pulled the brim of his felt hat lower to shade his eyes from the harsh September sun as he moved along the walk. He glimpsed, approaching him, the blue of a parasol and the sweep of a muslin dress. He looked up and mechanically raised his hat. He had recognized Kathleen McIntosh and saluted her, but he did not pause.

'Why, hello, Calhoun! How are you?'

He stopped. The greeting had come in the clear, cordial unaffected tone he knew so well. Kathleen had turned around to face him. She looked cool under her parasol, in spite of the sun. It had been almost a year since he had seen her at close enough range to speak to her. It had been more than twice that long since they had a conversation. The clear pitch of her *Calhoun* penetrated him—struck a vibration deep inside him. Impulse pressed him toward her, hat in hand. His deep-set eye took in the untarnished brightness of her hair and the smoothness of her face. Kathleen was impervious to more than time, he told himself. She was unchanged and unchangeable, in spite of the welter that had washed over him and carried them apart.

He said that he was awfully glad to see her. He said it in a voice deepened with feeling. But when they had repeated the casual rote of greeting there was an awkward pause. There seemed to be nothing else to say.

Still he could not walk on. After hesitation, he took a step closer and said, with easy vibrance, 'You are like the leopard's spots, Kathleen!' He felt a tinge of awkwardness, but smiled and went on: 'Not in looks, of course, but—but in claiming your friends. Once. Always!'

Kathleen did not smile. She had no ready reply. She seemed affected by his direct show of emotion. She said, at length, that she did not see how she could be expected to forget their friendship. She could never forget the great comfort and aid he had given her, in her need.

Calhoun's twisted mouth loosened and his eye glistened with gratitude. She would have moved off, but he followed her pausing step. He said he supposed that she was going to the ladies' meeting in the courtroom. He would be back shortly and would remain at the courthouse some little time. It would be a great favor to let him drive her home—just for old time's sake! Kathleen said uncertainly that it would be late when the meeting ended, beyond dinner-time—she could not impose on him. Calhoun assured her that he would be there, waiting.

He walked on slowly, his mind busy with pleasanter thoughts than he had known in years. There were dogs and cut-throats surrounding her and a flock of fair-weather birds, but she was untouched by them. There was no other person in the world like Kathleen, he thought, with a fleeting pang. His reputation in Lancaster had been pretty badly crumpled, and her father's crowd had done it. They had put him in the light of a conspirator against her group. His fortune had been snatched from his hands; still, she could say, 'Hello, Calhoun!' just as she had always said it.

But when Calhoun had reached his office and stretched his great legs out in front of him in his swivel chair, he was less emotional. After all, why should he try to disinter the corpse? Disinter! he snorted with a noisy twist of the chair. It had never been buried. Yet it was a corpse, and what could be gained by his trying to breathe life into it again?

He went back over the abortive love-affair with Kathleen. She had never been really in love with him, he supposed. Though he still felt she had been sincere and gently respectful of his emotion—sincere, in spite of the strange complication with Casement. He had been sure at one time that she was in love with Casement. Then he had believed, without ever quite knowing, that there had been a breach—there must have been a breach, or she had never loved him: they had not married.

Kathleen had never actually broken their own engagement, though they had not been formally engaged. He had taken the only overt action, in the winter of '84, after the company filed suit against him and she had said that she respected him for his attitude.

During the next two years he had thought of nothing, done nothing except fight that lawsuit. What a fool he had been to think he might win! Yet it looked as if he had set up an airtight chain of title to the land—and he had: their circumstantial proof was inconclusive. But they had an ace in the hole: Cassius Crow, the judge; that made the whole thing a perfidious farce! Crow had been the fourth member of their counsel and he sat at a far more advantageous place than the counsel table.

When he, Calhoun, saw how strong the wind was blowing against his Kiger, Kleeman, and Colfax heirs' claim, he had fallen back on the Indiana title nullification theory. He had borne down on it, thrown it right into the judge's face: Could the State of Indiana own a part of the State of Georgia? And Crow's answer had been that it might hold against all the world except the State. Then, a thrust at him—which Crow never overlooked an opportunity to take—'Can Captain Calebb say with Louis XIV: "I am the State"?'

The company had tarred and feathered his reputation with the respectable people of Coventry County. And Kathleen had been too close to the company for him to try to convince her of his innocence. Calhoun had told himself that several times since the court fight, and now he repeated it: Kathleen was too close to the company. Yet he was dimly conscious, as he had been before, of a fearless sincerity in her that he did not choose to reckon with.

But even more important than his loss of reputation was the fact that he had lost his fortune. Money, stables, his farm, his mountain cottage. All had gone. He had been able to hold on to his home only through desperate effort. He had done that only because of his mother—though she was too feeble and ill now for it to have made any great difference. And the pickings during the last three years had been pretty lean, though he had still been able to take it out of the hide of the company! He had to piddle along with chinquapin suits—one or two lot claims. He couldn't take a chance on anything big enough to get into federal court; there the decision of Judge Crow barred him, there he was an outcast. Calhoun pursed the lips of his wry mouth, tightened and released them quickly in nervous habit, then drew them into a viselike line. He faced the blank wall opposite and glared, his deep-set eye like a blown coal.

After a time he looked at his watch and found it was noon. He put on his hat and walked back to the courthouse. For a while he waited downstairs in the Ordinary's office idling with court minutes, but finally he climbed up to the courtroom and looked in quietly. The ladies were still there talking about schoolbooks and clothes for poor children. He went into the witness room adjoining the court chamber and waited, looking out of a window.

It was one o'clock when Kathleen came out, and the meeting had not yet broken up. Calhoun heard her voice on the other side of the witness-room door which stood ajar. He was about to open it and come out when her words made him pause.

'I was asking you about your trap, because I want you to take me home,' her voice was saying. 'You've got to stick with me, Pegota—I'm afraid Calhoun Calebb is waiting for me downstairs.'

Calhoun jerked back from the door involuntarily and leaned against a table beyond it. He made no effort to listen, but he could not stop his ears.

'I'll say anything you want me to,' a voice he recognized as Pegota Raff's replied.

'I hate to impose on you, Pegota, but I can't bear a long funeral and his morbidness. I feel finicky. I can't look at that face this morning!'

'You mean the meat-grinder's masterpiece?' said Pegota, concluding in smothered laughter. Another laugh joined in. It was Kathleen's! How keenly he knew the round, clear quality of it! Calhoun's elbows drew into his sides and his back hunched. The laugh seemed to get shriller and shriller—to go on and on. It stuck through his scarred cheek—like a hot hat-pin—again, again, again. He had heard—subconsciously—footsteps retreating down the stairway, but he could not stop the echo of the laughter. Pain thrust up from his cheek through his brain. His brain throbbed as if it would knock the top off his head. The room grew misty, swam before his eye. He vomited.

During the succeeding month Calhoun confined his interest to the practice of law. A little weary, but indefatigable, he defended the small land claims of his squatter clients against the company. Particularly in the Coventry County Court, trial had grown more difficult; Judge Cromwell was tougher here than in the other counties of his circuit, juries were less sympathetic. Even with the squatters Calhoun's prestige was not what it once had been. Near the last of October the State Supreme Court handed down a decision that would make his way much harder. It reversed a case he had won the year before in a lower court and, incidentally, held that the federal court decree sustaining the Coventry chain of title could be offered as proof in State courts.

On the day before Hallowe'en diversion came to Calhoun, unpremeditatedly. He had gone to Pineville to interview a witness and, asking about him, was directed to the McMillan boarding-house on the end of the main street near the mill settlement. He picked out the house by its green paint, its long ell, and the elm tree in its narrow front yard. As he approached the picket gate, he saw a young woman on the porch watering flowers. Her back was turned and he got an oblique view of her side. His mind tricked him with a quaint vagary.

Her hair, thick, yellow, and curly, was drawn up from her neck and piled on top. He was conscious of her head, only. It was in color, form, and effect just as he remembered Kathleen's on the night of his Christmas ball at Lancaster. He was conscious, too, only of that disconnected memory. The impression was not Kathleen, not their relationship, past or present—just the graceful, gleaming pile of hair that he had known—that he had seen in memory so often.

The young woman did not turn when he opened the gate, or as he walked up the path, and he continued under his spell until he ascended the steps and she jerked about, immediately confronting him with her watering-pot.

He was shocked to find the face of a stranger. He continued to stare a moment absent-mindedly, until her questioning look prompted him. He was somehow gratified to see that this wearer of the hair had beauty worthy of it. Her features were even more regular and well-formed than Kathleen's, and while she didn't have the eyes, hers—naively serious—wrinkled into a friendly smile that was disarming.

Calhoun wondered, when she went inside to call her sister, what so pretty a girl was doing in a mill boarding-house.

The firm, berry-eyed woman who preceded the girl to the doorway seemed to recognize Calhoun. He could not recall that he had ever seen her before, though he knew about her. She said that she was Araminta Corn, who had married Dan'l McMillan. And she introduced the girl: Jasmine, the youngest of the Corn children. Calhoun did not find his witness, but he tarried to inquire about the Corns and to ask Mit how she was making out running a boarding-house since Dan'l's death. Mit informed him that she set the best table in Pineville and it was sought after by visitors as well as mill hands.

It was not Mit's recommendation of her own board that brought him back there to dinner, though he told her so. His declaration did not deceive even Mit. Jasmine helped to wait on the table during the meal, and every time she approached his chair, he laid down his knife and fork and smiled at her. He asked her if she knew that they were cousins and he told her how proud he was to be kin to a girl with her looks. He asked her how long she had been in Pineville and what she did there for amusement. He said he would like to show her what the neighborhood really had to offer. When he left, Mit and Jasmine saw him to the door and he called them by their first names when he said good-bye.

277

It was not unusual for Calhoun to tease a pretty girl, who happened to be about, or even to be as extravagant in casual interest as he had been with his *Cousin* Jasmine. After he had seen his witness and had moved about the stores and was ready to go, he wondered that the incident was still so much in his mind. He was not given to delusions, like this vagary over her hair—it was a queer thing!

That afternoon he stayed awhile in pot-bellied Pete McClendon's general store talking to its proprietor and chewing on the end of a cigar. He was there because the meeting with Jasmine was still on his mind, though he talked of the cotton market. She did have a kind of simple loveliness, he reflected. And so fresh! She couldn't be more than twenty. And what in the name of common sense did he have to lose—in Lancaster, or anywhere else? She was young, but after all he was barely forty-four! The number of years sounded a little formidable to him. His nerves and muscles told him that he was really much younger.

Just what would he do to entertain a young flibbertigibbet who had scarcely been bussed the first time by a beau? Calhoun dropped his cigar butt into a sand-box and told McClendon he would have to be getting along back to Lancaster. Still he moved toward the door reluctantly. The prospect of Lancaster, his big empty house and his fly-blown office, seemed cheerless. He stopped to pick up a slice of dried apple from an open barrel. By God, the infant mind of the female young was not inscrutable! He would have to remember not to be an old fool. To play at the games she liked to play, to get down on her level. He had been on levels lower than hers—his ability to do so had made him the best trial lawyer in the circuit.

Calhoun interrupted McClendon's account of his wife's porely back, to ask for a pen and some writing paper.

Mit was more fluttered over Calhoun's note than Jasmine. Jasmine hadn't been around and didn't get things yet. Nobody had any ambition in the sticks. Pineville would bring Jasmine out. It had made a new woman out of her, Mit often told herself. She had enjoyed the year and a half since they had come to the old mill town more than anything she could remember since childhood. And the seven years of knocking about after they got run off their place had been a good test to make her know. She would never go back to the farm. Why, with Dan'l and D.J. working at the mill and her taking in boarders, they had had more money coming in every month than she had seen in a year on the farm. And there were all sorts of interesting people to meet with every day—she had one man boarding with her who came all the way from Sweden and two from Pennsylvania! She had more clothes and nice bought things in the house now than she had had in the rest of her life put together.

Dan'l's death had been awful and bloody and his going took away the biggest pay envelope, but Mit was bearing up under it with resolution. For some time her ambition had centered on moving into the fine painted house on the main street to enlarge her boarding establishment. Dan'l's death had made it more needed and she gone ahead quickly with her plans.

Pa had been very contrary about Jasmine's coming to Pineville and it was only supposed to be a visit, but Mit expected it to do a lot for her little sister. She had the looks and Mit had got her some right-looking sort of clothes. There wasn't any reason why she shouldn't marry a saw filer, or almost anybody. But Mit's hopes had never soared so high as a Calebb—not until after the note came.

'Must you go?' she had echoed Jasmine's question when she brought her the note in the kitchen. 'Why, yore Cousin Calhoun—he ain't much kin—is Colonel Calebb, one of the biggest lawyers in this whole country and he lives in the biggest house in Lancaster—and he ain't never so much as been married before. It was plain to see at dinner, he was taken with you. And why not? With yore looks—and clothes!'

Mit worked herself into a glow over Jasmine's invitation to go with Calhoun to a Hallowe'en cane-grinding near Pineville. She dictated the answer, coached Jasmine, even bought her a new pair of shoes, though she had misgivings over spending the money before her boarding-house was secure in its new place. Jasmine wouldn't know much of what he would talk about, Mit supposed. But she must just smile and say, Yes or No, if that looked like the proper answer. And Jasmine had sense. She ought to pick up a lot if she'd keep her wits about her and her mouth shut most of the time.

As an afterthought Mit could have wished it had been an invitation to go to some fine party in Lancaster, but Jasmine said she had much rather go to the cane-grinding. Jasmine wondered, retrospectively, how Karl Johnson, the Swedish boarder, would take it, but Mit dismissed that—he was only a lumber grader.

She waited up for Jasmine's return from the frolic, though it was striking eleven when Calhoun drove up to the gate with her. And she stayed up almost another hour to hear about it.

Excitement had been transferred to Jasmine. As she sat on a stool to take off her new shoes, which had been a mixed pleasure, her fair face was tinged with a graceful glow. Cousin Calhoun had proved the nicest surprise and the most fun! He was not stiff or wordy and preacherish at all. He had really been a cut-up at the party, though everybody showed him a lot of respect. Except for a big-mouthed, blowsy Quinn girl. Around the sirup kettle and when they were pulling candy, she had been just as forward as she could be, putting her hands on the boys and her face around to be kissed. She was especially after Cousin Calhoun, and he had bussed her, too, right on the lips. But he had put her in her place then, saying that he wanted her to get at least one smack, even if it was from a one-eyed man. He had been laughing, but he meant it. Jasmine reckoned he had to buss the girl, she'd put it up to him so.

But Cousin Calhoun could dance so smooth for such a big man—he was the best dancer there. And could play a fiddle and sing. He had sung that thing about:

> *Old farmer riding to town,*
> *Old horse with his hip knocked down,*
> *What you going to do when the meat gives out?*
> *Sit in the corner with your lip stuck out.*

He had sung that again with more verses and 'The Girl in the Homespun Dress,' riding back home, and had said silly nice things to her about her dancing and her candy-pulling, and her hair and eyes. He had a way of saying those things that was nicer than any boy's she had ever known. He had such a big soft voice. Jasmine said she didn't mind his scar;

281

you wouldn't even know it was there sitting on his right side. She neglected to tell that they had played holding hands under the laprobe, too.

Mit was a little surprised at Calhoun's behavior, but if he wanted to cut the fool, it was his privilege. She felt sure she could make the match and she took a close interest in it. Calhoun came back on the next Sunday night and took Jasmine to the Pineville union church. It showed his intentions were right, Mit said, but she hadn't thought else. After he had taken her to another frolic the next week, Mit asked Jasmine if Calhoun had kissed her yet. Jasmine blushed and bridled, and said what if he hadn't! Mit would ask her anything! Mit reflected that the only trouble was that Pa would be coming for Jasmine before long and she didn't have so much time, though of course, Mit didn't want Calhoun to think light of Jasmine. And Micajah did come, but Jasmine persuaded him to let her stay longer. By Christmas-time Calhoun had been back five times and had taken Jasmine once to Lancaster to see a minstrel show at the schoolhouse. Mit knew now he was seriously taken with Jasmine and must be just about to ask her to marry him, for he gave her a gold bracelet for Christmas.

But he called on her early in January, and then through that month and most of the next Jasmine did not see hide nor hair of him, nor hear a word. Mit wondered about it, though she decided she would wait for Jasmine to speak. She wouldn't say a thing; and she didn't—nothing, except to ask three times if they had had a fuss and occasionally about whether she had got any letter. But Jasmine was so close-mouthed.

'There shorely was a fuss, aer something—why don't you tell me, Jasmine?' Mit prodded one afternoon when her sister had listlessly declined to accompany her on her afternoon trip to the stores.

Sitting in front of the bedroom fire, Jasmine had raised her eyes to Mit's and had looked at her a long moment without seeming to see her. She had thought over the one little thing in their last ride together so many times. Calhoun was holding her tight and had kissed her on her mouth. Then he kissed her on the neck just below her ear and had murmured something in his deep rumble and his breath had gone along her neck. It made a rabbit jump over her grave and a funny feeling start up inside her. She had shuddered and jumped. He had turned her loose. There seemed to be a long time then when she couldn't say anything, but finally he had spoken, had said, 'You would be like a holly tree in my lonesome house.' But almost as soon as he said it, he broke off with foolishness, singing, 'Old farmer riding to town...'

'He must of pawed you too much, aer put you on his lap?' Mit pursued, her lower lip loosening.

Jasmine batted her eyes and looked back at the fire. Her skin showed a faint pink on either side of her neck.

'I thought so,' Mit said, staring at her. 'It didn't hurt you none, did it? Let me hear about it.'

At Mit's request, Jasmine—her face now shaded with pink—looked away from the fire quickly and anxiously. She shook her head slowly. 'Waunt nothin'.'

Mit continued to bore into Jasmine with her berry eyes. 'I wisht I knowed what I know and had yore looks. You virgins think if you a-let a man put his hands on you before you get married, he's got what he wants for nothin' and gone.'

283

Her lips were wet. 'Takes a lot to tie some of 'em. You can always keep 'em comin' back for more if you know how.'

Calhoun was snared in events more important to him than Jasmine's shudder, or anything that Jasmine might do or say. He got wind of the negro's turning on him about the middle of January. He should have had better sense than to deal with a nigger, he accused himself when he heard. And one he didn't know any too well! He had grown reckless in his need and his bitter aim to make the company suffer. The negro was already squatting on the land and had come to him about it. He had told him confidently that it would be simple to hold the land against the company in Telfair County. He had manufactured the deed himself, and let the negro know it. He had done everything and had sold the lot himself for six hundred dollars and had given the negro a hundred of it, which was more than the darky deserved.

Then McIntosh—or it may have been Casement—had got hold of the black scoundrel and they were taking him as a witness to the federal court. Of course, the negro could not have been induced to go into a State court. But he would go with the Yankees before Judge Crow, where he, Calhoun, had been enjoined from laying claim to any of the Coventry land or interfering with the company's land title in any way. Calhoun realized his predicament was serious and he employed a Macon lawyer with whom Crow was friendly to represent him.

Late in February he appeared in the walnut-paneled federal courtroom at Macon in answer to the bench summons. The trial was as urgent and brief as covert copulation, and as agonizing. The nigger was scared, but, flanked by the company

284

hirelings and encouraged by Judge Crow, he was defiant. The city lawyer didn't know how to handle him either, Calhoun discovered too late. Calhoun almost argued with his own lawyer at the counsel table and sweat dripped off his nose, despite the February weather.

Judge Crow was ominously elevated and unreachable, in his black robe, behind the massive judge's desk. Once, at a time less grave, Calhoun had said Crow was the only man he knew who could strut sitting down. Now his pale forehead and gray eyes gave him a look of cold arrogance.

It seemed to Calhoun that the trial had scarcely got under way when he rose at Crow's command to receive the verdict. Crow said that his violation of the court's injunction was too flagrant for the court to temporize or relent over. He said that Calhoun had shown not merely contempt for the court, but contempt for the order and morals of decent society.

Even in the high-paneled courtroom before the pyramid dais of the judge, Calhoun looked big. Beneath the ceiling lamp, his cross-bar mustache cast no shadow on his face: his chin was neither raised nor lowered. It was as if his head were fixed by a straight beam sent from his deep-set eye to the judge's face. His own face was pale and immobile, except for the sardonic scar-twist of his mouth.

Judge Crow pronounced a sentence of five months in the Savannah jail, and stopped speaking. Calhoun remained standing as he had stood, without the smallest movement. The pause lengthened. Finally the judge asked if the defendant had anything to say. Calhoun's reply was a smoky-sounding 'No.' The effort appeared to have roused his muscles. He sat down uncertainly. Mentally he remained standing. He was unwilling to accept the report of his senses. He refused to credit the meaning of the judge's words. The goddamn Yankees could not send him to jail, nor the goddamn judge! The whole thing was an illusion of his senses; an aberration! He did not speak or stir in his seat until the door had closed behind the whisking hem of Judge Crow's robe and an empty-voiced bailiff had oyezed court into adjournment. God bless the United States and this honorable court, he had said, Calhoun later remembered.

Afterward, Calhoun's lawyer got Judge Crow to assign Zenas Fears as custodian for the trip to Savannah. Fears permitted Calhoun to stop a day or two in Lancaster to wind up his affairs.

During the seven weeks since he had seen Jasmine, Calhoun had thought of her. He had thought of her several times and with moving desire, but he would not now have remembered her, nor have spent a part of his brief margin of liberty with her, but for the note. Jasmine had written finally and without Mit's knowledge. She was afraid, she said, that Cousin Calhoun was sick. She asked if she had done anything to offend him.

Calhoun read the note in his office, drew it slowly in with his fingers, and crumpled it. Poignant pain passed through the roof of his mouth and his throat ached. The goddamn company took his women away from him, too! Now he could never marry her! Later he picked up the wad of paper from the floor and unrumpled it. He read it over, slowly. The skin at his temples tightened. There was yet a little time, an evening he might spend fiddling above the fire.

27

KATHLEEN saw her image in her bureau mirror and looked away self-consciously. Then she turned back to it and gazed at her reflection, with her hands on the marble bureau top. A few minutes before she had left the library where she had been reading a new novel and had come up to her bedroom. She had come to be alone. Examining the mirrored face, she discovered tiny lines at the corners of the mouth and eyes and longer ones between the eyebrows. There was the impress of years about the nose and in the cheeks. Still these marks could only be detected by close scrutiny. She looked away. They had not been there then! There was greater change in her looks than the lines told. It was an intangible change. Kathleen could not see it, but she knew it was there. That change, too, had come in these six— more than six—years.

Looking backward on it all, it seemed a practical joke! Kathleen turned from the mirror and looked into the wavering blaze on the hearth. A joke whose crude deception was apparent to all, or would have been, except to herself—a joke that left nothing to cry about and no gusto for laughing.

She moved toward the cloth-covered easy-chair by her reading table, glancing up at the marble clock on her mantel.

'Mister John!' The name had stirred her fancy since girlhood. And almost as early the joke began, the joke of which, for all his knowing and her inability to guess, they both had been made the butts.

She had from the first, of course, wanted John Casement's love. And when he dared her with a show of his feelings, then fled before her response, it had made him seem all the more desirable—whatever that fight might have cost her vanity.

He had acted deliberately to keep her from escaping—it must have been deliberate on his part, though the malice was not his, she felt. From her easy-chair, Kathleen now stared at the fire. There had been the Trezevant boy. Left alone, she could have loved him, she believed. And life in Savannah would have carried her out of John's way. Then Calhoun. Even if she could never have loved Calhoun, and even if he was the swindler they had proved him to be, he had had something to offer.

A strange creature, Calhoun: like some ill-fated Cyclops. But he had been able to make her see his one-eyed world—to live in it for a time. He had been able to cloud the acts and motives of John, and even those of her father, without ever saying a word against them, and to make himself a self-effacing benefactor.

But John had *saved* her from Calhoun, too, had convinced her he was the scoundrel the court later decreed him. And that deliverance had undone John—had forced him to reveal the joke, though she could not then see that it was a joke.

There sounded the distant moan of a train whistle and Kathleen looked up at the clock again. She uncrossed her knees and sat upright in her chair, as if to rise, but she did not take her eyes from the fire and remained sitting.

She saw herself again, with John gripping her by the shoulders on that threatening afternoon on the timber-camp road. She had made her horse throw her to force a crisis, and John, his face as gray, as drawn about the mouth as a hawk's talons, had shouted, 'Kathleen—you damn fool!' But she must know at all costs, and he had told her: he already had a wife, a Catholic wife in Ireland, who, though she had not seen him for twenty years, would not release him from the bond.

Kathleen relaxed again in her chair and tapped her fingers on its arm. Forcing it into the open only convinced them both there was no joke. It was she who had proposed their course. On that first night ride in the pine woods: in the pine woods a white flake, through the dark, had moved across John's face. It was most of what she remembered now about that night. There had been other nights to remember, but it was hard to sift romance from soiled feelings of slipping out of suspected beds, of the fear of her family, of the savage circle of the community's suspicious eyes. And finally there had been ugly suspicion between themselves. The price there had been harsh. They had been fools to think they could get away with it. They had not believed in jokes. Even now those six months seemed a long time; distended with their dark and bright eventfulness.

The whistle blew again softly. She could hear the subdued roar of the train approaching the station. She turned her face to look toward the window, but she did not move.

During the last five years she had scarcely seen John, or had come not to see him. She had passed him often enough, but it was like passing a gatepost along the walk, where no gate swings.

She had heard the train stop at the station before she finally rose and, first walking uncertainly toward the bed, came upon the window. She listened and heard the low pant of the halted locomotive. A fragmentary sound of voices suggested the bustle of passengers and freight. John was getting into the vestibule of the parlor car behind a white-coated porter, bearing his new bags. She saw it not with her eyes. Those bags held his wedding-clothes. He had not told her directly, but she had known for some time that his Irish wife was dead. For a month she had known of his intended marriage. The woman, she had heard, was only nineteen. She had heard that she was a brunette and had once said that she thought croquet was a strenuous game.

Kathleen leaned against the window-facing until a final echo of the whistle lost the train in the distance. Then she came back to the hearth and poured herself a cup of tea. On the seventeenth of next month she would be thirty. What then? She sat down by the table and opened her novel.

On her birthday, Kathleen went with her father in the cars to Lumber City. Half-consciously she had been dreading the day. In her car seat, looking out of the window, the whirling acres of identical pine trees repeated her empty days of fearing it. Since the echo of the train carrying Casement toward Savannah had died at her window, they had been empty, she confessed, in spite of her effort to fill them. But now that she was thirty, that she could no longer escape the day, it did not seem different from the others.

From the Lumber City station they went immediately to a sawmill on a bluff of the Ocmulgee, not far from the town. The mill did not belong to the company, but her father had said he wished to buy some of its output. Kathleen accompanied him because she felt no interest in seeing anyone she knew in Lumber City. After Ian had gone into the mill office, she stood on the river bluff looking at the corduroy of logs floating inside the boom and at the squat figures of men moving below. On the bluff not far from her was a derrick. Its tall mast was braced by outspreading cables, against one of which she leaned. Every now and then the boom of the derrick swung out over the river and a cable let down from it. The men below fastened tongs around a log. The log was swung into the air and, as the boom drew up toward its mast, the derrick revolved and brought the timber to a logpile on the bluff. Kathleen had never before seen a big derrick like this one swing logs up from the river and she thought it spectacular.

In a pillbox in front of the mast a man pulled big levers.

Steam spurted from a pipe in the wall of the cubicle. Kathleen looked from it to the river below. This time the men on the logs were waving their hats as the cable drew taut. Then she saw that a man was standing on the log holding to the cable in front of him. Involuntarily she gripped the guy wire against which she was leaning and sucked in her breath. The log with the man on it was in the air. He balanced the uneven ends of the timber, slowly moving his legs. Up he came with the log—up over the edge of the bluff. Hardly a dozen yards from her. For a moment he swung there at a dizzy height above the river. She could see him smoothly shift pressure from one leg to the other and keep the log even. His cheeks had been creased in pleased excitement. Now he saw her and smiled, showing his teeth.

Kathleen smiled back. She raised her hand, scarcely knowing she had done it. For pure bravado, she believed she had never seen anything so fine. He looked like the hero of some melodrama, only harder and dirtier. Such fine shoulders; such a sinewy, vivid face; such reckless eyes. As the derrick turned and his swinging perch slowly moved away toward the log pile, he took off his black hat and waved it. His hair in the sunlight was shining bronze.

Elemental reflexes stirred in Kathleen. She felt the movement of blood in her veins. She could not remember when the sight of any man had excited her so much. She told herself it was his eyes. She had caught their look but for an instant. She had never before seen eyes so hard as his, nor so clear.

She became conscious of the shuffling of feet of a black, square-cut negro near her. His hat was off and he bowed. 'Ain't he a reckless devil, Miss?' he said, jerking the headgear in the direction of the logpile. His white grin somehow surprised her. An instant before his flaring nostrils and lips had looked menacing.

She smiled, and asked who the man riding the log was. 'Lawd, lady, ain't you never heerd of Mist Lit before?' The negro seemed too eager to tell her, to remember. 'He's the river-runningest rascal ever on the Ocmulgee, aer anywhere else!'

Mister Lit must have more of a name; but Kathleen decided that it wouldn't be important to her. She supposed she had better keep him the *river-runningest rascal* she had ever seen on a log in midair. Though momentarily she resented a world that forced this on her.

The negro was adding to his extravagant description of the man. He seemed to know Mister Lit well, Kathleen said. 'Know 'im,' said the darky, a little indignant, 'I'se been wid him in ever' kind of scrape he could get into!'

Kathleen smiled. His loose lips twitched and he looked upward reflectively. He recalled one time when he and Mist Lit were fishing shad nets in the mouth of Horse Creek and a big sawed raft had broken up on the point above. There was a lot of water, and swift. The sawn timbers floated out into the swamp and down the river. The white man and two negroes on the raft just about to give up. They were helpless in the freshet. They didn't even have a boat.

About that time Mist Lit came along and he was in the boat with him. Mist Lit, always as clever a fellow as you could meet, turned his boat around and helped them catch some of the timbers. Then he lent them his boat, saying he would just hold up on fishing his nets in the daytime until they got what they could of the raft together.

Those raft hands were the most appreciative fellows he had ever seen. Looked like they never would get over telling Mist Lit how they appreciated his boat. So they worked at running down the timbers all day.

Then at night he and Mist Lit got in that boat to do the shad fishing and they picked up the loose timbers all night. They snaked them around through the swamp and hid them in the old swamp lake.

The raft hands, after four days working at it, had got almost half of their raft together. Then they untied and drifted on for Darien, glad to have something to drift and thanking Mist Lit again before they left. Three days later, he and Mist Lit came on behind them on the bigger half of the raft.

The negro's laugh echoed across the river and Kathleen joined in. 'Yessuh, they ain't another un like Mist Lit, I tell yuh!' He paused a moment. Then he looked at her wisely and spoke with an air of mystery. 'I could tell yuh moah about 'im—and about how the company rafts got to' up.'

Kathleen's interest sharpened, but she maintained a casual voice. She would like to know more about Mister Lit. What rafts had been torn up?

The negro was laughing to himself. 'He don't think I knows it, naer his brother, Zeke. But I knew what they wuz gonna do that night when they sont me home. Even if I did jerk my finger out in de rope.'

He said it was right after that happened that the first one of the company raft trains got torn up. He attributed all of the company's rafting losses to Mist Lit, Mist Zeke, and their pa.

Kathleen looked off toward the mill office and then across the river. The wind from it was making her feel chilled now. She wondered if what he said were true. Would he tell such a thing to a stranger? She felt that he would. She ventured again her question about Mister Lit: what was his last name?

'Cawn—they's all Cawns,' the negro said casually; then he looked at her sharply. She was walking away.

Corn! Kathleen remembered the name vividly enough. So her bold man on the log was a Corn. And she had thought she wanted to know him. He would probably spit in her face!

Kathleen moved on with a feeling of minor disgust. She would stick with her father. After all, he was sufficient hero for her. She thought of the story she had heard at the company office at Christmas-time. The thing had happened more than a month before, but he had never said anything about it. And never did, except in response to her prodding.

The terrorism of the squatters in Telfair County had grown so bad in the fall that the mill bosses could not get crews—white or black—to go into the woods in the upper end of the county. Hozendorf, who had first told her about it, said that her father had roared around. He said that he wanted a white man who wasn't too sugar-coated to lead in a crew of negro choppers—the negroes would follow any white man with nerve enough to lead them.

Nobody had volunteered. Not even the top bosses in the office. He had said then that he would take them in himself. And he did, not even carrying a gun.

The particular tract of timber in question was being held by two men named Saunders. They had shotguns and threatened, first to shoot the negroes, and then 'any man who gets over that fence.'

The fence was a low fence. Her father had climbed over it, without a word. The men moved back, cocking their guns. They said loudly then that the first nigger who stuck an axe in one of their trees would be a dead nigger.

Her father had taken an axe from the hands of one of the choppers. Deliberately he had swung the blade. He did not stop until he had cut the tree halfway through. Then one of the hands touched him on the arm. The men with the shotguns had gone.

She had heard mention of this on the streets of Lancaster and Lumber City. Casement had said men who did not like the company admired her father's foolhardiness. But when she asked him about it, he had only said, 'Humph! I was caught at my awn br-ragging and had to—I was scar-red enough!'

28

LITTLETON Corn had been working at the Lumber City mill most of the winter. The river had been too low for rafting all of January and February, a rare thing, and trying to a man's patience. Micajah had sent for him to help with the plowing in the Sugar Field, rain had set in again.

It was near the end of April when Littleton left the mill, and then it was not to plow. The first of April had been dry, dry enough for an ox team to snake logs to the river bank. But toward the last of the month the rains were steady and general, and he knew a freshet was in the making. He did not go home, where the Sugar Field was under water, but to Zeke's.

Littleton had heard before he left the mill that the company had been hauling logs to Temperance and Coventry Booms all during the month. There would be big raft trains ready to ride the freshet. He did not mention this to Zeke when he saw him, nor when he suggested that they get a skiff together and start out to pick up. He hadn't even mentioned that at first, because King Charles was there working on an ox yoke for Zeke. Right off the nigger talked about a pick-up raft trip, but Littleton had told him he had to get back to the mill soon.

A thing had rankled in him since early the previous fall. When Micajah had refused to take another fling at the company raft trains, he had slipped off and set out with Zeke, without telling even Zeke what he aimed to do. They had got a dozen logs together for a pick-up, though they didn't cut any of Micajah's ash. Everything seemed to break wrong. Zeke had opposed the idea of bothering the company rafts. They had been slow catching up with the train. And three nights they had paddled back to the rafters' camp to find it too closely watched for them.

Zeke agreed to cut fifteen logs on his own land to start off with, after King Charles had gone. While they were at work cutting and hauling the logs to Horse Creek with a borrowed timber cart, Littleton talked about Micajah. He said Pa was getting old, though he wouldn't own up to it. He was really too old to run the river any more, let alone tackle the company rafts. The thing to do would be to just shove in and go ahead without saying anything to him about it. But Littleton did not say he aimed to tackle the company again.

Zeke and Littleton lost only two days getting their log skiff on the river. Already it overflowed the swamp at many places. Logs were afloat in the swamp and floating out of it. The pick-ups were plentiful and the Corns took their time.

They had been on the river a week when the first company raft train passed them. It was on toward sundown. They were tied-up on the swampy side of Piney Bluff in the Altamaha. Only Zeke was there to see the train pass, swinging cumbersomely around the wide bend close to the bluff side. He counted five rafts in the train and estimated that there were five or six hundred logs in it, all told. There were only four hands on it he could see. All were black. The pilot raised his arm, but they were too far off for talking. Zeke remarked it was the first time he had ever seen a canvas tent used for a lean-to. He asked Littleton, as he paddled out to the swamp towing two big cypress, when the company took to using tents.

Littleton got out of the swamp only in time to see the train, an alligator back in the distance. He couldn't say. The bottom of his dugout was mealed with May haw and crabapple blossoms. He said spring was blooming wide open in the swamp. The sun had been so warm that the moccasins were all lying out on the limbs. They dropped in his boat every time they got a chance. And the alligators were rutting and bellowing of a night in the moonlight. Zeke said he reckoned things out to be a-bloom. It was plumb May.

But Littleton kept up as they paddled across the river to the bluff to make camp for the night. He said the swamp blooms sifted down on him like a snow, though he'd never seen much of that. And they smelled sweeter than Miss Pearl's room at Darien.

It made him feel like calling on the Widow Hall's daughters over in the Piney Bluff settlement. Then he laughed and went off into a rice nigger song as he pulled his paddle deep.

The raft hand set his bare foots on the ground—
The raft hand set his bare foots on the ground,
All amongst the frost-er.
He tore lot of rope and wobble around.
I believe, be God, he's lost-er!

He had talked about tackling the company rafts all along the way, but while they were eating their fat-back at supper that night, he put it up to Zeke. They were sitting on the same log and Littleton wiped his mouth on the back of his hand and said as he swallowed, 'I aim to tear up them rafts that passed this afternoon.'

Zeke threw a lightwood chunk on the fire before he said anything, but he was firm. It wouldn't do at all. They hadn't been able to make it the last time. He wasn't going to try it again—not without Pa, or at least without Pa knowing about it.

He said for Lit to go on over to see the Hall girls; he'd keep camp.

This seemed to pique Littleton. He drew his neck in and sat hunched over, looking into the fire for awhile. When he raised up, his face was flushed and his nostrils flared. He spoke stiffly. 'I reckon, Zeke, if you'd been at Dan'l's with Jet, you'd a-kept watch under the bed!'

Zeke took it without any show. He said there wasn't any similarity between then and now. But when Littleton kept putting it to him, he finally agreed to go along.

Littleton said that they would be loaded for them this shot. They would tie up above the raft train and go down to it in the dugout. They would land and scout the camp carefully. If the hands were all asleep, good enough. If there was a guard on watch, they would slug him if they could get to him. If the guard was strong, he had another way. He had brought along two pistols. Each would take one in addition to his rifle. One of them would drop below the camp and one would stay above, but both would remain between the camp and the river. They would stay under cover and shoot up the camp, fast and wild. When the guard and the raft hands ran off into the swamp, he and Zeke would cut the whole raft train loose and dismember it as it went down the river. It was unlikely anybody at the camp would see them close enough to tell who they were, but they could black their hands and faces, just to be safe.

Zeke and Littleton had eighty sticks of timber in their raft and they didn't pick up any more. However, they spent the next day at Piney Bluff fishing and puttering around on the raft. It was a keen-bowed sharp-shooter and tight. Littleton had laid it right for speed. After dark they showed themselves at the commissary of the pepperbox mill in the Bluff settlement. It was near nine o'clock when they got back to camp and loosed the raft. The night was clear, but moonless.

Littleton took the dark, sweeping current as a blind man moves about his bedroom. He knew every bend, every eddy, every swing in the stream, every clay root. He never lost a foot on the turns, cut almost straight from bend to bend. They covered forty miles before sunup. After daylight they smutted their faces and kept the raft at the same clip all day. At sundown, Littleton called to Zeke to pull over. They tied up and made camp. Littleton did not speculate on where the company raft train was until after dark, when they went to get into the dugout. 'They'll be at Sister Pine,' he said, 'not a quarter of a mile from the round.'

Zeke, in the front of the canoe, sighted the string of rafts when they were a half-mile away. He caught a gleam of the campfire, too, high up on the hill. They turned directly to the swamp. The going on foot was precarious and they were three-quarters of an hour getting close enough to the camp to scout it. It was easy to find and plain enough to see. The company hands had made camp on the lower edge of the bluff, out in the open. The end of the lightwood log was still burning on the campfire. Littleton could make out two negroes, wrapped in blankets, just beyond it. They looked like 'possums over a barbecue pit.

The only bothersome thing was the tent. Under the edge of a big whiteoak, about ten feet from the fire and facing it, was the tent Zeke had seen when they drifted by Piney Bluff. Its flaps were drawn. Littleton couldn't understand why anybody would want to sleep in a tent, camping in May. It was a suspicious thing.

He wormed his way around to the whiteoak and came close to the tent. Everything was quiet. There was the flicker of the log blaze. One of the negroes beyond it snored. Listening, he caught the sound of heavy, regular breathing within the gray-shadowed canvas walls. He raised his head. There was a lumpish silhouette inside, brought out by the firelight beyond. It was low and spread out, like a mound of men in blankets. He could see the silhouette of the front tent pole and something hanging on it, like a hat. He thought there was a rifle leaning against the pole.

As cautiously as they came, Zeke and Littleton crawled away from the camp and picked their way down the side of the bluff to the river. The rafts were a good hundred and fifty paces from the camp. It looked like cracking a chinquapin. After a moment's close whispering, they decided to loose the rafts one by one and make a neat job of it.

They were standing by the upper tie-rope within the swamp shadow as they whispered. Littleton gripped the rope and he could feel the tug of the current coming around the bend against the rafts. There was no moon, but the air was so clear he could almost make out the swamp across the river. There were faint glints along the dark stretch of the raft bed below them.

He had a better sleight with a pike-pole than Zeke. They had decided he should go aboard the rafts to undo them and hold each off until it swung into the current. Littleton left Zeke feeling the slip of the tie-rope. He stepped back to tell him to keep his rifle close and he carried his aboard the raft with him.

When he reached the coupling chain, he stopped to feel its fastening. The chain was knotted and hard-taut from the pull of the rafts below. He stood up to signal Zeke to let off on the tie-rope a little. The edge of the swamp was a dim black wall, almost without form. He could see the rope from the raft disappear into it. Zeke, he knew, was standing there by it, but he could get no trace of him. He wondered fleetingly, as he raised his arms, if Zeke could get his signal.

The signal was caught. There was a rifle blaze and detonation. The flash in the swamp looked unreal like fox fire, but the noise ripped through the river wide open. Littleton started dropping at the crack of it. There must have been another shot almost at the same time, for he felt the sting of a bullet in his shoulder before he hit the logs. Then for a moment the swamp was black and invisible as ever. He thought he felt a tug at the

303

raft, stronger than the current. The jet of light he had seen went in Zeke's direction. He visioned Zeke's grip breaking from the rope.

But the swamp blackness and silence was momentary. A rifle blazed in his direction. And then another a little distance from the first. The bullets cut up bark close to him. He rolled quickly onto a sinking log and tried to make cover of the higher log beside it. It was not enough to shield him. He had his rifle now, and he fired back into the swamp in the direction whence the jets of flame had come. But he knew this was a waste of ammunition. His shoulder wound was little more than skin deep and didn't bother him. He wondered about Zeke. He had never fired a shot. Maybe he jumped in the river! But Littleton knew he had not heard the splash. A bullet riveted the log in front of him just at his head. If it had been an inch or two higher, it would have got him. He could not hold his place on the raft.

Gripping his rifle to him, Littleton rolled off into the river. The gun in his hands was heavy enough to keep him under water. He floated down the dark stream, still seeing with his eyes shut the unreal flash like a glow of fox fire.

29

THE head of Mathias Hurd's bay mare nodded energetically. In the buggy behind, beside her master, rode Calhoun Calebb. At Horse Creek Bridge, she had paused to let down one of the Ruskin boys, who had been riding behind the seat. Now the mare pushed on at a fast dig. There were ten miles more of the winding River Road to Jacksonville.

Mathias Hurd, still sheriff of Telfair County, talked in a pausing monotone about minor incidents in his career as a law-enforcement officer. His interest in the subject appeared to be lukewarm, yet he pursued it doggedly. He did not reflect upon his urge to talk, but subconsciously a vague fear that Calhoun might bare his suffering at Savannah jail held him to the subject.

Hunched forward laxly, his long legs buckled up in front of him, Calhoun gave divided attention to Hurd's conversation. He appeared restlessly tired and his glance roved soberly over the passing roadside. His imprisonment had ended on the second day of August. That day and night had been spent getting home and the next he had used in rest and adjustment, but now—the day after—he was taking up the fight.

Calhoun's jailing had humiliated him more than he believed it could. The suddenness of the court's retribution had given him no time to prepare for it. Lethargy had quickly overcome him and had held him fast during the first two months of imprisonment. The morbid suspicion that his whole world had turned its back had grown on him. It was not until he received Mathias' first letter in May that the gloom began to dissolve and the lethargy leave his mind. Mathias had written to say that the people of Telfair County were anxious to hear from him; the company had downed him, but they knew he had not quit the fight. It had been a sun bath for Calhoun. His correspondence grew active with Mathias and spread to many other political friends of Telfair and Coventry Counties.

Calhoun had laid the ground for it in his letters, but Mathias had actually suggested that he run for the State Senate upon his release. And there had been others in Telfair and a few in Coventry to second the sheriff. At first, Calhoun had felt a little uncertain of himself and more of the people of the district, but his confidence mounted rapidly. During the last two months of incarceration his desire for vindication, his will to fight, had accumulated in a smouldering passion.

Mathias had agreed to manage his campaign and preparations for its opening had already been made. The candidate and his manager now moved on Jacksonville to begin the speech-making. No time must be lost, for only a little more than a month remained for the canvass.

It was Saturday afternoon, but the people who milled about Jacksonville's ell-shaped main street at speaking-time were more than a Saturday crowd. People were there from as far away as Macville and Deacon's Courtyard and Shelton's Chapel. The gathering had a political flavor, though most of the crowd were backwoodsmen. There was a sprinkling of women and a few negroes loitered in the mouths of the alleys and around the cotton gin. Many were friends and acquaintances of Calhoun and others were there because of the side of the fence that he was on, but the number curious to see the big Lancaster lawyer in his first public appearance out of jail augmented the gathering. It was a bathed, black-hatted, clean-shirted crowd.

The porch of the old courthouse (now dilapidated) had been converted into a platform, by the addition of a table, a water pitcher, and four chairs. Calhoun and Mathias occupied two of them and the justice of the peace who would introduce Calhoun and a local constable were in the others.

Calhoun sat relaxed and did not look directly at the crowd. The jail had left its mark. He had lost flesh and his big frame showed it. His face was downcast and he was motionless, except for a nervous pursing and straightening of his lower lip. He had the look of a gaunt Great Dane, resting before the run.

He rose and approached the edge of the porch deliberately, not standing behind the table. In the afternoon sunlight his face showed a grayish pallor. The depression in his right cheek was deeper. The high cheekbone and deep-set eye gave it a cavernous look. In jail he had cut his mustache close, and now, on the other cheek, the scar beneath his eye-shield stood out like a purplish monster cutworm.

He looked carefully over the crowd, recognizing, among other familiar faces, those of Micajah Corn and his youngest boy. 'My friends and neighbors,' he began with the easy mellowness of wind, 'I'm mighty glad to see you—and mighty glad to be here.' He paused as if what he had to say was worthy of reflection. 'You are used to hearing speeches open that way and usually take it as just a polite howdy-de-do—meaning little.

'But today I mean that'—his voice was still slack and deep, but he brought it to a sharp halt, then went on in the manner of afterthought—'and you *know* I mean it. You know I mean it, because I have been in a place that would make me glad to see anybody and be anywhere else.' A smile moved across his wide mouth ending in a twist of its drawn side.

'I have been in jail.' He said it levelly, and stopped. The men standing near shifted in their shoes and some in the rear craned their necks to get a better look at him.

His voice took on a slightly histrionic flavor, but it still kept its natural depth and suggestion of latent power. 'I come to you wearing the jail pallor and the marks of shackles—the shackles of the Yankee jail in Savannah! I come to you because I know you are my friends—the kind of friends that won't quit me because I've been in jail.' He ceased, and his face became immobile. There was a very still pause. Then, with the justice of the peace back of him leading off, the applause began like falling rain and swept into a downpour.

While Calhoun waited in outward calm for the applause to die away, his gray eye kindled and his jaw slowly tightened. But he began again with even depth of voice. 'I wear the scars and pallor, friends, but I am not ashamed.' He suddenly raised his chin and his voice gathered sinew. 'I am still looking my persecutors in the eye. My head is bloody, but unbowed!'

His final words had come like a blow. He paused now and relaxed, dropping his eyes. Applause again filled the air.

He was still standing with his head bowed, almost as if he were not aware of the response, when the applause ended. Suddenly he drew to full height and looked up. His eye burned. 'Ashamed of them, my friends?' he paused on the inflection and his voice went up again, 'Ashamed?'

'They are my stripes of honor! I am proud to wear them!' Now his voice spread out over the crowd and to the stores beyond with prison force. 'Proud, because I wear them in your name—in the name of all the backwoods people!'

The men in front beat the justice of the peace to the handclapping this time. It went off in a sudden burst, rolled over the crowd and back, moved in surging waves. 'You are telling it, Calhoun!' shouted a voice below him. 'We are proud of you!' came farther back. A man on the outer fringe yelled, 'Give 'em hell, Cal!'

Micajah, close to the edge of the porch, had remained placid until Calhoun said that he was still looking his persecutors in the eye. Then a quiet tension had spread over his features and he had spit hard on the ground between his feet. Now he joined in the handclapping. Littleton, standing by him, blinked red eyes.

Calhoun knew that he had won his case. But he had no idea of stopping yet. There were things he had to say. There was a hard pressure within his chest that he must relieve. Moreover, his task had just begun. He must give them arguments to campaign with; he must make them want to fight for him.

He went on now, swiftly, in an even narrative voice. The oppression of the people in the piney woods had been long and wearing, he said. Twenty-five years ago the gray soldiers had come back from Appomattox defeated, but believing war was at an end and ready to remake their homes. Piney-woods people had believed that, too.

Then the hordes of carpetbaggers descended and, with the freed negroes and the blue-bellies, had continued an oppression that was worse than the war. Even that had ended *elsewhere* in Georgia when Carpetbagger Bulloch was chased from the State in '71.

In the pine barrens the oppression had continued—and twenty years later still went on. Big rich Yankees, supported by their court, came back. Everything else had been looted; they took the land.

Yankee-like, they had come wearing sheep's clothing; lawfully, they said—federal law. That term had come to have powerful ugly meaning amongst piney-woods people.

It wasn't long until the Yankees' thieving began, but the backwoodsmen had been slow to believe it and slower to take it up.

This was history they knew about: knew about it through poverty; knew about it through the stealing of their land; knew about it through buckshot in their backs; knew about it through the graves of fathers, sons, and husbands!

It was hard to believe, but some people were yet deceived by Coventry and Company. The foreign bosses were big rich and powerful respectable. The black-robed federal judges bowed to them and said, Yessir! Others were disheartened; said, 'You can't win against the company.'

Both were wrong. He had seen the light. He would show them. If they agreed, they should say so at the ballot box in September.

He had tried fighting the company through the courts, hard and long. Too long! Some had taken a more practical method. His hat was off to them! Here Calhoun stepped to the edge of the porch and shot his arm upward and his big voice came out with driving force. 'I tell you, here and now, if the buzzards found carcasses of more of these timber rats and their Yankee bosses in the swamps—if the gophers found more of 'em in their holes—this would be a better country to live in—and healthier for them as has a right to it!'

The crowd sent up a clatter. Some men shouted and striplings screamed, but more of the men stood and looked up at him with glinting eyes. Micajah, who had been gazing at Calhoun intently, broke away and moved restively about in the welter.

Calhoun went on. That way, too—he feared—could not win. They all wanted peace, preferred law. He gave his version of the history of Coventry's land title. When the State of Indiana came by the deeds in '44 for a bad Yankee debt, title had reverted to the State of Georgia and it had become free land. Their fathers had believed that and had handed that belief down to them. They had been right, were still right. All that was needed was a law, by their own government, for their own benefit.

The excitement of the crowd had been seeping into Calhoun. His gaze was fixed on the mass of eyes. His voice had developed the muzzle ring of a field piece.

He paused now without shifting his eye and went on more deliberately. He attempted the mellow depth of his early voice, but the metallic ring was still in it. Awhile ago he had said he knew their suffering, by his own. Because he spoke for them in court, he had been called a renegade, a jackleg; because he sometimes won their cases, he had been called a swindler and a scoundrel; because he said their cause was just, he had been called a demagogue and a liar!

He supported the Peace and Plenty Land Company when it showed some heart toward them, and the Coventry crowd had called him a pirate and used its all-powerful court to close his mouth. Here his voice rose and began to show strain. 'And to take away what little I had grabbed together over years of hard work,' he concluded.

Micajah, looking into his eye, noted now a mad dancing of the pupil. His speech became ranting and he breathed stertorously. 'These company agents—these Yankees—these foreigners, wanted to disbar me—take away my means of making a living—their women gossiped about me—attacked my character! Then finally—then finally—when they couldn't do more—they threw me in jail!' His shout had become a shriek. Micajah at first winced, then turned and walked away. Other older men looked off and shifted their stance. But some of the more hysterical shouted approval in high-pitched voices.

Calhoun stood quivering and looking at the crowd, silently. He saw that he had gone too far! He walked twice along the porch and back before recommencing. He asked forgiveness of his friends. Jail damp did not help a man's voice. A jailer's curses did not steady his nerves.

He moved on rapidly. He was very happy to be able to open his campaign in historic old Jacksonville, where their forefathers had laid the foundations of the county. In the shadow of old Telfair County Courthouse, where law was first made and justice meted out—'our law and our justice!' In sight of old Blockhouse Church, where men and women kneel to pray. And where, in an earlier day, they did their praying standing up with their eyes squinting down a gun barrel, because the Indians didn't take time out for prayer.

He wanted them to send him up to Atlanta to help put this country back in the hands of white men. 'And when I say white men, I mean white men!' he shouted.

A negro boy, who had wandered out of an alley, suddenly broke into a run at his shout. Two broganned backwoodsmen started after him.

'Hold up, men! Hold up!' Calhoun's voice broke forth with the violence of a gunshot. He raised an arm.

The pursuers stopped and turned back.

He stood at ease, smiling good-humoredly until the men had walked back to the mass and its faces had turned back to him.

'Boys,' he said, 'let's don't chase rabbits. We got big game in the woods!'

Micajah and Littleton were among those who shook hands with Calhoun on the old courthouse steps and pledged their support. Micajah was warm in his praise of the speech and unhesitant about joining in the campaign, when he shook hands. There was no denying that Calhoun was a powerful speaker. He saw all the way around a thing and he could make it as clear as morning sun. But Micajah had not gone up with the first. He had taken time to swap a chew with one of the Hattons and squat to whittle. He had never thought Calhoun was sound, or to be trusted, too much. Calhoun had proved that in putting off those Peace and Plenty deeds on him. And he wasn't too sure about what Calhoun could do up there in Atlanta in the legislature. But now Calhoun had suffered like the Corns and others. There could be no question about his being against the company. If there was a chance to do anything in the legislature, they ought to send him. Micajah would go in for anything that might help.

Littleton had already shaken hands and was standing by Calhoun when Micajah came up. Littleton had no reservations. He wanted to spend his time helping Calhoun; was ready to start that minute; just tell him what to do.

Calhoun made men want to work for him. He spent five days in Telfair County making speeches, handshaking and organizing it. Day and night he moved as if he were on a battle-field. The men he met felt it. In the stores, at a grist mill, in a cotton patch, outside a meeting house, he never overlooked shaking hands with a man, or asking about his folks if he knew him. He seemed as glad to see a fellow as any politician ever was. But they could tell that all the time the whole fight was on his mind. If he knew the man was *right,* he had something for him to do by the time he had finished asking about his crop and family. No personal favor. 'You can help win the fight,' he would begin.

From Telfair he moved into Montgomery, going first to Mount Vernon and Judge Cromwell. The old judge was cool toward Calhoun. They sat in his private law office with their

314

shirt-fronts open, fanning. Calhoun talked around a bit, but he didn't mince matters when he came to the point. Win or lose this fight, he said, he would control Telfair County when it was over. The time wasn't far off when the judge would need Telfair. Cromwell leaned over, put his hand on Calhoun's shoulder. He said that Calhoun must know where his heart lay, but he was so tied up with the company crowd, he would have to move underground. The judge could call his men in and put them to work in an undercover way, Calhoun replied. He would be back to attend the conference. Then he covered the county, handshaking, and he made four speeches.

He reserved his own county for the last. He would have to make a different sort of speech in Lancaster and he wouldn't speak at all in Pineville, but out in the county he could blast away.

After he had twice covered the whole district and the election was only ten days off, he and Mathias sat down at his headquarters in McRae and figured on the vote. Mathias agreed that they could get out from eight hundred to eight-fifty votes in Telfair, voting a few niggers and dogs, maybe. There would be two hundred, maybe two-fifty votes against them—votes in McRae and Lumber City and a few in Macville, they couldn't touch. Calhoun figured they would lose Coventry by two hundred and seventy-five, maybe three hundred votes. That would give him a margin of two hundred and fifty, by the most conservative estimate. All they needed from Montgomery was an even break. He believed he had shoved Cromwell so far out on a limb he couldn't double-cross him now. Even if he tried it, he couldn't shift enough votes. The judge couldn't take

315

them away from him down in old Sodom, nor over around Spring Hill, anyhow.

Opposing Calhoun was a McRae lawyer name Josiah Templeton Jones, 'Colonel' by courtesy of Georgia custom. He had concentrated his campaign in Montgomery County, but he had spoken in Telfair, too. Here he had attacked Calhoun's plan to reclaim Coventry lands for the State and redistribute them. He pointed out that Calebb had only had a change of heart after he failed in stealing them for himself. Calebb's plan was a nostrum to mislead the good people of his county.

But he found it hazardous to criticize Calhoun too strongly. Even in Macville at a schoolhouse he had had a mushy sweet potato flung at him. And there was always someone from the crowd to yell, 'Company candidate!' 'Tramroad Temp!' and 'Punch-and-Judy Joe!' Calhoun had scattered slogans that caught on. He had told the backwoodsmen, and they repeated it. This was not his fight, it was a Georgia Cracker crusade. 'Land for the Little Fellow' and 'The Barrens for Backwoodsmen' were phrases that spread throughout the district.

Littleton had attached himself to Calhoun at the outset of the campaign. He drove his buggy team, was present in the crowd at every speaking to start the applause if it seemed necessary. After Calhoun, on the platform, had finished with a heckler, Littleton led the bunch to throw him out. About the stores and dinner-houses he talked of Calhoun's great learning, said that he would be Governor one day. Calhoun had been reared on a one-legged bed, he told backwoodsmen—was in the race only to fight their fight.

Micajah was aroused, too, though he spent some of his effort in his neighborhood. For more than two months now—

with puke in his cup and salt under his hide—he had known he went wrong to even think of making peace with the company. He had been a fool, a pumpkinhead! He had let the company shake the bushes and draw him off. He had doubted his own devil; let Civil talk to him about God.

In the first days of the campaign he had gone at it, because it gave him a fight against the company. But as he worked and got about the county, and a little beyond a few times, he saw it was growing to be a big thing. In Telfair, off the railroad, the people were all one way. And anywhere in the district men didn't talk or fight about anything else. Micajah let his cotton drop out of the bolls without holding up. He told Civil and the Swilleys to keep at it the best they could. A week before the election he made a trip to McArthur, in Montgomery County, to talk to some of Civil's cousins, going by Lumber City and coming back by Spring Hill and McRae. It looked like Calhoun had it won, he told Ben Cameron, though you never could tell about an election. He was still dubious about what Calhoun could do in Atlanta, but with as many people worked up over a thing something must come of it.

The excitement extended to John Casement and Ian McIntosh and to the Coventry and Company offices in New York. Casement wrote the home office that Calebb could do the company little harm if he went to the legislature, but his election would be bad on account of the trouble it would create in the neighborhood. The company must stay out of the fight openly, but it could help.

Calhoun was confident of victory. He had gained weight on the campaign. In fact he appeared bloated. And during the last days his eye always had a feverish look.

Mathias was sure of his winning, too. He had never seen such an organization as they had in Telfair. They had taken over the Alliance all over the district. They had workers for every box, even in Pineville. He gave the credit to Calhoun. Calhoun was the only man he'd ever known who thought of everything. He didn't need a manager. All he needed was enough runners to carry his messages. During the last week before election, Benton Mills, the Lancaster banker, a McRae banker, and a dozen merchants dropped by Calhoun's head-quarters to wish him well and offer a little backing.

Eleventh-hour rumors made some of Calhoun's workers shaky. The word was out that the federal court had deputized a hundred marshals to be at the polls. Another report had it that the company had sent down ten thousand dollars in gold. Judge Cromwell was going through Montgomery County with a keg of whiskey tied on the back of his buggy and a meal sack full of gold dollars. Calhoun only laughed. The Squatters' Scarecrow had pulled a shotgun loaded with votes. It was votes, not rumors, that counted!

The squatters voted on election day, the backwoodsmen, the farmers. The townspeople voted, too, and the mill hands. When the election had ended and two men had been beaten and another shot in the course of it, the outcome still re-mained uncertain. One could learn from Calebb headquarters in McRae that he had won. With equal certainty, he could learn from Jones headquarters in Lancaster that that candi-date had been victorious.

It was not until the following Monday, four days later, when Micajah brought the Deacon's Courtyard box in to McRae that he got it straight. There had never been any question in Telfair, but it took the official count and a lot of figuring for the whole district. He waited late at the telegraph office in the depot. When the final report came in, Micajah climbed into his buggy without even a celebration dram.

30

I N Telfair County, Alliance men, Calebb workers, were unable to believe the election returns, not thinking of accepting them. All day Tuesday they were moving in and out of McRae and about the back districts of the county, singly and in bunches. At sundown most of the back district men had gathered by Cameron Shops and by twilight a formal meeting was under way.

The September weather was sultry. The evening was windless and the air was hot and as thick as bean soup. Bugs and night pests were everywhere. In Ben Cameron's long shop, the men in front squatted knee by knee and those to the back stood close. Most of them had their shirt-fronts open and fanned and fought bugs with their hats. The smelly body sweat broke through the stench of tobacco.

Outside the shop a tall blaze from lightwood logs snaked upward. It had been set going to draw away mosquitoes and night pests. There was no fire on the forge in the shop. A half-dozen brass lanterns flickered along the walls and one sat on the anvil in front of the forge.

Short Milt Hatton, with his chipmunk eyes and leather skin, was running the meeting, though Ben Cameron sat beside him. A Jacksonville man talked, standing near the anvil. He wore boots and held a riding-whip in his hand. His voice was high and thin, but not flat like those of the backwoodsmen. He was saying that the election had been stolen from them in Montgomery and Coventry Counties. There were more votes for Jones in the Pineville box than hands at the mill, white and black. Calebb had lost by only eighty-nine votes, but there had been hundreds stolen from him.

Micajah heard the voice, though he paid it little mind. He squatted at the side of the semicircle in front of the speakers and gazed across at the feet of other squatters. He was unmindful of the heat. His hat was on his head, and it was only now and then he struck absently at a mosquito on his neck. Except for ditches now slanting from the sides of his mouth, his face had changed little during the four years since he first gathered here with his neighbors. As he gazed now, these wrinkles tightened.

The smell was in his nose again. That sweet-sickening smell like nothing else in creation. It dived at him any time, anywhere, like a swarm of wild bees.

Then it had spread everywhere, overpoweringly—had been harder to face, to bore into, than a bee swarm. At the core of the smell, Micajah saw a rough pine-board coffin in his wagon-bed. He heard his horses sneeze and saw them stagger as they started to pull the wagon up the river bank from Bell's Ferry. He felt again the contraction of his throat and stomach when he had put his shoulder to the wheel. In spite of his hardest effort, he hadn't been able to keep his insides down.

Zeke had been dead nineteen days then. Poor Lit had paid for his rashness. It was better than two weeks before he found the body floating in the swamp. Then he had had to paddle with it sixty-odd miles upstream, going night and day. He had knocked the coffin together by himself at Beard's Bluff. Nobody could stand to help him. Though he didn't ask them. He had hired the mule team and had driven on to the ferry. The mules wouldn't hardly eat and were given out when they got there. Littleton was given out, too, and shriveled like a flint-dried hide. There was nothing to his face but his eyes.

Driving on to Lumber City and out across Telfair on the way home, Micajah had smoked and chewed at the same time, but it didn't do much good. He had puked from the wagon-seat until there wasn't anything left inside him. Still the retching in his raw guts kept up. Littleton was too weak to retch then, though he kept on shuddering every now and then when a hard chill hit him.

But they had buried Zeke in his rightful place—buried him thirty years before his time! With Zenas Fears' bullet in his back. Buried him. It was the littlest they could do for him. It was all they had done for him—yet.

Micajah squatted there, thinking all of this and did not join in the talk for some time. A half-dozen men had risen to voice their complaints or set forth their plans and arguments. Two of them wanted to file a contest with the Democratic Committee. Two had said they should wait until Calebb could get there. They themselves could file no contest. The others had said that there was no use: the company would control the politicians. Micajah knew what they would say, were saying. He knew it without looking up or listening. It was just talk.

Fears was a copperhead; he never rattled before he struck. It seemed like he didn't even raise his head!. . .Micajah shifted his eyes now. He looked toward the lantern on the anvil. It was a vague, troubled look. But he spat swift and sure between his knees onto the ground. He knew when to get a copperhead. It was the easiest when the varmint was slow and swelled with a frog inside him.

Micajah rose without being called on and walked around behind the anvil. He took off his hat and his long hair looked whiter than it had looked when he stood there four years before. He was close to the anvil and the lantern magnified the lines at his mouth and the jut of his chin. Light brightened his cheekbones and shadows from his curving mustache darkened his cheeks. It gave him a ghostly look, and a devilish look, too. But his eyes were calm.

'The time for electioneering is by us.' He said it definitely, not permitting question. His manner was shorter than usual, though unexcited. He waited deliberately for his words to soak in.

Then he began again. They were wasting valuable time, he said, sitting there like old women, stitching up the might-have-beens. They could not fight money with money, for they had none. He favored action and he had a plan. He asked if they wanted action, or only talk, and then he waited, quite still, to hear what they said.

'Hell, yes, action!' Milt Hatton started it, and there was loud agreement all the way back to the entrance.

Micajah was quite still until the noise had died down. Then his arm was raised, pointing at the front door of the shop. 'Pete Doster, shut that door and bar it! Clem, you bar the side

323

door.' His voice was sharp as a pair of shears, and he said nothing more until the doors were barred. When men looked around uncertain, questioning, he said that he took the precautions for their sake and for his own.

He went on. He wouldn't waste a lot of time telling them that they could not lick the company in the elections or in courts. If they didn't know that by now, he couldn't convince them. The load to give the company was not law. It was a bellyful—a bellyful at one crack.

There was a knock at the entrance. Micajah paused with a look of annoyance. Hatton stood up. He asked Micajah if they should open the door. Someone said it was probably Calebb. The door was opened, and Calhoun, followed by Mathias Hurd, Littleton, Cone and a stranger, came in. Their arrival dissipated the tension and Micajah asked the crowd, when it had finally quieted, if they wanted him to go on. Calhoun urged him to continue. His manner was insistent, but empty.

Micajah began where he had broken off. His voice was unchanged, though now his eyebrows were drawn together. There were two hundred and eighty-nine men in the shop, he said, before the last five came in. There were wagons, buggies, and saddle critters outside, enough to move them all. They did not want for strength.

It was sixteen miles to Pineville, the back way. Everybody there was drinking or drunk by now. Zenas Fears was drinking, or had been early in the afternoon. He would be at home with his whiskey.

Two hundred of them—under Calebb's lead, or whoever they wanted—would be enough to burn the mill. They could get ready and get on the road in thirty minutes and be there before midnight. Hatton could take the seventy-five left and rush Camp Six about the same hour, putting the torch to it.

If the other fourteen would ride with him, saddle-back, they would start off now for Fears' home. He supposed Mathias, Littleton, and the Ruskin boys would want to be included among the riders. They needed nothing to make ready, except their guns and twelve feet of rope.

There was a full half-minute of silence after Micajah ceased before anyone spoke. He remained standing behind the lantern with his eyes on the crowd. His face was in rigid stillness and his eyes were dark and luminous. He saw he was not holding them, for many glanced in Calhoun's direction as the pause lengthened. Finally, behind him he heard Milt Hatton's voice. Milt didn't know about taking the lead, but he would damn sure go with the crowd. Then there was silence again.

Calhoun came forward from the rear deliberately. At first his eye had batted in astonishment at Micajah's words. Then his face had tightened and he had breathed hard. His thoughts on the ride over had been hardly less violent. But before Micajah had ended, his jaw dropped a little and his lips twisted.

He now stood behind the anvil, where Micajah had stood. His eye was bloodshot, his skin was drawn at the cheekbone and bagged about the mouth. His voice sounded tired when he began, but it was still mellow. He had come out, he said slowly, to put fight into them—to cheer them on. He was late getting to the shop, much later than he had realized. They had got a long way ahead of him! He smiled good-humoredly and the tension was broken.

325

Calhoun looked about him and shrugged his head waggishly. There was frank uncertainty in the gesture. He, of course, didn't know what had been said before he came. He might be ready to go on such a ride if he knew more about it. Nobody had more respect for Micajah's judgment and leadership than he had. He supposed they had talked about contesting the election and decided against it. He was willing to agree with them. . .He talked on smoothly, thoughtfully.

Finally he asked Micajah if he had considered that Fears' lynching would bring a flock of federal marshals down upon them. He paused, and Micajah rose to his feet. Micajah spoke with deliberate dryness. The marshals could be no worse than they already had upon them.

Calhoun agreed, but shifted about and addressed his questioning to the crowd. Lynching Fears seemed to him like wasting rope on a yearling. Would not the company probably be glad to get rid of Fears now? He asked rhetorically what the result would be if they burned the mill? Would it not bring militiamen into Coventry and Telfair Counties? Would it not bring federal officers of all kinds and breeds there, to arrest every man they could get their clutches on? After all, did they have a quarrel with the hands who earned a living at the Pineville mill? The mill hands were not trying to steal their land and timber. Some of them were sons or brothers of men in the room. Micajah, there, had a grandson working at the mill.

Calhoun had looked in Micajah's direction, but not at him. Micajah, still standing, stared hard at him without moving or speaking.

If they burned the mill, Calhoun said, after a pause, there would be five hundred families without means of making a living. He paused thoughtfully again. It might be the thing to do. He didn't know, but he wanted to think with them about it.

There was no will to act among the men in the shop when he brought his meditative talk to an end. Micajah was alone.

Then, after a pause, Calhoun straightened up. His face grew more alert. He spoke more firmly. If he were to measure up to the trust they had already placed in him, he must not leave them stranded in the ditch. He fully agreed with Micajah and the others. There was nothing to be gained in contesting the election. He agreed with them that lawful means had been exhausted.

Calhoun's eye in its hollow socket glistened hot. His nostrils broadened and his lips drew in. He spoke with hard force. The company had many heads. Eyes in many places. Cutting a head off wouldn't stop it. And unless the closest caution was used, they would be seen. Even among themselves, in their own group, they must not let their right hand know what their left hand did. 'You know, and I know, that is true! It is the most important thing to know about our next step!' He spoke with sharp inflection and broke off.

Calhoun raised his arm, palm outward, as if taking an oath. His voice became fervent. No man, ever in all time, was more grateful than he for their trust and support. He lowered his arm and dropped his head in a gesture of humility. Their confidence had made him grateful; his responsibility had made him humble!

'Believe me, when I say I have only your interest at heart!'

He had thrown up his head and his big voice struck the walls of the shop. 'Trust me to do the right thing!'

He asked that they delay their action. Hatton adjourned the meeting.

Calhoun started toward Micajah as the crowd broke up, but Micajah had turned and was moving toward the side door. Over his shoulder he called back to Littleton to 'Come on,' and went out. Littleton did not follow him.

On Wednesday afternoon of the week following the meeting at Cameron Shops, Micajah worked at a new plow stock. The hickory beam was fast in the vise of his workbench by the tool shed. He moved his plane over the wood in steady regular strokes. First picking of his cotton had been finished the day before and he returned from the gin by noon. He wouldn't start on the scraps until the following week.

But he found work to do. A broad patch on the back of his homespun shirt was dark with sweat. And his body, its shoulders drooped, remained bent above the vise as he continued to plane. He did not pause or straighten up and his face seemed intent on the shaving, but occasionally it turned aside a little and he glanced off to his right. The glance was sidewise and brief. He did not seem to be looking at anything. It might have been sound, but he did not cock his ear. He appeared unconscious that he looked. Yet there seemed to be something approaching.

Two men were moving toward him, but they came from the left. Micajah heard them and straightened up, recognizing Littleton. There was a stranger with him. He had not seen his son since he left him at the meeting at Cameron Shops. Now he faced him silently.

Littleton managed a stiff grin. He said that the man with him was Trigger Fowler. He wanted to bunk him a few days in Rody's old cabin. They were planning a raft trip.

Micajah saw that the stranger was a negro, and not quite a negro either. He looked at him closely before he spoke. The fellow's face was light, but it was more of a copper-red than yellow and his cheekbones were high. His nose started out like a white man's, yet it was snubbed at the end and spread out. His eyes were the gray of dirtdauber's mud. They reminded Micajah of a bobcat's, only they had less yellow in them. But they looked fixedly at you and were still, until you almost thought they weren't eyes. Then they moved, slow, sure, taking everything in all the time.

Micajah knew that he had seen him somewhere. He couldn't make up his mind where. Littleton had bunked hands in the cabin before, but Micajah decided that this was a mean nigger. Not quite biggity, but worse!

'There's nobody in it now,' he said, without smiling, or offering more welcome. When Littleton moved off, he called him to come back by the tool shed. He kept wondering where he had seen that nigger before!

Littleton appeared at the tool shed alone and Micajah asked him whether he aimed to live at home or not. His manner was short. He said he himself didn't care, but Civil kept fretting.

Littleton lifted his chin. He said that he had to make a living. He had been out around looking for something. He and the negro and Peter Hurd were going to raft some timber as soon as Hurd got through with his cotton. Micajah wanted to know about the negro, but Littleton was guffish. He had

329

known him a long time, he said. Trigger was a smart teamster and bowhand.

A week passed. Micajah found work for every minute of it. He helped clean up his cotton, working harder than any hand he had. He bored into it from can till can't, without seeming quite able to go at it hard enough to suit himself.

Littleton and his hand were still there, though they didn't help with the cotton-picking. The negro remained in the cabin, scarcely moving about the place. And Littleton spent much of his time there with him. Once they had left together in the buggy and had taken the Pineville road, but they both came back that night. Micajah finally remembered that he had seen the negro in the jail in McRae, talking to Mathias once, way back just after Jet was killed. But he didn't know anything about him.

Littleton hadn't been acting natural. He was still too long and he was too close-mouthed. On an afternoon following the trip to town, Micajah stopped him at the well. Littleton had drawn a bucket of water and was going to carry it to the cabin.

Micajah wanted to know, point-blank, what he was doing, keeping that nigger there. They weren't getting ready to raft timber! 'What are you and the Hurds and Calebb up to?' He raised his voice, unnaturally. His pin-point pupils seemed to bore into Littleton's eyes. He was guessing.

Littleton denied that they were up to anything. He denied it with a 'Hell-no!' He was too stout about it.

Micajah kept looking at him until Littleton got his dander up. But Micajah did not wait for him to speak. 'Calhoun and Mathias is too fast company for you, son—they'll get you in trouble!'

Then Littleton gave his hard grin. He could always rail his father about Calhoun. He asked Micajah why he never could get over Calhoun's being half Yankee and a little kin to him. He oughtn't to condemn a man for that!

Micajah jerked his head up and walked off around the side of the house toward the martin pole. It looked like his last children—the only ones left!—would be nothing but a grief to him. Littleton never was much for farm work. And since he had taken to trailing around after Calebb, he wasn't worth a damn for anything. It looked like he'd just as soon lie to his pa as to a stranger!

He stopped to look up at one of the gourds swung from the top of the pole. It was broken. And there was Jasmine. He couldn't get her to stay any more! She hadn't come home from Mit's till nearly May. Then it looked like the town was in her head all of the time, or something. She wasn't satisfied with anything at home. It was hardly a month before she traipsed off to—of all places—Georgie's. Micajah winced a little at the thought of that. He hadn't seen her since they buried Zeke, and then it looked like she couldn't stay home a minute. Why she had rather live with Cones than in her own home was more than he could figure out.

Micajah shook the pole with his hand to see if it were solid. It was more of a jerk and he shook his body with it. There was a whole lot he couldn't figure out of late. It seemed the older he got, the less he could figure anything out. About man and God! He even wondered about himself, sometimes!

Micajah said half-aloud that he would put up a new gourd *then*. He was thankful to have martin poles to fix. He would fix the pole. But his thoughts plunged on apace. About himself—

well, the quarrel with the company had not been settled yet! Things were clouded up still. Something was making up to happen.

He held to the pole and looked off across the cornstalks in the cowpen field—he had watched it spread form a cowpen to nigh sixteen acres—and at his pine woods beyond the fence, still untouched by a turpentine hack. What was making up? Who was making it? He looked at the tree-line in the distance and at the sky beyond. The threat was there, but he could not say.

31

DARK came early on the first Friday in October, as the people of Pineville and the country surrounding later remembered. Rain fell, but first there was a foggy mist. Gray gloom seeped down from a low sky and dropped a curtain of invisibility to the ground. By six o'clock it was night and the mill hands had to finish their suppers by lamplight. They were glad for the cheer on such a night—a night that swallowed a man up ten feet from his door—and a little fire on the hearth wasn't bad. In Pineville the close rows of white-washed mill houses were a luminous-windowed mauve.

In the piney woods dark came quicker. The mist seemed to spread out of the deep pines, straight from the 'overcast' resting on their tops. And from the forest it drifted over the stump lands, softening their ragged desolation. Backwoodsmen relinquished their lonely patches to the mist and made themselves secure against the night in pole shacks with lightwood blazes in their stick-and-mud chimneys.

In the cheerless weather, two wayfarers led their horses from the road, feeling their way through the pines to an abandoned shack. It lay within the forest about two miles from Pineville. There was no door, and they led their horses behind them into the floorless hovel.

After a short time one of them emerged on foot. He moved through the woods invisibly. Only a hunter could have made out the padding of the cushioned balls of his bare feet. He moved deliberately, but with sure direction, and in less than an hour he was out of the woods and within sight of the lights of Pineville.

The mist had given way to a downpour. The man hesitated at the edge of the woods. He felt briefly the long oilcloth-wrapped bundle he carried and then moved on through the night rain like a shadow.

He did not enter the window-lighted streets of mill houses, but skirted around the edges of fields and a commons to the north side of town. When he had struck the Lancaster road, he turned back toward the village. Now there was a sidewalk and he moved along the grass-bordered path. Soon there appeared off to his right a tall, dim house with bright windows, and a little distance beyond it another house like it.

He moved along by the picket fence of the first house. His gait was neither slow nor fast. He seemed almost to float. He turned the corner to his right at the end of the picket fence and went in a right-angular direction; in a short while he reappeared approaching from the same way in which he had first passed. But this time he did not pass. When he was yet a distance from the gate, from which a bordered path led to high front steps and a luminous glassed door beyond, he halted. The long bundle rested inside the fence, as he tried two of the pickets to see if they were firm. Then he was over the fence with his bundle, moving off toward the house.

As he came close to the porch, he hesitated and looked briefly toward the oblong of light on it. The porch extended around the corner and for a distance along the upper side of the house. The light came from a side window. Then he turned in the opposite direction and moved off, keeping close by the house. He rounded it and came up on the other side. At a lighted window near its rear he halted and stepped closer. He could see inside only by rising on his tiptoes. Quickly he brought the bundle from under his arm and started to unwrap it, then he paused. His head shifted to the left and then on so that his view took in the oblong of light on the porch beyond him.

He moved swiftly now in the direction of the light. He stopped at the edge of the oblong and looked in through the window. Then he pivoted his head and looked around him. Rain still fell in a noisy downpour and rolled from the eaves of the porch in a ragged sheet. He shifted away from the light and approached the porch edge. For a moment he paused, then he quickly ducked his head and shoulders under the eaves. The roll of water continued to wash upon his back, while he carefully laid his bundle down and noiselessly eased himself up into the porch.

Lying prone on the floor he appeared to be in no haste. First he removed his shapeless dripping hat, folded it and stuffed it into his breeches pocket. Then he unfolded the dripping oilcloth that wrapped his bundle. But he did not remove it. He sat up and took from his pocket a square rag, almost as wet as his clothes. With this he wiped his face and hands, rubbing it hard over his hands again and again.

He came soundlessly to his knees and from the oilcloth wrapping brought with him the dark barrel of a shotgun. He moved without noise to a post at the edge of the window light. Leeched close to the shadow he faced the window. In the half-light, his face was a dull snuff color. Nothing about him took sharp form except the gun barrel beside his leg and his eyes. They were still ovals of white.

The room within the window was softly lighted from the ceiling. Around the walls were open bookshelves of light brown wood. And a glow came from a fireplace beside the window. There was a long low table and on one end of it rested a green-shaded reading-lamp. Within the cone of lamplight was a large, slant-backed easy-chair, upholstered darkly. A large man filled the chair. A fresh cigar smoked in his fingers and his gaze was on the newspaper in his hands. His firm cheeks were a reddish color. Above, his forehead shone white, except for a graying curving lock of hair. He was alone in the room.

All of this the eyes took in, though they were still but a moment. Then the gun barrel came up, paused for an infinite fraction of time, and spurted flame. There was a detonation and a splintering of glass through the dull roar of the rain. Then the porch was empty. The man was gone.

Kathleen was on the stairway. She had left the parlor a moment before and was on her way upstairs to inquire about her mother's headache. As she moved up the stairs, she kept one hand on a gold brooch at the bosom of her dress. With the other she held her skirt. The dress was low-cut and was made of wine-colored velvet. There had been only the two of them at the table, but she had dressed formally for dinner. Her father liked it. She was on the stairs when she heard the gunshot. It sounded remote, but she could tell the glass had been broken in some window of the house. Then there was a fall that jarred the floor of the library.

She looked toward the closed library door. The startled look remained on her face as she came rapidly down the steps and strode with free-sweeping skirt to the door. She did not hesitate, but swung it open. The same shocked curiosity was in her eyes, her mouth. There was no fear, no apprehension.

She could see her father's chair was empty. On the floor in front of it he lay, his head and shoulders resting against the chair. His head hung forward. She glimpsed splinters of glass beyond and felt a breeze without knowing that she felt it.

Her action was swift, unthinking. Time was brief. She did not assume that her father had been shot. She did not assume anything. Her face showed only agitation. She was still incredulous when she had taken his bleeding head into her lap. His shirt-front was dark and blood dripped from the back of his head, soaking into her velvet dress. Her eyes saw plain enough and her skin felt the warmth. Reflexes jerked her muscles taut, quickened her breath to gasping.

By his side a long cigar smouldered, burned into the rug. A crumpled newspaper lay beneath his foot. She glimpsed a black top line. Wheat, it said. She felt the sharp dampness of wind from the broken window. But her mind could find no sequence, make no inference.

The body in her lap struggled. The eyes opened briefly. Her father coughed. 'Kathleen!—I don't know—'

She continued to look at him, her mouth pried open, her face empty. As she looked, his muscles slackened, his jaw dropped. Dead! By whose hand? Why? Kathleen heard only the heavy roar of rain beyond the window.

At ten o'clock that night, in his law office at Lancaster, Calhoun was reading an abstract. A lean, black cigar had burned out on the edge of his desk. Deciphering the handwriting, he followed the chain of conveyancing down the long page with his finger. His eye was intent upon the lighted page, but there were drawn lines beside his nose and a stillness of suspense about his mouth.

Half-a-block away he heard loud noises. They came from the direction of the depot. Rising from his seat, he left the open book and dead cigar. He moved toward the window of his office, but halfway he paused. He returned to his desk and blew out his lamp. Then, moving rapidly to the window, he pulled up the sash and propped it. There was still a raised voice, calling back in his direction. '...at Pineville. Yeah, shot through his library window. Blew his brains out. Dead when his daughter got to him.'

Calhoun let the sash down noiselessly and moved back into the darkness. Without relighting the lamp, he found his hat and gloves and walked down the rear stairs from his office. In the open space of the hitching-racks behind the stores, he found his horse and quickly, methodically, laced her to the buggy. Then he drove briskly down the back street toward his home. When he entered his wide, high-ceilinged hall, a low light still burned at the back. He did not extinguish it, but moved swiftly up the carpeted stairway. The door to his mother's room stood ajar and he paused before it. He looked in. A lamp on top of a chest of drawers burned low and was shaded by an envelope. He could discern his mother's white nightcap and the yellow blur of her face. An inside door to an adjoining room was partly open. He could hear the snoring of the white woman he hired to nurse his mother.

Calhoun entered his own room. Without pausing, he lighted a bed lamp, then stooped down at the hearth and struck a match to the fire that had been laid. He leaned against the mantel and watched it kindle. The lightwood blazed high. Still he did not move. The big boss dead! He repeated the phrase half-aloud for the sound of the words. The active head, the secretary of the company—the iron McIntosh—the man who led choppers into the woods without a gun—got himself bragged about for his nerve! Death had dared to touch the company at its source!

Calhoun felt the heat and shifted. But he still looked into the blaze, his arms folded on his chest. He spat into the fire. A gunshot had belched from the piney woods. The backwoodsmen had finally shot true, for *he* had primed the gun and had aimed the shot.

Blew his brains out! The fire had burned low and Calhoun leaned on the mantel again. And blew her heart out, too! He rubbed his hand over his left cheek.

Micajah figured it was near midnight when he heard noise at the barn lot. His ear was sensitive to barn-lot noises. But Civil had waked, too, and was in his room before he had got out of bed. She had talked about Littleton's absence early in the evening. It had been on his mind also. Micajah had put on his breeches and got his gun, but he stopped on the shed-room porch.

Overhead the clouds had broken. The moon was coming through mistily. He could hear no noise when he had reached the porch. He stood there barefoot, peering through the glimmering night. Then the moon came out and he saw Littleton and the nigger climbing over the lot fence. They had those horses out till midnight!

Over the fence they swung shotguns up to their shoulders. Littleton was not turning back to the house. Both of them were moving off toward Rody's cabin. Going to sleep with the yellow son-of-a-bitch, too!

Micajah rubbed his chin and his forehead wrinkled. Littleton was headed for trouble—if he wasn't already in trouble. In trouble already!

32

B Y daybreak the people of Pineville were in motion again. Most of them had gone to bed the night before when darkness and the continuing downpour and lack of direction made their help seem useless. Few of them had slept much, for talk went on in the mill houses after they had withdrawn from the streets. Everybody was shaken up over the assassination of Captain McIntosh. Most of the men were violent in their feeling and speech about the assassins, though none could think of any proof. Among the women and many of the men, too, there sprang up a quick and unspoken apprehension. They would never leave their own windows unshuttered! No man, nor his family, was safe in his own house from these sneaking piney-woods murderers! They said that anybody low enough to sneak up in the dark could kill a man, but they were shocked to know that any of the squatter trash were bold enough to kill Captain Iron. Of course, no squatter had done it, they said. That was no great comfort to them, though.

This talk had gone on in the houses during the night. It continued when the mill hands came out in the morning to walk about the streets and the mill, or up as close as they could get to the McIntosh home. The sky was overcast again and light rain fell, but this kept no one indoors. They had to talk. There seemed to be nothing else for them to do. Except, every now and then, to go up to the mill office and to renew their offer of help to the bosses. Steve Cromarty, the big red-haired engineer, had unbanked his fires and stoked up the boilers at the mill the night before. He kept them going all night and continued into the day, though the mill remained idle. He said he didn't know but they might want to throw somebody in one of the fire boxes, and a head of steam was a mighty handy thing to have in any emergency.

At the McIntosh home, Zenas Fears had taken charge of the pursuit of the slayers the night before and he resumed that leadership when he returned in the morning. By the time he got there in the night with his dogs, the ground had been pretty badly trampled over, but he had established a guard around the place to keep people out. That night the darkness and rain had proved too much for his dogs and his men. They had decided to give it up until morning. He had been bitterly reluctant, but the hounds wouldn't work and the men couldn't stay together in the dark.

General headquarters had been established at the mill offices with Casement and Hozendorf in charge. The McIntoshes were given the privacy of their house, but Fears had kept his guard around the fence throughout the night and he and the Coventry County officers gathered there for the morning search. The sheriff had come down from Lancaster, bringing three of his deputies and the superintendent of the convict camp. And there was Mr. Pettigrew, Doctor Hernandez, and

342

Mills the banker, the newspaper editor, two preachers, turpentine stillers, merchants, lawyers. It looked like half of Lancaster had come. The solicitor for the superior court got there from McRae about breakfast-time, but the posse and the dogs were already out in the woods.

The known facts were few and simple, yet the people who clotted and milled about Pineville stores and the company offices, heard and passed on strange variations and additions. Someone had seen a bunch of men that looked like a mob moving along in the rain on a road south of Pineville the afternoon before. Somebody else had seen Ardel Cone on the streets of Pineville, drunk and bragging that the company was scared of him. Mathias Hurd had been seen—nobody knew by whom—riding a horse along Lancaster road just at dark. Calhoun Calebb was reported to have been too busy and mysterious around Lancaster lately. There was the story that McIntosh had been killed by mistake. The Ruskin boys had come to get Fears and were misdirected as to where he lived. Almost everybody agreed that there must have been a mistake. Captain McIntosh had been both patient and kind with the squatters. He should have no enemies. If there was one man connected with the company who was straight and aboveboard with everybody, it was McIntosh. But whoever it was and however they came to sneak up in the night and shoot him through his window, they ought to be caught immediately and lynched. Everybody in Pineville was agreed on this, though the preachers and a few others veiled the punishment with the vaguer word, Justice.

Fears listened to none of it, nor considered it. He talked to the lanky Coventry County sheriff under the oak trees across

343

the street from the McIntosh home as the sky in the east got vaguely lighter. A quiet, oilskinned group moved about under the thick boughs, their long coats sticking out in front over sheltered gun barrels. Two heavy-chested bloodhounds pulled at a leash Fears held. His face and body were fuller now than when he became a woodsman-agent ten years before, but somehow he seemed harsher. His nose and mouth looked grosser. He was still clean-shaven and his face was hard and drawn. There were depressions behind his eyes and beside his cheekbones. They appeared unnatural in the fullness of his face. It was as if he had sucked them in and held them there by grim resolution, or because of some unremitting emotion.

They waited for the convict boss to arrive with his dogs. Fears talked, but he did not speak his thoughts. He had been feeling bad and had gone to bed early the night before. The McIntosh place was trampled over like a herd of cattle had been turned into it when he got there. He doubted that his dogs or anybody else's could do much with the trail, though he intended to keep this opinion to himself.

The muscles at his cheekbones and mouth were taut with his anger. He hardly realized that he was angry. He merely kept repeating himself: 'Ian McIntosh, the loyalist man I ever knew!' This murder was a bold thing. He could think of no backwoodsman who had the nerve for it. There was Micajah Corn, but Corn would only shoot a man he had a grudge against. He doubted if Corn even knew McIntosh. The Ruskin boys didn't have the nerve, nor Mathias Hurd for that matter. He dismissed the thought of others. There was Ardel Cone, but he wouldn't have had sense enough to think of it. Could

344

Calebb have put him up to it? Cone was reckless enough to shoot, but he wasn't such a fool.

Three dogs from the convict camp were turned loose on the McIntosh side porch, while Fears held his at leash. They smelled around briefly and one of them led off across the yard with his nose to the ground. He was followed by a second and after he had leaped the fence and raised his muzzle in a yowl, the third struck in after them. The posse followed the dogs. There were more than thirty men in it in spite of Fears' effort to hold it down. The trail circled the block and carried them—dogs and men—into the house of the mill sawyer. They came back to the McIntosh home and tried again. They tried Fears' dogs separately and both bunches together. They tried them ranging free and at leash.

Fears' cheekbones and mouth grew harder and the copper-ringed pupils of his eyes stood out like gun muzzles. The barking of the hounds on the trail stirred him. He wanted the thin smell of gunpowder—the sight of a falling body. In his mind he continued to speculate on who the killer might be. He thought of Red Chauncy, the half-cracked turpentine woods rider the company had fired; of Lum Fussell, who had cut off the head of one of their nigger raft hands; of the Quincy brothers near Temperance, who had tried him with their shotguns once. Somebody had done it. Any one or all of the men he thought of might have been into it, probably were! Somebody had to pay. It was a damn certainty, these sneaking squatters were not going to get away with murdering McIntosh!

He mulled over the idea. When they had come back through the drizzle to the McIntosh home for the fifth time, he divided the posse. The bulk of the group he left with the sheriff and the convict camp dogs. He took only eight with him, mostly woodsmen he had used in the past, and his dogs at leash. Again his dogs trailed away from the McIntosh porch with their noses to the ground. They moved in a northwesterly direction, a course they had taken once before, but Fears held them close and walked along beside them. When the group came to the timber road where the dogs had given up the trail before, Fears drew the hounds in close and urged them on. He walked with the dogs down the dim road. The posse followed him. Nobody said anything. Fears was abreast of the dogs, sometimes ahead. In this fashion they tramped along for more than two miles.

Ardel Corn got up late on the morning after Captain McIntosh was killed and the country around Pineville was full of gun-toting possemen and bloodhounds. But Ardel knew nothing of the stir. He had been in the back country the night before at a frolic. The late hours and the liquor he had drunk made him lay abed. His women had not gone with him. They were in no shape to go. Besides, he didn't like a woman trailing him when he was out for a good time. He had trouble enough without that.

He quit the shack, where Georgie and her sister Jasmine were fussing around, as soon as he had pulled on his breeches. He went out to the well where he could get fresh water and plenty of it. He sat down on a wash log and drank from the cedar bucket. He sat there, reflecting. Trouble pursued him. It looked like all of his children, as soon as they got big enough to make hands around the place, took out for town, or somewhere. He had four at home now and another one coming, and except for Carrie, not a one of them was big enough to work, and Carrie was a girl! He had got the place he lived on from one of the Fussells nearly two years before. It wasn't worth a damn for farming and he hadn't been able to clear his claim to it enough to sell it, or the timber on it. The sheriff had a warrant out for him about the last lot of land he sold! And here a month ago, his house had burned down. Lucky his wagon shed had a good roof on it and he had been able to get hold of enough lumber to make it tight, but living on the ground in a wagon shed was pretty tough. And his fiddle had burned up in the house. Of all things, for Georgie to let his fiddle burn!

He had quenched his thirst for the time, but he still sat wearily on the wash log, his matted hair about his eyes. Then he heard the thud of feet behind him on the trail to his gate. He twisted quickly around and was suddenly tense. Gun-bearing strangers were approaching and not a hundred yards away. He recognized the superintendent of the convict camp and thought of the warrant for his arrest.

He glanced behind him. It was fifty steps to the wagon shed. 'Dothan, bring my gun!' His voice was sharp as a buggy whip and urgent. Already he had squatted behind the log.

The son he had called to came from the shed at a run with a rifle in his hands and his shirt-tail flapping. He was too tall and too old to still be in shirt-tails, but Georgie had never got around to cutting down any breeches for him.

When the men in the lane saw the boy, they ran, too, and shouted at Ardel. They came heavy-footed, cocking their shotguns. They warned him not to get his gun. But Dothan got to Ardel before they could come abreast of the rail fence in front of the yard. The fence and the log, both, were between him and the men. He saw that there were seven of them. They were still thirty feet from the fence. They were hesitating. All, except Rand, the convict keeper. Thinking about cover! Rand yelled at him again, paused to bring his gun up.

Ardel raised up a little and reached backward to grab the gun in the outstretched arms of Dothan.

In right-angular rows behind the wagon shed a sugar-cane thicket stretched out. It was behind Ardel and fifty yards away. He may have heard the rustle of the cane fodder when he reached for his rifle but he could not have seen Fears, or the man with him. Both of them raised their guns from within the foliage at the same time.

Dothan fell flat before he could give Ardel the rifle and Ardel toppled over. Yet he was up again and on his knees quicker than light, with the gun in his hands. He fired almost even with Fears' second shot, but he was going down when he pulled the trigger. He had been hit again.

The posse came over the rail fence. Now they lowered their guns and started closing in. Ardel lay still. The boy was bellering on the ground. He couldn't get up. His arm was broken. The smoke had lifted, was thinning out.

Suddenly from the door of the shack across the yard, a woman was running. It was Georgie. Her loose dress flopped behind her and her big dugs flopped in front. She held her distended belly as she ran and hollered in short breaths.

The men in the posse pulled up to a halt. They hesitated an instant, not sure what to do. But Fears was already out of the canebreak, racing toward the gun that lay on the ground by Ardel.

Georgie beat him to it. She was coming up with the gun muzzle when Fears got there. He knocked her to the ground, went down on top of her. They wrestled for the rifle, Georgie screaming and crying. Dothan, on his knees, tried to help. He hit Fears with a shingle back. But Fears got the rifle. He came up, holding Georgie flat on the ground with his foot on her belly.

When the posse got back to town, Fears did the talking. They had got the man who killed Captain McIntosh—one of the men. The man who actually pulled the trigger, Fears said.

They had tried to take him alive, but he started shooting as soon as he saw them. They had been forced to kill him.

The word went in shouts over the town, 'They got the murderer!'

33

MICAJAH had seen Littleton and the negro move off toward Rody's cabin in the night, but they were not there when he visited it after breakfast. He had not looked for them when he fed the stock. He had not even replied when Civil wondered where they were at breakfast-time. But now the empty cabin troubled him. He saddled the gelding and made a round by Cameron Shops before returning to the house. Ben Cameron was dry and straight-faced in telling about McIntosh's death. The news dried Micajah's face, too, when he heard it. McIntosh was a respected man and liked by a lot of people who had nothing to do with the company. He wasn't a Yankee but a Scotchman. The Scotch were thick at Macville and pretty well scattered all over the country.

It was mid-morning when Littleton appeared on the place. Micajah was at the well, pulling the sweep down. He had been filling up the horse trough. He saw Littleton come into the breezeway of the barn, moving cautiously and looking off toward the house and front fence. He stopped, and Micajah went to meet him. They stood at the front of the breezeway, where Littleton had a clear view of the place.

Littleton looked a little red-eyed and as uneasy as a turkey at daybreak, though he kept himself still. He said that he and Trigger were laying out in the creek-fork swamp. They would be moving on soon, but they hadn't had anything to eat since dinner the day before. Trigger was hungry. Micajah's eyes kept their melancholy. His manner was casual but withdrawn. He said that Civil had plenty of victuals in the kitchen. All Littleton had to do was ask her. She was complaining about his absence, anyhow. But Littleton did not want to go to the kitchen to get food. He did not want to be bothered with Civil's complaining, though he didn't quite say so.

Micajah's casualness did not alter when he spoke of his trip to Cameron Shops. He looked mildly at Littleton. 'I reckon you a-know McIntosh, the mill boss, was shot last night in Pineville—through a window?'

Littleton had looked off toward the cowpen field when Micajah began. After a pause, picking cockleburs off his jacket sleeve, he responded, 'They a-got any idee who done it?' He also asked if anybody had been caught. Micajah's eyes did not shift. He made no reply. Littleton looked at the pines beyond the cowpen field closely, then broke the gap of silence to ask if Mathias Hurd had been by. When Micajah shook his head, Littleton went on to say that Mathias would be by to see him, or rather the negro. He asked Micajah if he would bring Mathias to them up in the creek fork. Give a hog call there by that old stooping bee tree.

'What business you a-got with Mathias, son?' Micajah raised his voice. It was as smooth and sweet as the edge of a

351

lancet. Littleton glanced at him a moment, then looked beyond at the wellsweep. He did not speak. Micajah's voice was now less casual. 'Can't the nigger settle his own business with Mathias? How come you a-havin' to nurse him?'

Littleton was looking again at the distance about him. He looked over his shoulder to the rear, too. Finally, he asked if his pa couldn't leastways tell Mathias where to come.

'You a-call me, pa, Littleton, but it looks like I'm just a hand to tote word for you.' Micajah's voice was firmer, and he now put his hand on Littleton's shoulder to draw his face toward him.

Littleton would not meet his father's gaze. He said that he would be all right. Anyhow, it wasn't only his business: he couldn't talk about it.

Micajah's eyes and voice sharpened. He asked if Calhoun Calebb were in it, and Littleton nodded. Micajah said he thought so. His voice showed feeling. That eely devil had put Littleton up to doing the shooting!

No, the nigger did the shooting, Littleton said defensively, now returning his father's gaze. Micajah's drooping eyelids lifted and his face stiffened, but Littleton went on. Calhoun had shown them where it was smart to use a nigger. It was a tough job. All of them were under suspicion. It would be hard to keep it from leaking out if any of them took part. Calhoun and Mathias had planned it all; he hadn't. Now Mathias was coming to pay the nigger off.

It took a little time for Micajah to resume his casual attitude. He was incredulous. Pay a man to kill your enemy—and a nigger at that! Only Calebb would think of doing such a thing! But he merely asked Littleton how he came to get mixed up in such doings. He asked who was putting up the money.

Littleton said Trigger had agreed to do it for six hundred dollars. Calhoun, Mathias, and his brother Peter, Red Chauncy, a fellow from over in Coventry County named Barnaby, and Runcie, the middle Ruskin boy, had put up money. Ardel Cone had been in on the first talks, but he said he didn't have any money to put up. Littleton hadn't put up any either. His job was to point out McIntosh and the McIntosh house to Trigger, to get him there and get him away.

There was anger in Micajah's voice when he spoke, but he held himself tightly. He asked what Littleton was sleeping and laying around with the nigger for now? His job was done. Mathias and Calebb could pay the yellow bastard. They were putting up the money. He, Littleton, had no interest in whether the nigger got it or not.

Littleton's eyes were hard and no longer evasive. He said that his job was not yet done. Calhoun didn't go into anything half-cocked. He saw all the way around it, first—left nothing out. They couldn't risk leaving the nigger to run around loose and get picked up. He might talk. He had to be got rid of. He, Littleton, and the nigger were heading for the Altamaha soon as the money came. They were supposed to be going on a raft trip.

Micajah wanted to know why they had to wait in the creek fork. It was within four miles of Camp Six. They ought to get on down the river now. Littleton said that the nigger wouldn't go without the money. Micajah observed that the money wasn't going to do him much good.

Littleton's lips twitched with the hint of a smile. 'The nigger don't know that.' He faced away, his chin coming up a trifle. Anyhow, he said, the crowd shouldn't mind paying up. The thing went off just as it had been planned. He had done his part and so had the nigger. They hadn't touched it, or had any trouble over it. Mathias ought to be along almost any time, now.

He looked back and met Micajah's pin-point gaze. He dropped his eyes. There was a bulging silence. Finally, Micajah broke it. 'I'll go get you the victuals,' he said.

When Littleton had disappeared among the pines beyond the barn lot in the direction of the Sugar Field, Micajah stood awhile looking after him. Then he dropped his dry tobacco cud into his hand and threw it away. He went over to the horse trough and washed his hands, rubbing them roughly on the lick of rock salt.

He beat his wet hands on his breeches legs. His eyes looked almost black. His nostrils curved at the back and pinched together at the end. Littleton, his son—just a corncob for a flat-butted Calebb! And a second corncob at that! He went a little way toward the barn, then wheeled around and headed for the well. His son, taking son-of-a-bitch money! Taking it second-hand! From a dead man's hand!

He paused a moment at the wellsweep before putting his hands on it. The muscles across his chest were so tight that he felt it would be an effort to raise them. Killing a man for money! Just a hired hand! Not the killer, either—the nigger did that. Just the nigger's whore! His son a hired nigger hand's whore—killing for pay! He remembered hearing about some rich men during the war hiring hands to go to war for them.

354

He'd never heard of a man hiring another man to kill his enemy.

He doused the bucket below the distant surface of the well and let it up rapidly. He sluiced the water so sharply into the wooden run extending to the horse trough that it spilled over both sides. Then he pushed the bucket down again. He worked desperately at drawing water, his cheeks and forehead corded. What, in the name of God and creation, had Calebb done to his boy! He was his boy. Had been his boy. Maybe, he'd been pretty lazy, trifling too much river, but at bottom he had been sound.

Water was running over the edges of the horse trough. Hell, he had filled it once before that morning! He jerked away from the well and walked toward the barn again, then he stopped in his tracks and turned back to the house. Calebb was a half-Yankee, half-bastard renegade! Tainted meat that spoilt every piece in the box it touched. From the back porch he got his drawknife and riving iron and walked back to his workbench by the tool shed. Here he found hickory poles and a split-oak post. He set about making another pole-yoke for Sook, the wild cow who jumped his fences. He had finished one three days before. He tightened the oak post in a vise, laid his riving iron on it. Littleton was already rotten clean to the heart. And this was the Corn left to carry on, to farm their land and protect it, to get Fears—if he failed! Out sleeping with a nigger! Carrying his gun to kill a man—*for the nigger to kill a man,* for money! A man, he, Littleton, had scarcely ever seen, who had never done him any harm.

This was the Corn left to do the job—if he failed! Micajah's wooden maul hung in midair and he straightened up. He looked before him at nothing. He said the words half-aloud: "If I fail!' The words were strange on his lips. How had he come to say them? They meant defeat. Defeat! He had never acknowledged it before, but it had been there all along. He had seen the gray thing from the corner of his eye, seen it stealing up, had heard the padding feet. Micajah dropped the maul.

Civil complained at Micajah's going off squirrel hunting that day. He had come to the house in a hurry, but his eyes had an absent look as he gazed at her with the gun on his shoulder. She did not believe he was going squirrel hunting— who ever heard of hunting squirrels in the middle of the day. And she did not want to be left alone on the place. Micajah disappeared over the cowpen fence and into the pine woods without ever answering her. But he did not hunt. He did not look for squirrels. And the walking and the trees did not quiet him. They brought him no sureness or belief. They gave him no token now. He was back in a little while, back before Mathias got there, though Mathias didn't bring him back. Micajah told Mathias where to find Littleton and the negro in the creek fork. He would not go with him.

Micajah and Civil were alone in the house that night. They went to bed, in their usual beds at their usual time. They had been in bed two hours when Georgie got there. Micajah had not slept. He had felt too much muscle-bound for sleep. Georgie's 'Pa!' and hammering on the dog-run had brought him out of the four-poster at a jump.

Georgie and Jasmine and the four children had been on the road ten hours in that ox cart, bringing Ardel's body with them. They were whipped down, and Georgie and Dothan were ailing. Civil got them to bed in the loft. Micajah laid out

Ardel's body in the front room across the dog-run. Georgie was brief with her talk, but he had heard enough. Ardel had a right to come—his body, or his spirit.

It was past six o'clock before Civil rang for breakfast. Georgie and her crowd were so tuckered out, she wanted them to get a long sleep. Micajah had kept watch over the corpse and had not gone to bed. He was finishing his meal when Georgie got to the kitchen with her four trailing behind her. Civil was frying more eggs. The two women exchanged a look, and Georgie said Jasmine needn't hang back any longer. She'd go get her.

Micajah was blowing a saucerful of coffee and sipping it, when Jasmine followed Georgie into the kitchen and stopped just inside the doorway. Her face was sallow and her eyes were puffy. She stood before him downcast and silent. She wore one of Georgie's loose floppy dresses and her belly pointed out in front enough to fill it.

Micajah got his saucer down to the table, though he spilled the coffee. He sat straight in his chair, staring. The pupils of his eyes slowly widened and the flesh in his cheekbones began to twitch. His voice cut like a plowshare through frozen ground. 'Who done it?'

Jasmine's head hung lower. She did not speak or move. Civil told her to come around and sit down at the table.

She had scarcely taken a step when Micajah came out of his chair, kicking it over behind him. His nose was pinched hard at the end. His face looked frozen. His breath whistled. 'A slut, too!' He was moving swiftly toward the door. He turned back. 'There's an end to it!' He was gone.

357

Micajah was gone, but the women heard him plundering about the house. They had expected to. Civil had hid every gun and everything else that resembled a weapon. They heard him outside racing around the dwelling. They heard him cursing at the woodpile. Then he started for his tool shed. Georgie, watching from the shed-room door, ran out after him. She ran ahead, holding her heavy belly, and stood in his path. He side-stepped her, but she blocked him again. 'Kill me—don't kill her, Pa!' Georgie yelled it at him, then went on yelling. She was not afraid. It wasn't right to kill Jasmine. It wasn't right to do anything until he had heard. Until he knew who had bigged her, and how.

Micajah did not seem to hear her. He strode on relentless-ly. Georgie ran around in front of him again. She shouted into his face. 'It 'uz Calhoun Calebb done it!'

When her words were out, Micajah stood there before her, stock-still, as if his legs were posts driven in the ground. Be-neath his curving mustache his mouth jerked open.

He followed Georgie without a word, followed her as a hound might have followed her, into the kitchen. Jasmine was sitting by the fireplace. Her eyes were lowered. Micajah stood in front of her and asked her if it was Calebb. Her long lashes brushed her sallow cheeks and she was silent, then, without looking up, she nodded.

It was like the last breath of dying—expected, inevitable, yet blowing a world to bits. Micajah sucked wind shrilly through his mustache. His eyes jerked and his body trembled. He wheeled and disappeared through the shed-room door.

358

Micajah knocked planks off the back of his potato house for the coffin. He could not face Ben Cameron at the shops. He decided to plane the boards for the sides and the lid. The planning was some help. Bent over his workbench, he pushed the jackplane steadily. Each stroke was rigid, and ended with a jerk. The hard lacing in his chest would not loosen. His heart pounded in a closing vise. But he told himself that he must face things; he could not let them keep whirling him around. He must hold his mind to the track. Sweat trickled over the creases of his forehead, dribbled from the end of his nose.

A box for Ardel Cone's carcass! His would be the fourth one Fears and the company had planted on the place for him—sure, all of them, somehow, had been put there by Fears and the company. He ought to know: he had been the gravehand!

He spat and wiped sweat from his face with a sweep of his sleeve. For ten years now Jet had lain there, rotting and leaching back into the ground—his wife gone to another man's bed, taking his son with her! Gone, and his place taken. Nothing left to remember him by except a lightwood post and the lead between his eyes!

And the gun that sent it there, spitting lead still—still in the same man's hands!

Micajah lifted his head and straightened a little, as he knocked the plane on the side of the board to shake the shavings out of it. There was Dan'l. He could only feel sorry for Dan'l—too slow to take it all in. He got mixed up—ate his own dung, and it poisoned him! But behind it all was Fears and the company. Dan'l dead two years!

The gun that got Jethro, got Zeke—and the gun hand. It had not even been slowed up! Zeke lay beside them now: rotting too. He was rotten when they got him there—shot in the dark—in the back—and nothing done about it! Micajah's plane stopped mid-stroke, and for a moment his dark eyes stared before him, then he drew a harsh wheezing breath and went on.

And now came Ardel. A pretty rough fellow, Ardel. He didn't care much for anything, lived like a hog sometimes, but a clever sort, too, in his way. He had a right to live. Would have lived if Fears had been settled with!

Micajah's plane strokes shortened and came faster without his knowing it. If Fears had been settled with! If he himself hadn't failed! By God, he had tried! It couldn't be said he hadn't tried. What was there to Fears? What was there to the man? He was a man—lead would cut his guts, bust his brains! Was it just Fears? There was Rhea before him, and another one after him. They kept coming—kept coming!

Micajah dropped his plane. He had finished the board. He raised it on edge and nailed an end plank to it. He had been ten years with his gun barrel ahead of him, trying to slip up on this man!

The thoughts that were veering down on him set up a jumping in his stomach. Not minding his backside, he had been got at from the rear. A damn, sneaking, egg-sucking dog had grabbed him in the privates!

Micajah had the physical feeling of being unmanned. He straightened up. It hadn't been Fears alone who got Cone. Calebb had put him in the way. Calebb didn't give a damn for man—or woman! He made a nigger's whore of Littleton—made his own whore of Jasmine!

Micajah's hammer came up with a convulsive jerk. He held it there. He lifted his face to the sky. He shouted at the sky:

'Not Calebb, either—Goddamnit!—Goddamnit!'

He threw the hammer from him. He felt his palm tingle as the handle left it. Then the tingling spread, up into his neck. There was a prickling in his right cheek. He looked down and saw that his right arm was hanging by his side. There was a prickling in his leg. He was falling to the ground.

34

THE death of Ardel Cone did not appease the company and it enraged backwoodsmen all over Telfair and Coventry Counties, and even Montgomery and Laurens. At most, Cone could have been only a tool for more powerful and important enemies of the company. Casement, Lechleiter, Hozendorf, all of the company bosses agreed that his removal had settled nothing.

By the middle of the week following, the word that Cone was the wrong man was widespread. There were witnesses to swear to it. Ardel's oldest boy, who had been working as a turpentine hand over in Montgomery, came to Coventry and visited the widow Rucker's place, where his father had been frolicking on the night before his death. The widow and her daughters said that Ardel had come there by first dark and had remained until the frolic broke up in the early morning hours. There were twenty people who could swear to having seen him there most of the evening. On Thursday the *Telegraph* sent a reporter all the way from Macon to see about it. He talked to people in McRae and saw Dothan with his arm in a sling and rode all the way out to the widow Rucker's. When it came out in the paper that Cone was the wrong man, even the mill hands at Pineville believed it.

But even before the newspaper had published anything, Alliance men gathered in McRae to storm the Pineville mill and burn it. A bunch came back from Coventry County with Ardel's boy. Others walked or drove their carts and wagons into McRae from all over Telfair during Wednesday. Five or six hundred of them had gathered at Steve McRae's cotton warehouse by dark. They wanted to lynch Fears, but the word was out that he had skipped the country. It was a noisy crowd and wild to fight or burn and wreck things. Milt Hatton was there and the Ruskin boys. Still the Alliance men were short of leadership. Calhoun Calebb was said to be in Dublin at court. Micajah Corn was flat of his back at home with a stroke of paralysis.

Mathias Hurd got there late, and then he came to hold them down, not to lead them on to Pineville. Hurd told them he had just got word from one of his deputies who had been there. The mill was guarded by a thousand men with shotguns and pistols. They would be fools to march on such a stockade. There was still a lot of noise going on, but that quieted most of them. Then Hurd brought in the solicitor for the circuit who told the men that the lawful way was the best course. He said it looked as if Cone had been murdered without cause. He was bringing witnesses before the grand jury then and he expected indictments against every man in the posse.

John Casement was disgusted with Fears. The slaying of Cone put the company on the defensive. It deprived Casement of Fears' help when it was most needed, for Fears had to go

363

into hiding, first to escape the mob and then to avoid arrest by the State.

In the welter of rumor and wild talk, of bad feeling and violent threats all around, Casement worked collectedly, incessantly. Evidence was circumstantial and fragmentary, but he believed that the assassination of McIntosh was the result of a conspiracy which doubtless involved all of the company's worst enemies. It was very important to the company's future to prove such a conspiracy. And there was more than the company involved for him: Ian McIntosh, his truest friend, must not go unavenged!

At first the chances of getting to the bottom of the matter, or of serving the company's interest, seemed poor. The Coventry County sheriff was a willing but almost useless aid. Casement did not believe the solicitor for the circuit really wanted to get at the bottom of anything. He lived in McRae. He was close to Hurd. He had been elected largely by the Alliance.

But on his way down from New York, Lechleiter had stopped in Macon and had talked to Judge Crow and to the district attorney. Through their influence the marshal had sent down a half-dozen deputies. Lechleiter had brought two Pinkerton men with him. Casement wondered, too, if the federal court could not be used to far more important advantage.

He would not have given Fears for all of the outside helpers, however. They didn't know the people or the country. A week passed, and neither the federal men nor the detectives had turned in a scrap of real evidence. The only direct information gleaned was the report that Calebb had appeared before a meeting of Alliance men soon after the election and had prevented their moving on Pineville to lynch Fears. It was the

364

deepest Casement had been able to penetrate the piney woods, to uncover its secrets. And he had no witness for that. Moreover, what did it prove?

On Wednesday of the second week following the assassination, Casement went to Macon to see the district attorney. The district attorney was willing to help, but dubious. His down-slanting features, which reminded Casement of the fingers of a drooping glove, were more pensive than usual as he listened in his office to what Casement had to say.

Casement's self-assured eyes were none too clear. He went over a list of big and little suspects. Most of the names had been furnished him by Fears before he left. But he could offer no proof to involve them in the assassination except that of their hostility toward the company. Casement wanted a strong show of force. The little one, he thought, might be frightened into talking.

The district attorney was uncertain of his jurisdiction, but he agreed that the federal injunction protecting Coventry landholdings provided him a possible interest in the case. Having agreed, he joined in Casement's plan. He would arrest suspects in the name of the Government. Anybody Casement suggested, within reason. He would snatch them into the Macon jail. See if fear of the federal court and strange surroundings would not break them down.

Casement had no complaint to make about the support given him by the district attorney. During the next week that officer took twenty-five backwoodsmen into custody at his nod. In Telfair and Coventry Counties, deputy marshals descended at night, took men from their tables, beds. They were hurried by buggy to Lancaster, transferred to the early morning train for Macon.

Toward the end of the week it grew harder to find the suspects. Word about the marshals got around. Backwoodsmen with any reason to believe they might be nabbed went to the swamps or hid out in the shanties of their friends.

Chiefly, Casement suspected Calhoun Calebb, Mathias Hurd, Dake Barnaby. They had more reason to want to destroy the company than anybody else. But that wasn't evidence. He directed the arrest of their friends, followers, anyone who might know about their recent comings and goings. But his suspicions did not end with these. There were a dozen others who might be involved—almost any one of them might have been the killer. The number of suspects grew, and with it the herd of backwoodsmen in Macon jail. Around McRae and Lancaster the backwoodsmen's stories of the *kidnappings* by United States marshals made boys scared to get out at night. They gave grown people chill bumps, too. Men who answered knocks were dragged through their doorways into the night and were never heard of again. The circuit solicitor protested against the district attorney's activity, charged that he was arresting the State's witnesses and obstructing investigation. The arrests went on. The district attorney ignored the circuit solicitor's protest.

But the end of October approached and Casement had uncovered no conspiracy; the district attorney had brought charges against no one. They had not even been able to support the claim that Ardel Cone was involved. Casement felt shaky and worn out, though he was still desperately intent.

When the criminal docket had been cleared, the district attorney made a visit to Lancaster and Pineville. He and Casement talked the case over on Sunday night and spent Monday in questioning Pineville people, anybody who had a report or rumor. Late Monday afternoon, they returned to the company offices at Pineville to review recorded statements, depositions. They sat at a long table in the office provided Casement and read excerpts aloud to each other.

The slant sunlight had already withdrawn from the window and Casement had risen to light a table lamp, when a knock at the door halted him. He touched his match to the wick and replaced the chimney before he opened the door.

A lean, white-whiskered, black-hatted man stood in the doorway. He was yet tall, though his shoulders drooped and he leaned on the arm of a half-grown boy. Casement did not know him. At once he gave his name. He was Micajah Corn. He had business to talk over with the company lawyer.

Casement introduced the district attorney, but Micajah continued to stand just inside the doorway, his hat on and silent. Casement asked if he wished to see him alone, and Micajah nodded. The district attorney withdrew, Micajah turned to the boy, telling him to wait outside in the buggy. With the aid of a walking-stick he moved to a chair and remained standing before it.

He removed his hat. His hair, the stubble beard on his face, and his mustache all had a dead-white look. His skin was livid and puffy about the eyes. His manner was brittle. He moved stiffly.

Still standing, he spoke. His voice had a dead, dry sound. It was a high, old-man's voice. 'I come to you,' he said, 'by the help of God.'

Three days before, Micajah had risen from his bed for the first time since the Sunday he was carried to it. For nearly a week after he was stricken, he had lain on his back, motionless, staring at the ceiling. Then Civil had found tears streaming down his cheeks one day. He made no response to her questions, but the tears had come with frequency until after he regained some use of his limbs.

Civil had waited on him in awed silence. She never told him that his stroke was a punishment. She was not sure that it was. But Micajah was sure. He did not talk to her about it, though once he asked her to pray for him. And more than once at the sound of his voice in the night, she had crossed the dog-run to his door and had heard him calling on God.

As the frost cleared from his head and a little strength came back to him, Micajah knew without reflection that God had struck him down. God never held with killing, and he had harbored it in his heart then for ten years. It became plain, too, that the company was on the side of the law and right. This was not for him to question. Micajah had agreed to forgive his enemies. Still God had not given him peace of mind!

It was days before he came to see that he had had a share in the death of McIntosh, the company boss, and he had been responsible for the escape of the killers. An innocent man had been murdered. The murderers had broken God's law. Calebb had destroyed his daughter and his son, and those sins were against the law of God, too.

Littleton was no longer a Corn, but a part of Calebb. God wanted Calebb punished. He had sought out Micajah to be His instrument. Micajah could have no peace until he did God's will.

Micajah sat down in the chair across the table from Casement after he had announced his mission. As he began to unburden himself, Casement winced. The man must be mad! He wondered fleetingly if this were some wild backwoodsman's joke or trick. It was too fantastic!

But as he got under way, Micajah's voice lowered and began to sound more natural. What he said made sense. It fitted with the circumstances Casement knew. It was the conspiracy he had suspected—exactly the plot he wanted to uncover.

Casement hadn't prayed over this case, but he had been desperate enough to pray—and no prayer had ever been so fully answered!

He overcame Micajah's reluctance and called in the district attorney. Together they went over Micajah's story again. The prosecutor questioned Micajah closely about Calebb's speech at Cameron Shops after the election. He wished Micajah had gone with Hurd to see him give the money to the negro. But with the circumstantial evidence they had developed, it was enough to make out a case.

Micajah had started to rise, when the district attorney stopped him. Micajah's life would be in danger, he said, if he attempted to return to his home now and remain there. But Micajah replied he had rather go home. The district attorney said that, as an officer of the federal court, he would have to detain Micajah. It would be necessary for Micajah to go to Macon. He would have every attention to his comfort.

369

Finally Micajah agreed to go if the boy could go with him. He had sent for Big Bud, the oldest of Zeke's flock, soon after he was able to sit up in bed. He had kept him by his bedside, and when he grew able to walk with assistance, he had used the boy for support. Big Bud was now his constant companion.

When the matter had been settled, the district attorney ran a hand over his thick mop of gray hair. He looked pensively at the table top. The attitude seemed in contrast with his brisk voice. Micajah had done his duty as a citizen, he said. He had performed a very great service for the company, too. The company should certainly clear the title to his farm.

Micajah was sitting relaxed in his chair, with his hands on the arms, his head against the high back. The side of his face toward the prosecutor was frozen still by paralysis, but he did not turn his head or move. Slowly his eyes moistened.

35

ON the morning of December eighth, Calhoun Calebb and his six confederates sat in the federal courtroom in Macon, facing trial. They were there through a sequence of events too astonishing for them to reckon with. Ian McIntosh was now cold in his grave, foully murdered two months before in Coventry County. But they were not charged with his murder. Nobody was.

If they had killed McIntosh, or caused his death—or whoever had done it—the Coventry County Grand Jury should indict them and the circuit solicitor prosecute them. That was unquestioned in law practice. But the solicitor said that he could not accuse without evidence. It was hardly to be expected of Calebb and his friends if they were guilty—or if they were not, for that matter—to help him in making a case against them. His own efforts had been futile. The *evidence,* before he could get to it, had been bodily dragged out of his circuit and lodged in Macon jail by the district attorney for the United States.

And while it seemed that nobody was going to suffer for the murder of McIntosh, the men commonly believed to be responsible for it were here to be tried on a charge of conspiring to violate the property rights of Proudfitt Coventry, a citizen of the State of New York. Proudfitt Coventry, who had never set foot in Coventry County and whom none of them had ever seen before he appeared in the courtroom to accuse them!

The twist of events had exceeded all of Calhoun's calculations. It was too much for him. He had given over his fate and that of his co-defendants to the hands of the more accomplished lawyers.

The subdued gloss of the walnut-paneled courtroom gave it an air of solemn elegance. Its softness was broken only by the provocative red of two gold-fringed American flags crossed on the wall behind the judge's dais. The courtroom was filled to its last seat and paunchy court officers stood at its studded leather doors holding back an outside crowd. There were the rough hair and whiskers, jackets and brogans of a few backwoodsmen in the chamber. For the most part the crowd was city-dressed and uncommonly well-dressed. There were company bosses from Pineville, people from Lancaster and McRae, but almost as many from Macon.

From his lesser desk, under the massive pyramid of the judge's dais, a pendulous-lipped clerk stood up and raised his hand for the spectators to rise. Amid the rustly scrunch of a rising crowd, black-robed Judge Cassius Crow ascended his bench without looking to the right or left. First to resume their seats were four newspapermen at a table beside the clerk's desk.

At two long oak tables, separated by a reading stand, sat the numerous lawyers on each side. Calhoun and Mathias Hurd sat alongside their two attorneys. Peter Hurd, Littleton,

Dake Barnaby, and Runcie Ruskin sat in chairs just back of them. Red Chauncy was remote in a chair not far away from the district attorney. With the prosecutor were Proudfitt Coventry, the two lawyers representing him, and Casement, Lechleiter, and Hozendorf. Kathleen McIntosh, under a black veil, sat with her friend, Pegota Raff, behind the company group amid the front row of spectators.

They were gathered, not yet for trial, but to contest the tribunal chosen. This was to be a battle between lawyers, a battle of words, with a judge in the referee's seat. And not of words, either—nor of lawyers, as these participants vaguely felt. Words would be merely the symptoms, the fever and the pockmarks, of the struggle in the pine barrens, now under way sixteen years. A struggle of strong prejudices, of social beliefs, of political alignments.

It was called a preliminary action, but Judge Marcus Dreighton, who now stood at the reading stand, regarded it as being more important than the ultimate fate of the clients he represented. Judge Dreighton had acquired his title as a member of the State Supreme Court, from which he had resigned to re-enter private practice. He was lean and erect. His high forehead was topped by a thinning thatch of gray hair. His manner was reserved and dignified. His voice was calm, his diction faultless.

Judge Dreighton reviewed briefly the charges in the indictment. A conspiracy, unlawfully and feloniously entered into with the object of injuring Proudfitt Coventry because of his previous exercise of rights secured to him by the Federal Constitution and laws of the United States. To the counts for conspiracy was added the charge, that in pursuance of the

373

conspiracy one, Trigger Fowler, on the seventh day of October, within the jurisdiction of the court, did kill and murder Ian McIntosh, agent of Coventry.

Judge Dreighton, continuing, read the defendants' demurrer to this indictment in a monotone. The matters charged did not constitute an offense against the laws of the United States and did not come within the true meaning of the Act of Congress of May 1, 1870. The decree, mentioned in the indictment as a buttress of Proudfitt Coventry's title, was not set out or proved to be so. The indictment failed to specify what law secured to Proudfitt Coventry the right supposed to have been interfered with.

Judge Dreighton still stood behind the stand on which his voluminous bill was laid out, but now he did not read. He looked toward the massive bench of Judge Crow. His voice was unchanged and his expression neutral, except that the nostrils of his long thin nose seemed to curve out slightly.

The defendants did not question Proudfitt Coventry's general right to come into federal court, but they did question his right to come in under the injunction decree of 1886. That decree had been in favor of Dexter Coventry.

The defendants did not, to be sure, question the Coventrys' desire to seek the shelter of the federal court. That had become manifest as far back as 1877, when the legislature of Georgia passed an act requiring corporations holding more than five thousand acres of land to incorporate under Georgia laws within a year. Before the law could take effect, Coventry and Company had deeded its great landholding to Dexter Coventry, a natural person, to avoid becoming a citizen of the State.

Proudfitt Coventry was now the title-holder, but it was not proved that the benefits of federal decree went with the land.

Judge Dreighton asked, his nostrils now curving, what federal law protecting Proudfitt had been flouted. He had searched the record of the injunction issued to protect Dexter. That was the protection alleged in the indictment. Protection even there had been extended by the court through a contempt proceeding. Trial for contempt was inherent in any court of record and was not dependent on the Constitution or on any statute.

Judge Dreighton came to the end of his legal discussion without having broken the evenness of his voice. Other aspects of the question he would leave to his distinguished associate in the case. He assembled his papers and, with a stiff, slight bow, sat down.

Pegota Raff whispered in Kathleen's ear. Littleton yawned. Courtroom spectators shifted their feet and waited. Only the lawyers seemed tense.

The district attorney read the Government's answer from the same stand where Dreighton had stood. He pushed back his hair before he began speaking. His voice was fuzzy, and he cleared his throat. He read briskly.

The Government had proceeded under the statute of 1870. It would be well to review this law. If two or more persons conspired to misuse, oppress, threaten, or intimidate any citizen in free exercise or enjoyment of any right or privilege secured to him by the Constitution or laws of the United States—or, if they went in disguise on the highway or premises with intent to prevent free exercise of these rights, they were guilty of conspiracy.

Further, if, in the act of conspiracy, another felony or misdemeanor were committed, the offender should be punished for it, with such punishment as the laws of the State where it occurred prescribed. The district attorney laid down the code from which he had been reading and glanced toward the defense table where Calhoun whispered to Judge Dreighton. The law itself was iniquitous, he had said. Dreighton replied that it was really unconstitutional.

But the speaker heard only the noise. He went on. The indictment did not charge that a conspiracy was formed on account of the right of Proudfitt Coventry to proceed in federal court, but that he had already instituted proceedings and the conspiracy was formed to interfere with his right. He discussed this right.

Finally he approached an end. He raised his pensive face to survey the judge and the defense counsel. The principle of the procedure was that when an offense was committed against the State and federal courts, the court first getting the offender had the right to prosecute. He sat down.

The prosecutor was followed by counsel for Coventry, Judge Eustace Druillard, a former federal judge of Maryland. He was tall and slender and wore a white flower in the lapel of his frock coat. His face was finely formed and mobile. His eyes were black and liquid.

As he straightened his papers at the reading stand, Casement, who sat at the table to his right, leaned over and clasped the district attorney's hand. He said in a sandy whisper that the prosecutor had come off well. It seemed to satisfy Judge Crow, from the look in his eye. Casement smiled and took hold of the attorney's arm. If they won this demurrer, it was all over! He'd clean out every squatter in the piney woods and never set foot inside another state court! There was sudden stillness around them and the prosecutor shook Casement's grasp. Judge Druillard and the courtroom were waiting for them to finish. Judge Crow was rapping gently and smiling.

Druillard began speaking in a low voice. His voice was as liquid as his eyes, ran easily up and down the scale, increased and diminished. Dreighton had said that this was not a conspiracy case. He thought, when the case was brought before a jury, that he would be able to convince even the skepticism of Dreighton. Here his voice swelled to a ringing baritone. Convince him that it was a conspiracy as damnable as ever conceived by human depravity and as far-reaching as the rights of Proudfitt Coventry extended—a conspiracy against his rights, in which the murder of Captain Ian McIntosh, cruel and heartless as it was, played no more important part than would the death of a faithful watchdog on the premises of his victimized owner.

He reviewed the long history of the Coventry injunction lawsuit in federal court, through which Proudfitt Coventry was now proceeding. He reviewed it fluently and with colorful flourishes.

'I will not quibble with counsel on the use of words,' he said, with an indulgent smile at the defense table. 'I prefer to plant the Government's case on language used by the Supreme Court of the United States in One-hundred-and-twelve U.S. Reports, while construing this very section.' Here he paused an instant gracefully, then went on to read from an open book. Proudfitt's right to proceed was a constitutional and a statutory right. He emphasized his point by closing the book and sat down.

When Major Leighton Troupe rose and walked around to the reading stand to conclude the defense argument, spectators stirred in their seats. He was the most popular trial lawyer in Macon. His reputation as a speaker was widespread throughout South Georgia. He stood before the stand with a cavalry-man's stout-legged stance. He was barrel-chested and powerfully built. His bold aquiline nose and his short pointed beard were raised as he faced the judge.

Judge Crow's copiously robed bust had pressed forward against his desk a little, too. His smooth jowls, molding into the robe, did not lose their remote immobility. But his cold gray eyes sharpened.

Troupe's voice, as he began, was surprisingly soft, but deep and heavy with latent power. He bowed and addressed the judge and opposing counsel simply, yet there was an emotional quality to his tone that set apart these casual words. Now he paused abruptly and stretched a hand toward the lawyers at the Government table. His words were in polite contrast to his gesture. He sought their copy of the federal injunction decree.

The district attorney skittered hastily among the litter on the table to search for it.

Judge Crow's eyes batted quickly. As Troupe took the document from the prosecutor's hand, Crow spoke with testiness. Were there any marks on those papers which would prevent their getting mixed up with other defense papers?

Troupe took hold of the reading stand with both hands and looked directly at Crow. 'I was perhaps a little too confident,

Your Honor, that my honesty and that of my associates would have prevented any such mishap.'

Crow remained immobile and cold. He said it was always well to be careful in these matters. In fact, one could not be too careful. He ended with a hard inflection.

Troupe bowed deeply and handed the papers back to the district attorney. As he turned again to the stand, Judge Dreighton was coming up out of his seat, his eyes snapping. Troupe leaned over, pressing him back into the chair. He whispered that Dreighton must take it. Of course the black-guard would not dare make such an insinuation off the bench. It seemed that Crow was out to harass him, to make him mad. The situation was too serious for personalities.

Troupe appeared unruffled when he resumed. He referred to the technical questions involved in the demurrer briefly, and in a perfunctory voice. He would devote himself largely to discussing the equity of it, he said.

Resting his elbow on the reading stand, he now pointed a finger toward Judge Crow. His voice was still soft, but there was sinew in it. The question was simple. Had the rights of Proudfitt Coventry been invaded? That was the whole question as far as the federal court was concerned. That was the limit of its rightful interest.

But as a matter of fact that was not what the federal court was undertaking to try. His forearm and finger had stiffened. Now his voice showed force. It was murder—a question entirely peculiar to the State courts.

He stood spraddle-legged behind the stand and held to its top with both hands. His voice rang out. This was an attempt, pure and simple, to invade the rights of the State of Georgia—

by the federal courts—to usurp the prerogative of the State to punish all crime within its limits!

Crow leaned back in his high-backed chair and rocked it a little.

Troupe went on in a clear, swift voice. The Act of 1870 was directed against conspiracy to deprive a citizen of the United States of the rights secured to him by the Federal Constitution or laws. It referred to rights originating with or created under the Constitution, not rights which were the common heritage of the people prior to the framing of that document and which were simply recognized by it.

He cited Supreme Court rulings. He quoted John Marshall. It was no more the duty or within the power of the United States to punish for a conspiracy to murder within the State than it would be to punish for murder itself. He raised his arm above his head, closed his fist. 'These rights are in our Magna Carta!'

People were sitting up straight in their courtroom chairs. Their faces were sharpened with emotion. Crow leaned forward against his desk and his eyebrows puckered.

He interrupted Troupe. His voice was still cold, but it showed constraint. The Constitution had created the federal courts and limited the persons who could bring suit therein. The rights enjoyed by such persons to bring suit was conferred by the Federal Constitution.

Troupe's sharp voice shot into the pause. A specific conferment to a specific class did not rob others of already existing State rights.

His tones now became casual. Conceding that Proudfitt Coventry had a right to sue in the federal courts, the case of

Cruickshank plainly showed that a conspiracy to interfere with that right did not fall within the terms of the Enforcement Act under which this indictment was framed. Nor would the institution of contempt proceedings in a case to which Proudfitt Coventry was not a party fall within the terms of the act. The right to punish for contempt was not conferred by the Constitution.

His voice ended in a soft, pervading bass. He raised a clenched hand. He spoke in sharp, ringing periods, which he punctuated with jabs of his fist. The real purpose of this indictment and prosecution was to bring citizens of Georgia into the federal courts—to try them under the charge of murder—of which the State courts alone had jurisdiction—so that the attention of the court and jury would be absorbed in the question as to who had committed the foul, iniquitous murder, so that Proudfitt Coventry would be lost sight of in the trial on such an issue. Proudfitt Coventry was, in fact, nothing but a sham and a pretense—a stalking horse, a decoy duck—to bring this case into court and thus give the court a jurisdiction without which there could be no pretense of jurisdiction in the federal court!

Troupe dropped the hand he held clenched and raised the other in a repelling gesture. There was contempt in his voice. This contempt seemed to be aimed directly at Crow. He said that the State of Georgia did not need the aid of federal courts to punish the commission of crime within its borders. It had the power and the will to mete out proper punishment in such cases. It was due the State that she be allowed, with her own people, to vindicate her honor and punish those guilty of the foul crime.

'This is invasion!' Troupe's voice smote the walls. A finger of his raised arm pointed toward the ceiling. It was as if he accused the Government of horse-stealing. Spectators in the courtroom batted their eyes and looked at Crow. Troupe's voice held the pitch strongly. 'No one has a right to say the people of Georgia are unable to bring to justice those who perpetrate crime within her borders!'

There was a tense pause. Troupe's hand dropped. He held on to the reading stand, his body relaxing. His voice was soft, gently indulgent. 'But I know, Your Honor, how difficult it is to put away power.'

Crow had been sitting forward. Now he batted his eyes and shifted back into his seat quickly. He opened his mouth and swallowed without speaking. His voice was a little fuzzy when he began. 'Not at all, sir, not at all. This court has often put away its power.' He regained his self-control as he spoke: 'And on this, your motion, I only wish you to confine your argument to the legal question and not allow it to assume a political air!' He had completely regained his composure.

Troupe's voice carried a tone of mock apology. He said if his argument were not to the point, he was mistaken. A murder had been committed in Georgia and the prosecution of it lay with the people of Georgia. The slender excuse upon which it was brought into this court should not be allowed to wrest it from the hands of the people of Georgia. He did not think there was any politics in that.

The court was not interested in the power of the State, Crow replied. The question before them depended on nothing except the letter of the law.

Troupe paused. There was bafflement in his eyes. An offense had been committed against the State, he said silkily, and in arguing as to the jurisdiction of this court, was it not proper subject-matter to introduce the State? If this court took jurisdiction, the State court would be ousted.

Slowly, his hands holding either side of the reading stand, he gathered strength. His voice was restrained, but tensely vibrant when he began speaking. 'If this case is decided as asked under the indictment, it will be the greatest and most sweeping revolution that has ever occurred in the history of the United States. The books do not contain anything to parallel it!'

He began again with a grimness that made his body tremble. He stood with his legs astride. His short neck was drawn down between his shoulders. His cheeks were twisted. 'I have never, in all my years of law practice, stood upon my feet to address a court on a question as grave as this! If the decision of the court should hold that the court is without jurisdiction, I feel that it will be a very wise one. But if the court takes this case—and is affirmed by the Supreme Court in taking it—there has never been a decision so radical or far-reaching, or one that will so deeply invade what we consider to be the sovereign rights of the people!'

He paused and spoke again, solemnly: 'A war between the States was fought over a lesser invasion!' With his voice still ringing through the chamber, he sat down.

Judge Crow's cheekbones were sharp, his mouth shut tight like a pod. He said that he would take the question under advisement.

36

JUDGE Crow took twenty minutes in which to announce his decision, when court reconvened after two hours' recess, though everybody concerned knew what it would be as soon as he began speaking. The defense had lost its most important battle.

The case went on trial quickly. Judge Crow's hostility became increasingly apparent to Troupe and Dreighton, to Calebb and his fellow defendants, as it proceeded. When the jury picking began, Dreighton asked for the twenty challenges allowed by Georgia law for each of his defendants. Judge Crow would allow but twenty for the seven. During the noon recess of the second day, as the Government was preparing to begin presentation of its case, a group of backwoodsmen and Pineville mill hands had a scuffle at the entrance of the federal building. Officers arrested only the backwoodsmen, including three defense witnesses. When Troupe protested, charging that the Government was intimidating his witnesses, Crow treated his protest lightly. When Troupe demanded a hearing on his charges, Crow reluctantly agreed, postponed the hearing indefinitely.

After the Government had presented it foundational proof, Micajah Corn was called. A bailiff preceded him and Civil walked behind, but he entered the courtroom unassisted. He came through a doorway near the judge's bench and walked slowly around the press table and across the parquet to the witness stand. He leaned on a stick and dragged his right foot a little. His jaws were clean-shaven and his blue coat and gray wool shirt had a tidy appearance. Except for the deep wrinkles about his mouth, his face was smooth and a little puffy.

He did not look about him until he was seated in the chair. He sat forward. His glance shifted rapidly from the jury to the blurred faces of the courtroom crowd, to the appraising eyes at the counsel table. The glance was hurried, shrinking, and yet quizzical. His eyes found Civil, seated beyond the clerk's desk. He had wanted her closer. Casement spoke to him from the Government counsel table where he sat with the district attorney. The left side of Micajah's face wrinkled with recognition. He slipped back into his seat.

Casement stood up. He began asking Micajah questions and Micajah answered them, deliberately. They were reasonable, Micajah found, and kept closely to their previous talks about the case. Casement kept saying that he wanted him to look at the jury when he gave his answers. Casement was across the room. That made it a nuisance, but Micajah tried to follow directions. He had trouble with Casement about his questions only one time. Referring to something he, Micajah, had said, Casement had Littleton getting over the barn-lot fence last that night after the killing. It was the nigger who got over last. Micajah had to check Casement up twice about that.

Littleton, sitting a little distance back of the defense counsel table, never took his hard eyes off of Micajah but once. His father looked strange to him. It was difficult, somehow, for him to know that it was his Pa. The dead white of his mustache and hair didn't bother Littleton so much. It was that dead half of his face that took no part in what he was saying or doing. And his eyes. They had a staring look in them. Micajah had looked at him calmly soon after he sat down, then his glance passed on. Littleton could not be sure that his father had even seen him. He could not see how Pa could face him so calm.

Toward the end of his direct examination, Micajah had looked again at Littleton. Littleton sharpened his eyes and gazed back as hard as he could. Micajah continued to look at him. His eyes did not glare, nor shrink, but Littleton could not penetrate their stare. Suddenly, incredibly, Micajah laughed. There was no sound, but his mouth came open in a cacklish smile. Littleton dropped his eyes and a blush crept up his neck into his cheeks.

On cross-examination, Major Troupe asked Micajah if he had not suffered a paralytic stroke. Micajah said he had been sick, didn't have much feeling in one side. Troupe asked him if he were not still sick. Micajah replied that he didn't have good use of that side yet. Troupe told him he could go.

During Micajah's examination, Civil had sat with her hands in her lap and her eyes bent upon her hands. She had never once looked in Littleton's direction until she rose to follow Micajah out. It was a quick look then, hurried by the fear of seeing him. Then she walked behind Micajah in bowed silence.

Red Chauncy finally decided not to testify for the Government, though the district attorney used against him the confession he had given. He took the witness stand in his own behalf, along with the other defendants, and agreed, when the major asked him, that the confession had been extracted from him under duress.

All the lawyers agreed that Calhoun made the poorest witness for himself. He started out all right, but he talked too much and he lost his temper on cross-examination. He even argued with the judge. He was there, he said, a defendant on trial, because he had spoken for the people when the Coventrys tried to steal their land. That was the only part he had played in the land troubles, but the Coventrys were trying to make a murderer out of him to get rid of him.

Judge Crow reminded him that he was testifying, not arguing before a jury. But Calhoun broke forth again later. The third time the judge reprimanded him Calhoun got up and shook his fist at the judge and yelled out that he was part and parcel with the Coventrys and had persecuted him for years.

The bailiffs grabbed him and Crow held him in contempt of court. His own lawyers apologized. They said that he was a sick man.

Somebody in the audience yelled, 'Give 'im hell, Calhoun!' Judge Crow had the courtroom searched, but the bailiffs couldn't pin it on anyone. The judge threatened to have the courtroom cleared, but he didn't.

The case wound up two days before Christmas. After seventeen hours of argument and a long charge, the jury took it about two o'clock in the afternoon. Micajah told Civil they might ride on the afternoon train and get to McRae before

387

dark. Civil wanted to wait. They sat in the witness room. Micajah talked, but Civil had no answers. Micajah did not press her. She had been like that ever since he told the company lawyer about Littleton's part in the murder, although she had said at the time that she believed he was doing God's will.

Listening through the witness-room doorway, they heard the judge repeat the jury's verdict. The lights were on when it came and there was a bee swarm of noise. Littleton was sentenced to the federal prison for life. So were all the rest, except Chauncy. He got ten years. As they got up to go, Civil held back. She wondered if she couldn't see Littleton once more before they took him away. Micajah said it wouldn't do. Littleton, along with the others, was being led out of the side door by the bailiffs.

Micajah and Civil went on to the depot to wait for the night train. They had a six-hour wait. They whiled it away sitting, most of it, because Micajah couldn't get about much. Civil got up a few times to get them water and to ask about the train to McRae when the station man hollered out things she could not understand. And all sorts of people came in and out of the big, drafty waiting room. Micajah did not look at them. He kept his seat in the back of the room near a spittoon. He sat there with his hands cupped on the head of his walking-stick and leaned over to drop the ambeer from his mouth. 'I've got a pretty good sleight to it,' he said once, wiping his chin, and gave Civil a one-sided smile.

Later, as he gazed off over the tops of the benches, he spoke again. 'I wonder if Big Bud's been a-feedin' that old weevilly corn to the hosses?' He twisted the stick in his hands, and after a moment added, 'I reckon not, shorely—it 'uz in the crib with the shucks and fodder.'

Civil brought him a cup of water and stood before him, holding it. He did not move to take it immediately. He lifted his face toward hers. 'Just a-figurin'—I been nigh two months here in Macon.' The crowfoot at his left eye creased. He looked off over the benches. 'I ain't been away from home that long before since the war,' he said. 'I a-reckon them gourds on the martin pole'll look good to me when I get there,' he finished, reaching for the cup.

When he had rinsed his mouth and had drunk a swallow or two of the water, he handed it back. 'I a-won't take much of this,' he said with a one-sided smile. 'Fore long I'll be where I can get good water.'

Civil looked down quickly without smiling. If he didn't drink more water, he'd dry up, she said. When she had restored the cup, he went on. 'I 'uz a-lookin' at it 'fore I left home—the stock's chewed one side of the barn trough plum out. Think I'll start work on that old poplar log by the shed—I cut it for a trough.'

He stretched out his sound leg and, laying aside his stick, moved the other with his hands. 'It a-won't take much walkin' 'round. Reckon I'll get started on it soon.'

Limping back from a final trip to the water-closet before the train came, he let Civil help him get down into his seat again. 'You ain't got Big Bud's sleight to it, Civil—I reckon you ain't as strong.' His lips twitched as he looked up from the bench. 'That aer stringy yearlin's stout. Ye wouldn't think it, just a-lookin' at 'im, but he is.'

He looked off across the room before he turned back to Civil with the creases still at the corner of his mouth. 'Apt as not he'll be at the McRae depot to meet us—you a-writin' him that letter we 'uz a-comin' home. You don't have to prompt him much.'

Big Bud wasn't at the depot when they got off. It was five o'clock and barely light. There was only a negro helper and a baggage cart. Micajah held to Civil's arm and fumbled in the dimness. 'Hadn't figured it 'ud be so dark—city mixes you up,' he muttered. 'Should've known the boy couldn't get here from home.' They went over to an eating-house to get breakfast. They sat on stools at a counter. Micajah had to prop his bad leg, but he made it. He handed Civil his hat to hang up and pulled at his mustache. A flat-faced, sniffling woman brought them coffee. Civil pushed her cup away from her and sat looking at it, but Micajah carefully steadied his hand and poured black coffee into his saucer. He leaned over it. 'Smells good,' he said, his cheek wrinkling. Then he looked up at Civil and around the room and his face straightened.

A man wearing thick-lensed spectacles came into the restaurant. He slumped onto a stool farther down the line and turned his face toward the waitress. Micajah stopped blowing his coffee and looked over his saucer at him. The man was taking a cup from the woman's hands. He shoveled a spoonful of sugar into it. Micajah turned back to Civil. 'He a-looks like the man who took Zenas Fears' place. He's out early for a company man.' He raised his saucer again, then paused with his elbows on the counter to look toward the man. The fellow looked like a turtle with his neck and back bent like that. He was pouring milk into his cup from a pitcher. He looked up, met Micajah's gaze, and glanced away. The next minute he was getting off his stool. He came over and touched Micajah's arm.

'You're Micajah Corn, ain't you?' he said; then, without awaiting a reply, looked at a slip of paper in his hand. 'You been making a claim to lot 180?'

Micajah lowered his saucer and nodded slowly.

The man looked down at the paper. "Lots 180, 181, 145, and 146 in the Savannah District, and lot 47 in the Fifth?' He read the numbers briskly, following the line on the sheet with his finger. He raised his eyes and peered at Micajah and Civil through thick lenses. 'You're just the man I'm looking for, Mr. Corn. You make the eighty-ninth. I got four hundred of these to serve before I get through.'

Micajah opened his mouth, but he did not speak.

The man handed Micajah the slip of paper. 'Served eighty-eight of these summons in the last six days,' he said. He stood a moment with his hands on his hips, rocking back on his heels. 'The company's bundled the whole lot of land cases into one ejectment suit. They're going to try it in the Macon court.'

Micajah fumbled with a piece of paper in his hand. He lowered his gaze, but he did not look at the paper. He stared beyond the man, at the counter, at the cup that still sat there full of coffee.

'Macon?' he said. 'Macon Court.'

THE END

391

Brainard Cheney
A Biographical Sketch

Brainard Cheney, the author of *Lightwood*, was born in Fitzgerald, Georgia on June 3, 1900. The family soon relocated to nearby Lumber City. His father and namesake, Brainard Bartwell Cheney, who practiced as a successful attorney, inherited extensive land holdings in the Lumber City area of Telfair County. He assigned the administration of the estate to overseers while he pursued his legal career.

In Brainard's eighth year, his father died unexpectedly, leaving his widow to raise their children on her own. Cheney's mother, Mattie Mood, came from an old and prominent Charleston family. Though a long way from Charleston, she chose to remain in Lumber City to administer the estates. Brainard remembered an idyllic childhood living in the small river town. His days included school work and playing and swimming in the Ocmulgee River—a boyhood he recalled as not unlike that of Tom Sawyer, one of his literary heroes.

A childless couple took young Brainard under their wing and introduced him to the world of literature. In a 1982 interview, Cheney remembered visiting their home and enjoying free rein to borrow books from their library. The house contained books in every room, he recalled, even in the closets. He read Mark Twain and Charles Dickens, and then Thackeray, George Meredith, Trollope, along with many others. One must consider the time, circa 1910, and the place, a very small town hundreds of miles from any large city, to fully grasp the isolation a child may have experienced. Cheney recalled a striking image. He remembered his literary patron reading on the front porch, pacing back and forth while holding a book. Because of a back injury, he was uncomfortable sitting down. Looking back on this time, almost a century in the past, one marvels at the transformations wrought by the modern world. Those days of leisurely reading oneself through the private library of one's own, or of a friend, absorbing as a young person the great literature of the age, conjure images of a lost and golden time vastly different from our own.

Cheney's mother managed the family estates, depending on Robin Bess as overseer. Mr. Bess, a black man, occupied a farm located on the holdings. This arrangement, with Robin as overseer, was unusual for those times in the segregated South. Cheney regarded Mr. Bess as an essential influence in his life, tantamount to a father figure. He recalled their fishing and hunting trips. They often traversed the river swamps and cypress forests belonging to the Cheneys, known as the Cheney Woods. Cheney's third novel, *This is Adam*, is based on Robin and the professional relationship between Mr. Bess and Cheney's mother. It celebrates the friendship between Brainard and Robin. He dedicated the work to Mr. Bess.

As a young teenager, Cheney considered training as a steamboat captain on the Ocmulgee River. A lively steamboat transport system plied the Ocmulgee and Altamaha Rivers as late as the 1930's, reaching as far north as Macon—that is, when the river's water level was high enough to accommodate the boats. Cheney sought an apprenticeship with a local steamboat captain. That captain, Mr. Ashburn, discouraged him, correctly foreseeing the coming demise of the steamboat era.

World War I began in 1914 just as Cheney entered the Citadel in Charleston, with vague notions of pursuing a military career. He counted his time there as the unhappiest period of his life. Small in stature, he was hounded by upper classmen and officers. He recalled being addressed incorrectly as "Cheeney" by one particularly unpleasant teacher. Military life and discipline aggravated the young man, who rose to the occasion and transformed his frustration into rebellion.

An English professor at the Citadel encouraged Cheney's interest in writing, an interest destined to lay dormant for a few more years. The War ended before Cheney finished the Citadel and by the same token deflated his ambitions for a military career.

After the Citadel, he attended one quarter at Vanderbilt University. Family financial straits required that he return home to Lumber City. He went to work in the family farming and timber business, at one time running a timber camp with some success. He also worked as a school teacher, functioning as an educator at three successive "one-room" schools in as many years. His teaching career ended when he decided to return to college at Vanderbilt University.

Vanderbilt offered the young man a new world of possibilities. There, through chance connections and a lot of hard work, Cheney became a writer. He worked as a journalist while attending classes. One of those classes was taught by the renowned poet, John Crowe Ransom, who introduced him to the Fugitive and Agrarian literary movements of southern writers. Another important mentor was Caroline Gordon, a professor and author. When he first tried writing fiction, Gordon steered him away from journalistic prose and into the creation of literature, as Cheney related in 1982.

At this time, Cheney also became friend and roommate with the young poet, Robert Penn Warren, known as "Red" among his friends. Warren later published the acclaimed novel, *All the Kings Men*. On many occasions he acknowledged Cheney's critical assistance with some of the political speeches contained in the famous work. Robert Penn Warren went on to become an eminent poet, author and teacher, as well as Poet Laureate Consultant in Poetry at the Library of Congress. Their friendship endured until Warren's death (one year before Cheney's) and included not only literary collaboration but also field trips for research to local rivers and rural areas.

Brainard married Frances Neel, a young woman just then embarking on a prominent career as a librarian and author. They settled in Nashville. Among their friends, Frances was known as Fannie, and Brainard was called Lon, after the silent movie star Lon Chaney. Many of Cheney's autographed works are signed "Lon."

Cheney left Vanderbilt before graduation to forge a career as a respected newspaperman in Tennessee and later worked for various political figures as a speechwriter and advisor. Frances began her career in the library world, becoming an eminent librarian, respected professor and author of a famous textbook on librarianship. During World War II, she worked as Allen Tate's assistant when he accepted the post of Poet Consultant at the Library of Congress.

In 1936, Cheney took a year off to write a novel. He embarked on a journey to his home town of Lumber City. An old story of the timber wars in the area drew him back and he commenced work on the novel which became *Lightwood*, his fictional retelling of that story.

Fortune presented Cheney with a cousin whose insurance office once served as the last office of the Dodge Company. Those tenants left behind a mass of papers documenting the complete record of nearly half a century of legal wrangling. Cheney recalled sitting in this office, situated in a back room, reading through thousands of pages of musty legal papers. From his study of this archive and additional research, he created *Lightwood*, the story of an epic battle between the proverbial haves and have-nots, the timber barons and the land squatters. Published in 1939, the book sold respectably and this encouraged him to write his next novel, *River Rogue*.

Lightwood was reviewed nationally, including in the New York *Times*. The November 5, 1939 issue contains a favorable review by Edith H. Walton, who called the work a "superior novel of the South, exceedingly well written." *Time* magazine summed up the novel as having "the unimpeachable honesty, goodness, flatness, of a mouthful of cold excellent corn bread."

Cheney traveled to the south Georgia area and signed many copies of the novel for local friends and family. These autographed copies of the original 1939 hardcover edition surface in the area periodically. They usually contain dates ranging from late October to early November, 1939.

In 1941, Cheney received a Guggenheim Fellowship. This enabled him to research the novel *River Rogue*, which is also based on events and people he knew from the Ocmulgee area. The book sold respectably and garnered a movie option from MGM, though it was never produced. After 1941, Cheney concentrated on his journalism career, later moving to speechwriting, working for Tennessee governor, Frank G. Clement, among others.

Fannie Cheney inherited a family home near Smyrna, Tennessee which they called Idler's Retreat. There they hosted many prominent literary and political figures through the years. Through Caroline Gordon's introduction, the Cheneys befriended Georgia novelist Flannery O'Connor in 1953, with whom they exchanged visits and letters until her death in 1964. Selections from this correspondence were collected into the book, *The Correspondence of Flannery O'Connor and the Brainard Cheneys*. They shared common interests in both literature and Catholicism, to which the Cheneys had converted. O'Connor is on record as saying that Brainard Cheney is the only reviewer who 'got the meaning' of her first novel, *Wise Blood*. Over the years they discussed and critiqued one another's work.

Cheney published two more novels, *This is Adam*, in 1959, and *Devil's Elbow*, in 1968. Both of these works take place in the Ocmulgee area, based on autobiographical events in Cheney's life. He continued to work on additional fiction, but no new titles appeared during his lifetime.

In 1982, Dr. Delma Presley, of Georgia Southern University, conducted Project RAFT, also known as the Restoring Altamaha Folk Traditions project. This grant-funded project gathered together the few surviving timber rafters of the area. The events rekindled interest in the works of Brainard Cheney, specifically at that time, *River Rogue*, whose main protagonist was a timber raftsman.

In the spring of 1982, Dr. Presley and other project personnel actually built a timber log raft and navigated it down the Ocmulgee and Altamaha rivers to Darien. They recreated the experience of many of the old piney woods settlers who rafted timber for supplemental income. Brainard Cheney participated in the festivities, even traveling on a portion of the raft trip. He was 82 years old at the time. Through the efforts and support of Dr. Presley, a new edition of *River Rogue* was published to coincide with the project. This renewed interest in Cheney's work led to the republication of *Lightwood* in 1984, spearheaded by his nephew, Roy Neel.

Brainard Cheney remained an author to the end, passing away at age 89 in January of 1990. Several unpublished works, primarily fiction and plays set in his native Georgia, remained. Fannie Cheney passed away in 1996 also at age 89. These two remarkable people bequeathed a rich legacy of literature, authorship and teaching, and left many friends.

By Stephen Whigham

Excerpted from: *The Lightwood Chronicles: murder and greed in the piney woods of south Georgia, 1869-1923, being the true story of Brainard Cheney's novel,* Lightwood

This version of *Lightwood* designed by Josh Sheffield

Printed on acid-free paper in Georgia font

Made in the USA
Lexington, KY
28 May 2016